Cliff Farrell

divided his time between newspaper work
and writing fiction after he was lured out
West from his job as a newspaper office boy
in Zanesville, Ohio. He worked as an editor
on several California papers, including the
Los Angeles *Examiner*. More than six
hundred of his stories appeared in such
magazines as *Liberty, Collier's,* and *The
Saturday Evening Post*. His more- than-
twenty novels include DEATH TRAP ON
THE PLATTE, and PATCHSADDLE
DRIVE/SHOOTOUT AT SIOUX WELLS,
published in Signet paperback editions.

SIGNET Double Westerns For Your Library

COMANCH'
and
RIDE THE WILD TRAIL

by
Cliff Farrell

Ø

A SIGNET BOOK

NEW AMERICAN LIBRARY

TIMES MIRROR

Comanch' Copyright © 1966 by Cliff Farrell

Ride the Wild Trail Copyright © 1959 by Cliff Farrell

Comanch' and *Ride the Wild Trail* are published by arrangement with Doubleday and Company, Inc. Originally appeared in paperback as separate volumes published by The New American Library.

SIGNET TRADEMARK REG. U.S. PAT. OFF. AND FOREIGN COUNTRIES
REGISTERED TRADEMARK—MARCA REGISTRADA
HECHO EN CHICAGO, U.S.A.

SIGNET, SIGNET CLASSICS, MENTOR, PLUME, MERIDIAN AND NAL BOOKS are published by The New American Library, Inc., 1633 Broadway, New York, New York 10019

First Printing (Double Western Edition), June, 1982

1 2 3 4 5 6 7 8 9

PRINTED IN THE UNITED STATES OF AMERICA

COMANCH'

Chapter ONE

Standing on the gallery of Casa Bonita, Mike Bastrop tossed a scatter of gold coins among the riders of his trail crew, and watched with amusement as they scrambled for the money.

They were saddle-hardened men, made savage by long-denied wants. They were ragged, with bellies wolf-lean after months on the drive to Kansas and return.

It took five days of riding to earn a five-dollar gold piece. Five dollars would buy whisky enough to drown a man's memories of the hardships, hire a woman's kisses for a night, blank out the fears of the future for a few hours at least.

They fought like wild dogs for the coins, cursing and sweating. It was the law of survival. The biggest and strongest among them came up with the major share of the booty.

"That's a little extra to blow in on the fandango gals," Mike Bastrop said. "But be mighty sure that such of you as I'm keeping on the payroll will be in shape to ride when you show up for work. I'll give you two days to have your fling. Then, we're shaping up a late drive and heading north again."

His eyes rested briefly on one of the riders. Lee Jackson was the only man who had not joined in the melee for the tossed coins. He had remained apart, watching the others maul each other in the struggle.

It had always been that way with Lee Jackson. He had ridden with them to Kansas, lined up with them at the chuckwagon for his meals, shared tobacco and canteen water with them when those items were in short supply. He had more than shared the work and the miseries.

Mike Bastrop, who acted as his own trail boss, had a

habit of giving Lee Jackson the worst of it. Come a dry
stretch where the dust hung in the blazing sun, it would be
Lee Jackson who rode drag, breathing through a neckerchief as he prodded the laggards along.

More often than any other member of the crew, he
drew the graveyard shift on which a man was awakened in
his blankets two hours before daybreak to stand the last
watch on the bed grounds until the herd was thrown on
the trail. Then he rode swing or drag until dusk, sixteen
to eighteen hours a day during the long June marches on
the road to Kansas.

"Good enough for him," Mike Bastrop had said more
than once. "The nerve of him, trying to palm himself off
as the son of my poor, dead wife!"

There were other things Mike Bastrop said about Lee
Jackson. "He's all Indian," Bastrop had declared repeat-
edly. "He looks like 'em. He thinks like 'em. He'll act like
one, sooner or later. He's Comanch', I tell you."

Even Bastrop never said anything like that in Lee Jackson's presence, and he was not a man to spare the feelings
of underlings. He was big, powerfully built, and in his
forties. He was handsome in a hard-cut way, with a clipped
black mustache and sideburns. He had appeared in the
Punchbowl not long after Appomattox, wearing the tat-
tered tunic of a Confederate major. He was said to have
served under Jubal Early, but there were whispers that he
had actually been one of Cantrell's guerrillas.

He now owned Rancho Verde. Its range stretched from
the breaks of the Pecos River on the west to the dry plains
beyond the Armadillo Hills, with the bluffs of the Staked
Plains rising in the distance.

Comanch'! The last man who had used that term in Lee
Jackson's hearing had revived in Dr. Obey Peters' office in
Punchbowl. Lee Jackson's fists had dealt the damage.

"Next time, cowboy," Obey had said as he patched up
the victim, "pick on somebody that don't turn into a buzz
saw. You ought to have seen the last feller they carried
in here after he'd called Lee Jackson a Comanch'. He was
a worse sight than you."

However, no matter how many men Lee Jackson fought,
nothing was changed. Behind his back they still had a term
that, in their minds, was an epithet. Comanch'.

He walked to the corral, cut out a powerful blue roan, and cinched down his worn saddle. He owned the roan personally, and had left it at the ranch when he had headed for Kansas with the drive. The wrangler had brought his horse in from pasture that morning. It was fat and in need of work, but Lee had never seen it reach the end of its endurance.

He mounted to ride away. In the pocket of his weathered duck jacket were twelve gold eagles. One hundred and twenty dollars. His pay for the months he had spent shaping up two beef herds and helping drive them north from New Mexico.

Two gunny sacks lay on the big cedar table in the main room of Casa Bonita. They had been brought back from Kansas in the chuckwagon, with the crew armed and acting as outriders, while Mike Bastrop and Bill Tice rode in the wagon with buckshot guns across their knees.

Mike Bastrop could afford to toss away a few extra coins after paying off the trail hands, for the sacks contained more than a hundred thousand dollars, the proceeds from the sale of the herds at the shipping point on the Santa Fe Railroad.

"You there, Jackson!" Mike Bastrop called. "I want you back here tomorrow. Kinky Bob tells me he's fetched in a string of green ones off the range to be broke. There's no time to lose. We'll need horseflesh in a hurry, what with one more drive to shove up the line before snow flies."

Lee did not answer. He wheeled his horse to head up the trail to town. He was long-legged, lean-fibered, with thick black hair, skin burned the color of rawhide, and very dark eyes.

A big man, who had stood in the background, excluded from taking part in the scramble for the money, called out,

"See you tomorrow, Jack-Lee!"

The speaker was the wrangler, a black man who had no other name than Kinky Bob. He was a former slave, and his job was handling young, unbroken horses at Rancho Verde. He was even better at that art than Lee Jackson, whom he always addressed as Jack-Lee. That meant that Kinky Bob was the best rider of bad horses in the Punchbowl. Some cowboys said he might be the best in the world.

Lee Jackson grinned at Kinky Bob and nodded. He and Kink always worked together with the greenies. Shaping up Rancho Verde livestock took muscle and guts. A twister who got by a season without breaking a leg or an arm considered himself ahead of the game.

Mike Bastrop, a man who did not spare humans when it came to working cattle, had learned that it paid to have his riders mounted on strong, powerful horses that had been expertly broken and trained so that they would not stampede a herd on the bed ground or cause trouble at the branding fires. He bought the best Morgan stallions and would have nothing to do with the broomtails that ran wild on the Staked Plains or beyond the Pecos.

Still standing was Bastrop's offer of a thousand dollars for the return of a big Barb stud that he had imported from Spain three years previously at a cost of more than six thousand dollars. The stallion was pure white, a rarity in Barbs, and had come from the stable of a grandee. It had jumped a high corral fence a few days after its arrival at Rancho Verde and had vanished. There were rumors that a white stallion had been sighted occasionally beyond the Armadillo Hills, but the big reward had never been claimed.

Lee watched Bastrop join two men who had been waiting in the background. The trio vanished into the cool dimness of the main room. El Casa Bonita had been built when the range was ruled by old Mexico. The beautiful house. It was adobe-built, shaded by galleries and vines and ancient oaks, mesquite and cottonwood. Hayfields were ripe beyond the spread of buildings. Ample water glinted in irrigation ditches.

Bill Tice and Judge Amos Clebe held drinks in their hands. Bill Tice owned the prosperous BT outfit a dozen miles northeast toward the Armadillos. He pooled his beef-raising with that of Rancho Verde and always went up the trail with the drives, acting as Mike Bastrop's *segundo*, or second in command.

Amos Clebe presided over court in Punchbowl, which was the county seat. The judge also held the office of county clerk and recorder. He and Bill Tice were Mike Bastrop's poker and drinking companions. Their poker games sometimes lasted for days and the stakes were said to be very stiff.

The hot, late-afternoon sun beat down on Lee as he rode toward Punchbowl. As usual he rode alone. He never felt comfortable with men who didn't seem to feel comfortable around him. And that meant almost everyone except Kinky Bob.

They believed Mike Bastrop was right in saying that Lee Jackson was a Comanche. There were strains of Spanish and white blood in some of the tribes that cropped out after generations. Throwbacks, handsome and proud like this one. But Comanch', nevertheless. There was scarcely a person in the Punchbowl who had not lost a mother, a father, or other close kin to the lances and hatchets of raiding Comanches in the past.

The Comanches were now on reservation. They had not come down from the plains to raid and terrorize in more than a dozen years, but the memories remained. And the bitterness. Above all, the bitterness.

It had been some eighteen years ago when Lee had been brought to Rancho Verde by a cavalry sergeant and an Army scout who acted as interpreter. They had come from Fort Gilman, nearly two hundred miles away.

Lee had been about six years old. Instead of the breech-clout to which he was accustomed, he was clad in smothering homespun breeches and shirt that the wives of Army officers had forced upon him.

He spoke only the Comanche tongue, but from the facial expressions, he followed the gist of the conversation and any missing segments were explained to him later by the scout.

Mike Bastrop had stood on the same gallery from which he had tossed the coins, inspecting the ragged child with distaste. "What's this, sergeant?" he had demanded.

"A scoutin' detail come across this young one, alone an' runnin' for his life up north on the plains a few weeks ago," the soldier explained. "He was being chased by three Comanche warriors. They turned back when they saw the troopers. He told the interpreter he was the son of Quin-a-se-i-co. That's old Eagle-in-the-Sky, the big blue devil of the Comanche Nation. The boy seems to hate the chief, an' wanted to get away from Eagle's village."

"What's this got to do with me?" Bastrop demanded.

"The records show that this ranch was hit by the Comanches about four years ago," the sergeant explained.

"Your wife, the former Señora Margarita Calvin, was killed along with three other adults, who were all that were at the ranch that day. You were in town on business, Major Bastrop. There was also a boy, less than two years old, whose remains were never found. There was the chance he had been taken with them by the Comanches. He was the Señora's son. Your stepson. He was named after his father, John Calvin, who was killed in the last few months of the war, fightin' for the reb—beggin' your pardon, sir—for the Confederacy. Colonel Graham thinks this boy might be your stepson."

"Ridiculous!" Mike Bastrop snorted. "This brat is Comanch'! You can see that for yourself."

Mike Bastrop grasped Lee by the hair, jerked his head back. "Why, he's not even a breed, by the looks. He's all Injun. You don't think I'm going to let the Army palm off a murderin' Comanch' whelp on me as my stepson, do you? This one, when he got old enough, would murder us in our beds."

"The Colonel thought it was worth a try," the sergeant admitted.

Mike Bastrop laughed. "I figured it that way. Your Colonel thought this would be an easy way to get an Indian off his hands."

"I wouldn't know anything about that, sir." the sergeant said with a smirk.

Mike Bastrop scornfully shook Lee by the hair. "What's your name, Injun?" he demanded.

Lee only glared at him, afraid, but defiant. He did not like this man.

"He doesn't seem to know even his own name," the sergeant said.

"My poor wife's son is dead," Bastrop said. "He was killed the same day Margarita was murdered by those red devils. I'll never stop mourning the fact that I happened to be away from the ranch that day. Otherwise I might have saved her and the child. Or, at least, have died with them."

Bastrop added, "But, in memory of Margarita, I'll look after this boy, at least long enough to give you fellows a chance to find his people—if he really has any white blood, which I doubt. He looks like he could stand a few square meals."

The Army had been only too happy to settle the problem

in that manner. Lee had been made a ward of Mike Bastrop and had been placed in the hands of stern-minded Mexican women who helped with the kitchen and housework at Casa Bonita. They did not like Comanches, either. They treated him as an inferior and gave him the most menial tasks to perform.

"I'll give you a name," Mike Bastrop had told him. "After two of the greatest men that ever lived. I don't reckon an Injun ever heard of General Robert E. Lee or General Stonewall Jackson. But it might give even an Injun luck to be named after them. From now on, you're Lee Jackson. Don't ever try to make out that you're any kin of mine, or of my dead wife. I'll feed you and look after you, but I reckon you'll go back to the Comanches at first chance. Once an Injun, always an Injun."

Mike Bastrop had been wrong. Lee hadn't gone back to Indian life. He remembered the cruelty and hardships he had suffered at the hands of the Comanche chief and his squaws. He had tried twice previously to escape from Eagle's village. On both occassions he had been overtaken and carried back to Eagle-in-the-Sky's lodge.

Between the chief and the nameless youngster had been a deep, puzzling animosity. On Lee's part it had been a feeling that Eagle had committed an unforgivable wrong, but the exact nature of the act always escaped him.

In return, Eagle held toward him an emotion that was even greater than aversion. Fear, perhaps. But why would the great Quin-a-se-i-co, the Eagle chief of the Comanches, fear his own son, a mere boy?

Lee's determination to escape had never been quenched by his failures and the punishments Eagle had inflicted on him when he had been brought back. He wanted only to get away from Eagle and the silent *something* that lay between them. In his young mind had been only the intention of joining some other Comanche village where life might be easier. He had held no thought that he was other than a Comanche until the Army had brought up the question.

Each time he had made his bid to free himself from Eagle's cruelty he had struck southwesterly across the Staked Plains. It had seemed to him there was a tribe in that direction, or a haven, where he might find peace. A place where he belonged.

From the moment of his first meeting with Mike Bastrop he had made up his mind to flee from Rancho Verde and continue his attempt to find the Comanche village that was his imaginary place of safety.

For reasons he had never understood, he had kept putting off his departure. He grew to manhood and became a full-fledged vaquero. He still did not understand why he had not gone back to the Comanches. That was where he belonged. He had never been accepted here. The war trail was no more, but there were still remnants of the buffalo herds in the breaks of the plains. The Comanche spearmen would ride as long as meat was needed. He could be a spearman also. He would be accepted there. It was only Eagle-in-the-Sky who had persecuted him.

He rode now to town with white men's money in his pocket. Money was for spending. All he wanted was the sting of whisky in his throat, to drink until there were no memories in his mind, to forget the bitterness, to forget the ambitions he secretly held in his mind.

He stabled the roan at Ed Moorehead's livery. He rented a box stall and bought two measures of bran, ears of flint corn, and straw for bedding.

"You-all must purely think a heap o' that roan," the hostler said. "Spendin' almost a whole dollah on a hawss."

"Here's two bits more to see that he's pampered tomorrow in case I'm detained," Lee said.

The hostler hesitated. Lee had seen that expression in the faces of other men. Many times. Sam Barker, who was a bleary derelict, still had pride enough to feel ashamed of taking a gift from an Indian.

Lee pocketed the quarter. "Don't ever look at me like that again," he said.

He walked away. At the entrance to the wagon tunnel a high-stepping bay mare with a young woman in the side-saddle came racing into the barn at a gallop. He leaped aside to avoid being hit by the horse, but went sprawling in the dust. He looked up to see the disdainful delight in Clemmy O'Neil's gray-green eyes. She pulled the mare to a halt inside the barn, slid to the ground, and tossed the reins to the hostler.

"The mare will need a rub after she's cooled," she said. "I'm going back to the ranch tonight."

She removed her spurs and hung them on the saddle. She wore a gray riding habit and a straw sombrero held on her head by a chin strap. She pulled off the sombrero and arranged her unruly mop of red-gold hair.

Lee got to his feet and began whisking dust from his breeches. Their eyes met briefly. Then Clemmy O'Neil turned away, offering no apology.

Lee walked out of the barn and headed down Summer Street. He heard the crisp tap of the heels of Clementina O'Neil's riding boots a few paces back of him. He found himself walking faster. Nettled, he slowed to his former pace. She was trying to hurrah him. He wasn't in any hurry, and damned if he was going to let a vixen like Clemmy O'Neil prod him into dancing to her tune. She was always going out of her way to snub him and try to set herself a peg above him in the scale by which Punchbowl rated its people.

The peg for both of them was very low. That was one thing, at least, they had in common. She overtook him and walked past with a swish of her riding skirt. She had a figure and knew it. She was slim, and taller than average, with a healthy crop of freckles above a small nose in a very comely face. She always seemed to have a chip on her shoulder.

Lee saw the eyes of men along the street swing to watch Clemmy O'Neil as she walked past. She turned into Lucy Miller's sewing store. Now that she was out of sight the male onlookers began making remarks to each other. Their faces bore smirks.

Lee felt pity for Clemmy O'Neil—an emotion that would have touched off her short-fuse temper if she had known. He knew she would resent pity from anyone, most of all from a Comanche.

He walked into the Silver Bell. Combined music hall, gambling house, and saloon, it was a sizable establishment, the biggest between Denver and El Paso. Girls in bangles and beads were already on duty at this early evening hour, for everybody in Punchbowl knew that Mike Bastrop and Bill Tice had paid off their riders, and the crews would soon be hitting town with money to spend.

Lee moved to the bar. "Whisky," he said. "A bottle. The best you've got."

He saw in the bartender's eyes something of the same

question the livery hostler's face had held. Every bar carried an Injun list, as it was called. Alcoholics, deadbeats, and squaw men were on the list. No liquor was to be sold to them. It was against the law to sell alcohol to an Indian.

Lee rarely had entered the Silver Bell in the past, for he knew he was not welcome there. He had made a point of appearing at its bar on occasion, but had never ordered more than a glass of beer. He knew his name was not officially on the Injun list. There apparently was still some doubt in the minds of some of the citizens of Punchbowl, at least, in spite of Mike Bastrop's attitude.

The bartender decided it was not up to him to make an issue of it. He wanted no trouble with the lean, dark rider with the burning challenge in his eyes. He produced a bottle. Lee paid for it and carried it to a table and sat down.

A percentage girl came sidling up. He looked at her and said, "What's your name, sweetheart? Susie?"

"Why, sure," she simpered. "Susie's a good name."

"I've met you before," Lee said. "In other places."

The liquor was fire and thunder. It eased the hurts, dulled the memories of cold rain and harsh wind and bitter nights on the trail. But that was all. It did not answer the questions he had asked himself all these years of growing up.

The arms of Susie were soft, clinging. Money was to spend. He spent it. It was only metal with which to buy forgetfulness and the company of these Susies of the world.

He drank again. And again. But the memories stayed with him. He gave Susie a gold piece. "Good-by, Susie!" he said. "Go away. That's for your own good. You don't want to be put on the Injun list do you?"

"Injun list?"

Lee laughed at her. She suddenly backed away from him. She was a stranger in Punchbowl. She hadn't known who he was.

He left the Silver Bell. Tomorrow he would be back where he belonged. At Rancho Verde, breaking wild horses with Kinky Bob. Having his guts jolted into his throat, his lungs hammered by the antics of an animal until blood showed on his lips.

He had drunk far more than he had ever drunk before.

He had failed in his purpose. He had failed to erase the bitterness. He was not a part of the conviviality that was increasing in the town, for the crews were now pouring in, not only from BT and Rancho Verde, but from other outfits. But he was not one of them.

Chapter TWO

Four riders came down Summer Street, pulled up in a flurry of hoofs, and swung down at a saloon ahead. They were from Bill Tice's BT outfit.

Bill Tice's two sons were in the group that came onto the sidewalk in Lee's path, stamping the kinks out of their legs after their ride.

Merl Tice recognized Lee. "Hòwl!" he said, lifting a palm in the peace sign. It was a common form of greeting among friends, meant to be humorous. It wasn't humorous the way Merl Tice said it.

The brothers hadn't gone up the trail with the drives in the spring, staying home to oversee the ranch. Lee had worked cattle with them in the past and had gone up the trail with them the previous year. There had never been any real trouble with them on his part. Neither had they become friends.

Merl, a couple of years older than Gabe, was the one who set the pattern for their thinking. The brothers were prototypes of their father—bony, lantern-jawed, and boisterous. The Tice ranch was making money, big money, and the Tices were the kind who believed that money gave them the right to ride roughshod over less fortunate neighbors.

There had been a time, so Lee had been told by older men, when the Tice ranch had been a starving, patched-saddle outfit in the coulees and dry benches along the toe of the Armadillos, with Bill Tice suspected of riding with a long loop on moonlit nights and with a running iron hidden in his boot.

That day was past. Bill Tice was now in virtual partnership with Mike Bastrop's mighty Rancho Verde. The Tices rode expensive saddles and owned race horses and wore handmade shirts with big pearl buttons, foxed breeches, and smoke-gray sombreros that cost fifty dollars a throw.

16

Gabe Tice, taking the cue from his brother, moved into Lee's path. Lee did not swerve. He shouldered Gabe aside and continued on down the sidewalk. Gabe took a stride to overtake him.

"Who'n blazes do you think you're pushin' around, you lousy In— !" he began.

His brother halted him. "Don't spoil a big evenin' by barkin' your knuckles on Lee Jackson," Merl Tice said. "He's drunk. Drunker'n a skunk."

Gabe subsided. "It's about time they quit sellin' whisky to some folks in these parts," he said. "There's a law ag'in it an' it ought to be heeded."

Lee's stride slowed. Then he kept going. He heard another word from the group. Comanch'!

The four men walked into the saloon. Which of them had uttered the word, Lee didn't know. It didn't matter. Either of the Tice brothers would be a handful in a fight. The chances were that he'd have all four of them on him if he took up the issue.

The whisky was having its effect. He wanted to stand in the middle of the street, lift a war whoop, and dare them to make the most of it. If he was Comanche, he was proud of it. The Spearmen were a proud race of warriors, marred only by the evil that was in Eagle-in-the-Sky.

He swallowed his anger. A sooty lantern burned in the tunnel in the livery stable. Sam Barker was playing solitaire in the lamplit cubby that served as an office. The hostler poked his head out of the door, scowled when he saw that it was Lee, and went back to his game.

Lee was fuzzy-headed as he began rigging the roan. He heard a new arrival enter the livery. "You can get out my mare for me," Clemmy O'Neil's voice spoke.

The hostler yawned and continued to riffle the cards. Lee remained out of sight in the box stall.

"Please hurry!" Clemmy O'Neil said.

"What's all the rush?" the man drawled. "Why go home so early? Ain't you missin' all the fun? All the boys are in town from the outfits tonight. Maybe you ought to stop in at the Silver Bell."

"Get my saddle on that mare as fast as you can!" Clemmy O'Neil's voice was shaking with humiliation.

The hostler laughed. "There was a time when the Bell got a bigger play on nights like this than all the other traps put together. They flocked to see Rose O'Neil like bears around spilled honey."

Clemmy O'Neil ignored that, waiting as the hostler slowly saddled her mount.

"All right," she finally exploded. "You can go back to your rat hole. Charge the fee to the BT account."

"Come on, dearie," the hostler said. "I'll lift you onto the saddle. It'll be a pleasure."

"You touch me with your filthy hands and I'll take a quirt to you," Clemmy O'Neil said.

"Suit yourself," the man said. "Maybe you'll change your tune. That mare's mighty skittish. She ain't in the mood to be rode home tonight, if you ask me. There's a stallion in the corral outside an' the mare knows it. You'll need luck, climbin' into that sidewheel hull. Just call me when you need me. An' say pretty please when you do."

The hostler was right. The girl had her hands full. Lee peered out. The mare was wheeling, pulling away, each time the girl tried to mount. She was dragged to her knees in the dust. She hung to the reins.

The hostler laughed again. "Say pretty please."

"Merl and Gabe will beat you to jelly if I tell them how you're acting," the girl gasped.

The hosler's amusement ended and he retreated hastily out of sight into his cubby.

Lee watched the struggle continue between the girl and the mare. She was weakening and was faced with the choice of releasing the reins or risk being trampled.

Lee had made up his mind not to interfere. Clemmy O'Neil had never treated him as anything better than the dust that was marring her garb. If anything, she had been even more disdainful of him than the majority.

Maybe that was because, like himself, she was listed on the lower end of the social scale in Punchbowl. Women made a show of drawing aside the hems of their skirts when she passed by. Their husbands pretended that same brand of superiority, but only when their wives were around. Whenever they encountered Clemmy O'Neil alone, they eyed her with a different expression.

She was the daughter of Rose O'Neil, who had been the toast of the music halls from Denver to El Paso. Rose O'Neil was said to have had a fortune showered at her feet during the half-dozen years she had been known as the Golden Nightingale of the frontier towns. It was legend that she had squandered the money on clothes and jewelry as fast as it came into her hands. She had lived life to the full and had died tragically.

Ballads were still sung in line camps and around chuck-wagon fires:

> . . . lay still an' dead
> There on that silent stage.
> Lay dead there
> In ol' Punchbowl town,
> Our beautiful Rose O'Neil.

Rose O'Neil had been killed by a stray bullet while she was singing on the stage at the Silver Bell when a gunfight broke out among drunken cowboys. The man accused of firing the wild shot was lynched by a mob, but Rose O'Neil "lay still an' dead there on that silent stage."

When her will came to light it was learned she had a six-year-old daughter who was being raised in a convent in Santa Fe. As a young woman, Rose Shannon had been a seamstress and choir singer in Punchbowl, the daughter of a hard-working freighter. Against all advice, she had married a handsome, reckless Virginian named Clement O'Neil, who speculated in cattle and cotton and raced fast horses. He was killed in a horse race only a few months after their marriage, when his mount fell.

After the death of her husband, Rose O'Neil vanished for a time, then reappeared as a music-hall entertainer. Because of the beauty of her voice, men rode hundreds of miles to see and hear the Golden Nightingale.

Her will contained other surprises. It developed that Rose O'Neil's only other living relative was Bill Tice, owner of the BT outfit. The relationship was not of blood. Bill Tice had married Rose O'Neil's older sister when he was a young man. The sister had died a year or so after the marriage. Bill Tice had married again and Merl and Gabe were products of the second union.

As the only legal relative, Bill Tice was named guardian of the six-year-old Clementina O'Neil. It was understood that the Golden Nightingale had died almost penniless, but Bill Tice had made it known that he was a generous man who would see to it that his ward always had a roof over her head and a Christian upbringing, no matter how wild the blood that ran in her.

Therefore, Lee had not been the only one regarded as outside the social pale in the Punchbowl. Clemmy O'Neil carried the same burden. And with the same refusal to acknowledge that any living being was better. Or to let anyone say a word against her mother in her presence without regretting the error.

Clemmy O'Neil was losing the battle with the mare. She was blinded by dust and in tears. She was being dragged around like a doll. She wasn't quitting, but her strength wasn't equal to the demand of her will. The reins slipped away. The mare started to bolt from the barn.

Lee emerged from the stall, caught the reins, dug in his heels, and brought the animal to a halt. "All right," he said. "Easy now. Easy, I say."

The animal began to calm. Clemmy O'Neil got to her feet, panting and quivering, and brushed her skirt.

"After you get your breath, I'll give you a hand up," Lee said. "She won't try to unload you. If she starts thinking of getting rank again, lay a quirt on her. Hard! Let her know you mean business."

Clemmy O'Neil approached. She was still breathing hard and was trembling. When Lee offered her a hand to assist her to mount, she straightened. The spitfire pride had returned.

"I need no help," she said. "Please stand aside."

The liquor as boiling in Lee. He was an angry as he had ever been in his life. To be scorned by the likes of Clemmy O'Neil.

"What you mean," he said, "is that you don't want to be touched by an Indian. Now, aren't you the proud one!"

She was near. Too near. She with her green eyes that held such scorn. Don't touch me, you outcast, she was telling him with her eyes.

He caught her in his free arm, pulled her against him, and kissed her on the mouth. It was done before she realized what was coming, before even he knew what he was doing. It was the whisky, perhaps. It was life, perhaps. It was his answer to Clemmy O'Neil's scorn, and to all the world.

She tore free. She snatched the quirt from her saddle and raised it to lay the lash across his face. Then she paused.

"You're drunk!" she cried. "Drunk!"

She pulled herself aboard the sidesaddle, fury giving her

strength. She struck the mare with spurs and rode out of the barn. Lee heard the hoofbeats fade down Sumner Street.

He saw Sam Barker's leering face peeking out of the cubby. The man had seem him forcibly kiss Clemmy O'Neil. He turned unsteadily away. What did it matter? He made his way to his horse, pulled himself into the saddle, and rode out of the barn.

His thoughts were addled. Time seemed to be slowed so that impulses passed sluggishly across his mind. The truth was that he had never been drunk before. He had seen drunken men sing and dance. He wondered why he did not feel like singing or dancing. He had seen others weep in their cups. He did not feel like weeping. He only felt empty. And alone.

He ran his hand over his lips. His lips which had touched the lips of Clementina O'Neil. He regretted what he had done. He had treated her in the way most men wanted to treat her—as the daughter of the flaming Rose O'Neil.

He felt deep pity for Clemmy O'Neil, an attitude that he knew she would resent bitterly. She would want pity from no one, least of all Lee Jackson.

He found himself standing at the bar of the worst dive in town. He was drinking whisky he didn't remember ordering and it was bitter in his throat. What he sought was oblivion. From everything. From all memories, and especially from the thought that he had added to Clemmy O'Neil's burden.

He fumbled for his watch. It was a cheap, nickel-plated piece with a buffalo-tooth fob that he had bought from a peddler on the trail to Kansas. It was missing from his pocket.

The banjo clock on the saloon wall said ten o'clock. He left the place, mounted his roan, and headed down the trail toward Rancho Verde. That was all he remembered. After that came the oblivion that had been eluding him all evening.

Dawn was in the sky when he awakened, stiff, cold, and forlorn, with a throat as dry as alkali. His horse was nuzzling for forage nearby, its reins dragging. He had slept in high grass near a shallow stream.

He identified his location. Soldier Ford. Casa Bonita was still five miles south. The trail forded the creek nearby, but he and his horse had been hidden by brush and darkness from any travelers who might have passed by during the night.

He drank from the stream. And drank again. He buried his face in the cooling water. He reached for his watch. When he failed to find it, he recalled that it had been missing before he had left town. He decided that he must have dropped it in the livery barn.

He had slept here five or six hours. A period of total oblivion. That realization now appalled him.

He mounted and rode to Rancho Verde. Full daylight had come, but lamps still burned back of the curtains in Casa Bonita. Judge Amos Clebe's varnished buggy stood, shafts hoisted, alongside the house. Bill Tice's silver-trimmed saddle was stored on a tree on the gallery of the house. The poker game was still on.

The bunkhouse stood a considerable distance west of the main house. It was dark and deserted, for all hands were still in town. Only a few line riders at lonely shacks out in the range were on duty.

Kinky Bob appeared. He lived alone in a low, dirt-roofed adobe shack near the barn and wagon shed. His home had once been the quarters of a slave family. He had just cooked and finished his breakfast and had a tin cup of coffee in his hand.

Lee dismounted, drew his rig from the roan, turned it into the corral, and saw that it had water and feed. Kinky Bob came closer, took a long look at him, then whistled and hurried back to his shack.

He returned with another tin of black coffee. "You sure look like you need it, Jack-Lee," he said.

The coffee helped a little. "There's a woodpecker hammering on my skull," Lee sighed. "And danged if I can scare him away."

"You look like you're goin' to enjoy bronc twistin' a lot less than usual," Kinky Bob said.

Lee groaned. "My head's going to sail right off into the tules the first time a horse sunfishes on me today. And good riddance."

"You git any sleep atall, Jack-Lee?"

"I woke up in the brush at Soldier Ford. I must have snored there for hours. You ever been drunk, Kink?"

"I ain't sayin'. But I know you'll be all right. You young. You come back in a hurry. Wait 'til yo're old. Like Kinky

Bob. Older'n sin. I kin hear my bones creak every time a
snuffy horse humps his back under me."

Lee grinned weakly. He had no idea how old Kink really
was. Nor did Kink. Frost was in his tough, curly hair, but
to Lee he was a powerful rock that would never change.
In his youth he had been trained as a boxer. No man had
ever defeated him.

Lee ate the flapjacks and grits Kink cooked for him.
They saddled up, each picking as his mount his smartest
cutting horse, trained for assisting with green animals. They
loaded a pack animal with food and bedrolls.

The poker game evidently was still going on in Casa
Bonita. The wan light of lamps continued to burn back of
the velvet curtains even though sunup was at hand.

At this hour the air was keen and bracing. It drove the
last of the murk from Lee's thoughts. They rode in silence
for a time, heading westward for the horse pasture two
miles away where there were pole corrals and squeezers to
help with handling rough horses.

"Why'd you do it, Jack-Lee?" Kinky Bob finally asked.

Lee didn't bother trying to evade. He knew what Kink
meant. "I guess things just got to closing in on me a little
too snug," he said.

"Such as de boss orderin' you out to bust horses the very
next day after you got back from de long trail?"

"Maybe," Lee replied.

"Seems like, bein' as he tuk you to raise, he don't show
much mercy to you."

Lee looked at the big man. Kinky Bob met his gaze. "He
hate you, Jack-Lee."

"I've never done anything to him, Kink."

"Comanches, dey kill de lady dat was his wife as she sat
right in dat house, so I was told. Dey tried to burn de
house itself, but de walls an' big beams was too old an'
tough. De Majah, he remember who done dem things."

Lee was silent for a time. "I see your point. Mike Bastrop has reason to hate Comanches. But he took me in and
raised me. Why? He could have sent me to an orphanage."

"Or had you sent back to Eagle-in-the-Sky," Kinky Bob
said. "He tried to do dat."

"Back to Eagle?" Lee exclaimed. "What are you saying?"

"De Majah, he made a trip to Fo't Gilman not long
after you was first brung here when you was a button. He
tried to talk de Colonel into sendin' you back to de chief.

He said Eagle was yore father. Said you was Injun an' you belonged with your people."

Lee peered at the big man. "How do you know this?"

"I was breakin' hawsses for de Army at de fo't when he come dar. De Colonel's orderly tol' me all about it. I didn't pay much 'tention at de time. I didn't come here to Rancho Verde 'til a few years afterward to work for dat man. Since den I been doin' a lot of seein'. An' thinkin' about you."

"What did the Colonel say?"

"Said he wasn't convinced that you was a Comanch'. He said he'd have you put in an orphanage somewhere. Majah Bastrop changed his tune. Said he'd look after you 'til you was big enough to fend for yourself. De Colonel was happy to let it stand dat way."

Kinky Bob was silent for a time. "Why don't you pull out, Jack-Lee?" he finally asked. "Change yore name. Go somewhere else. Forgit de Punchbowl. Forgit de Majah. He give you all de tough jobs. Everybody know dat. It's like he wants to make you pay for what happened to de lady."

Lee rode for minutes without speaking. "What you're advising me to do, Kink," he finally said, "is go somewhere, change my identity, and never let anyone know I'm a Comanche."

"I didn't say dat, Jack-Lee."

"You believe I *am* a Comanche, don't you, Kink?"

"Kink don't believe nothin'," the big man exclaimed.

"I'm not pulling out," Lee said. "At least not yet. I don't savvy why I hang on. I've decided to leave. A hundred times. But something keeps holding me here."

Chapter *THREE*

They reached the fenced pasture where the new crop of unbroken horses was held. The animals were all five-year-olds that had been cut from the main herd and brought off the range for training.

Lee and Kinky Bob began their task. Working animals in groups of half a dozen, they sought, first of all, to win their confidence by moving among them, accustoming them to the presence of humans. Next would come the critical period of letting them smell saddle blankets and of submitting to the feel of a halter.

It was a tough day's work, with animals rearing and striking with lightning hoofs. Patience and more patience. Try and try again. Dust and blistering sun. Gain an inch, lose an inch. Start over. Talk gently, confidently. Beware of the slash of savage teeth. Teeth that did not always miss.

They quit at sundown. Bone-weary, they had a respectable string of horses submitting to the weight of a saddle blanket, and a few even accepting a halter.

They stripped and reveled in the cool water of the irrigation ditch. They washed their dust-caked garments, hung them to dry on brush, and donned clean replacements.

They had set up camp in the horse pasture in order to accustom the animals to the presence of humans and to the smells and sounds of a cookfire. It developed they had failed to include salt in their food pack. Kinky Bob saddled up and headed for his shack to fetch the essential condiment.

Lee, with half an hour to wait, rolled another cigaret, opened a can of tomatoes, and tested the contents. It was without zest, lacking salt. He went to the ditch, scoured the Dutch oven with sand and water in order to pass time.

He straightened. Riders were approaching. Several riders. The sun had gone down and the range was sinking into a sea of purple mist. The riders who loomed out of the dusk

were miraged to the stature of giants on mighty horses.
But they were mere men.

There were five of them. Mike Bastrop was the nucleus
of the contingent. With him were his poker-playing cronies,
Bill Tice and the pudgy, gray-bearded jurist, Amos Clebe.
For once, the fastidious Judge was riding saddleback, rather
than in his gleaming top buggy which was more suited to
his paunchy, soft physique.

The other two were Bill Tice's sons. Merl and Gabe Tice
held Lee's attention as they dismounted. They had the
attitude of avengers on the prowl. They bore the flinty
glare of pursuers who had overtaken their quarry.

Bill Tice also dismounted, but Mike Bastrop and the
Judge remained in the saddle. All five were armed with
pistols. Rifles jutted from slings on the saddles of the Tice
brothers.

Kinky Bob loomed up in the background and halted his
horse. Evidently he had turned back when he had met the
five on their way to the pasture. His face was ashine with
uneasiness.

"All right," Mike Bastrop said. "There he is, men. It's
your pleasure."

Lee, astounded, stood staring. Merl and Gabe Tice came
walking toward him. Not until too late did he comprehend
that they meant harm. However, they made no move to
draw their pistols. His own .44 and his rifle were out of
reach.

Merl snarled, "You filthy copperpot, if you live a million
years, you'll never quit bein' sorry you tried to lay a hand
on our kind of women."

Merl and Gabe came at him from left and right. Lee, still
stunned by the suddenness of it, only partly warded off the
first fist that came at him. Gabe seized his arm and whirled
him off balance. He was exposed to the smashing blow
that Merl drove at his jaw, staggering him.

He braced his heels and pivoted. Gabe was many pounds
heavier, but Lee lifted him clear of the ground and whip-
cracked him, sending him slithering into the fringe of the
fire.

Gabe uttered a grunt of fear, but rolled clear, brushing
away sparks, without serious damage. Lee ducked, twisting
aside, for he sensed that Merl was coming at him from the
opposite side. He felt Merl's arms slide over his head, failing in an attempt to pin his arms to his sides.

The brothers circled him. He moved in on Merl and rammed a fist to the stomach. Merl reeled back with a wheeze of agony.

Bill Tice now came to the aid of his sons. He leaped on Lee's back. He was a powerful man, and Lee, his lungs already burning from the stress of the battle, was unable to shake him off.

Gabe moved in, fists poised. "Wait a minute!" Lee panted. "What's come over you people? What's this all about?"

Mike Bastrop spoke. "You know what you did, you whelp. You ought to be hung. Tie him to that mesquite snag over there, boys. Use my quirt if you want."

Kinky Bob spoke in his deep voice. "You ain't goin' to horsewhip him? Not dat!"

Bastrop whirled on the black man. "What have you got to say about it? Maybe you'd like a taste of a quirt, too. We don't stand for white men trying to break into the sleeping rooms of our women, let alone an Indian."

"What are you talking about?" Lee demanded.

Merl Tice slapped him savagely. "You know," he raged. "You insulted my sister last night at the livery, then followed her to the ranch, knowin' she'd be alone. You tried to bust in on her."

Lee quit struggling to escape from Bill Tice's arms. "Your sister? You mean Clemmy O'Neil? No! No! I couldn't do a thing like that!"

Merl slapped him again. "You grabbed her ag'in her will at the livery! Don't deny that. Sam Barker saw it. You followed her out of town."

Ice suddenly rushed through Lee's veins. He was thinking of those hours of blankness the previous night. Had he really lain asleep in the brush at Soldier Creek all that time? The Tice ranch house was little more than an hour's ride from the ford.

They saw the uncertainty in him. Merl struck him again. He felt blood flow from a split lip.

"All I ask is that I get first whack at him with the quirt," Merl gritted. "We ought to drag him by the heels back to the BT so that Clemmy can see him pay for scarin' her out of her wits."

"You mean she says I was there?" Lee demanded. "She saw me?"

"O' course she saw you. You ain't goin' to add to your troubles by callin' my sister a liar, are you?"

His father spoke wrathfully. "She ain't your sister, Merl, an' I don't want you claimin' the likes of her as such. But, even so, she's a woman an' is entitled to protection from the likes of this one."

"She's lying," Lee said, and suddenly he was sure of it. "She couldn't have seen me at BT last night. I wasn't within miles of your ranch."

"Then how do you explain why this was found in her room after she fought you off?" Merl demanded.

He dangled an object in front of Lee's eyes. It was the pocket watch with the buffalo-tooth fob that had been missing from Lee's pocket. He could only gaze at it, bewildered.

Amos Clebe said, "I reckon there wasn't any real harm done to the gal. I say to give this fellow a hiding, then run him out of the country. As a legally elected representative of law and order, I don't want to be a witness to anything like this, much as it's deserved."

Amos Clebe rode away, kicking his horse in the ribs, the skirts of his long, black linen coat flapping around his fat legs.

"Let's get this over with," Mike Bastrop said harshly. "The Judge is right. No use hangin' him." He pointed a finger at Kinky Bob. "Slope out of here, you. This is no place for you to linger."

Kinky Bob did not stir his horse. "I'm stayin'," he said. He was inviting death by his defiance and knew it. He had seen men of his race shot down for less.

Bastrop gazed at him with deadly speculation. Whatever the pros and cons that he weighed, the decision went in favor of the black man's survival.

"Stay and be damned," Bastrop said. "Maybe it'll be a lesson to you as well as to him."

Lee began fighting. He was sure they were wrong. Clemmy O'Neil was wrong. She had lied. This, no doubt, was her way of paying him off for humiliating her with the hostler watching. Chances were she had found his watch in the livery.

He wrested free of Bill Tice's grasp. But it was no use. The three Tices piled on him. Their weight carried him to the ground.

Mike Bastrop, from the saddle, flipped a loop around his

ankles and yanked it tight. Bastrop gigged his horse and Lee found himself being dragged through brush. His shirt was ripped. Thorns drove into him. Rocks punished him.

He had no real strength to fight back. He was spread-eagled against a dead tree.

Merl Tice got his wish. He was the first to use the quirt. Lee felt the heavy, brutal force of the lash. Felt it strike again. And again.

He saw Kinky Bob, still mounted, gazing at him. It seemed to him that Kinky Bob was also feeling each blow of the lash. It was as though he was trying to add his own power of endurance to Lee's.

Gabe used the quirt also. Their father took a turn. Kinky Bob cried, "In God's mercy! Dat's enough!"

Mike Bastrop spoke. "I reckon that'll do, men." Bastrop was ashen and beads of cold sweat stood on his forehead.

The punishment ceased. Bastrop dismounted, came to where Lee was sagging, seized him by the hair, and twisted his head around. "Get out of this country, Comanche," he said. "Don't let sunrise find you in the Punchbowl. You got off lucky this time. Go back where you came from. To the people that murdered my wife."

They rode away. Kinky Bob cut Lee free and supported him until his knees steadied. Lee made his way to the ditch, waded in, and let the cooling water wash away some of the blood, some of the pain. Kinky Bob doctored the welts on his back, using a cooling ointment they carried in the medical kit.

"What you aim to do, Jack-Lee?" Kink finally asked.

"You know the answer to that, Kink."

Kinky Bob sighed. "I'm afeared I do. I see it in your face. You ain't a forgivin' man."

"One thing kept me from passin' out," Lee said. "It was the thought that I had to live through it, live through anything so as to give them a taste of the same medicine."

"They'll only kill you. Hang you, Jack-Lee. Maybe torture you."

"I want to see how much Merl Tice will take before he caves in. And Gabe. They're tough. But how tough? I'll find out. And their father used a quirt on me, too."

"Vengeance is fer de Lawd, Jack-Lee."

"The Tices aren't the only ones. There are others."

"You mean *him*, don't you, Jack-Lee? De Majah?"

Lee didn't answer that. No answer was needed. Mike

Bastrop had not actually swung the quirt, but he had refused to defend Lee or seek a fair hearing.

Then there was Clementina O'Neil. If that was her way of paying him back for the episode at the livery, she had more than succeeded.

He stumbled to where his roan was picketed and picked up his saddle.

"Where you goin'? Kinky Bob asked.

"It's better that you don't know," Lee said. "You'll hear from me some day."

"Take me along, Jack-Lee. With you gone, there's no friend o' Kinky Bob's here at Verde."

"I'd be doing you no favor, letting you go with me."

"You can't ride off like dis—nothin' but de clothes on yore back."

"That's about how I came here. At least I own my own horse. And my own packhorse. Where is that buckskin devil? If he's handy, I'll take him with me tonight."

"He handy. I fetched him in from de range along with yore roan. I'll bring him in."

Kink rode away into the early dusk and presently returned, leading a tough, short-coupled buckskin. He accompanied Lee to the ranch bunkhouse and waited moodily while Lee collected his personal belongings and loaded them on the buckskin, which had been equipped with a packsaddle.

The big man went to his shack and made up a pack of food and blankets from his larder. He added a skillet, Dutch oven, and a battered coffeepot. Also an ax, a water bag, and a skinning knife.

"Make sure you got yore razah," he advised. "An' soap an' such. A man feels more like a man if'n he keeps shaved an' lookin' respectable. Then he *stays* respectable."

"That might take more than a razor and soap," Lee said.

"I got more grub cached out in the brush," Kink said. "An' other possibles. Keep dat in mind in case o' need."

"Thanks, my friend," Lee said. They shook hands, and Lee rode off into the darkness.

He had been deadlined out of the range where he had been raised, deadlined by the man he had hoped would come to look on him as a son. Kink had been right. Mike Bastrop hated him. At first there might have been a doubt in Bastrop's mind, but, evidently, as the years passed, he had become certain that Lee was a member of the tribe that had murdered his wife.

Lee began mapping his future. To the west lay the Pecos. Except for stage stations at the few fords, the only habitations along the lonely river were the dugouts of Indian traders or professed hunters who were in reality men hiding from the law, or road agents who preyed on whatever quarry they found on the few trails. Outlaw country. Law officers rarely crossed the Pecos, except in numbers, and usually returned empty-handed and often with empty saddles.

A man with vengeance in his mind could operate from beyond the Pecos. But a man who crossed the river was a lost soul. He had only one course—to become as savage and harsh as the land itself. It was said that, even in the days of the great herds, not even the hardy buffalo ·had ever grazed west of the Pecos.

Southward was Mexico. A land where a man could take a new name, cloak himself in a new life, and erase the past from his memory. Mexico was a place for forgetting, if a man really wanted to forget.

Eastward lay another lonely land that men avoided. The Llano Estacado it had been named by the early Spanish travelers. The fenced plains. Ranchers called that area the Staked Plains. By either name it was a bitter land—a wasteland where lay the bleached bones of the buffalo that had grazed there, and the bones of soldiers and explorers and Indians who had died there of starvation or thirst, or had frozen in the blizzards that howled across its swells in winter.

To Lee's knowledge no cowboy had ventured more than a few miles beyond the high, dry bluffs that frowned down on the range east of the Armadillo Hills. That particular area of the Staked Plains was written off as a waterless desert for a hundred miles, swept by sandstorms. Punchbowl people called that area the Devil's Garden.

However, it had been from the Devil's Garden that the Comanches had come in the days of the war trail, sweeping down on the border settlements to scalp and pillage.

No white man had ever crossed the Devil's Garden, it was said. But the Comanches had traveled it, and Lee, as a child, had crossed it with war and hunting parties. He knew its secrets.

If he was to need a hideout, it would be the Devil's

Garden. With that decided, he set his course in the direction
of BT ranch. After a few miles, he camped for the night in
thick brush.

He remained camped until twilight the next day. Saddling the roan, he left the buckskin on picket in the brush
and headed toward the Tice ranch. He had treated the welts
on his back. They would require attention for a time, but
he doubted if there would be any permanent damage.

It was still early evening when he came in sight of the
sprawling, many-winged Tice place. Windows in the main
section glowed with light, but the bunkhouse, which stood
a distance away, was dark. The riders were still in town,
spending their pay and trying to forget that the majority
of them would soon be heading for Kansas again, riding
the harsh miles of the trail.

A late cattle drive was a gamble, but it paid off, if successful. If caught by an early winter, such herds could be
held along the Brazos or the Red River, but that meant
extra crew expenses and the possibility of loss from blizzards.

Although Bill Tice gambled with Mike Bastrop on these
drives and had at least a quarter interest in the bags of
gold that had lain on the big table in Casa Bonita the
previous day, Lee had been told by old-timers that the man
didn't know any more about the art of raising cattle than
a hog did about ballroom dancing. And never would,
they had always added with a sniff of scorn.

Bill Tice had a gift for gab and impressing the ladies. He
had always seemed to find time to spend in town and the
money to be well-dressed and barbered, even though what
few cattle he had owned in the early days had been scrub
stock, afflicted by worms and ticks.

Rose O'Neil's older sister had been an unsophisticated
girl of eighteen who was dazzled by Bill Tice's surface
manners. She had died within two years after their marriage
of neglect and a broken heart. Bill Tice had soon remarried.
His second wife had born him two sons before succumbing
also to hardship and loneliness at the squalid ranch in the
hills.

However, a change had come in Bill Tice's fortunes some
years in the past. Some said it was the death of his second
wife that had caused him to turn over a new leaf. Whatever
the reason, Bill Tice and his ranch began to prosper. Mike
Bastrop, who had inherited Rancho Verde after the death

of his wife at the hands of Comanches, began to find better qualities in his neighbor than other Punchbowl people had seen. He helped Bill Tice grade up his cattle and widen his range by installing windmills and tanks and check dams along the flanks of the Armadillos.

Within a few years, Rancho Verde and BT were in a pool that was a virtual partnership. An imposing ranch house stood on the site of the former tumble-down house where two wives had died. It was said that Bill Tice had leveled the shack and plowed under the soil so that he would never be reminded of his days of poverty.

He kept adding to the house each year. It was now an amazing polyglot maze of wings and galleries and turrets and gables. He built new wings and rooms on the structure constantly. Cowboys rode far out of their way to take a look at the bizarre collection. It was said there were more than thirty rooms in the place that had never even been occupied.

There was a superstition that some of those rooms were inhabited by the ghosts of the wives Bill Tice had buried. And it was said that Clemmy O'Neil's mother also haunted BT ranch. There were freighters and mule packers who had stopped near BT overnight who declared they had heard Rose O'Neil singing in the midnight blackness. More practical persons said that what those fools had heard was Clemmy O'Neil, who had a voice almost as sweet as that of the Golden Nightingale.

Lee had never been inside the huge ranch house. Ahead, it bulked enormously in the starlight as he dismounted and picketed his horse. It crouched beneath a full moon that was ballooning above the Armadillos, as yellow as a jack-o'-lantern. There were several wings, separated from the original main house by roofed galleries and breezeways.

The original house, where the lights burned, was where the Tices held forth. Lee moved cautiously into the ranch yard on foot and scouted the place.

He could hear voices and the clatter of dishes and utensils. He moved to the east wall and stepped silently into the shadow of the gallery. The curtains of the main room had not been drawn.

Bill Tice, Mike Bastrop, and Judge Amos Clebe sat at a big, linen-spread table which bore the residue of a meal along with wine and whisky bottles and glasses. Mexican servants moved about. Bill Tice, flushed with liquor, embraced a comely servant girl, who escaped, giggling, from his grasp. Amos Clebe, his fat, bearded face expressionless, sat toying with a whisky glass. Mike Bastrop was smoking a cigar and had a wineglass in front of him.

A smaller table in a corner of the room bore poker chips and a deck of cards. There were three chairs at this table. Evidently the game that had started at Rancho Verde had been adjourned to Bill Tice's ranch.

Tice tried to arise drunkenly to pursue the giggling girl who was little more than a child. Mike Bastrop moved. He placed a big hand against Tice's face and shoved him roughly back in his chair. "You're drunk, Bill," he said scornfully. "Swill some coffee instead of booze. Sober up, so we can play a few more hands."

Bill Tice wore the garb of a gentleman—a dark sack coat, white shirt, and string tie. He had a black-velvet sash around his waist in the Spanish style. A pistol and a dagger with a carved gold handle were thrust in the sash.

The two men sat glaring at each other. Bill Tice wanted to go for a weapon but didn't have the courage. Mike Bastrop, who had his six-shooter in a holster on his thigh, smiled mockingly as though daring the BT owner to come at him. Tice quieted and carefully let his hand drop away from his sash.

Judge Clebe had made no move to interfere. When he saw that the crisis was past, he reached for a bottle and refilled his whisky glass. His pale blue eyes did not seem to change expression. However, Lee had the impression that the Judge was disappointed.

Lee moved to a better position which gave him a full view of the table. He discovered that Merl and Gabe Tice were also guests at the supper. The brothers were scowling at Mike Bastrop, but that was as far as they went in resenting his treatment of their father. In fact, Lee believed Merl and Gabe had rather enjoyed seeing their parent humiliated, even though they seemed to hold no particular regard for Mike Bastrop.

Clemmy O'Neil was present at the feast. She sat at the far end of the table, as distant as possible from the others. She wore a modest supper dress and had her hair done in a mature style, but there was taut distaste for her companions in the set of her lips and in the way she stonily ignored them with her eyes. Lee surmised she was here against her will.

She waved away a servant bearing wine. Her glass was turned down. Merl reached across the table, righted the glass, and angrily motioned the servant to fill it.

"Drink up, honey!" he demanded, his voice carrying through the open window. "Here's a toast to the prettiest gal in New Mexico. Come on! Let's clink glasses."

He held the glass to her lips. She suddenly seized it and tossed the contents into his face.

"Why you little hussy!" he exploded. He seized her wrist and started to drag her to her feet.

Mike Bastrop spoke. "Sit down, Merl, before I blow an ear off you."

Bastrop had his six-shooter in his hand. He was one of the best pistol shots in the Punchbowl and usually won the target shooting at the Christmas and Fourth of July festivals.

Merl subsided abruptly. "I was just funnin'," he growled, and went back to his seat. "No need for peelin' out a hog laig on me, Major."

"You carry your funning too far," Bastrop said. "You said she was a sister to you. Treat her as such."

"You know I didn't mean that," Merl growled. "She's not of my blood. You know what she is."

"Shut up!" his father roared, seizing a chance to show authority over his son. "An' I warn you not to try no foolishness with her. You'll git your eyes scratched out. I don't want no scandals in my house."

"Let's go back to the game," Mike Bastrop said. "We've all drunk too much already. What we need is action."

Clemmy O'Neil walked from the room. She walked with dignity, but Lee sensed that she was deathly afraid and wanted to run.

Gabe and Merl downed their drinks and pushed back their chairs. "It's too danged early to turn in," Gabe said. "I'm goin' to town an' maybe play a little monte. How about you, Merl?"

Merl laughed sneeringly. "That monte game wouldn't be at Pedro's place where that little, black-eyed señorita who calls herself Lola Vasquez hangs out, now would it?"

"You ridin' with me or do you just want to keep runnin' off the mouth?"

"I got nobody in Punchbowl I figure worth ridin' fifteen miles to take a look at tonight. I'm turnin' in."

"An' you better do the same, Gabe," his father blustered.

"I've heard of Lola Vasquez. An' nothin' good. There ought to be decent girls you can take up with. You hang around that Mexican tamale an' some day you'll likely get a chiv between yore ribs."

Gabe ignored him and stamped out. Lee retreated around a corner of the structure and waited until Gabe had saddled and headed away toward town. By that time Bastrop, the Judge, and Bill Tice were back at their poker game.

Merl Tice came to the front gallery, smoking a cigaret while he watched his brother ride away. Presently Merl headed away through the house, evidently bound for his quarters to turn in for the night.

Lamplight showed in two windows in an east wing of the sprawl of rooms. Lee decided that marked Clemmy O'Neil's rooms. He debated whether to stalk Merl, confront him, and pay him off for the quirt whipping. That was what he had come here to do.

But Clemmy O'Neil was also on his list. There could hardly be physical punishment of a girl, of course, but he at least meant to confront her, and force her to admit she had lied.

He waited until sure Merl was out of the way, then moved to the wing where the light showed. It was separated from the main building by a roofed, tile-floored patio, which was more popularly known as a dogtrot.

Light seeped around the curtains of the windows. They were casements, open for the sake of coolness. The curtains moved slightly in the draw of the warm breeze. One window overlooked the dogtrot. An arched, wide doorway led into a red-tiled hall that served all the rooms in this wing. The heavy double doors stood open.

Lee crouched beneath the window. He could hear movement inside the room. The rustle of garments. He tiptoed into the hall and to the first door. He put his ear to the panel; the faint footsteps he could hear inside were those of a woman. Clemmy O'Neil, beyond a doubt.

He debated it for a time. From the main wing came the muted sounds of the poker game—the riffle of cards, the clack of chips, an occasional word from the players.

He made his decision. With painful care, he tried the wrought-iron thumb latch that held the heavy cedar portal. The door did not yield. It was bolted inside.

Despite his caution, the latch gave a faint sound as he

released pressure. Sounds in the room ceased instantly. He could hear the drive of his own pulse. Or was it the frightened pound of Clemmy O'Neil's lungs he was hearing? He could imagine her terror.

She spoke, so afraid her voice was faint and shaky. "Merl? Is that you?"

Lee did not answer. He began slowly, soundlessly drawing away from the door, taking a backward step at a time. She spoke again. "Merl? If it *is* you, go away!" She added quaveringly, "I've got a gun. I'll use it! You know I will!"

On a sudden hunch, Lee spoke softly. "It isn't Merl."

There was a space of silence. Then she said, "It's Lee Jackson, isn't it." It was more a statement than a question.

To Lee's surprise, the bolt in the door grated and the door opened. He stared. In the short time since she had left the main room she had changed from the supper costume to denim riding breeches and boots, a cotton shirtwaist, and a neckerchief. A false riding skirt lay on a chair, ready to be pinned around her waist as a sop to convention which considered riding astride unladylike.

She had rearranged her hair in a tight, coiled plait, so that it would fit beneath her sombrero which lay on the bed. She had a pistol in her hand, her finger on the trigger. It was a short-muzzled .32, such as might be carried in a purse or handbag. At this range it could be very deadly.

She did not point the gun at him. She merely gazed at him, waiting, her eyes jade green with the stress of her emotions.

She studied him for a time. Then, as though satisfied of something, she motioned him to enter. "Quick!" she murmured. "Someone might see you!"

Astounded, Lee stepped into the room. She closed the door. He saw that this was a sitting room, comfortably furnished with easy chairs, sofa, books, an oil reading lamp, and rag rugs.

An open door led to a bedroom, where the sombrero lay. A bedroll was lashed in a tarp for packing on a saddle.

"You act like you might have been expecting me," Lee said.

"Maybe I was," she responded. She kept her voice down to a whisper.

Lee followed that example. "Don't you know it's bad luck to put a hat on a bed."

"I'm not superstitious," she said.

"Why did you figure I'd come here?" he asked.

"I heard what happened yesterday. They whipped you."

"That ought to have made you happy."

"Happy? What sort of a person do you think I am?"

"I wonder. What sort of a person would do what you did to get square? I'm sorry about kissing you. I apologize. I was drunk. I didn't really mean to."

"You mean no man would kiss Clemmy O'Neil unless he was full of booze and didn't know what he was doing?"

Lee cocked an eyebrow. "You said that. I didn't. At any rate, I don't figure it was worth fixing to have me flogged and run out of the country. They might even have strung me up. That's what usually happens to a man accused of what you said I did."

He added, "You lied, didn't you?"

"This is why I knew you'd come here," she said. "To tell me I lied. That's why I guessed you were the one outside my door just now."

She was continually jabbing him off balance by her coolness. "Better put that gun down," he said. "You might touch it off and hurt somebody."

She lowered the gun slightly. "That's better," he said. "They've deadlined me out of the Punchbowl, because of what you told them. But I'm not leaving. I'll hang around. You can tell Merl and Gabe that. And their father. They were the ones who swung the whip on me. Tell them that sooner or later they'll know how it feels."

"I don't suppose you'd believe me if I told you I had nothing to do with it," she said. "I never said you were the man who broke into my room that night."

"The Tices told it different."

"They were the ones who lied," she said. "Someone did come in here that night. Through the window. I had gone to bed. I heard him. He had a pillowcase over his head, with eyeholes cut in it. He grabbed me and we fought. I managed to scream like a banshee. That scared him away. He scrambled back through the window and got away before anybody showed up to help me."

She added, after a space of silence, "I never said you were the man. It was Merl who found your watch in my room."

She paused again, then remarked, "At least he *said* he had found it there."

Lee eyed her questioningly. She nodded. "I'm sure it was

Merl in that pillowcase. I've been afraid of him for a long time. He came back from town in a wild rage that night after I'd been in Punchbowl. The hostler had told him about seeing you kiss me. He was like a wild man. He accused me of awful things. He said he'd make you the sorriest man alive."

"He almost did," Lee said.

"You don't want to believe me, do you?" she asked.

The trouble was that Lee *did* find himself believing her, against his will. Evidently the hostler had found his watch and had given it to Merl Tice when he had gone to Merl with the story of what had happened in the livery.

She was watching him. "I could be lying, of course," she said. "I could be stringing you along so that you won't harm me to pay off for what they did to you at the horse camp. That's why you came here, wasn't it?"

"Maybe," Lee said.

"That's why I expected you," she said.

"I wanted to get a close look at a girl who'd tell a lie like that," Lee admitted.

"Are you getting a close enough look?"

"Closer than an Indian is supposed to look at even—"

He broke off. He hadn't meant to say anything like that.

She said it for him. "—at even a person like Clemmy O'Neil. About the only thing lower than Clemmy O'Neil is an Indian."

"Again you're the one who said that, not me," Lee said.

"Some things need saying."

Chapter FOUR

Lee eyed her garb and gazed around at the evidence of preparations for a journey. "You going somewhere?" he asked.

"I'm leaving BT," she said.

"For keeps?"

"For keeps."

"You don't like it here?"

She gave him a wry smile. "That's putting it mildly."

"Where will you go?"

"That's none of your concern," she said.

The sounds from the poker game had become more audible. The voices of the players had risen. They were in angry dispute.

"It's Bastrop and Bill Tice again," Lee said. "They don't seem to be the pals everybody thinks they are. I saw the Major push Bill Tice in the face at the supper table. I was peeking at a window."

"Window peepers can get shot," she said.

"I'd say, from the sounds, that somebody else might get shot," Lee remarked. "What caused 'em to fall out?"

"They're always quarreling," she said. "But that's as far as it goes. They despise each other."

"But they're partners."

She shrugged. "Wolves run in packs. And eat each other if the chance comes."

"I hear they play for big stakes," Lee said. "And they say the Major loses pretty heavy to the Judge and Bill Tice."

"Bosh!" she sniffed.

"What do you mean, 'bosh'?"

"All three of them are so miserly they wouldn't risk more than a few dollars in a card game."

"What? But everybody says—"

"I know. Everybody thinks thousands of dollars change

hands in those games. If so, I've never seen it. They like to play poker, but only to pass time. But none of them wants to lose. They're that kind."

"How do you know this?" Lee demanded.

"I spy on them. I'm a window peeper, too. I've spied on them since I was a child. Uncle Tice caught me at it years ago, and beat me. Oh, how he beat me. I couldn't sit down for days. He told me it would go harder on me if he ever caught me eavesdropping on him and his friends again."

She gave him another of her little, dry smiles. "Since then I've been more careful. He hasn't caught me at it."

Clemmy O'Neil was no longer speaking in the brittle, superior manner that Lee associated with her. He understood suddenly that this had been a defensive armor, the image she showed to a world that was trying always to snub her.

Her voice was clear, musical. There was a Spanish flavor to the way she formed her words. This was due, no doubt, to her training at the convent and at the hands of Mexican housekeepers at the Tice ranch.

The sounds of quarreling faded. But the poker game was not being resumed.

The girl moved to the window and listened. "They're finally quitting," she said. "Major Bastrop and the Judge are leaving." She added, "You must wait. They'll be gone in a few minutes."

Lee scowled at her. She was as much as dismissing him, and even directing when he should leave. She seemed to be taking it for granted that he believed the story she had told about the intruder in the pillowcase.

He waited. Bill Tice was bawling an order for the Judge's buggy and Mike Bastrop's horse to be brought up. A wrangler evidently was still on call.

"What will you do?" Clemmy O'Neil asked as they waited.

Lee shrugged. *"Quien sabe?* I haven't decided."

She was silent for a time. "I think you *do* know," she said abruptly. "You've made up your mind." She added, "Don't do it!"

"Do what?"

"Become an outlaw. How is it they say it, ride the trail where the owls hoot?"

"What makes you think I'd do a thing like that?" Lee demanded.

"It's written on you. You've already taken the first step."

"And what was this first step?"

"You didn't come to this ranch to window peep. You came here to pay off for what they did to you. To use force. What will be your next step? And the next?"

"You aim to preach to me?" Lee snapped.

"Now that would be something, wouldn't it?" she replied. "Clemmy O'Neil preaching, standing up for the straight and narrow path. Isn't that a big laugh?"

Beneath her mockery was pathos and loneliness. That angered Lee. "For God's sake!" he exploded. "Don't start pitying yourself! Not you, of all people. Don't let them break you!"

She straightened, stung. The defiance returned. "I don't pity myself," she said. "And nobody will ever break me. I'll promise you that."

"Nor me," Lee said. "And that's another promise."

He heard the crunch of wheels and hoofs as Amos Clebe's buggy and Mike Bastrop's mount were brought to the front of the house.

Bill Tice's voice sounded. "Be careful, Clebe, you old sot. You'll bust a laig gettin' into that buggy if you ain't careful. Maybe I better tie you down in that thing, else you might fall out and break your fat neck. You can sleep it off while the horse takes you home."

Lee heard stealthy movement in the hall. Clemmy O'Neil heard it also. Someone was at the door. The latch was being tested. The door was opening slightly. She had failed to bolt it after Lee had entered the room.

Lee drew his .44. She gave him a frightened look, then moved to the lamp on the dressing table and blew out the light. "Who's there?" she called.

The door swung open. Faint light seeped in from the windows in the main house. The intruder had a pillowcase over his head. From his size, Lee was certain it was Merl Tice.

He holstered his six-shooter. Reaching out in the darkness, he caught the intruder by his mask, dragged him into the room, and kicked the door closed.

He sent a fist smashing into the face beneath the mask. He struck again, and a third time. He was remembering the agony of the quirt Merl had wielded on his back. He felt a measure of fierce, primitive satisfaction as his fists crashed into bone and flesh. At least part of the debt was being paid.

His target was smashed to the floor and out of his grasp. The masked man was Merl Tice, right enough. Merl mumbled in a shocked voice, "My God! Is that you, Gabe? It's me. Merl. Don't hit me ag'in. I'm——"

Merl must have realized that he might not be talking to his brother. He probably was armed and reaching for his gun. Lee could not chance an attempt to locate him in the darkness. If they began trying to find each other with bullets, Clemmy O'Neil might be in the line of fire.

Lee jerked the door open, ran into the hallway and out of the building.

Merl Tice raised a frantic shout. "Stop him! Paw! Major Bastrop! There's a man runnin'! Stop him! Shoot him!"

Lee veered, followed the shadow of a gallery, and circled two sections of the sprawling maze of wings and additions. He paused in shadows against a wall.

Merl's voice was rising to almost a scream. "You trollop! Who was it you had in here? I'll kill him! I'll roast him over a slow fire! He's broke my nose. Knocked out my teeth. I'll skin him alive!"

Merl added, his voice rising still higher in a burst of fury, "It was that damned Comanch', wasn't it? Lee Jackson! I might have knowed!"

Merl's screeching was bringing answering shouts from his father and Mike Bastrop. Lee could hear them running, but they were confused as to direction.

Lee retreated to the west side of the house. He could hear them concentrating on the east wing. A man ran past, within a dozen feet of where he crouched, but kept going to join in the confusion on the opposite side of the buildings. Lee guessed it was the wrangler who had returned to the bunkhouse after rigging the Judge's harness horse and Mike Bastrop's mount.

Lee darted across the open ranch yard and reached a haystack. From there he made his way to the barn. He crouched there, trying to suppress his breathing. He could still hear Merl making wild explanations.

Then he heard them scatter. The search was on. A man came running from a dogtrot into the open ranch yard. It was Bill Tice. He had a pistol in his hand. He halted, peering around, crouching slightly as he tried to pick up any sign of movement in the shadows or any sound.

A gun flamed from the dogtrot not thirty feet beyond where Bill Tice stood. It roared again. And a third time. The shots were spaced a second or two apart, as though the marksman was making very sure of his target.

Lee had the impression the flashes came from the window of Clemmy O'Neil's sitting room which opened onto the dogtrot. The reports were lighter than would have come from the .44s that most men carried, or even a .38. Lee was remembering the .32-caliber pistol that Clemmy O'Neil owned.

He heard each slug smash into Bill Tice's body. The sounds were like the spaced blows of a hammer on wood.

Bill Tice uttered a choking moan. He gasped, "Don't— don't—! Oh, my God! I've always been afeared you'd—"

Bill Tice was reeling as he spoke. He fell on his face and Lee could hear the agonized wheezing fade away as his life ended there in the dust.

Lee circled the barn and retreated from the ranch, keeping the barn between himself and the scene of the murder.

For it had been murder! The person who had fired the shots could not have been mistaken as to the identity of his target.

Wild shouting arose again in the BT ranch yard. Lee could hear Amos Clebe's voice, shocked and shrill. And Mike Bastrop's deeper tones.

Merl was shouting, "It's Paw! He's dead! He's dead!"

Again Merl's voice rose to a frenzied screech. "That hellcat! That vixen! She's the cause of this! Maybe she even done it herself! She hated Paw! I'll tear her to pieces!"

Lee had started to circle to where he had left his horse. He paused and stood listening. The sounds indicated that Merl was raging through the rambling ranch house in search of Clemmy O'Neil. He heard Judge Clebe trying to calm the infuriated man.

Merl would not listen. "Where are you, Clemmy?" he yelled. "You can't hide so deep I can't find you an' drag you out! Where are you?"

Lee heard the sudden pound of hoofs of a spurred horse. Mike Bastrop's voice sounded, "She's taken my horse and is pulling out!"

The rider came in Lee's direction. A mounted figure loomed against the stars. Clemmy O'Neil was astride with the false skirt adding to her mount's wildness.

The horse reared when it saw Lee in its path and nearly

unseated the girl. She had a pistol in her hand and was trying to bring it to bear on him.

"Don't shoot!" Lee exclaimed. "It's Lee Jackson!"

"Get out of the way!" she panted. "They'll be after me. They'll kill me!"

She added, "And they'll hang you for sure, now. Why did you do it?"

"Do what?"

"Why did you shoot Uncle Tice?"

"Me?" The horse reared again and tried to strike Lee with its hoofs. He caught a grip on the saddle and vaulted up behind the girl.

"Let's ride!" he said. "We'd make a pretty pair, strung up together for buzzard bait, now wouldn't we?"

She had no alternative, for he clamped his left arm around her waist and slapped the horse into motion. It was a big, powerful black with thoroughbred blood in it, the pick of Mike Bastrop's stock. He slapped the animal into a gallop.

"I heard Merl say that maybe it was you who killed his Paw," he said.

She began trying to talk, but she was weeping and unintelligible. Evidently no one at the ranch had been able to mount pursuit as yet. Lee took the reins from Clemmy O'Neil's shaking hands and guided the way to where he had left his roan. His horse was still grazing peacefully on picket. He slid from the black and swung into the saddle.

"Where are you going?" she asked.

"I'm going to where the owls hoot," Lee said. "That's where you said I would wind up. As for you, we'll cross the trail to town a mile or so ahead. You can ride into Punchbowl. You'll be safe there. At least from Merl Tice."

"Safe! Safe! I'll never be safe as long as any Tice is alive. Only from Uncle Tice. And that's because he's dead! And then there's that slimy Judge Clebe and—and that awful Major Bastrop!" She was hysterical, frenzied.

"What do you mean?" Lee demanded. "Amos Clebe and Mike Bastrop? Why would you be afraid of them?"

"They suspect I know too much because I eavesdropped on them," she wept.

"Too much about what?"

"About why they play poker and never really win or lose, I suppose."

"You suppose? Don't you know? Why don't they ever win or lose?"

"I don't know!" she blubbered. "And quit pestering me. I tell you I don't know. And I'm too tired to talk about it."

"Then where can you go?" Lee demanded.

She dabbed at her eyes in the darkness. "You tell me."

Lee peered closer at her. "Oh, no you don't! he exclaimed. "You're going to Punchbowl!"

"You wouldn't really want me to do that."

"*Me? Why* not?"

"You ought to be able to figure that out, Lee Jackson. I'm the only person who really knows that you were the man who slugged Merl in my room. They'll try to force me to tell who it was."

"Oh, so it's me you're worrying about," Lee snorted. "Merl guessed right from the start that I was the one who gave him that beating."

"It takes more than a guess to convict a man of murder."

"Murder?" Lee seized her arm, shaking her. "Are you still trying to pretend that I killed Bill Tice?"

She refused to answer. His grip tightened, but she would not ask for mercy, although he heard her draw a sharp breath.

"I ought to drag you off that horse and set you afoot," he raged. "Bill Tice was shot by someone at the house. I saw the flashes. They came from inside the dogtrot. Just where *were* you at the time?"

"I tell you I didn't do it."

"I'm asking where you were. Or don't you have an answer thought up?"

"I—I don't know where I was," she wailed.

"Now you don't expect me to believe that."

"I don't expect you to believe anything good about me. I followed Merl when he ran out to chase you after you had left. Merl had a gun and would have killed you. Then the shooting broke out. I thought it came from the other side of the house, for I was some distance away. Merl ran in that direction by way of the front of the place. I decided I'd better go back to my room. Then Merl began screaming that Uncle Tice had been killed and that I was to blame. He was coming to get me. So I ran back to the front of the house, took Major Bastrop's horse, and rode away."

When Lee remained silent, she took that for disbelief. She pulled away from his grasp. "I don't care whether you believe me or not," she cried. "It's the truth. Don't you dare try to twist things around to make it out that I'm lying."

"There's always been talk that Bill Tice found a gold mine when he became your guardian," Lee said. "Some people believe your mother wasn't penniless as advertised."

"I'm sure Uncle Tice has robbed me blind," she said grimly. "It's only been since I grew up that I realized it. Now, it's probably too late."

"You told me you were afraid of all the Tices. Of your uncle, especially. He was shot with a small-bore gun. I'm sure of that. You had a purse-gun in your hand when I saw you in your room. Isn't that the same gun you've got in your belt now? Let's take a look at it."

She suddenly struck him in the face. She had little strength and the blow did no damage. It was like a frightened child lashing out at fear itself—at a phantom in a nightmare.

"You're trying to build up quite a case against me, aren't you?" she choked. "Don't try to touch me. I'll shoot you. It's clear enough. You killed him and intend to put it on me."

Lee drew away from her. "I'm not trying to put anything on you that doesn't belong on your conscience," he said. "Bill Tice was shot in the back. Deliberately. Coolly. *That* is why it was murder."

The wagon trail that led to town loomed ahead in the moonlight. "You better go into town," Lee said. "Go to the sheriff. Tell him your story. Tell the truth. They say Fred Mack is an honest man."

"But he's a man, isn't he? And I'm the daughter of Rose O'Neil. Every man seems to want to paw over me. He'd send me back to BT, most likely. Gabe and Merl are there. That'd be even worse."

"But—"

"Let's face it," she said. "I can put your neck in a noose, Lee Jackson. You know you wouldn't have a chance if I testified that you came into my room tonight to get even for the whipping they gave you. Merl would testify against you. Who'd believe your word against even the likes of me? Everybody says you're a—a—"

"Comanche," Lee said. "And I've decided they're right."

"Right or wrong, we've got to hide someplace. They'll trail us. Where can we go?"

"I tell you that you can't go with me."

"We're two of a kind. Dirt under their feet. You had already made up your mind to ride long. There's no other choice for me. If you're an outlaw, so am I."

Lee began another refusal, but she halted him. "I'm staying with you whether you want it that way or not. It's all I can do. I don't like it any better than you do. You must know of a hiding place. Otherwise you wouldn't have come to the BT tonight. You meant to pay off the Tices for what they did. You knew you'd be trailed and maybe hanged if they caught you. You're wasting time trying to send me back. I would only follow you."

She was right, of course. Every minute lost in debate meant that pursuit would be closer on his heels by daybreak. Circumstances forced him to let her have her way. For the present at least.

He urged the roan ahead. "All right," he said. "You've asked for it. Here we go."

He set a steady pace until they reached the thicket where he had left the buckskin and his camp gear. Leading the packhorse, they pushed on.

They had not spoken in nearly an hour. "If you don't mind, you might get rid of that cussed thing that keeps flapping like the wings of an owl," Lee finally said. "Your horse doesn't like it one bit, and neither does mine."

She removed the false skirt and bundled it on the saddle. "But I'll wear it in daylight," she said. "The horses will have to get used to it. I don't feel decent, riding like a man."

"This is hardly the time to get choosy," Lee commented.

"I imagine I can find a store somewhere, so I can buy myself a dress or two," she said. "I had to leave without taking any of the clothes I'd laid out. I'll need a few other things, too."

"Store? Do you know what you're saying?"

"Oh, I see," she said. "I forgot. We just can't ride into some town and go shopping."

"Not unless you want to go to jail. But there are other ways of getting what we need."

"How do you mean to—?" she began. Then she understood. Again she said, "I see." She said it slowly, wearily.

"You gave it a name a while back," Lee said. "Outlaw.

That's what we are. Outlaws. But you don't seem to have given much thought to what it really meant."

"I'm afraid not," she said. "But I'm learning."

They said nothing more for a long time. They reached Flat Creek near the Armadillo Hills after midnight and followed its bed of heavy gravel and bedrock in order to blind their trail. The stream bottom offered tricky going in the patches of moonlight. Hoofs sent water flying, dampening riders as well as animals. However, the night was so warm they both felt refreshed.

After more than an hour of this, Lee let the horses rest and drink. He dismounted and helped Clemmy down.

"We'll take a breather," he said. "How are you making out?"

"If you're asking if I'm tired, the answer is yes. If you're asking if I want to turn back, the answer is no."

They found a sand bar where they could lie on their stomachs, drink, and dip their faces in water. The horses blew noisily downstream.

"How far away are they?" she asked.

"How far away are what?"

"The Staked Plains. I've never been east of the Armadillo Hills, and so I have no idea of the distance."

"Who said anything about going into the plains?"

"You didn't have to say it, but I know that's what you've got in your mind."

"And how would you know that?"

"Now, how could I answer that? I'm just guessing, of course. But that's what you're planning, isn't it?"

Lee believed he had the answer. The Staked Plains had always been looked upon as Comanche country. It was into the plains the Spearmen had usually vanished after their raids. A Comanche, in need of a hiding place, would instinctively turn to that refuge even now. She had been aware of all this.

"You don't really believe I'd let you go there, do you?" he asked roughly.

"Not if you could help it, I suppose. They say it's a fearful place. I've heard of the Devil's Garden all my life. But you can't help it. If you feel that you'll be safer there, then I'll feel the same way."

She added, "Hadn't we better be traveling?"

Lee found that he had no grounds on which to debate

the matter. He helped her into the saddle of the black horse.

They rode steadily eastward through the night. At daybreak they emerged from the hills into view of a wild stretch of country. In the distance stood a low, forbidding line of bluffs.

"Caprock," Lee said. "There are your Staked Plains."

"You've been there?" she asked.

"Yes."

"With the Comanches?"

"Yes. As a child, to help flense robes and cure buffalo meat." He added, "And, on one trip to wait while the warriors went ahead on a raid. They came back with a lot of stolen horses. And scalps."

"But, is there water?" she asked after a pause. "I've been told there's none for miles and miles in the Devil's Garden."

Lee eyed her. "Do you still intend to follow me in there?"

"Yes. You don't intend to stay in that awful place all your life, do you?"

"That might depend on how long a man stays alive."

"You can't scare me," she said, but there was a quaver in her voice.

"It'll be weeks before they quit looking for us," Lee said. "Months maybe. They'll see to it that men will be watching for us if we show up beyond the plains in any direction. We might have to tough it out in there for a long time—if you're still bent on making an Indian of yourself."

"Indian?"

"That word does something to you, inside, doesn't it?"

She gave him an icy look. "No. If I were an Indian, I'd be proud of it."

"That's the only way anyone can live in the Garden. The Indian way. You don't stay alive there just by wishing. You work for it. Maybe fight for it."

"Anything would be better than what I'd be up against back there."

Lee reached out, took the .32 pistol from her belt before she realized his intention. He released the cylinder and punched out the shells. There were two live shells and four empties. Three of the exploded cartridges bore fresh powder burns. The fourth was blackened by time and evidently had been carried as a safety under the hammer.

She stared at the evidence. What color there had been in her face faded away as she understood what this meant.

"Do you still want me to believe you didn't shoot Bill Tice?" he asked. "He was hit by three shots from a light-caliber gun."

"It's—it's impossible!" she gasped. "I don't know how . . . !" Then a thought occurred to her. Scorn and accusation came into her face.

"Very clever," she said. "I didn't know you were a sleight-of-hand artist."

Lee laughed grimly. "Meaning that I palmed those empty shells in place of live ones? That's too ridiculous to talk about."

He held the gun to the light. "How about the powder stains? This gun was fired recently. I couldn't have done that by hokus-pokus, now could I?"

"I suppose not," she snapped.

Lee waited for further denials, but she turned her back on him and sat rigid and scornful on the horse. It was plain that she had made up her mind to offer no further explanations nor to submit to any more questioning.

He expected her to weaken and decide to turn back, but she kept pace with him, riding in dogged silence all during the stolid heat of the afternoon. He kept to cover as much as possible, often swinging far out of the direct line eastward in order to stay below the skyline or to follow stands of brush. Whenever they were forced to cross exposed areas, they dismounted and walked close to the sides of their horses.

"There are lots of mustangs in this country," he said. "If anybody spots us at a distance, let's hope they figure they're only seeing a wild horse or two."

The grim bluffs drew closer. Lee knew that she was peering at them with increasing apprehension.

"How long . . . ?" she finally began, then left it unfinished.

It was the first word she had spoken since the incident of the empty cartridges in the pistol.

"How long since I've been on the Llano?" Lee said. "Is that what you were going to ask? Two years. I took a *paseo* there, just to see if it really was like I remembered it."

"And was it?"

"Yes. For all I could tell, nobody had been in there since the last Comanche war party came down the plains years ago."

"How was it when you were with—" she hesitated, then plunged ahead, "—with the Comanches?"

Lee studied it. "With most Comanches it was a good life. With me it was a different story."

"In what way?"

"Eagle-in-the-Sky, who said he was my father, had a taboo on me. He seemed to be afraid of me. He hated me for some reason and did his best to make life miserable for me."

"You mean he tortured you? But you were only a child. I've heard that Indians are very kind to their children."

"Then I was the exception. The one who said she was my mother was the worst of all. She was Eagle's eldest wife. Her name was Wau-Qua. I never knew what that stood for in the Comanche language. To me it meant cruelty."

"What was your name in the Comanche tongue?"

"I don't know. It was never spoken in my presence. It was taboo. Many things are taboo to Indians."

He gazed northward into the distance. "They're still up there. Beyond the Llano. On the Comanche reserve on the Clear Fork of the Brazos River. I was told a few months ago that Eagle-in-the-Sky is still alive and chief of his village. I had hoped that he was dead."

He looked at her. "There are times when I get to remembering, and then I want to kill him. But he might be telling the truth when he said he was my father."

Clemmy was silenced, frightened by his bitterness.

Chapter *FIVE*

They camped at dark. Clemmy accepted the tarp and blanket Lee handed her and slept in the shelter of a boulder, protected from the wind that changed from warmth to thin chill before dawn. It was a lonely wind, which whispered and moaned in the brush. It drove white clouds across the face of the moon. Clouds that formed phantom shapes.

Lee was soddenly tired, but sleep evaded him for a long time. He lay looking up at the difting clouds. His life had been like that. Driven this way and that at the whim of savages and white men.

That part of his life was finished. His days of drifting were over. Comanche, Spanish, Mexican, white—whatever his blood, he would not only meet every man eye-to-eye, but would take from them what he needed and what he wanted. By violence, if necessary.

He became aware of faint sounds in the darkness. Clemmy O'Neil was awake also. She lay weeping, trying to silence her grief. She wept for all the slights and wounds that life had inflicted on her.

Lee lifted his head. "There'll be no more tears," he said harshly. "If tears are to be shed, let others do it."

They resumed their journey at dawn. At mid-morning they emerged from a canyon after a hard climb that tired the horses. Before them lay a vast, silent land. Its swells were a frozen sea, extending to the horizon and broken by low buttes and wrinkled hills that were like the hulls of sinking ships.

Neither of them spoke for a time. Clemmy broke the silence. "Lead the way," she said.

There was a new soberness in her. A steadfast quality. Her eyes were gray now, and cool.

Together they rode into the Devil's Garden. The swells

enclosed them. The buttes and eroded hills never came nearer.

At intervals, when Lee believed she was not aware of it, he glanced back.

It was late afternoon when she finally spoke. "Are they still trailing us?"

"I didn't think you knew," Lee said.

"I've known it since morning. I glimpsed them far back on the flats when we were climbing the canyon. And they're gaining."

"They're punishing their horses," Lee said. "They're less than an hour's ride back of us now. If they don't quit soon, I'll discourage 'em."

"It's Gabe and Merl, isn't it?"

"That's my guess," Lee said. "But there are three of them. I think the other one is Mike Bastrop. They seem to be the ones who want us bad enough to follow us into the Garden."

They continued their steady pace for another hour. Their own horses were growing foot-heavy.

"All right," Lee said, pulling up in the shelter of uptilted slabs of rock that shaded them from the westering sun. "You'll be all right here. You know how to use a rifle, I imagine."

"Yes," she said. Her voice was faint, shaky.

"If they show up, keep them at a distance until dark. Shoot their horses. You can get away from them if you put them afoot. Go back to Verde and get in touch with Kink. Do what he tells you. That's about all the advice I can give you."

He took a swallow from the water bag. "There's enough left to get you back to Flat Creek," he said. "Rest the horses a few hours until moon-up. It will be up late, but you can travel farther and faster in the cool."

"I'm going with you," she said.

"No. I intend to come back. But there's always the chance of bad luck. Do you remember that barranca we crossed back there a quarter of a mile or so? It was what I've been looking for all afternoon."

"How?"

"I don't intend to kill them. Only set them afoot like I just told you to do. I'd really be doing them a favor. They'd never make it out of the Garden if they followed us much farther. They're probably already worse off for water than we are."

He walked away, carrying his rifle. She was still standing in the shade of the rocks, watching, when he looked back before brush intervened.

He descended a broken slant, keeping to cover, and reached a wide, dry flat, sparsely sprinkled with saltbush and rabbit brush. A shallow barranca, cut by runoffs from thunderstorms, curved into the flat from the base of the descent.

He had marked this gully as a likely place for his purpose, for its presence had not been apparent until they were almost upon it.

He made his way along the shallow gully until he came to the point where he and Clemmy had crossed with their mounts and the packhorse. He found a clump of brush growing on the rim which offered an observation point and settled down to wait.

There could be no question but that the pursuers knew they had been sighted by their quarry. Therefore they would be alert, no doubt, for the possibility of an ambush. However, their approach to Lee's hiding place would bring them across nearly half a mile of this unbroken flat which offered little chance of concealment.

He was gambling on the hope they would not discover the presence of the gully until too late. If they did become aware of the danger in time, the tables would be turned. It would be Lee who would be caught in a trap, for, with three of them to deal with, it would only be a matter of time until he would be outflanked and wiped out by crossfire.

Minutes dragged by. Lee chanced another glimpse and hastily withdrew his head. The three riders had appeared. They were still a long rifleshot away. When he chanced another look, they were nearer and miraged by heat refraction and the background of the steel-blue sky to fantastic proportions. Their horses seemed to be walking on stilts, but the riders were flattened to froglike shapes.

Suddenly they took on normal shapes. Merl Tice rode in the lead. Even at that distance Lee could see the white strips of medical plaster that bound his nose and jaw, the result of the beating Lee had given him. He rode with the hungry attitude of a hound on the scent of its quarry. His horse was caked with alkali. The animal was nearing the end of its strength, but was still being pushed by spur and quirt.

Gabe Tice and Mike Bastrop were lagging a trifle, but were being forced to prod their mounts to keep pace with the eager one. Lee sank back out of sight. The route Merl was following would bring the trio to the wash within yards of where he crouched.

Presently he could hear the scuff of hoofs and the creak of saddle leather. Mike Bastrop's voice, surly with weariness, sounded. "Take it easy, I tell you, Merl. What are you trying to do, kill these horses?"

"It's nearin' sundown an' unless we get that Indian before night, he might slip away," Merl answered. "I ain't stoppin' until I get my hands on him an' beat him to a pulp. Turn back if your guts have gone yellow on you, Bastrop. Gabe an' me can handle him. An' that girl, too. It'll be a pleasure."

"Then why didn't you take care of him when he busted that buzzard beak of yours the other night?" Mike Bastrop said scornfully. "If you could fight as big as you talk, I'd let you go on alone. If you ask me, that Comanche devil would make you crawl and whimper if—"

Bastrop's voice broke off. "Look!" he exclaimed. "There's a gully . . . !"

They had discovered the possible danger of an ambush. Lee emerged from concealment. They were less than a hundred feet away and were yanking their jaded horses to a stop.

Bastrop, reacting faster than the Tice brothers, was trying to get at his six-shooter. But he had pushed the holster back and out of position for the sake of comfort.

Lee shouted, "No!"

Bastrop continued to twist, trying to draw his pistol. Lee fired the rifle. The bullet drove through the peak of Bastrop's tall hat. The hat was torn from his head and toppled across the face of his horse.

Bastrop was riding one of his fine black saddle-mounts, a cross of quarterhorse and thoroughbred. The animal was weary, but the gunshot and the flight of the hat brought an explosion. It humped its back instantly and swapped ends, trying to unload its rider.

Bastrop was caught off balance. He grabbed the horn, but was partly unseated. His weight spilled the horse. Man and animal went down in a sprawling fall. The six-shooter was jolted from Bastrop's holster and fell out of reach. He lay stunned, a leg caught beneath the horse which had rolled partly on its back, the saddle wedging it in that position so that it was unable to right itself immediately.

Lee levered another shell under the hammer. Merl and Gabe Tice had sat frozen by surprise for a second or two. They were now making frenzied, belated attempts to get at their weapons. Gabe's choice was a rifle in the boot on his saddle, while Merl's preference was a six-shooter in a holster.

Lee sent a bullet within inches of Gabe's ear. "No!" he shouted again. "Lift your hands!"

The brothers froze. For a space the only sound was the gasping of Mike Bastrop. Then the hands of the two Tices went suddenly in the air.

"Pile down!" Lee commanded. "On this side? Slow! Keep your hands up!"

The brothers complied, sliding from the saddles with arms stretched high. They were almost ludicrous in their stiffness and apprehension.

Mike Bastrop's horse managed to roll into position and lurch to its feet. It trotted away a few rods, its trailing reins finally bringing it to a halt.

Bastrop, still gagging for breath, located his pistol lying nearby and scrambled toward it.

His path was blocked by Lee's boots. Lee jammed the boot heel into the man's face, shoved him back, then picked up the weapon and thrust it in his own belt.

He continued to keep the Tices covered. "Turn around," he ordered the brothers. "Keep your hands high."

When they complied, he moved in and disarmed them. Both had rifles on the saddles. In addition to a six-shooter, Merl's sleeve yielded a slingshot. Gabe had a knife in an armpit holster and a set of brass knuckles in his hip pocket.

Lee dropped all the captured weapons into the barranca, out of reach. The horses the Tices had been riding drifted away to join Bastrop's animal.

"Put down that rifle, Jackson," Bastrop said hoarsely. "We're taking you back to Punchbowl. Alive, if you give up peaceful. Dead, if you want it that way."

"You've got things twisted, Major," Lee said. "It's my choice, not yours. I've decided to let you stay alive—this time at least. You can make it back to Flat Creek by noon tomorrow if you keep walking all night. That's your first chance at water. There's none in the direction I'm heading. So there'd be no point in following me any farther, although I'd be happy to see you try."

They eyed him, their mouths tightening as they realized what this meant. A water bag hung on one of their saddles. Lee walked to the horse, lifted the bag, and tossed it at their feet. It seemed to be more than half filled.

"That's better than you deserve," he said.

He jabbed Merl in the back with the rifle, sending him staggering. "You too, Major," he said. "Walk! On the double!"

He shoved the man into motion. "Not you, Gabe," he said. "You're staying here for a while."

Gabe Tice had started to follow his companions. He paused, scowling, not understanding.

"We've got a matter to settle," Lee said. "You're the last of the three men who used a quirt on me. Merl paid off some of what he owed me the other night when I took a few swings at him while he was wearing that pillowcase over his head. He got off easy that time, but there may come another day. The other of the three is dead. Maybe he's lucky. But you're the one I'm after right now."

Gabe looked at Lee's weapons and his lips were suddenly ashen. "You ain't goin' to kill me like you killed Paw?" he protested, his voice hoarse. "You wouldn't shoot me down without givin' me a chance?"

"If I was going to shoot you, you'd have your chance," Lee said. "And you'll have your chance now. But not with guns. You've got a reputation as a tough man in a fist fight. This is going to be with fists."

Gabe didn't believe him for a moment. Then hope began to rise in him. And distrust. He turned and looked at his brother and at Mike Bastrop who had paused a short distance away and were listening. They, too, apparently were doubting their own ears.

Lee motioned with his rifle. "You two keep going," he said. "You can wait out there a ways if you want. But far enough away so that you won't interfere in this little affair. This is between Gabe and me. Don't stop until you're a long shot away."

It dawned on them that he might actually mean it. Merl uttered a croaking laugh. "Give 'im the boots, Gabe," he said. "But don't stomp him clear under. I owe him plenty. I want a chance to pay off."

Lee put a bullet between Merl's feet. The slug chewed into the hot earth, missing the man's toes by a thin margin. "Move!" Lee said. "You too, Major."

Merl was stampeded into a trot. Mike Bastrop refused to bow to Lee's will to that extent, but he could not resist lengthening his stride as he followed Merl.

Lee waited until the two men were some distance away. They halted and he drove them still farther out in the flat with a bullet close over their heads. They paused, and he sent a final shot as a warning not to return.

He placed his rifle against a bush and shed his pistol and the weapon he had taken from Mike Bastrop, leaving them at a distance.

Gabe Tice hadn't really believed Lee would go through with it. Now a wicked flame blazed in his eyes. He had beefy shoulders, with a stomach that folded just a trifle over his belt. He had greasy hair the color of faded straw and his whiskers grew in patches on a coarse face. He rubbed his palms down the sides of his breeches and then clenched his fists in greedy anticipation.

Lee moved in. He knew that Gabe had experience at roughhouse fighting where a man could bite and kick and gouge and take any other unfair advantage. But he also knew his own strength. And this would not be his first try at this sort of conflict.

He knew it would be Gabe's plan to overwhelm him with weight, strength, and ferocity right at the start. Gabe probably would also attempt to plan the battle so that he would be in a position from which he could get to the weapons Lee had set aside.

Gabe came in slowly for a few strides and then erupted with a headlong dive at Lee's knees, intending to bowl them both to the ground where his superior weight would come into play.

Lee had expected something like that. What Gabe encountered was a knee. It was driven into his chin. Teeth were loosened and lips were mashed. Gabe clawed frantically for Lee's legs in an attempt to bring him down, but missed.

Lee caught his man by the hair, lifted his head, and drove a knee again to the face. Gabe joined his brother in misery with a shattered nose.

Gabe's strength told. He managed to clamp both hands on Lee's left arm. He tried for a hammerlock, intending to dislocate the shoulder. Lee twisted, dived forward, carrying Gabe off balance, and broke free.

Gabe sprawled on the ground. He rolled over and over with Lee trailing him. Lee leaped on him, his knees driving into Gabe's stomach. He smashed Gabe in the face with his fists.

Gabe had wanted a fight with no quarter asked, and this was what he was getting. Lee caught him by the hair again, rolled him over, knelt on his back, and jammed his face into the hot earth. "Eat dirt!" he panted. "Eat! And then some more!"

Gabe gagged and choked. Lee hammered his head on the earth. "Eat!" he raged.

He became aware of a frightened voice screaming, "Please! Please! You're killing him! Please stop!"

Clemmy O'Neil was tugging at him, trying to drag him off his victim. He looked at her for seconds before he fully realized who she was. Such was the haze of fury. He had been remembering the agony of the quirt as Gabe had laid on the lash.

Clemmy seemed to be praying. Praying that he would come to his senses.

That shocked him out of his moment of madness. He stopped jamming his victim's head into the earth and got to his feet. He was gasping for breath, retching with the aftermath of the struggle.

Gabe lay dazed, blubbering with pain. His shirt had been torn from his back. "You busted my ribs," Gabe moaned "You're no human being. You're a devil!"

Lee looked at Clemmy. Her eyes were dark gray in a colorless face. She acted as though she expected she might be the next object of his fury.

He saw that Bastrop and Merl Tice were returning. They were moving hesitantly, as though expecting to be ordered back. Clemmy had a rifle in her hands. She had followed him, against his wishes, and evidently the rifle had made sure that the two men out there would not interfere in the fight.

Lee rounded up the three horses and tied to the saddles the rifles and pistols he had seized. Gabe was sitting up, his face buried in his hands. Blood was flowing and flies were gathering. Gnats began to swarm. Bastrop and Merl Tice were still wary about moving closer.

"He's all yours," Lee called. He had manhandled Gabe with more anger than he had intended, but the man was big and tough and should be able to make it back to safety with the help of his companions.

Clemmy still bore that blanched look. "Maybe you had better head back the same way they're going," Lee said. He motioned toward the horses. "Pick the one you want. No need for you to walk. That's for scum like them."

She shook her head and silently mounted the black horse Bastrop had been riding. Lee swung into the saddle of one of the other mounts.

"You must know what you're doing by this time," he said. "You saw it. That's the way a Comanche would have worked him over. So now we both know for sure."

Still without speaking, she followed him as he rode away. Mike Bastrop shouted after them, "Girl, are you crazy? You'll die in that country. There's no water for eighty miles. Don't stay with that red devil."

Clemmy did not look back, nor answer. Lee presently turned in the saddle. The three men were walking westward across the flat into the setting sun. Gabe Tice seemed able to keep up with his companions without help.

Chapter *SIX*

Leading the three captured horses, they rode through sand dunes whose undulating swells were bathed in a wash of gold by the sun. There was no wind, and the tracks of their animals stretched out in a wide swath behind them.

Lee answered the question in Clemmy's eyes as she looked back. "The wind will spring up tonight. By morning there'll be no sign we came this way."

They left the dunes. Lifeless, barren hills closed in around them. The horses, dispirited these last several miles, seemed to find something to enliven them. They crossed a rincon and descended a narrow canyon that was little more than a slit in the hills.

Willows and green grass began to appear. The defile widened suddenly and they emerged into the open. A band of deer went bounding away.

Clemmy uttered a little surprised cry. A long basin, enclosed by the barren hills, was spread before them. She could see the shimmer of a sizable lake in the purple twilight. Geese and ducks squawked in reedy marshes.

"The Comanches had a long name for this place," Lee said. "It meant The Place Where the Spirits Walk. I've also heard them use a Spanish term for it. *La Ciudad Sombra.* The City of the Ghosts."

She shivered a little. "A fearsome name for such a pretty place," she said. "I've heard stories about a place like this out on the plains. There's a legend among cowboys about a waterhole that only dead men can find. Some riders who make up their own songs, tell about the Spirit Lake that nobody ever reaches."

Lee nodded. "I know. And there's a legend that a wagon train, heading for California during the gold rush, went into the Devil's Garden, led by a Comanche guide, who told them there was a waterhole ahead. Nobody ever heard of them again. The truth is they were massacred here."

"Massacred?"

"I found the remains of burned wagons when I scouted this place two seasons ago. They're scattered over a stretch of ground beyond the lake, along with bones and skulls. I remember that when I came here with Comanche hunting and war parties they never went near that part of the basin."

Clemmy shuddered again. "I assure you that I never will either."

Lee urged the horses ahead. "That goes for me too," he admitted. "We'll camp as far away as possible. Ghosts, I strictly want nothing to do with."

As darkness came they found a pleasant camping place amid willows along a small, rushing stream that fed the lake.

"This water comes from a spring that boils to the surface less than a mile up the basin," Lee explained. "I guess it goes underground again in that marsh below the lake, for there's no sign of water on the plains south of those hills."

"Why is it that only Comanches know about this place?" she asked.

"The hills we just came through look like scores of others that crop out for a hundred miles," Lee said. "Rough, dry, worthless. There's no real reason for anyone to travel the Devil's Garden by the way we came, and any cowboys or explorers who tried it would swing around these hills instead of going through them. That is, if they were in their right minds. I don't think even the Comanches know how they learned about this basin. It is a secret handed down from the old ones."

He added, "White men don't always see what's right before their eyes. For instance, I saw evidence there is plenty of game around this basin. Deer, wild horses, elk, even a few buffalo. I saw fresh sign. Where there's game there must be water."

"I didn't mean it that way," she said. She was sorting through the food supply in order to plan a meal and wasn't looking directly at him.

"Mean what?"

"I didn't mean that you had to be a Comanche to know about this place."

"You still can't have any doubt in your mind, can you?"

"What difference would it make what your blood might be?" she said. "It's what you are that matters."

They dropped the subject. Another matter that they never discussed was the killing of Bill Tice. Since the time Lee had found the empty shells in her pistol a truce had been declared in that respect.

But that did not mean it was forgotten. The questions kept bobbing up in Lee's thoughts. Had she really fired the shots that had taken her uncle's life? And, if she had not, did she really believe that he was the killer?

In her attitude he could find no answer to the puzzles, no hint as to what she was thinking. She evidently had decided to let the matter rest while their more immediate problems were faced.

Circumstances had forced her to share with him the hardships and dangers of living outside the law. She was devastatingly attractive, but theirs could only be an alliance of necessity and nothing more. Between them lay the shadows of two men—the slain Bill Tice and the Comanche chief, Eagle-in-the-Sky, who said he was Lee's father.

After he had cared for the horses, Lee picked up his rifle. "I'll try for a deer while it's still light enough to notch a sight," he said. "They should be watering now. We'll have to get along tonight on what Kink gave us, for any meat I bag will have to cool for a time. Later on, we can have ducks and geese for the taking with clubs."

He answered the question in her eyes. "Don't worry about a fire being seen or a shot being heard. I doubt if there's another human being within seventy miles, excepting, of course, our friends who are hoofing it back to Flat Creek."

He did not have far to hunt. The wild game that came into the basin for water had not learned to fear humans. He dropped a young buck, gutted it, and carried it to camp where he hung the carcass on a limb to cure.

The fire was burning. He heard splashing in the stream. Presently Clemmy returned, dressed and refreshed from a bath.

"That idea stacks up like a thousand dollars' worth of blue chips," Lee said. He found the pool, stripped, and let the cool water drive some of the fatigue out of him. Rancho Verde, Punchbowl, the Tices and Mike Bastrop seemed far, far in his past. For the moment, at least.

When he returned to camp, Clemmy had smoke-meat

sizzling in the skillet and biscuits in the Dutch oven. Grits and canned tomatoes completed the fare.

"I never sat down to a better banquet," Lee said fervently.

"You'll have to get used to it," Clemmy said. "Our larder doesn't offer much variety. Nor much of anything, for that matter."

The saddlebags on the three horses they had taken from Bastrop and the Tices had yielded a meager supply of jerky, tortillas, and coffee, along with an additional skillet and a coffeepot.

"They didn't aim on going too far into the Garden," Lee had commented on the scant rations the trio had carried. "And they didn't intend to bring anybody out with them, I'd say—alive, at least."

Kink had provided tin plates in the pack. They balanced these on their knees as they ate. "I'll fix up some sort of a table and benches tomorrow," Clemmy said. "Later on, I can do a better job when I get rawhide to work with. You'd be surprised what a person can do with rawhide and willow twigs."

"Rawhide? What do you know about working with rawhide?"

"The nuns in the convent at Santa Fe taught us to cook and sew and provide. Maria, my wonderful duenna at the BT, was Mexican-Indian. She taught me to tan hides and make clothes of deerskin. I can even make a moccasin, but that is very hard on the teeth. The best way to soften the leather and weld a watertight sole is to chew them together."

"Squaw work," Lee said.

"Yes, squaw work. Maybe you ought to be thankful I had that training. We might be here for some time."

She began washing the utensils at the stream. "What did the squaws use for soap?" she asked. "And I could welcome a dishpan."

"The same as you're doing," Lee said. "Sand and elbow grease—when they were in the mood to wash dishes at all. As a rule they weren't as particular about it as you seem to be. What else do you need?"

She twisted around, looking up at him. "What do you mean, what else do I need? I need a lot of things."

"We'll soon be out of flour and salt," Lee said. "And coffee too. We can't live always on just venison and wild duck. We need more blankets. More cook pots. And an ax. You could stand some other kind of clothes. Dresses, for instance."

"And just where are you going to get such things? From the ghosts?"

"The same way I intend to get everything else we need."

"Oh!" She added hastily, "I didn't mean to complain. I can get along. I don't need anything. We can make out for quite a while. You know very well they'll be watching all around the plains in case we make it through alive."

"Every place except one, maybe," Lee said.

"Where would that be?"

"The one place they don't expect us. At Punchbowl."

"It's too dangerous, of course," she said.

Lee let the subject drop. But nearly a week later, as she was again scouring the cooking utensils at the stream, he brought in his roan and the buckskin pack animal and began rigging them.

She straightened, the skillet in her hands. "What size dresses do you wear?" he asked, without looking at her. "And boots and shoes? The boots you've got on won't last much longer."

"Dresses? Boots? Where are you going?"

"To Punchbowl to do a little shopping at Sim Quarles' place, like I told you."

"That's crazy! You can't just ride into town and take what you want."

Lee continued saddling the roan. She dropped the skillet and came running. "What—what if you don't come back?" she wailed.

"I'll leave two loaded six-guns and two rifles with you," he said. "And plenty of shells. I'll be gone four, five days. If I'm not back in a week, ride out and get in touch with Kinky Bob, like I told you before."

"I don't need anything," she protested. "Not a thing. I told you before that we can get along."

"You know we can't. We're already about out of everything. We can't live like animals."

"I'm going with you," she said.

She silenced the refusal he tried to voice. "Do you believe I could stay here alone, just waiting? Waiting and worrying! What kind of a person do you think I am? I'd die."

Lee suddenly found a lump in his throat. "Of course,"

he said. "I should have understood that. I'm sorry. Of course you must go with me. I was thinking that you'd be safer here."

"Safer? Safer?" She shouted it with scorn. "There are things worse than being safe. Haven't you ever been lonely?"

"Yes," Lee said. "I've been lonely."

She hastily began arranging the camp, hanging what little food they had out of reach of animals, covering their other belongings with the tarp.

Lee saddled the black Bastrop horse that she had taken when she fled from the Tice ranch. "One thing's for certain," he commented. "Mike Bastrop's got plenty of good horses, but he sure must be running short of those fancy saddles he has made special from him at San'tone. We've got away with two of 'em already."

He turned the other three horses out. "They'll stay in the basin on graze and water," he said. "That is, unless they decide to join the wild bunch."

They had sighted wild horses once or twice, always at dawn and always far down the basin where they watered and grazed, then retreated to the plains before sunrise. A white stallion with his *manada* of mares had aroused Lee's curiosity, but the glimpses he had of the animal had been too distant and too fleeting for anything more than speculation. He was remembering the big white Barb stallion Mike Bastrop had imported from Spain three years ago which had escaped from the corral at Rancho Verde.

Leading the packhorse, he and Clemmy pulled out before the sun was well up. They followed a different route westward off the plains and reached Flat Creek shortly after midnight. They rested and resumed their journey at noon, heading toward Punchbowl and keeping to cover, avoiding all habitations and blinding their trail as much as possible.

Early darkness had come when the lights of the town appeared ahead. They dismounted in brush along Punchbowl Creek near the outlying structures of the town. Lee helped Clemmy down and steadied her, for she was saddle-numbed after the long miles. "This is as far as you go," he told her. "I'm going in on foot. I'll follow the creek brush into town. You stay right here. Is that a deal?"

"Yes," she said reluctantly. "That is, unless something happens."

"Nothing's going to happen," Lee said. "I've got it all planned. I'll be careful."

"How long will you be gone?"

"No telling. An hour, at least. Longer, most likely. It depends on how late Sim Quarles' stays open."

"You're risking your life just to try to make things easier for me," she said.

"I tell you I'll be back," he said gruffly. He hesitated, then patted her awkwardly on the shoulder. "That's a promise," he said. "I'll be back."

He moved away through the willows. The stream wound into the heart of town between brushy banks. Stars were blazing in the sky when he reached the wooden bridge that spanned the stream at Sumner Street within a block of his objective.

He climbed the bank and chanced a look into the street. Punchbowl was quieting down for the night. The four gambling houses were brightly lighted and busy, but the majority of the stores were closed.

However, Sim Quarles' Mercantile, the largest structure in town, was still lighted, as Lee had expected. Sim was always the last to shut his doors to the chance of earning another penny.

Waiting until sure the way was clear, Lee left the brush and made his way along the rear of buildings toward the mercantile. He paused in a vacant lot on a side street which he had to cross to reach the store.

The mercantile was an unpainted, barny, one-story structure. It had a loading platform at the rear which overlooked a hitch lot where patrons could leave horses and rigs while shopping. The hitch lot was dark and vacant, although sounds indicated there were still patrons in the store.

Footsteps warned that someone was approaching along the side street, and Lee retreated deeper into the lot, crouching down in darkness.

The passer-by loomed up as a vague shadow on the sidewalk. The man suddenly halted. Lee eased his body around so that he could get at his six-shooter in a hurry if need be, for he feared his presence had been discovered.

However, the man merely stood there for second after second. His attention seemed to be fixed on something in Sumner Street. Lee decided the man was entirely unaware of him. The fragrance of bay rum, of good cigar smoke, and of fine whisky came to him. That identified the stroller. Judge Amos Clebe. Those expensive items, whose fragrance always seemed to surround him, were his trademark.

Suddenly the Judge turned. Reversing his course, he walked quickly away down the dark side street in the direction from which he had come. He lived in that direction, in an ornate house on the outskirts of town, and evidently had decided to return home.

Lee waited until sure the street was clear. He emerged, mystified as to what had caused the Judge to change his mind, and peered into Sumner Street. Only three or four establishments were in view at that limited angle on the opposite side of Sumner Street. All were dark except one and that was the ornately painted front of the Silver Bell, which never closed its door.

A ranch wagon and four saddlehorses stood at the hitch rail of the gambling house, for business was always slack at this mid-week hour. Lee recognized one of the horses. It was a sleek sorrel that was in Mike Bastrop's personal string at Rancho Verde. It bore a stock saddle, glaringly new and untarnished.

Lee debated it an instant, wondering why the discovery that Mike Bastrop was in the Silver Bell seemed to be so important to Judge Clebe. Important enough to cause him to change his mind about his own destination, which evidently had been the Silver Bell. Amos Clebe might have wanted to avoid a meeting with the Rancho Verde owner. Or, perhaps, he had forgotten something of importance, and had turned back to his house to get it.

Lee crossed the street and reached the darkness of the hitch lot. He tiptoed up the steps to the loading platform of the store. There was a door for the convenience of patrons and also a wide sliding door that served the storage room. Both were closed, but when he cautiously pressed the thumb latch on the smaller door, the portal opened with scarcely a sound.

A passageway led into the main room. To the left, a door opened into the storage room which was a jumble of packing cases and barrels.

Sim Quarles was waiting on a woman in the dry goods section of the mercantile. The patron was fussily trying to decide on the purchase of material for a dress from the bolts of material the storeman was laying out.

Lee could hear their voices, although they were not in

sight at the angle from which he was looking into the main room. He slipped into the unlighted stockroom and waited.

Finally the transaction was completed. He heard the woman leave. The bolt creaked in the street door and all lights except a night lamp were snuffed in the main room. There was a long delay while the storeman carried his cash drawer to his office, counted the day's receipts, and closed the door of the iron safe.

Quarles left by the rear door, which he padlocked on the outside. Lee waited until certain the man was gone, then made his way into the main store.

A supply of gunny sacks was always kept under the counter for the use of riders who were outfitting. Lee helped himself. Keeping below the counter level as much as possible, he snatched items from the shelves. The night lamp gave light enough, but it was also a danger, for he might be discovered by passers-by on the street. The blinds on the street windows had not been lowered.

He tried to take his time until his mental list of necessities was completed. "Soap," he mumbled. "Dishpan, two cook pots. Matches. Let's see. What else?"

He added another slab of bacon from the meat cooler. That stuffed the first gunny sack.

With a second sack, he moved to the dry goods side of the store. He helped himself to a blanket, a quilt, and a rubber tarp. He moved into women's wear. He sorted through a rack of cotton dresses, growing more and more bewildered as to size and style. In desperation he finally stuffed three dresses into the bag. Boots and shoes were another problem, so he finally took three pairs of each, hoping that at least one pair would be within the right size range.

He was so carried away by his success that he left a note on Sim's pad at the cash register which said:

"Charge it to Rancho Verde."

He discovered that the two stuffed gunny sacks would be too much of a load to attempt to spirit out of town. He left by way of the big sliding door which had been bolted from the inside. He left the bundle of clothing beneath the loading platform. Shouldering the other bag, he made his way to the creek brush unseen, and returned to where Clemmy waited.

"For goodness' sake!" she breathed. "You look like Santa Claus."

"I got you the dishpan and soap," he said proudly. "And you haven't seen the half of it. I'll be back with more before you can say pronto."

He returned by his devious route to the mercantile. He was dragging the second bag of booty from its hiding place under the platform when he again heard footsteps approaching in the street. He retreated, crabwise, beneath the platfrom, lowering the gunny sack, and crouched down.

To his dismay, the arrival once more paused in the street. Lee believed he had been discovered. But the man, instead, turned off the street into the hitch lot and halted in darkness at the corner of the loading platform.

Again it was Judge Amos Clebe, redolent of barbershop tonic, tobacco, and whisky. He merely stood there, leaning against the platform in the darkness, little more than an arm's length from where Lee was huddled.

Minutes passed. The Judge waited, motionless. More minutes. Lee's nose itched. He did not dare move. His legs began to ache because of his cramped position.

In addition to his discomfort, he was puzzled. There was something in the immobility of the portly figure that held a grimness and a threat. Amos Clebe seemed to be waiting tensely. Lee sensed there was a seething impatience within the man.

More minutes passed. He could hear only occasional activity in Sumner Street. On two occasions, wheeled rigs rattled out of town. A horseman came in off the west trail and entered a saloon down the street. Two riders left town and headed north, talking over their experiences in the fleshpots.

Still, the Judge waited, motionless, silent. A man came down the side street on foot and the Judge retreated deeper into the shadows until the citizen had passed by, evidently homeward bound. Then Amos Clebe returned to his vigil. Lee was sure it was the Silver Bell that held the man's attention. He was remembering that the Silver Bell had seemed to spark some thought of importance in Amos Clebe's mind not many minutes earlier.

He wondered what Clemmy was thinking because of his prolonged absence. And what she might be doing about it. He began doing some wishing on his own account. He wished fervently that she would do nothing.

Amos Clebe moved suddenly. He straightened and took a stride away from the platform. He was outlined against the reflection of light from the Silver Bell.

Lee was startled to see that the Judge had a six-shooter in his hand. It was cocked and he was raising it. There was in his attitude the tautness of a hunter who had waited patiently for his quarry and was now about to make the kill.

Lee heard the scuffle of a horse's hoofs in Sumner Street. Someone had emerged from the Silver Bell and had mounted. He realized that person must be Amos Clebe's target. And that target was, perhaps, Mike Bastrop. Amos Clebe had recognized his horse at the rail of the gambling house and had hurried home to get a weapon in order to assassinate the man everyone believed to be his crony.

This was cold-blooded murder. Instinct caused Lee to intervene. Mainly it was the normal aversion to seeing a human being slain in cold blood. But also there was, deep within Lee, the belief that Mike Bastrop held secrets that were vital to his own life, his own future.

He dived headlong toward the Judge, shouting, "No!" as he moved.

His voice startled Amos Clebe just as he pulled the trigger. The six-shooter roared as Lee's shoulder crashed into Clebe's knees. They both crashed to the ground.

Fear and desperation galvanized the portly Judge. He tore free of Lee's grasp and lurched to his feet. He had clung to the six-shooter and he tried to bring it to bear on Lee, rocking back the hammer.

Lee, on his knees, plunged forward again, taking the Judge at the knees. The six-shooter exploded almost in his face, but he only felt the sting of the flash and of burning powder. Once again he brought Amos Clebe to the ground. This time he found a grip on the Judge's arm and twisted. Clebe uttered a gasp of pain and was forced to drop the gun.

Lee drove a fist into the Judge's throat and a knee into the man's soft stomach. He felt his victim collapse.

There was shouting in Sumner Street. The voice of Mike Bastrop became audible, rising to a hoarse thunder of fury. "Somebody tried to murder me. I've got a bullet in my arm. I need a doctor before I bleed to death!"

Lee began running. Because a freight shed blocked the rear of the lot, he was forced to use the side street. Confusion gripped Sumner Street. Men were shouting for a doctor. Apparently nobody knew from where the shot had come that had been fired at Bastrop.

Then Amos Clebe began shouting hoarsely, "Stop him! Stop him! This way! It's that Comanche! The one that murdered Bill Tice. He just tried to kill Major Bastrop."

Lee ran desperately. Amos Clebe had recognized him. Men came racing into the side street. A six-shooter opened up. Lee suspected it was Amos Clebe who fired the first shot. He must have found the gun Lee had shaken from his fingers and was emptying the weapon.

A slug tore a long furrow of dust at Lee's feet. Another twitched at his sleeve. He kept thinking, "That gun must be about empty. It must—"

Amos Clebe, however, had one more shell to fire. Lee felt the impact of the bullet. It was as though someone had struck him on the side with a heavy hand. He staggered, reeled ahead, then regained his stride.

He fought for breath. His lungs seemed to be deflated. He could not stop now. Men were pursuing him on foot. He knew that if they overtook him, the chances were they'd hang him on the spot. He kept going.

Chapter *SEVEN*

He was fleeing from the shadow of death, from the faceless violence of a lynch mob. For this was a mob that had now formed. The screeching was that of men who wanted vengeance—and blood.

He felt his strength ebbing. He had instinctively headed for the fringe of town toward where he had left Clemmy and the horses in the thickets along the creek. He veered down a side path. His thoughts were growing as sluggish as his failing strength. He was sure of only one thing. He must not lead them to her. They might take vengeance on her also.

He rounded a shack. A small figure loomed in his path. He tried to swerve away, tried to lift his pistol.

"No! It's me! Clemmy!"

"I told you not to come in here," he mumbled. "Hide! Hide! Quick! They're—"

She was supporting him. "You're hurt!"

The pursuit had hesitated, unable to decide in which direction its quarry had turned in the darkness.

Lee tried to push Clemmy away. "Get out of here!" he said. "Don't let them catch you."

She hurried him along with her. "I've got the horses handy," she said. "I brought them in closer when I heard the shooting start. They're right here. Are you able to ride?"

Lee found a measure of strength returning. He was bleeding, but he hoped he had sustained only a rib glance. He saw the horses in the darkness. Even the buckskin pack-horse, with the bulging gunny sack lashed to its saddle, was there.

Men were now moving in their direction, but still uncertain and peering into the darkness. Discovery was only a matter of seconds.

"I'm all right," Lee said. He pushed her toward her

mount, waited to make sure she was in the saddle, then pulled himself on his roan. They raced away.

Wild shouts arose. "There they are!" a man screeched. "They got horses! There's more'n one of 'em!"

A pistol opened up. More joined in. "Hold your fire, you danged fools!" an aggrieved voice boomed. "You just busted a window in my own house. Remember, there's innocent folks around here. I've got kids in there sleepin'."

The shooting ended. The pursuers had no horses within quick reach. Lee and Clemmy reached the creek brush north of town and followed it for a time. They were well away from town and swerving into open flats before they heard evidence of riders on their way out of the settlement. But the pursuit was far away, evidently scattered and confused.

Clemmy pulled alongside Lee, peering anxiously at him. "How about it?" she demanded.

Lee had explored his injury. "Only a graze," he said. "Knocked the wind out of me for a minute."

He fought back the desire to groan with pain, for that was what was driving through him. His injury was far more than a scratch. The bullet had glanced. But it had broken a rib, at least, and perhaps two. He was sure, however, that it had not damaged a lung.

His manner deluded Clemmy. "We'll take a look at it in a little while to make sure," she said. "There's a BT windmill tank above Turtle Flat in the direction we're heading. There should be water in it. It'll take half an hour or so to get there. Can you hold out until then?"

Lee said that he could. But he was mighty thankful when the windmill showed against the skyline ahead. He reeled drunkenly when he slid from the saddle.

Clemmy, with a gasp of fright, came with a rush to steady him. She searched his pockets and found his book of matches. She handed them to him. "Are you able to give me some light?"

"Somebody might see us," he protested.

"That's a chance we'll have to take," she said. "Some light, please."

Lee complied, but even that took effort. She pulled off his blood-stiffened shirt. He heard her draw a deep breath.

"Just a graze," she said shakily. "You idiot!"

If the sight of blood and bullet-torn flesh terrified her, she refused to let it give her a pause. There was water in the windmill tank. She used his shirt to clean the wound, then formed a bandage.

She tried to help him into the saddle when they prepared to ride again. He huffily refused assistance.

He managed to pull himself on his horse, but he reeled and was forced to cling to the horn. Clemmy mounted and pulled her horse alongside so that she could place an arm around him to steady him.

His head cleared. The world quit spinning. "Next time," she said huskily, "Don't be so proud. Even a woman can be of some help."

He tried to pull away from her. "What am I?" he mumbled. "A child?"

"Even a child would have brains enough to accept help when it's needed," she snapped. "Don't be a fool."

She stayed close at his side as they headed away, but Lee found a measure of strength returning.

He looked around after a time. "What's this?" he demanded. "If we keep riding in this direction, we'll land at the BT."

"Yes," she said.

"Have you gone loco?"

"The BT might be the last place they'd think of looking for you," she said. "They'll expect you to head back to the plains. Merl and Gabe probably will join in the hunt as soon as they get word. Maybe we could hide in that rabbit warren that Uncle Tice built. There are rooms that haven't been used in years. I know my way around the kitchen and the pantry. We won't starve, and I'm sure they'll never know they have guests."

"Besides," she added, "I still need some clothes, as long as you seem to have bungled the job."

Events had been so crowded that Lee had not been able to sort them out in proper order. Now some of it came back. He began laughing crazily. Clemmy spoke. "Are you all right? Can you hold out a little longer? It's only a couple of miles."

"I haven't gone off my rocker. I was only thinking about what I left lying under the platform at Sim Quarles' store," he said.

"What was it?"

"Well, to mention a few things, there were three of the most fashionable dresses I could lay my hands on in a hurry."

"Dresses? You didn't really—!"

"And slippers and a new pair of boots. And a few other items to wear that I won't describe."

"I should just think you wouldn't *dare* describe them. The idea, you trying to pick out what I'm to wear!"

She added, "What will people think when they find those things?"

Then they both were laughing. They were a little fey, a trifle lightheaded. "At least you brought a dishpan," she gasped. "But I'm afraid I've already put a dent in it when I threw that gunny sack on the packsaddle."

After a time they sobered. The gaiety faded. Lee became aware of the grinding pain of his wound, of futility, of complete weariness. Clemmy rode slumped in the saddle.

"I heard someone in that mob that was chasing you say you had tried to kill Major Bastrop," she spoke, breaking a long silence. She was picking her words, trying to be casual about it. But he knew it was important.

"Would you believe me if I told you that man was wrong?" he asked.

"Why shouldn't I believe you?"

"You didn't really believe me when I told you I didn't kill Bill Tice. Or pretended not to believe me."

"Pretended? Oh, I see! You're still trying to say that I was the one who shot Uncle Tice. And that I'm trying to hang the guilt on you."

"If you didn't do it, then who did?"

"There you go again!" she exploded. "That's as much as saying I did it. *You* had more reason to do a thing like that. At least Uncle Tice never used a quirt on me."

"Maybe not, but you still might get it unless you simmer down," Lee warned. "Quit screeching before somebody hears you. And ease that horse down before I take the both of you in hand."

"You just try it," she panted. But she lowered her voice and slowed the pace of the horse.

"That's better," Lee said. "Now, tell me something. Why would Judge Clebe try to kill Mike Bastrop?"

She had intended to ignore him, but that brought her around. "What?"

"You heard me."

"You must really be out of your head!" she exclaimed.

"The Judge was the one who took that shot at Mike Bastrop. Winged him in the arm. If I hadn't jumped the

Judge he might have punched the Major's ticket for keeps. Then Judge Clebe tried to kill me too. And almost did."

He told her the details. She listened in silence. He took that silence to mean disbelief.

"You think I'm making all this up, don't you?" he demanded. "I know it sounds crazy. Why would the Judge try to drygulch Major Bastrop? He's always been a pompous, soft old windbag. Harmless as butter. He never even packed a gun in his life."

"Maybe he wasn't as soft and harmless as people believe," Clemmy said.

"You got any particular reason for saying that?"

"I told you I used to peek at the poker games they played at BT. And eavesdrop. There was something horrible about it. The danger, I mean. I always felt they'd skin me alive if they caught me. And Uncle Tice nearly did when he finally pounced on me one night."

"What do you mean, horrible about it?"

"Those three men played as though they hated each other," she said. "And it wasn't because of the game. That meant nothing. There was something else between them. The poker game was only an excuse for them to get together. And to divide up money."

"Divide?"

"I saw that happen. Only twice. But I'm sure it happened many times. That was what bound the three of them together. It wasn't poker. It was something bigger than that. Everybody knew that Uncle Tice was a sort of partner of Major Bastrop. I'm sure Judge Clebe was in on it also. Secretly."

"There's no law against being partners in marketing beef," Lee said. "Maybe the Judge, being as he sits on the bench, figured it better to keep it under his hat."

"I don't know what was in his mind," she said, "but, as far as Amos Clebe being a harmless old windbag, that couldn't be farther from the truth. I was deathly afraid of him. He was always looking at me with those wise eyes. I'd rather be watched by a wolf. Also, as for him never carrying a gun, the fact is that he *was* armed. Always. At least when he played poker at BT."

"Amos Clebe? I never saw a gun on him in my life!"

"He carried one of those wicked, little pistols with two barrels, fastened to a metal device up the sleeve of his shirt."

"A double-barreled derringer with a spring clip!" Lee exclaimed. "Good Lord!"

"He also had a horrible dagger in a sort of sheath that hung at the back of his neck."

Lee whistled, amazed. "Throw-knife! Are you sure you're talking about Amos Clebe? How did you find out about these hideouts?"

"One night he shed his coat when they played poker. He said it was because of the heat, but that wasn't the real reason."

"And what was the real reason?"

"I'm sure he wanted them to know he could defend himself. Uncle Tice and Major Bastrop wore weapons, too. Six-shooters in holsters. But they always carried them openly."

"While they were playing poker?"

"Yes. Well, not at first. You see, I started spying on them way back when I was small. It was different then. They actually seemed to be playing a friendly game. Nobody carried weapons. But, as I look back on it now, I can see how the atmosphere changed. Not suddenly. Those three men came slowly to distrust each other. And fear each other. But something bound them together."

"What you're actually saying is that it could have been Judge Clebe or Mike Bastrop who murdered Bill Tice that night."

"Yes," she said.

"At least that explains why Judge Clebe came back a second time to the mercantile. He hurried home to get a heavier gun when he saw that Mike Bastrop was in the Silver Bell. The range was too long for a derringer."

"I know that they hated you, also."

Lee's wound had been taking toll, along with the hours of great physical stress. His mind had been too numbed to try to puzzle out an answer to the problem Clemmy had presented.

But he now straightened, startled. "Me?" he exclaimed. "You mean Bill Tice and the Judge. I always knew Mike Bastrop had it in for me, but he might have had a reason. But the other two . . ."

"I heard your name mentioned only once," she said. "That was a long time ago. I don't know why it was brought up. It seemed to touch off some sort of a fury in Uncle Tice. He upbraided Major Bastrop. He seemed to be blaming the Major for something he'd failed to do. Judge Clebe got between them, or they might have gone for their guns. Judge Clebe was very angry. I don't know what he told them, but it quieted them down. I never heard them mention you since that night."

At that moment they topped a rise and lights showed far ahead. "There's the BT," Clemmy said.

"We can't hole up there," Lee said.

"Why not?"

"What would we do with the horses? That just occurred to me. We can't just stake them out in the brush. They'd likely be found, sooner or later. And if we turned them loose, it'd be a dead giveaway, for they'd head for their corrals."

"You're right," she said wearily. "I wasn't thinking straight."

"I've got another idea," he said. "As long as we're here, you ought to get what you need in the way of clothes. I'll sneak in with you to sort of take care of any trouble that might crop up. If we're quiet, we might have luck. I didn't have much trouble injuning in that night. It's late. The bunkhouse ought to be asleep, and the Tice brothers, too, if they're home. It looks like word of the ruckus in town hasn't got this far as yet."

"What is this plan?"

"We'll head for Rancho Verde."

"Verde? But I don't see—"

"That's another place they likely won't think of looking for us. I've got a friend there we can trust. Kinky Bob. He's got a shack of his own. He likely can hide the horses for a day or so while we rest up enough to head for the Llano."

He added, "We've got no time to debate it. If we don't make it to Verde before daylight, we're as good as cooked."

"All right," she said. "I'll hurry. I hope you know what you're doing."

They left the horses at a distance and moved in. The huge, rambling house was dark, but as they passed the main wing, they could hear a sleeper snoring.

"That's Merl," Clemmy breathed. "He always snores. Gabe is probably home, too. Dear God, don't let them wake up tonight!"

They crept to the wing where she had lived. The door of her quarters was locked, but one of the windows was open.

Lee helped her scramble across the sill. He waited outside until she handed him a bundle wrapped in a quilt and slid over the sill to join him.

"I tried to leave things in place, hoping they won't suspect I've been here," she whispered.

They returned to where they had left the horses and mounted. Clemmy drew a deep breath when they were at a safer distance. "We've been lucky—this far," she said.

It was perilously near daybreak when they again left their horses and warily approached the adobe hut where Kinky Bob lived. Their cautious tapping on the door brought action. Kinky Bob opened the portal a few inches.

"Lawd A'mighty! I knowed it was you, Jack-Lee, when I heard you at de door. And if'n it ain't Missy Clementine with you. Folks are sayin' dat both o' you must be daid."

Kinky Bob was wrapped in a quilt he had snatched from his pallet. "Get inside!" he breathed, "afore somebody see you. Don't you two know yo're wanted fer murder?"

Chapter *EIGHT*

Kinky Bob led their horses into hiding in thick brush at a distance from the spread. It was a temporary concealment. Dawn was breaking when he came stealing back to the shack.

"Dey'll be safe enough where I picketed 'em today," he said. "Nobody rightly go near dat brush. Tonight I'll move 'em to better cover. I know a few places where dey kin be handy when you need 'em."

"We're only asking you to cover us until we can get some rest," Lee said. "We'll pull out tonight."

"If'n you ask me, Jack-Lee, you don't look like you can do much more ridin' for a few days. You just make up your mind to lay low here 'til things clear up."

Clemmy spoke. "It's too much of a risk for you, Kink. We wouldn't ask you to hide us even for a few hours if we weren't desperate."

Kink pulled aside the pallet that served as his bed and removed a trap door that was fitted so carefully in the plank floor, its existence might have been overlooked.

"Dug myself a root cellar, years ago," he explained. "Dat's why I put in a plank floor in de shack. Used to be a clay floor. Dar's a crawl tunnel out of de root cellar dat you can find if you know where to dig. I mudded up dis end of it. If'n you foller it, you come out under de old hay rack dat's stored in de wagon shed out dar about a rope throw. De openin' in de floor o' de shed is covered by old planks what look like dey been dar fer years."

Kink grinned reassuringly at Clemmy. "Missy, you cain't find a safer place dan right here, now kin you?"

"Why did you build this tunnel, Kink?" she asked.

"I was born a slave, Missy. I don't never want to be one ag'in. I aim to make sure I kin run fer it if'n dey ever come for me."

"They'll never come for you for that again," Clemmy said.

Lee was fighting to stay on his feet. Clemmy saw his ashen color and uttered a little cry of contrition. "We stand here talking while this man is suffering," she exclaimed.

Kinky Bob had long experience at emergency treatment of broken bones and the injuries that were a part of the rough life of cowhands. Caring for bullet wounds was not exactly a novelty for him, either.

With Clemmy's help, he doctored and bandaged Lee's injury. Lee sat, enduring the pain, while they dressed the wound. When it was finished, Clemmy helped him to the pallet. "Sleep now," she said. "You'll be all right soon."

He was adrift for a time on a sea of pain and feverish dreams. Clemmy stayed at his side. Kinky Bob had left to go about his daily task of gentling the rough string in order to avoid arousing suspicion.

"Ain't much chance anybody'll come near de shack," he had assured Clemmy. "Kink don't have any visitors. But, if'n anybody shows up, you'n Jack-Lee kin hide in de root cellar, or git away through de tunnel."

Nobody came near the shack all day. Lee was aware that Clemmy was trying to soothe him, for he was fighting phantoms in his fever. He knew he was babbling wild things in the Comanche tongue and that she was pleading with him to be quiet. At times, reality would return. He would look up at her, knowing he had been raving.

"What was I talking about?" he would ask.

"Nothing that anybody could understand," she would answer. "Sleep now. Sleep." He could see her weariness. He could see her strength. Her determination.

He finally sank into real sleep. When he aroused, darkness had come. His fever was broken. Kink was back in the shack, cooking a meal, with an oil lamp burning. Clemmy lay sleeping on a blanket in a corner, curled in a childlike posture.

Kink put a finger to his lips when he saw that Lee was awake. "Let de missy sleep," he whispered. "She stayed awake all day, 'til I come home."

Lee tried to move. He failed. It seemed to him that minutes passed before he could form words. "Nobody came?"

"Nope," Kink whispered. "But dey's sure lookin' fer you an' de missy. I sighted riders a couple o' times durin' the

day, way off on the range in the direction o' the Armadillos. All de riders in de crew pulled out to join in de
hunt. I rode down to the stage road a while ago to talk to
a freighter. Pretended I'd run short o' matches for my
pipe. Done some talkin'."

"What did you find out?"

"Somebody put a slug in Majah Bastrop's arm last night
in Punchbowl. But only a gouge. He'll be all right in a few
days. Them kind never die."

"Who do they say did it?" Lee asked.

Kink didn't want to answer that for a time, but finally
he did. "Jedge Clebe says he seen you do it."

"He's lying, Kink. You'd never believe me if I told you
who really winged the Major."

"De Majah's put a price on yore haid," Kink said.

"A reward? How much?"

"A hundred dollars if yo're brought in alive. Five thousand dead."

Clemmy had awakened. She sat up, wide-eyed. "How
terrible!" she cried.

"It's like I tol' you before, Jack-Lee," Kink said. "De
Majah want you in yore grave. Who'd bring you in alive,
when he could git rich by packin' in a corpse?"

"Nothing adds up," Lee said. "Why would he want me
dead?"

Neither Clemmy nor Kink had an answer.

Within twenty-four hours Lee's wound was well on the
mend, but he was forced to admit that Kink and Clemmy
were right in insisting that he continue to take it easy.
However, within another day or two, his restlessness grew
as the injury improved.

He and Clemmy could only venture out of the shack at
night and after they were sure the ranch was asleep. On
the surface, Rancho Verde was resuming a semblance of
its normal routine. The Mexican housekeeper and her husband, who cooked and carried on the chores at Casa
Bonita, came and went in their duties, but never approached Kink's shack.

Two riders were still on duty, combing the range and
taking care of the *remuda,* but four others were still with
the posses hunting the fugitives. These four showed up
late on the third day. They were unshaven, saddle-stiffened,
and tired. They remained only overnight, pulling out the
next morning on fresh horses and leading remounts. They

were carrying rifles and six-shooters and had a packhorse loaded with food.

"They're still trying to earn that five thousand," Lee commented to Clemmy. "I rode to Kansas and back with those cowhands. Now they want my scalp."

"How long will they keep looking for us?"

"No telling," Lee said. Mike Bastrop had not returned to the ranch. Kink, who continued his normal daily work with the young horses, talked to the two men of the riding crew and picked up information.

"De Majah's ridin' with the posses, his arm in a sling," Kink reported. "He's called off the late beef drive. Won't be no horses needed, but I ain't got orders yet to quit shapin' them up, so I keep workin'. Everybody in dis part o' New Mexico is too busy tryin' to git rich by killin' a man to 'tend to de cattle business."

"You always been quite a lady's man, Kink," Lee observed. "Do you happen to be acquainted with that pretty girl that keeps house for Judge Clebe in Punchbowl?"

Kink grinned, flattered. "You know danged well I been courtin' Celia for a long time. What you drivin' at, Jack-Lee?"

"You need some supplies in town, Kink," Lee said. "Tobacco, or horseshoe nails, or such. It'd do you good to take the day off and see the sights. And call on Celia. I wonder if Judge Clebe is still holding court. And I'm concerned about his health. The Judge was looking poorly the last time I saw him."

Kink eyed him. "I reckon dat won't take much doin'," he said.

He rode away the following morning and did not return until long after midnight. "Ain't no trials bein' held," he reported. "Court is 'journed 'til de Judge gits back from El Paso. He was called dar on important business."

Lee and Clemmy looked at each other. "We might not be the only ones that are running scared," Lee commented.

Kink said the manhunt was still on, but it was beginning to slow down. "Town's full o' riders nursin' saddle blisters," he said. "A lot of 'em figure you two are daid out beyond de Caprock. Either dat or you've made it into Mexico. A lot of 'em are goin' back to their outfits."

"What about Merl and Gabe Tice?" Clemmy asked.

"Celia says she guesses if it wasn't fer dem two rascals an' Majah Bastrop dar wouldn't be anybody but maybe a few lawmen still out in de brush. I heard say dat de Tices swore on their father's grave dat dey'd git you, Jack-Lee, an' roast you over a slow fire."

In addition to news, Kink brought Lee a clean shirt and underwear and three pairs of socks. "Me'n de Judge wear about de same size shirt," Kink explained. "He got so many clothes he never miss what Celia give me. I reckon you kin use some of 'em, even if they ain't quite as snug as what you like."

When Kink prepared to leave the shack for his day's chore at the horse pasture the next morning, Lee said, "We'll pull out tonight, Kink. Can you bring in the horses for us?"

"Where'll you an' the missy go?" he asked mournfully.

"We've got a place. It's better that you don't know."

"You mean dey might try to squeeze it out'n me? I reckon dey would if they ketched on dat you'd been here, but I tell you now dey'd never git it out o' me."

"I know that."

"Ol Kink hankers to go with you an' de missy."

"For your own sake I can't let you do anything like that," Lee said. "Let's face it. You know that the chances are against us. Anybody who is with us will be given the same treatment if they catch us."

"I still hanker to go."

"Kink," Lee said abruptly, "you know I'm Comanche, don't you?"

Kink was taken by surprise. "I don't know nothin'," he exclaimed fearfully. "If you Comanche, if you Mexican, if you white, what difference. We friends."

"You know something," Lee insisted. "Something you've kept from me. You're sure I'm Comanche. Why?"

Kink refused to answer. He picked up his chaps and the bucking strap he used in riding the young horses and left the shack. Peering from a corner of the window, Lee watched him stride to the corral, rope out his day horse, and head for the horse pasture.

"He knows," Lee said. "He knows for sure."

The morning dragged by as had the other mornings since their confinement in the shack.

"You're not!" Clemmy spoke sharply, breaking a long silence.

"Not what?"

"What you said a while ago. Comanche."

"I feel that Kink is sure that—"

"He's wrong. And do you know what else I think? I'm sure you're the baby the Indians stole the day they hit this place. I think that the Señora Margarita Calvin, the widow of John Calvin, was your mother and that John Calvin was your father."

"If so, it'll never be proved," Lee said. "They're dead. How could you prove anything after so many years?"

She stamped her foot. "I tell you there's no Comanche blood in you. Spanish, yes, but very little even of that. Your mother was a Lopez before she married John Calvin, but Americans had married into the Lopez family for generations. Her mother was an American, and so was her grandmother."

"How do you know all this?"

"Maria, my duenna, had a tongue that swung like a bell clapper. She knew all about everyone in the Punchbowl. I could tell you considerable. You'd be surprised at some of the things."

"I'll bet that more than one reputation has been ruined by Maria. But what does all this add up to?"

"You're deliberately pretending to be dense, just to get my temper up," she said. "John Calvin's widow owned all of Rancho Verde. It was part of the original Spanish grant. The Lopez grant, one of the biggest in New Mexico. Now, do you see what I'm driving at? Or do I have to draw a picture and push your stupid nose into it so you can understand that—"

The door of the shack was flung abruptly open. Days of monotony had lulled them into carelessness. They had failed to bar the opening.

Lee whirled. He had been standing near the wall to the left of the door. The intruder who came leaping into the room was Gabe Tice. His beefy face still bore the blotches and healing wounds of the punishment he had taken at Lee's hands. He had a six-shooter in his hand. However, he was momentarily at a disadvantage, for his eyes were fixed on Clemmy. She shrank back, terrified.

Gabe's puffy eyes darted around the room in search of Lee. Lee was already leaping. He brought his left hand smashing down on Gabe's right arm. The pistol fell to the floor. His right fist drove into Gabe's stomach. It was a paralyzing blow. Even so, Gabe tried to retrieve the gun.

Clemmy darted in and snatched up the weapon. Another

man loomed up in the doorway. Merl Tice. He had a brace of six-shooters in his hands, but he could not fire because of the danger to his brother.

Lee caught Gabe by the waist and propelled him bodily into Merl. The brothers were driven through the door and sprawled on the ground outside.

Lee also fell to his hands and knees. He glimpsed at least two more armed men who were running from the corner of the bunkhouse toward the shack to help the Tices. He recognized them as BT riders.

Clemmy slammed the door shut an instant before a bullet smashed into one of its planks. The shot had been fired by the oncoming BT men.

The two strong wooden bars that Kink used to secure the door stood in a corner. Lee jammed them into place. More bullets beat at the portal, but none of the slugs penetrated the heavy oak planks which had been wedged together with wooden dowels by Kink, who evidently had defense in mind in every detail of his reconstruction of the shack. The walls were of adobe, eighteen inches thick. Only the door, and the three windows, which also had heavy wooden shutters, were at all vulnerable.

Lee pushed Clemmy forcibly to the floor. "Stay down!" he warned as he barred the window shutters.

The shutters were equipped with loopholes. Lee chanced a look. Merl and Gabe Tice were running toward the wagon shed. That offered the nearest shelter. The shed, in which Kink said his tunnel emerged, stood a short distance southwest of the shack. Gabe was doubled over, the wind still knocked out of him by Lee's violence, unable to keep the pace his brother was setting. But Merl kept going.

Lee could have picked off both brothers, but he let them reach cover in the shed, whose crooked double doors stood open, facing north. The two cowboys were doing the shooting. They had halted beyond the wagon shed and were crouched, emptying their weapons.

Lee heard the hammers click on spent shells. He pushed the muzzle of his gun over the ledge of the window and fired one shot. The bullet tore dust between the pair.

"Start running!" he shouted.

They obeyed. One lost his hat in his haste to make it back to the safety of the corner of the bunkhouse. By that time Merl and Gabe Tice had reached the shelter of the shed.

There was a moment of silence. Then Merl Tice shouted, "Come out o' there, you damned copperhide! We've got you dead to rights this time. Come out, or we'll smoke you out an' that featherheaded girl along with you."

Lee looked at Clemmy. "You ought to get out of this."

"And you're going to stay, of course?" she snapped.

"I'm not giving up to those two, at least," he said.

"That makes a pair of us featherheads. What do you think would happen to either of us in their filthy hands?"

Merl Tice opened up with a six-shooter. He screeched profanity and threats as he fired. The slugs died in the heavy adobe walls.

"If we can hold out until dark, maybe we can fool them," Clemmy said shakily. "Remember what Kink said about his tunnel?"

"I remember," Lee said. "Does that still make me a featherhead?"

"That remains to be seen." She picked up a rifle and moved to a window. The west window covered the wagon shed and bunkhouse. A rambling barn also stood in that direction, south of the bunkhouse. The door of the adobe shack stood in the west wall, overlooking these buildings.

The south window faced toward the irrigation ditch and hayfields. The main house was some distance to the northeast, and there was little cover for attackers from that direction.

Lee saw the frightened faces of the Mexican housekeeper and her husband peering from windows in the main house.

More bullets pounded futilely at the shack, coming from windows in the bunkhouse where the two BT riders had posted themselves.

"Quit wastin' caps," Gabe Tice shouted from the wagon shed. He addressed the shack. "You ain't got a chance, Jackson, an' you know it. We'll send for some more men an' we can hold you there 'til you an' the gal starve. Might as well make it easy on yourself by comin' out now."

For answer, Lee put a rifle bullet through the flimsy plank wall of the wagon shed. He could hear the Tice brothers scrambling around, hurriedly arranging bulwarks to protect themselves. Lee was familiar with the interior of the shed. He had a sinking feeling. If the Tices happened to discover the entrance to Kink's tunnel, any hope of escaping from this trap was ended.

He could see that Clemmy was entertaining the same fear. They waited. Merl Tice was talking to the men in the bunkhouse, but Lee could not make out the words.

However he began to breathe a trifle easier. There was no indication the tunnel had been found. If there really was a tunnel? The thought came that perhaps there never had been one. It might have been only an invention of Kink's imagination in order to give him a sense of security, so that he would remain in the shack until he had recovered his strength.

Silence came for a time. Then they heard a horse leaving the ranch. The rider was one of the BT cowboys who had retreated to where they had left their mounts. The man kept buildings between himself and the adobe shack until he was out of range, then headed north in the direction of Punchbowl.

"How do you suppose they found out we were here?" Clemmy murmured.

"I should have known they'd get around to suspecting Kink sooner or later," Lee said. "Another thing, I should have seen to it that the door was barred."

Gabe Tice confirmed Lee's surmise a few minutes later. "We'll make that black traitor sorry he was ever born when we get our hands on him," Gabe shouted, breaking the lull. "I should have guessed right from the start he was hidin' you here. You two have always been mighty friendly."

"At least that gives some hope for Kink," Lee said. "They haven't got him—yet. Let's hope he's heard the gunfire and knows what it means, and that he's had sense enough to pile a horse and head for Mexico."

Silence came again. Both Lee and Clemmy knew that the cowboy who had ridden away had been sent to bring reinforcements.

Chapter *NINE*

Hours passed. Late afternoon came, with the sun blazing down. The heavy dirt roof, on which bluebonnets and wild flowers bloomed, and the thick adobe walls insulated the interior of the shack. The room remained fairly cool.

However, the wagon shed, which had no windows, evidently was a furnace. Its double doors stood open, facing to the north, but this was of no help to the Tice brothers because the breeze was not drawing from that direction.

Lee heard them smashing a way of escape through the west wall. He sent a bullet into the shed, but aimed high, for he had no desire to kill—not even the Tice brothers. He wanted to help drive them from the shed. He was answered by bullets that beat at the heavy window shutters, bullets that sought his life.

He withdrew from the window. He pulled aside the pallet and lifted the trap door to the root cellar. "I hope Kink wasn't dreaming when he said he'd dug a burrow out of here," he said. "It's time to find out."

He descended the short ladder into the excavation. The space was so low he had to duck his head to avoid the beams that supported the plank floor. He could almost span the width and length of the cellar with his outstretched arms. The last of Kink's potato supply lay in a barrel, adorned with long sprouts. A supply of jerked beef that was as hard as leather, a bag of black-eyed beans, and another of cornmeal, along with a few cans of vegetables, rounded out Kink's cellar larder. However, Kink had said that he had a larger food cache hidden out somewhere. Kink's main purpose in life seemed to be to make sure he could get away "when they came for him."

At his request Clemmy handed down the lamp and matches. He lighted the wick. He could hear her moving from window to window, keeping watch. He explored the walls with his hands, but the earth seemed solid.

Clemmy gave him the stove poker, with which he began probing the west face of the cellar. That got results. The poker pierced deeply into softer earth. Lee widened the opening until he could thrust his arm into it at full length. His fingers touched nothing.

He doused the lamp and climbed back into the room. "I found it," he said. "Kink closed it up with small rocks and plastered it with wet clay. There's no use opening it entirely until we're sure there's no other way. We've got to hang on until dark. Then we will have a chance, at least."

He saw her swallow hard. "That ground looks solid enough," he said reassuringly. "Kink knows it's safe."

"I'm not afraid," she said. Then she drew a deep breath and tried to force a smile. That failed. "That's a fib," she said. "I *am* afraid. I've always been afraid of dark places, tunnels and such. I've had nightmares about being trapped in caves."

"We won't have any trouble," Lee said. "Kink built it. He's almost as big as both of us put together."

"Of course," she said.

"Maybe Gabe and Merl will give it up as useless," he said. It was a lame thought and he knew it.

"Maybe we can wish them away," she said.

"Wish them away?"

She again tried to smile wanly. "It's a game I used to play as a child. Well, not always as a child. I still wish for things. I used to wish that Merl and Gabe would vanish. I would sit by the hour, just wishing."

"Did you ever win?"

"Oh, yes. Not as far as Merl and Gabe were concerned, of course. Sometimes things turned out the way I wished."

"What, for instance?"

Color suddenly rose in her throat and she wouldn't look at him. "Oh, it doesn't matter. It was just a lot of foolishness. To pass time. I've always been left to my own devices. Maria, my duenna, was about the only person I ever knew whom I could confide in, or go to for advice. But Uncle Tice sent her away after I became old enough to look after myself."

"You never knew your mother?"

"I remember a beautiful woman who came to the convent and held me tight in her arms. A woman who kissed me and told me how much she loved me and that very soon we would be together always. She said she was earning money enough so that we could go somewhere and live comfortably. She mentioned San Francisco."

Tears were glistening in her eyes. "Yes, I knew my mother. She was good. She was an actress, but that doesn't mean that the things evil-minded people say were true. It's only that most women were jealous of her because she was so beautiful, so talented. It was the tongues of women that crucified Rose O'Neil. Women are so cruel to women."

"And they haven't changed," Lee said. "They've got another Rose O'Neil to crucify because she's young and pretty and is everything they wish they were deep in their hearts."

She looked at him through swimming eyes, surprised. "Thank you for the pretty part of it, even though you're only trying to cheer me up. They've hurt me. I wouldn't ever want them to know that. They have, but I'll never kneel to them. That's all they want. To humble me, so they can patronize me."

A bullet smashed into the door, breaking a long lull. Lee moved to a peephole. Powder smoke was fading in the hot sunlight from where a rifle had been fired from a knothole in the weathered side of the barn beyond the bunkhouse.

Gabe Tice's heavy voice rose tauntingly. "That's just to let you know we're still around, Comanch'. No use tryin' to wriggle away toward Casa Bonita. Ken Burns is hunkered in the barn, an' he's got all that stretch o' ground covered. You know Ken. An' you know he can shoot straight."

Merl took up the theme. "We're askin' you once more to come out peaceful. Clemmy, why did you pick up with an Indian? We're goin' to blast him out o' there right soon. You might git hurt."

"Start blasting," Clemmy responded.

Gabe cursed her. She clapped her hands over her ears. Gabe finally fell silent. No more shots were fired.

"Don't get careless," Lee warned her. "They're getting anxious. It's almost sundown, and nobody's showed up to help them."

He peered from a loophole. A bullet struck within two inches of the opening.

"They've got the loopholes spotted," he said. "Don't linger at one, like I just did, for more than a quick look. If that fellow had been a better shot, I'd have got that .44-40 right between the eyes."

The north window gave them a view of the trail to Punchbowl. It had remained empty since the messenger had vanished in the direction of town hours earlier.

Lee looked at the sun which was now touching the rims of the buttes to the west. "Won't you ever go down?" he blurted out.

He returned to the north window after a time to watch the trail. He remained there so long, Clemmy joined him. They both gazed in silence.

Riders were approaching on the trail. They were still nearly a mile away, but the setting sun caught the glint of rifle steel.

The trail carried the horsemen out of sight into timber. After a time they reappeared, much closer.

"Six, seven, eight!" Lee murmured, counting. "With the Tices, we're up against ten, eleven men, at least."

The sun went down at last. The sky darkened. The riders had left the trail and circled to a point beyond the buildings where their approach would be covered by the barn and the bunkhouse.

Lee and Clemmy waited. They could visualize what was going on. The arrivals would have left their horses at a distance and moved in on foot to confer with the Tice brothers as to the strategy they would follow.

Twilight lingered. Clouds became masses of gold. The weathered shakes on the buildings were the hue of hammered copper. Their splintery plank walls became a rich russet shade.

Lee speculated on Mike Bastrop's whereabouts. He had recognized the majority of the reinforcements. Sheriff Fred Mack had been leading the group, but Bastrop had not been present. Evidently the Rancho Verde owner was still out on the range, seeking trace of the fugitives elsewhere.

He felt Clemmy's shoulder touch his arm. She had moved close to his side. There was now no shadow of doubt between them. He no longer entertained the slightest belief that she had slain Bill Tice. He was certain also that she no longer suspected he might have been Tice's killer. In fact, he felt that she had never really believed it from the first.

A voice began shouting in the barn. "This is Sheriff Mack speaking. Can you hear me, you two in the shack?"

Lee delayed his reply for seconds. He was playing for

time. That was their only ally. Darkness was their only hope.

"I can hear you," he finally responded.

That brought a stir of boots and a subdued rumble of voices. Men were stationed in the barn and bunkhouse. Others, no doubt, were spotted along the irrigation ditch to prevent escape in other directions.

"Come out, unarmed, with your hands up," the sheriff yelled. "In the name of the law."

"And be shot full of holes in the name of the law," Lee answered.

"You'll be taken to town with the privilege of facin' a trial, fair an' square," Fred Mack said.

Lee was certain the officer was making a promise he knew he could not keep. He was asking a man to show himself so that he would likely be shot down or seized and hanged.

Lee remained silent. He kept watching the sky. Deep shadows were forming in the draws on the flanks of the Armadillos. The range below was fading into a sea of mauve light.

"Are you comin' out, or do we come in an' drag you out by the heels?" Merl Tice shouted, infuriated.

Lee spoke to Clemmy. "Take the poker and the lamp. Go down and open that tunnel. Don't light the lamp until I cover the trap. Here are the matches. We can't let any light show. They'll rush us as soon as it gets dark. We've got to be gone before they shoot down that door. Douse the lamp the minute you've got the tunnel open."

She complied. She was pale, but calm. She had the presence of mind to take with her into the root cellar the bundle of garments she had brought from her room at BT.

Lee replaced the trap door and shoved the pallet over it to mask any trickle of lamplight that might betray their plan.

"If you're any kind of a man," Fred Mack shouted, "you'll let that girl come out. We don't aim to hurt even such as her."

Clemmy heard that. "Tell them that such as I will put a bullet in the rotten hide of the first one that tries to rush this place," she said, her voice muffled.

Lee didn't relay the message. He was still buying time. He could hear the rasp of quarreling voices. The officer was engaged in a dispute with the brothers. Lee got the gist

of it. Fred Mack was hesitating about leading an assign-
ment where a girl's life might be at stake. The Tice brothers
were furiously demanding action and denouncing him as a
coward.

The Tices prevailed. A six-shooter opened up. Other
pistols and rifles joined in. A storm of bullets smashed
savagely at the door. The roar of guns went on and on. It
was plain that the posse had a definite plan, and also had
the ammunition to see it through.

Slugs began to chew through the planks. Lee heard spent
bullets buzzing in the room. Some were coming through
with such force they buried in the opposite wall. The door
could not sustain that torrent of metal much longer. The
upper hinge was torn from its supports.

"I've opened the tunnel!" Clemmy spoke during a brief
lull in the uproar.

Lee said, "Put out the lamp." He pulled aside the pallet,
lifted the trap door and passed down rifles and ammunition.

He moved to the west window, his rifle loaded. Gunfire
spurted from the barn and bunkhouse, but there was no
indication that the wagon shed had been reoccupied.

A new rain of slugs beat at the door. It began to sag,
and yells of triumph arose from the posse.

Lee lifted his rifle and emptied it at the bunkhouse and
barn. He spaced his bullets along the length of the structures. That slowed the shooting as men scrambled for cover.

He reloaded, making sure they could hear the metallic
click of the mechanism. Again he emptied the rifle. He was
seeking only to make them cautious, to delay the inevitable
final attack.

He dropped into the cellar, reached up, and slid the trap
door back in place.

"The tunnel isn't very big," Clemmy said in the darkness. Her voice was quivering.

"We've got to try it," Lee said. "Where is the blasted
thing? I'm turned around."

She guided him to a wall. His groping hands found the
opening. "All right," he said. "I'll go first and take the two
rifles."

He crawled into the opening, pushing the weapons ahead
of him. "It's plenty big enough," he said. "Come on."

He heard her following him. The tunnel was braced with
lengths of cottonwood or mesquite. "Kink did a good job,"

he whispered. "He's got enough timbering in here to hold up a mountain."

"I hope so," she quavered. "Don't go so fast. Don't get too far ahead of me."

The depth of earth dimmed sounds from above, but Lee could still hear the faint thud of bullets smashing at the door of the shack.

His head collided with a solid object. This time it was not one of the braces. It was a wall of unyielding earth that blocked the way.

He felt freezing despair. "Stop!" he breathed.

"What's wrong?" Clemmy chattered.

Lee did not answer. His first thought was that the tunnel ahead had collapsed. If so, all they could do would be to retreat to the root cellar.

The blackness was so impenetrable it seemed to have substance. Lee found himself fighting panic. If the tunnel had collapsed ahead, it might also cave in behind them. Or upon them. He could hear Clemmy breathing fast. She spoke again, her voice high-pitched. "What is it?"

Lee groped in the darkness. His hands met only hard, rough walls of earth on either side. He explored overhead. He touched nothing. And he could now distinctly hear the roar of guns that were being fired in the bunkhouse and barn.

Suddenly, he stood erect, feeling his knees quivering. His head touched wood. Wooden planks!

He suddenly wanted to yell, but managed to suppress that to a mumble. "Of course! Why, we're there! We've reached the end of the tunnel. I didn't realize we'd crawled that far. I'm standing almost straight and there are planks overhead. We must be under the wagon shed!"

Clemmy began babbling unintelligibly. He placed the palms of his hands against the obstruction and pushed cautiously. At first there was no result. He used more force, and one of the planks yielded. Any sound it made was lost in the roar of gunfire—now startlingly loud. He could see the flickering glow of the explosions, for the double doors of the shed still stood open, although facing at right angles to the buildings where the guns were flaming.

He wriggled out of the excavation and found himself beneath the spidery outlines of the hay wagon. "Give me your hand," he said. "And watch your head. We're coming out right under the hay rick."

He lifted her to the surface. She lay beside him, clinging to his hand like a terrified child. She was sobbing. He placed an arm around her, holding her tight against him until she calmed.

"I'm all right now," she breathed huskily. "I'm sorry I'm such a weakling. Afraid of the dark. I—"

The roar of guns reached a crescendo. Wild yelling swelled up. Lee moved to the open door and peered out. Clemmy joined him. The adobe shack was lighted by the crimson flash of gunfire. Its door was tilted drunkenly, its hinges torn away by the storm of metal.

Fred Mack's voice shouted, "Quit shootin' for a minute! Maybe the cuss is ready to come out now."

The gunfire tapered off. The officer shouted a demand for Lee's surrender. Silence came.

"I'm sick o' stallin' around!" Gabe Tice roared. "Come on, such of you as ain't made of jelly. Me an' Merl are goin' in there an' dig him out."

Guns were reloaded and the firing was resumed. Fred Mack continued to shout for Lee to give up, but his voice was lost in the uproar. Gabe and Merl Tice were shouting orders, organizing the others for a rush.

Lee and Clemmy retreated from the door of the shed. "Here they come!" Lee breathed.

The posse had left cover and were running toward the shack, spreading out to engulf it from three sides. They were shooting as they charged.

Men, crouching and zigzagging, ran past the open door of the shed. One paused, taking shelter back of one of the sagging doors for a time. He had two six-shooters in his hands, and was firing like a madman. Then he charged ahead again, but he was now in the rear of the rush. Lee recognized him. He was Gabe Tice. Gabe was letting other men go in ahead of him.

Lee said, "Let's go!"

The wave of attackers had gone past and their attention was concentrated on the adobe shack. "Stay close to me!" Lee said.

He had his rifle in his hands. He almost fired into a shadow that darted suddenly into the shed through the open door.

"Dat you, Jack-Lee?" a deep whisper sounded. "You dar with de missy?"

Lee felt ice in his veins. He had come within an ace of

shooting Kinky Bob. "I'm here, Kink!" he breathed. "Miss Clemmy's with me."

"Praise de Lawd!" the big man said. "I been layin' out dar all afternoon, prayin' you'd hold out 'til dark. Couldn't do nothin' but wait a chance to come in. I follered right behind dem men when dey started to rush my place."

His heavy hand touched Lee's arm. "Let's git out o' here afore dey find de tunnel an' ketch on that you two has got away. The horses are waitin'. It's about a mile away."

The shooting and screeching was at its height around the shack. Someone chanced entering the structure and began bawling a frantic plea for his companions to quit shooting.

Lee and Clemmy followed Kink as they darted out of the shed. They veered until they had its bulk between them and the shack. They headed away and passed the bunkhouse and barn. They were not challenged. All members of the posse apparently had joined in the attack on Kink's adobe stronghold.

Confused shouting arose back of them. It was dawning on the attackers that the bag was empty. Angry accusations were flying. The Tice brothers were frenziedly berating Fred Mack and others for carelessness, accusing them of letting their quarry slip past them in the darkness. This was being angrily denied.

"Dey'll find the tunnel pretty soon," Kink panted as they broke into a run. "But dey'll have plenty trouble pickin' up our trail in de dark. Come daybreak, we be long gone."

The shouting became fainter in the distance. Kink slowed the pace. Weight and age were telling on him. "I never was very light on my feet," he admitted.

Lee was also happy for a respite. Clemmy, realizing they were safe for the time being, said faintly, "I'm bushed!"

She was reeling, exhausted. Lee discovered that, in spite of everything, she had brought with her the bundle of clothing, which she clung to tightly. He lifted her in his arms and carried her, bundle and all.

After a time, she strengthened. "I can travel on my own feet now," she said. "I'm being a baby again."

Kink led the way through brush. Presently, Lee heard the stir of tethered animals ahead. There were seven horses in all, three of which bore saddles. One of them was the buckskin packhorse, bearing a sizable burden.

"I lifted my cache o' grub," Kink said. "I helped myself to some o' de Majah's best ridin' stock—such as you two ain't already got away with. We'll need remounts. It's quite a fur piece to Mexico, so dey tell me, an' we got to git there in a hurry, fer they'll be after us."

"You better head for Mexico alone, Kink," Lee said.

"What you mean, Jack-Lee? Don't you want to ride with me?"

"If you were caught with me, it'd only go harder on you."

Kink laughed scornfully. "How you talk! Dar ain't nothin' dat would help Kinky Bob now, if'n he was caught. Dey would hang me for stealin' horses, if nothin' else. Dey know it was me that kept you an' de missy hid out at my place while dey was ridin' dar horses down to skin an' bones huntin' you."

He added, "I cain't go back, but if you don't want me to travel with you, I'll haul out on my own."

"You know better than that," Lee said. "But I'm not going to Mexico. Not yet, at least."

"Whar you go, Jack-Lee?"

"Into the plains. Into the Garden."

"De Debbil's Garden? Nobody go dar, Jack-Lee! De imp-ghosts git you! Dey ride on de sandstorms!"

Clemmy spoke. "I've been there. No imp-ghosts better come around me. I'll tweak their noses for them."

"Don't talk like dat, Missy," Kink begged. "De hoodoos, dey'll hear you."

"We're going into the Garden," Clemmy said, "and you're going with us. You'll be better off with us than alone. They might catch you before you could make it to Mexico. We could never forgive ourselves if that happened."

"Of course," Lee said. He slapped Kink on the back. "That makes three of us now. Mavericks. Outlaws!"

"I got a hoot owl charm that I bought from a witch doctor," Kink said. "An' magic powder to sprinkle on de fire at night to keep de hoodoos away. I ain't skeered to go to Spirit Lake with you an' de missy, Jack-Lee."

"Spirit Lake?" Lee asked quickly. "You know about it?"

"Nobody know where 'tis," Kink said, "but I 'spect you think you do. Dar's no such place, but if'n you believe you kin find it, Kink will go along. But I ain't goin' to like it. None whatever."

They rode eastward. Back of them, distance erased all sounds. If they were being hunted, there was no sign of their pursuers. They veered northward to set up a blind trail, then headed again directly for the Devil's Garden.

Chapter *TEN*

Dawn was bright on the ridges when they rode out of the arid wastes of the Devil's Garden into view of the green basin. Spirit Lake lay still and gleaming, reflecting the glow in the sky.

Kink pulled up his dust-caked horse and stared for a long time. "De Lawd watch over us all," he finally said. "Dis here is a place dat ain't supposed to be."

His awe increased as they moved toward the camp site in the willows that Lee and Clemmy had used previously. A band of antelope went hop-scotching ahead of them, pausing at intervals to peer at them, and then take off again. Deer moved in the distance. Water fowl squabbled in the reeds.

The horses Lee had turned loose when he and Clemmy had left for Punchbowl had not joined the wild bunch. He sighted them grazing not far away.

However, he stood up in the stirrups, then sank back. "Hold up!" he said. "There are wild horses down the basin, but so far away they likely won't spot us if we stay still. They're starting to pull out for the day."

The wild ones were mere specks at that distance. Among them was a band of mares which was now being herded eastward toward low hills beyond which lay the open plains. Their master was a white stallion. Lee watched until the stallion and his *manada* had vanished into the hills.

The other bands of mustangs, having had their fill of water and grass, retreated to the hills also for the day.

"Remember that big white Barb stud that Mike Bastrop imported from Spain a few years ago, Kink?" Lee asked. "He offered a thousand dollars to anybody who would bring in that stallion. Do you suppose . . . ?"

He let it stand unfinished. Kink drew from inside his shirt a wrinkled object that was attached to a silver chain.

102

"Don't let de hoodoos fool you, Jack-Lee," he implored. "Dat's one o' dem ghost-devils in de shape of a horse."

"If it's a ghost-devil, it just might be the ghost of the Barb," Lee said. "There was no way of being sure at that distance. It likely will turn out to be a tough old broomtail. But I want a closer look at first chance."

They camped, and watched Kink sprinkle powder from a green glass vial onto the fire. The powder burned with an ugly purple flame and sent up a puff of pungent smoke.

"No ghost-devil will hurt us tonight," Kink said.

"I'm afraid the witch doctor who sold that voodoo charm to Kink wasn't exactly honest," Clemmy whispered to Lee. "Kink thinks it's the foot of an owl that was shot by a silver bullet in the light of a full moon. It looks more like the claw of a Plymouth Rock rooster to me."

But they all slept in peace that night. No ghost-devils came to hoodoo them.

Lee and Clemmy spent the major part of the next two days sleeping. It was the toll they paid for so many days of tension. Kink let them eat and sleep and sleep and eat. He mumbled over his hoodoo charm, sprinkled powder on the fire, and remained alert for sign of flesh-and-blood intruders.

Lee was beset by many questions, but there was one, above all, for which he had no answer. What of the future? They had escaped to a domain of their own where they could exist indefinitely, if necessary. For months, at least. Even for years, perhaps.

But that was unthinkable. There was water and game here. The outside world could be raided for other necessities. But there was also loneliness here that would grow with the passing of time.

They were fugitives. Outlaws! A murder charge was never canceled by time. Even worse in some ways, especially for a girl, they were outcasts—unwanted by society.

Lee kept thinking of the relentless hatred the Tice brothers seemed to hold toward him. It went beyond the bitterness that sons might naturally show toward a man they believed had murdered their father. In fact, Lee doubted that the brothers had held the great affection for their father that they now proclaimed. Nor for each other, for that matter.

Then there was Mike Bastrop. His animosity seemed even greater than that of the Tices. The five thousand dollars he had offered for Lee's death seemed bloodthirsty beyond all bounds of reason.

Also puzzling Lee was the mystery of Judge Amos Clebe's attempt to ambush Mike Bastrop. He had never given much thought to the corpulent, pompous judge. To the best of his knowledge, Amos Clebe had ignored his existence whenever their paths had happened to cross. The Judge had plainly considered himself in a walk of life far above that of the tall, black-haired cowboy who was tabbed as an Indian.

Now, looking back at these things in the light of the moment when he had prevented Amos Clebe from committing murder, he wondered if the Judge hadn't been far more aware of him than he had pretended.

None of these questions had an answer. And, as the days passed, they seemed to grow more and more remote. In contrast to the past period of danger and tension, the three of them settled into an existence that was almost Elysian.

Food was no problem, at least for the time being. Their horses grew sleek on rich forage. The heat of summer lay over the basin, but there was always the stream and the lake in which to swim for the sake of coolness. They built shelters under the overhang of boulders for protection from the drenching thunderstorms that occasionally raged across the land.

Kinky Bob, perhaps for the first time in his life, felt really free. His mood changed. Light broke through the somber way of his life. In the evenings he would sing as he helped with the camp work. Songs that Lee nor Clemmy had ever heard. Songs of the mighty Mississippi River. Of the plantations. Songs that were praise of creation and the Creator. His voice was deep and melodious.

Clemmy quickly learned the words and joined in the spirituals. Lee listened. He knew now why the legend of Rose O'Neil was kept alive around the wagon fires. The magic of Rose O'Neil had not been lost when she had died.

Kinky Bob confirmed that. "You make ol' Kink want to cry when you sing like dat, Missy," he told Clemmy. "It's like de Golden Nightingale was here with us ag'in."

"You mean you heard my mother sing?" Clemmy exclaimed.

"Suah did, Missy. Many times. Never tired o' listenin' to de voice o' Rose O'Neil. I worked as handy man in a playhouse in San'tone, way back in Texas, where yore mother was singin'. I follered her to El Paso an' got a job swampin' in a music hall where she was appearin'. I heerd her sing in Denver City, too. She knowed me by name. She used to smile at me."

He was silent for a moment. "An' I saw her lay dead on de stage in Punchbowl," he added. "I wished I hadn't."

"What was she like?" Clemmy asked slowly. "What was she *really* like?"

Kink sought for words. He gazed around at the basin. It was sundown. Broken thunderheads were like golden ships in the sky, propelled by massive sails. They cast great, drifting shadows on the lake and on the flats of grass that rippled in the warming wind.

"She was like all dis," he said. "Beautiful! Happy! alive! She liked everybody. Why, she even smiled at me. Treated me like I was a person."

Clemmy didn't ask any more questions. She busied herself with preparing the meal. But Lee saw that she was brushing away tears. Tears of happiness. And of sadness for a mother who was only a sweet memory from childhood.

Another week went by. During daylight hours, Lee and Kink, spelling each other, kept watch over the surrounding plains from a lookout point in the hills to the west which commanded the route by which they had entered the basin. No sign of pursuers appeared.

At times Clemmy took over the monotonous task. The lookout point was on a ridge nearly half an hour's ride from their camp along the stream. It commanded a full view of the basin as well as the sea of plains to the west and north.

Lee, arriving at the ridge to relieve Clemmy of the duty one afternoon, found her sitting cross-legged, her hands clasped back of her head, gazing at the basin. She was so absorbed, she did not seem aware of his arrival. She emerged from her thoughts with a start when he spoke.

"Daydreaming?" he asked.

She smiled. "Something like that."

"Wishing?"

She laughed again, self-consciously. "I'm afraid so."

"For what?"

"What does anyone wish for when they're daydreaming?"

He sat down beside her. "When I came to this basin two years ago I stood right on this spot for a long time, wishing for a lot of things. I pictured myself building a ranch house down there where we're camped. Of owning my own brand."

He paused for a long time while she sat silent, waiting. "I wished for other things," he finally said. "For everything a man wants in his house."

Neither of them spoke for a long time. Neither of them dared. For they knew what was in their hearts.

"Why didn't you apply for—?" she finally began.

She broke off the question, seeing the expression in his face.

"Indians can't take up land," he said. "In Texas or in New Mexico either. We're in Texas now. You know that."

"But I told you—!" she began angrily.

"I know. But that doesn't mean it's that way."

He added grimly, "Kink believes I'm Comanch'. He's sure of it, in fact."

"He can be wrong. If he's so sure, why doesn't he say exactly why he is?"

"I'm afraid to ask," Lee said.

She arose. "There's no need to ask. And what difference would it make either way?"

Lee walked with her to her horse, saddled it, and gave her a hand when she mounted.

"You told me once that you had a wish come true," he said. "Was it worth wishing for?"

Again he saw color rise in her throat. "Yes," she said. Then she rode away.

He watched her emerge from the hills and head across the flat toward the camp. She looked back, and raised a hand, as though sure he was watching, as though she knew how much he had wanted to take her in his arms and tell her that she was all that mattered in life. But, because he loved her, he could never say these things to her.

They had seen no sign of the white stallion since their return to the basin until the day Clemmy, coming in from lookout, reported sighting the horse and its band of mares.

"I spotted them north of the basin, out in the plains," she said. "They were foraging, but I'm sure they had come out of the basin. They must have been in for water last night."

"Around daybreak, most likely," Lee said. "That's the time the real wild ones usually come to water, especially a horse that's gone mustang after knowing what it's like to be in a corral. Those kind are the hardest to trap."

Kinky Bob's head lifted. "Trap?"

"If that's really Mike Bastrop's Barb stud, it's worth a try," Lee said.

"Ain't much chance it's de Barb," Kink argued. "Jest another broomie, most likely. Dar's white broomtails, jest like any other color. Not many, o' course. Anyway, what you aim to do, even if you ketched dat horse an' he turned out to be de Barb?"

"In addition to being a horse nobody could run down if one of us needed a real ride in a hurry, it's worth money," Lee said. "A lot of money." He eyed Clemmy.

"We can't live like this forever," he added. "And they won't keep on looking for us forever, either. It's my guess that they figure by this time that we've either gone under on the plains or have managed to get out of the country. And that's exactly what we'll have to do. We'll have a better chance now."

"To get out of the country?" Clemmy asked.

"Yes. We've got to try for Mexico. Maybe we can swing back in a year or two. Maybe into California. Or into the upper Missouri River country. They say people don't ask too many questions in either of those places."

Clemmy gazed at him. "If we weren't with you, would you try to hide in Mexico?"

"What else?" Lee demanded.

"I'll tell you what else. You'd stay here as an outlaw until they ran you down. That's what you'd do. You'd die before you'd let them run you out of this range. You believe this is your home. That you belong here. You're talking of going to Mexico only because you think Kink and I would be better off there. That's the truth, isn't it?"

"Why wouldn't I be thinking about my own neck?" Lee snorted. "After all, they want to hang me for a murder I didn't do."

She wrinkled her nose at him. "Maybe. But you also know they might try to put Uncle Tice's killing onto me. In fact, it wasn't very long ago that you acted like you believed that yourself. For all I know, you still do."

"That's for you to worry about," Lee said, grinning. "But I believe we were talking about trying to get a rope on that white stallion, instead of around our own necks. A trader would pay a thousand or more for that horse on sight, if it really is the Barb. Some of those rich *hacendados* down around Chihuahua might pay a heap more for him, and no questions asked."

"So you want to add another horse-stealing to your record?" she said.

"They can only hang me once," Le answered. "If that's Mike Bastrop's Barb, it now ought to belong to anyone who can catch it. It's been running wild for three years. If that's stealing, so be it."

Kink uttered an uneasy guffaw of derision. "Yo're ridin' a horse you ain't caught yit, Jack-Lee. If dat's de Barb, he's a ghost horse, I tell you, If'n you git a rope on him, he'll turn into a skilligan with a hoodoo ridin' him."

"That's a chance we'll have to take," Lee said.

"Worse'n dat, if he ain't a ghost, he'll suah be a killer, Jack-Lee. I don't want no more part o' dat stallion. The Majah blamed me for lettin' him git away. Dat Barb busted two o' my ribs when I tried to ride him. Left me layin' in de corral, an' jumped an eight-pole fence. Jest disappeared into de sky. You remember dat, Jack-Lee."

"I heard about it," Le said. "I was up the trail with a drive when it happened. How old would that Barb be?"

Kink counted on his fingers. "He were only a three-year-old when he was shipped acrost de ocean. He'll be goin' on seven, I reckon."

"Right in the prime," Lee said. "I've got a hunch that white speck we've sighted is the same horse. What was it he was called?"

"El Rey somethin' or other," Kink said. "Nobody could make out the rest o' the name them foreigners had registered. Majah Bastrop said pure-white Barbs are mighty scarce an' was rode only by kings an' nabobs in de old days. Ordinary folks was put to death for even tryin' to own one."

"We've got to stake out before daybreak down the basin until we can get a good look at that stud," Lee said. "The chances are that we're riding a blind trail and that horse will turn out to be a broomtail after all. The Barb's likely been dead for years."

It was still pitch dark the next morning when Lee and Kinky Bob crawled to a rise of ground that would give them a closer view of the meadows south of the lake where the wild horses grazed after coming in for water.

What breeze was drawing was light and intermittent,

and in their favor. "Let's hope it won't shift," Lee murmured. "One scent of us and we'd never again get close enough to have a chance, if that's really the Barb."

They lay motionless and silent. Dawn was faint in the sky when they heard the wild ones coming. The horses were more than a quarter of a mile away, mere shadows in the dim light as they drank in the shallows, then scattered to graze in the marshy flats.

They finally could make out the ghostly figure of the white stallion. The animal stood motionless at a distance, head poised, legs braced. It was standing guard while the mares in its *manada* drank and grazed.

But, was it the Barb?

Presently it moved to water and drank deeply. It threw up its head suddenly and stood like a statue, muzzle keening the air. It had caught some hint of danger.

Daylight had strengthened so that the true magnificence of the animal was apparent. It was the Barb!

Lee glanced at Kink, and saw confirmation in the big man's face. And superstitious dread also.

The stallion left the margin of the lake. Its call came loud and imperious. The mares obeyed. The band wheeled like a cavalry troop, and then was off and away, heading out of the basin, eastward toward low hills beyond which lay the rolling plains.

"Dat debbil horse, he knew we was here," Kinky Bob whispered.

"Maybe," Lee said. "Maybe not. I've got a feeling it was something else that spooked him."

He watched the receding band of mares. He could not make out the white Barb among them. Suddenly, he pointed and said, "There's your answer. Loafers. The Barb picked up their scent, not ours."

Two gray wolves were moving in the wake of the retreating *manada*. Big, savage plains wolves.

As they watched, doom suddenly materialized in the path of the loafers. The white stallion had leaped from hiding. The wolves tried to whirl and escape. But it was too late for one. It was trampled to death by the hoofs of an animal that had turned into a screaming, savage-eyed demon. The second wolf, which was the female, managed to flee into the brush.

Kinky Bob drew a long breath as they watched the

stallion continue to vent its fury on the carcass of the wolf. The wind brought the wild, eerie bugling.

"Like I said," Kink whispered. "Dat's not a horse, dat's a debbil."

"But he'll come back to the basin," Lee said. He had never seen an animal as magnificent, as free, as self-sufficient.

They returned to camp. "He's a horse fit for kings to ride, sure enough," he told Clemmy.

"Or for a war chief to own and brag about," she said.

"War chief?"

"Such as a Comanche chief," she said. "Such as Eagle—"

Kinky Bob, who had been busy at the cookfire, straightened. "No!" he boomed. "No, Missy. Don't you never—"

"Such as Eagle-in-the-Sky," she continued.

There was a space of silence. "Eagle can tell you the truth about what you are and where you came from, Lee Jackson," she went on. "The only one who can. He says he is your father. But he never treated you like a son. He's a chief. He won't talk unless it's worth while. He might—"

"Don't listen to her," Kinky Bob implored. "Let sleepin' dogs lie still, Jack-Lee. Let's all take ourselves into Mexico an' be safe."

"Eagle might talk if you dangled something in front of him that he really wanted," Clemmy went on relentlessly. She added, "Such as the Barb."

"Don't do it," Kink wailed. "You saw what dat debbil horse did to de wolf. He kill you too, Jack-Lee, if'n you try to ketch him."

Lee stood gazing almost unseeingly at Clemmy. She watched him for a time, then said, "It's got to be faced. It's got to be settled."

"You know what it might mean, don't you?" he asked.

She was suddenly ashen. "Yes. It doesn't have to be that way. But it will be. I know you too well to expect anything else."

What she meant was that she was aware that if he learned that he really was the son of the Comanche chief, she would never see him again.

"I can't go on this way," she said. "You know how it is with me."

Lee turned to Kinky Bob. "You're not as afraid of that

Barb as you try to make out," he said. "But you don't want me to talk to Eagle, do you, Kink?"

"What good would it do, Jack-Lee?"

"It would settle many things. You've refused to tell me why you are so sure I'm Comanche by birth. Why are you so certain, Kink?"

"I tell you I don't want to talk about it, Jack-Lee."

"You're going to tell me. Now!"

Kinky Bob was cornered. He said grimly, "You are Co-manch', Jack-Lee. Nothin' kin ever change dat. Don't ever try. 'Taint no use."

"How do you know this? Why are you so sure?"

"One o' dem Comancheros tell me."

"Comanchero?"

This was a term for men who traded mainly with the tribes, but sometimes with settlers. Although it was a fading occupation, now that the Indians had taken reservation, there were still a few of these nomads around. The majority of them were of mixed blood, usually of Mexican-Indian extraction. They were trusted by the tribes and had often been the only link of communication between the settlers and the hostile Comanche Nation.

Kinky Bob nodded. "This one come by Rancho Verde years ago when you was still a young sprout. He stayed with Kinky Bob a few nights to rest his mules. He seen you. He told me de Army tried to run a high blaze on de Majah an' that he knew you was an Injun."

"He was sure of that?"

Kink nodded. "He'd lived in Chief Eagle's village. Seen you dar as a child. He even knew your Indian name."

"My Indian name? Even I never heard that. It was taboo in the village."

"De Comanchero say your name was "Wa-no-lo-pay," Kink said.

Lee's lips were taut, colorless. Despair was in his eyes. "Wa-no-lo-pay?" he repeated. "That settles it."

Clemmy spoke, "You mean you had heard that name?"

Lee nodded. "Once, when I was a child, after I had been brought to Rancho Verde that name popped into my mind from somewhere. From a long way back. I don't know where. I suppose I'd heard it before the taboo was ordered in the village."

Memories crowded him, harsh and unwanted. "I uttered that name. Wa-no-lo-pay. Mike Bastrop went wild.

He beat me with his belt. He told me it was a bad word and I was never to mention it again."

He looked at Clemmy, and there was utter desolation in his eyes. "I'm sorry," he said.

"And I'm glad," she replied. "Glad for you and for myself, John Lopez Calvin."

Lee stood gazing at her. She repeated it. "John Lopez Calvin. That was the full name of the little boy they took away with them when they raided Rancho Verde."

She added softly, "Juano Lopey. John Calvin's widow was Spanish, remember. She was a Lopez. Don't you understand? John Lopez Calvin. Juan Lopez Calvin. Wano Lopey. That's the Spanish way of giving a pet name to a child. You weren't much more than a baby when the Comanches stole you, but you could repeat your name. The only name you knew. The one your mother used. Juano Lopey."

Lee rolled a cigaret with shaking fingers, spilling some of the treasured dry makings from his dwindling supply. Clemmy lifted a burning twig from the fire and held it to the quirly, and she and Kinky Bob stood waiting for him to speak.

He pulled smoke deep into his lungs. "One of you is right," he finally said. "You, Clemmy—or the Comanchero."

He looked around. "First, we've got to catch the Barb," he said.

Kinky Bob spoke, almost hopefully. "Maybe he won't never come back here." The big man plainly believed Clemmy was giving Lee a path that would only lead to disappointment. "Maybe he already know we after him. Maybe he lay fer us like he did for de wolves."

"How would he know we're after him?" Clemmy demanded.

"If I could answer that, Missy, I'd be able to vanish in a flash of fire. Dar are things that know everything. Some has the shape o' humans, some look like animals. But they ain't neither human nor animal."

"I don't believe you take any stock in such things yourself," Clemmy said. "You're just trying to stop Lee from talking to that Comanche chief."

However, the Barb and his *manada* did not return the next day. Nor the next, nor the next. Lee and Kinky Bob lay on watch as each day dawned. Except for the scrawny, long-tailed mustangs that came in, the marshes remained deserted.

There had been evidence of thunderstorms out on the plains. That could mean that the stallion and his mares had no need to come into the basin for water.

Hot, dry weather set in. Searing weather.

Chapter *ELEVEN*

It was the fifth morning of their vigil. Dawn was a promise in the sky when Lee came suddenly to attention. Kinky Bob sighed. Clemmy, who had come out with them in the darkness, tired of being alone in camp, drew a deep breath.

The wild ones had returned to the basin. And the big Barb was there with his *manada*.

"All right," Lee said, after the horses had headed back to the plains. "This is going to take time. Weeks, maybe. One mistake and he'll be gone forever out of reach."

The Barb came back the next morning, and the next. Lee mapped out the route the stallion used in coming in from the open plains. Through one area in the hills, the Barb and his mares followed a dry wash for more than half a mile. The wash was wide and flat for the most part, but narrowed at one point for a distance of nearly two hundred yards between cut banks eight to ten feet high.

"There's our only chance," Lee said. "And that's the Barb's mistake. He's used that path so many times he's sure he's safe and has grown careless."

There were ample deadfalls of willow and ash and cottonwood and wild pecan available in the basin. The three of them, with the help of the horses, spent their days moving poles, roughly ax-cut to ten-foot lengths, into position on the flats above the bottleneck in the wash.

Lee and Kinky Bob killed deer, doing their hunting far up the basin and only when they were sure the wild ones were out on the plains.

From the hides, the three of them laboriously cut strips, which they braided into rawhide thongs. Using the thongs, they laced the poles together into crude sections that could be handled by two persons, and lashed to form barricades. The green hide shrank as it dried in the hot days, clamping the poles rigidly.

Every move was made with extreme caution. The major part of the task was performed in the blazing heat of midday when the quarry was least likely to return. There were periods when the Barb and his mares failed to appear in the basin for days at a time. When this occurred they were beset by the fear the stallion had become suspicious and their labor had gone for nothing. But, always, the wild band would show up again, following the same route along the wash.

"We gittin' mighty low on flour, salt, an' a lot o' other things," Kinky Bob said one morning. "Looks like Kink bettter take a *paseo* fer a few days to see what he kin round up."

"Where would you do this rounding up?" Lee asked.

"Might hit a line camp or two in de Armadillos," Kink explained. "All de outfits will be stockin' de camps with grub this time o' year to git ready fer winter. Cain't clean out a camp, o' course. Jest take a dab here an' a dab there. Don't want to make 'em suspect we're still around. I'll finish up with whatever else we need from Judge Clebe's pantry."

"Judge Clebe's pantry?"

"He got plenty o' supplies an' he'll never miss what Kink takes. Celia say he never even check up on what she buys."

"I thought so. All this urge to fatten up our larder is only an excuse to ride into town to see your lady friend. You fool, if you're caught they'll string you up."

"Ain't goin' to be caught, Jack-Lee. An' if you're worryin' about Celia, I kin tell you dat she won't never tell nothin' to nobody."

Kink added, "An' she kin tell us what's goin' on. She'll know whether they're still lookin' fer us, or whether they've give up."

It was this argument that swayed Lee. They were desperately in need of news. "I'll give you four days," he said. "If you're not back by then, I'll come looking for you."

"Don't never do dat, Jack-Lee," Kink said grimly. "If I ain't back in dat time, it'll be 'cause dey got me. An' dey will figure you'll come in, lookin' for me. Dey'll be waitin' for you."

Kinky Bob returned only a few hours ahead of the four-day limit that Lee had set. He was saddle-worn, but grinning. He had a bulging bag of supplies on his horse.

"De Majah's give up any idea o' startin' a late beef drive up de trail dis year," he reported. "He seems to have too many other things to keep him busy. You ain't de only one what's got a price on yore head, Jack-Lee. I ain't one to brag, but de Majah is offerin' a thousand dollahs in gold to anyone what fetches in ol' Kink, dead or alive. Now who'd ever have figgered I'd be worth that much on de hoof?"

"We've been worrying ourselves sleepless, waiting for you to show up, and you come back swelled up because you've got a bounty on your scalp," Lee commented. "What about Judge Clebe? Is he still in El Paso?"

"No. He back in Punchbowl, presidin' over court, which is back in session. But he brung back three tough gentlemen with him from El Paso. Bodyguards. Celia says she's gittin' mighty tired o' them bein' always around de house an' havin' to be fed an' took care of."

"Bodyguards? For the Judge?"

'Gun quicks. Bad men, dey is, Celia say. Dey go wherever de Judge goes. De Judge says his life has been threatened by some pals o' a bunch o' rustlers dat he sent to prison about a year ago."

Lee and Clemmy looked at each other. "Maybe Mike Bastrop knows it was the Judge and not me who put that slug in him," Lee said.

"I'm sure of it," Clemmy said.

"You mean dem two are gunnin' fer each other?" Kink demanded disbelievingly. "De Majah an' de Judge? Why would dey do dat?"

Lee shrugged. "I wish I knew." There could only be conjectures. Only one thing seemed certain. Whatever the cause, it went back to the night Bill Tice had been killed. The easiest answer was that the feud had been touched off by a quarrel over their poker game.

But Clemmy had said big money was never involved in the games, contrary to popular belief. Perhaps the stakes were higher than she believed. At least Amos Clebe was certain to have some sort of income aside from the modest salary the county paid its presiding judge. It was assumed that he had investments, which, along with his poker winnings, permitted his way of living—a luxuriously furnished mansion, diamonds, fine cigars and whisky, and elaborate entertainment of flashy ladies on his trips out of town to El Paso and San Antonio and Denver.

"What about the Tice brothers?" Clemmy asked Kinky Bob.

"Celia said dem scamps spend de most o' their time in town now, drinkin' an' gamblin'. Dey got plenty o' money, now dat dey've inherited BT. Dey've gone an' hired themselves some gunpackers too, dat hang around with dem all de time."

"More bodyguards?" Lee exclaimed. "The Judge, and now the Tices! It looks like a lot of people we know are out to punch the tickets of somebody. With bullets."

"Are Merl and Gabe still looking for us?" Clemmy asked. "Personally, I mean."

"Maybe not personally, Missy, but Celia say somebody is seein' to it dat notices o' Mike Bastrop's reward offer is bein' posted all over Texas an' New Mexico. She say she heard dat de word has gone down even into Mexico dat de Majah will pay anybody who fetches you back across de river, Jack-Lee."

"Strapped dead to a pack mule, of course," Lee said.

"I reckon dat's de truth of it," Kink said gloomily. "Dat man still want you dead, an' he ain't goin' to give up 'til you is. Looks like we'll have to find someplace else to go an' hide."

"You think they'll find this place?" Lee asked.

"Five thousand dollahs keeps men thinkin', Jack-Lee. I don't reckon we kin keep on robbin' line camps, or depsendin' on Celia to supply us from de Judge's kitchen without somebody gittin' on our trail."

"You're right, of course," Lee said. "I've got a feeling we've about run out our string here. Sooner or later, somebody will remember stories about a Spirit Lake out here, and really begin to look for it."

"We got to go a long, long way to git away from de Majah," Kinky Bob said. "He a stubborn man. Where dis place I hear men talk about at times? Dis Argentina place. Lots o' outlaws go dar when things git too hot for dem around here. Is it in de United States?"

"No," Lee said. "But maybe we better go there. It's far enough away so that even Mike Bastrop isn't likely to ever have us brought back."

He added, "But we'll need money to travel that far. We're about all set to try for the Barb. We'll make sure we know exactly what to do, and then make our move when the sign is right."

The sign seemed right three days later. The three of them crouched close to earth, listening as the wild ones streamed down the wash toward the basin.

Lee kept restraining hands on both Clemmy and Kinky Bob, forcing them to wait, for they were as taut as drawn bowstrings. The thud of hoofs came abreast, then moved steadily on down the defile toward the basin.

Dawn lighted the ridges. A cold wind rattled the brush. The drumbeat of the hoofs of a single horse sounded in the wake of that of the main band. Lee chanced a quick glimpse and sank back. He waited until all sounds had faded into the distance.

"All right," he said. "That was the Barb, following his *manada* in. Let's go!"

They burst into activity. He and Kinky Bob, working at a run, carried, one by one, the sections of the barrier they had made and hidden beyond the rim of the coulee. They set the sections, bracing them with poles, and Clemmy lashed them together to form a barricade across the outer end of the bottleneck.

They were spent and soaked with cold sweat when Lee was satisfied that that part of the trap was as secure as possible. They hurried to the inner end of the bottleneck and crouched in hiding in brush above the rim.

Other sections of the second barricade lay close at hand. These were of lighter poles because there would be little leeway in time when they must be set in place. A stumble, a few seconds' delay, and their plan would fail.

They lay waiting, listening. Their laboring lungs quieted. Daylight strengthened. They did not speak, for Lee had warned them against conversation. He had seen samples of the acuteness of hearing of wild horses. The Barb, once having been dominated by man, would be quick to identify such an alien sound and would be gone with the wind.

The wait went on and on. Lee, watching the first rays of sunshine glint on the rims of the Armadillos, began to fear that the wild ones were not following their normal routine.

Then they heard the wild ones returning. The sound of hoofs came nearer. Lee fought back the urge to rise to his knees and take a look. That might have been fatal.

The Barb should be bringing up the rear, as usual. His habit was to remain well back of his harem, both to avoid dust and to punish any straggler.

The roll of hoofs came abreast in the coulee and receded eastward. A few seconds later they heard the lone horse pass by.

"Now!" Lee breathed.

They had rehearsed it several times at a distant spot and using imaginary items.

They arose, carrying the sections of the rawhide-bound barrier, slid over the lip of the cut bank into the wash, and frantically began bracing the sections in place to block the route of escape.

Up the wash, a bedlam arose. Mares were milling and screaming in confusion. They had found their path blocked by the upper barricade.

"Hurry!" Lee panted, jamming more poles in place to brace the new line.

A demon appeared in the draw. The Barb! The stallion had whirled to return, hoping to escape by the way he had entered the trap. He screamed in almost humanlike fury when he saw that his retreat was blocked by another of the terrible contrivances that had panicked the mares.

He came at the barrier, rearing, striking the poles with savage hoofs. Lee saw white teeth bared, grinding at the poles.

The mares also came thundering back, seeking escape. This was the moment Lee had forseen as decisive for success or failure. For victory and freedom for the Barb, or capture and submission.

"Get out of here!" he shouted at Clemmy as he continued to push more poles in order to brace the barrier. "If they knock down that fence, you'll be trampled to jelly."

For once, she obeyed, scrambling to the lip of the cut bank to safety. "You too, Kink!" Lee gritted. "Get in the clear!"

The big man did not answer, but continued jamming braces in place. A moment later a mass of frenzied wild horses came against the barrier.

The demoralized mares in the forefront reared back at the sight of the barricade, recoiling on the other animals. That saved the crude stockade, for Lee knew that it would never have stood against the full weight of the stampede. He knew that it also had likely saved his life and that of Kinky Bob's.

Once halted, the animals were victims of their own panic and indecision. The Barb was imprisoned among his own *manada.* He was rearing and bugling, but was almost help-less, jammed in among the mass of mares that stifled his efforts.

Lee and Kinky Bob scaled to opposite rims of the coulee and seized up the throw ropes they had placed there. The Barb screamed again—mournfully, despairingly. He re-membered ropes! He remembered men!

As Lee spread the loop there was a sudden sickness in him. Up to this moment the Barb had been only an objective—a means to serve his purpose. A quarry to be outwitted and taken.

Face-to-face with this splendid creature, he was stung by guilt and self-reproach. It was as though the stallion was pleading for death rather than capture. This, he could un-derstand. He, too, was a wild one who had fled to the plains to escape the confinement the Barb feared.

Clemmy was at his side. She sensed his hesitation, and its reason. "Please!" she screamed. "Throw!"

Lee flipped the loop over the rim of the cut bank and it settled precisely. Kinky Bob's rope joined it. Between them they had the Barb their captive.

The mares recoiled from their master who fought the ropes with appalling ferocity. They milled against the bar-rier, and it went down, opening a way to freedom. The *manada* fled down the draw and scattered on the open flat, heading for the plains.

But the Barb did not follow his mares. He was a pris-oner. Lee and Kinky Bob finally brought the stallion to earth and hobbled him. He lay there for a long time. El Rey, the king, was no longer free.

"He goin' to die," Kinky Bob muttered and fingered the hoot-owl charm. "He'll come back to ha'nt us."

Lee stood looking down at their captive. The sickness and the self-reproach increased. He and Kinky Bob and the horse were matted with sweat and dust.

The Barb did not die, whatever its own hope might have been. At last it drew a long, heaving breath that was almost a moan and struggled to its feet. It was prepared to fight to escape, but was forced to stand, trembling and helpless. The hobbles on its legs were the emblems of its despair.

Suddenly, Lee moved in, a knife in his hand. The stallion tried exhaustedly to strike at him, but failed. The blade slashed a hobble. Before he could continue, Clemmy rushed in, wrapping her arms around him, forcing him with her young strength away from the horse.

"No!" She had the same fierce spirit in this moment as the stallion, the same primitive determination.

"I can't do this," Lee said. "Alive or dead, that horse would haunt me the rest of my life. He doesn't deserve this. He won his freedom. He's been so alive, so free. It isn't worth it."

She continued to cling to him, pinning down his arms. "I know how you feel," she sobbed. "But you've got to do this. *We've* got to do this. Both of us. For your sake. For my sake. You can't be an outlaw all your life. They'll catch you sooner or later, just like the Barb was caught. I've felt from the moment we sighted this horse, that this was the right thing to do. The only thing. Maybe it sounds crazy, but it's as though this is an answer to a prayer. To my wish. As though this horse was here because you needed him. And because I needed him."

She added, her eyes warm and tender, "I have wished this. Night and day. Oh, how I've wished it."

She kissed him. She drew her head back and looked up at him. "You've got to try to make Eagle tell what you really are," she said. "For that's the only hope of having my wish come true. I love you, whatever you are or will be. I believe you love me, but I know that until you are sure what you are, I will always be lonely. It would make no difference to me what you are, but you'd always let it keep us apart. Destroy us both."

She continued to cling to him. He held her tight against him for a space, then his arms fell away. She had told the truth. He had seen what had happened to white women who had married Indians. He could not bring this on Clementina O'Neil, daughter of Rose O'Neil. Clemmy, the loyal, the gentle, the one who would remain steadfast through all hardship, through all eternity.

"There may come a time," he said hoarsely, "when we will never see each other again. I want you to always remember that you will be the only one—the only love in my life."

She began to smile. She held a happiness that was pure and joyous. "I'll begin wishing once more," she said.

"For what?"

"The same thing for which I've been wishing ever since

we came to this place. That some day this is where we will
live and be happy. And free."

She added, "And that the Barb will come back here
with us. I can wish that. I've told you that some of my
wishes come true. Like the one in Punchbowl that day."

"In Punchbowl?"

"When you kissed me. I was wishing you'd do exactly
that."

"You *are* a vixen, aren't you?"

"If that's what I have to be to get my wish, yes."

Chapter *TWELVE*

"Behold!" Clemmy said dramatically. "Admire the handiwork of the two best bronc peelers in New Mexico, and maybe all points east and west, not to mention north and south."

More than a week had passed since the capture of the Barb. The stallion stood, hipshot, on the fringe of camp, held by a hackamore and a picket rope, in addition to a hobble. He seemed to know he was the object of Clemmy's remark, for he came to attention, arched his neck, and cavorted.

"He's a showboat," Lee said. "Stands around admiring his own shadow. A real biscuit eater. That reminds me, and listen to what I say, girl! Quit feeding him biscuits. Let him rustle his own grub. You're spoiling a great horse by spoon-feeding. I don't want any fat on him. We may have riding to do."

"Who'd have thought he could have been gentled so soon?" she said.

"There's no such thing as gentling him. He's smart enough to act contented and ride the grub line—as long as there's a rope around his neck. All he's really waiting for is a chance to go back to his mares. Back to the plains."

He added, "And that's where he belongs."

Clemmy said nothing. It was sundown on a late August day. They were breaking camp.

They pulled out as dusk came. Clemmy rode her horse astride. Kinky Bob hazed the loaded packhorse ahead of them. Lee led the Barb. The stallion pranced along, skittish as a colt, plainly pleased to be on the move.

Lee and Kinky Bob had brought to bear everything they knew about the art of taming a horse, and had succeeded far more quickly than they had anticipated. Too quickly, Lee sometimes warned himself. The Barb, after a day or two of refusal, had abruptly decided to bow to the inevi-

123

table, and had accepted discipline without more than the expected protest. He had not objected to a bit and saddle, and had fought only mechanically when he was first mounted by Lee.

"Speed!" Lee had said in awe. "And strength. What a horse! I've never sat anything like this one."

"An' never will ag'in if'n you git careless," Kink had warned. "He's only waitin'. Don't let him fool you by actin' like he's given in. Remember, he was a tame horse at first. He knows humans, an' how to git along with 'em. An' how to wait for de right minute to go bad ag'in."

They headed northward, along the lonely stretches of the Llano Estacado. The thunderstorms of August were sweeping the plains regularly, and the natural basins and water tanks were full.

Their destination was the Comanche reservation on the Clear Fork of the Brazos River in Texas. The direction was generally northeastward over a country where there were few trails and where they saw occasional sign of the buffalo that were a vanishing breed. Lee said it would be more than a week's travel by the circuitous route they would be forced to follow in order to avoid settlements and ranches.

The moon was coming full. They intended to travel at night by its light as long as was feasible. An August moon. The Comanche war moon. For all its beauty, this was the moon the settlers had feared in the past because it had brought the Spearmen off the plains.

"Ain't no hostiles come down to kill an' skulp folks fer quite a spell," Kinky Bob said, "but dat don't mean dey won't paint ag'in, an' jump de reservation. What chance would we have if'n we run into a war party?"

Kink had never ceased opposing this mission. "Better to head fer Mexico, like we first said, Jack-Lee," he had argued. "Now dat we're comin' out into de open, sooner or later somebody's sure to ketch sight o' us. Den we'll have reward hunters on our trail. Even if'n we make it to dis Comanche camp dat you talk about, what den? Dis chief, Eagle, likely is daid after all dees years."

"I heard only a couple of months ago that Eagle-in-the-Sky was still alive and still head man in his village," Lee had said.

"But how you know he'll tell you anythin', even if you git to talk to him? How you know he won't turn you over to de law? Maybe even de Comanches know you is wanted."

Lee had no answer. The same misgivings were heavy in his mind. The risk was great, and there was only a gambling chance that Eagle would divulge anything helpful. In addition, Kink might be right about the chief being dead. Eagle was now a very old man who could have been taken since Lee's last news of him.

There might be a few other oldsters in the village whose memories went back to the raid on Rancho Verde, but Lee's knowledge of the Comanche character told him that his chances of getting information that could be relied on from anyone other than the chief were remote indeed.

Eagle was his only hope. The chief woud speak for all the village. He was above average in intelligence. Although he could speak Spanish and English, he usually scorned those languages and took the position that only the Comanche tongue was worth using.

Lesser members of the tribe would, no doubt, disclaim any connection with the Rancho Verde raid. Indians who had admitted such things in the past had been hung by the Army, or sent to the big, stone-walled lodge at Fort Leavenworth, never to return.

However, in spite of the cruelties he had suffered at Eagle's hands, Lee remembered the chief's pride. Eagle had fought for his people and his hunting grounds. He had a warrior's vanity in regard to his feats. He would be too proud to fear retaliation. Therefore, he might talk about the Rancho Verde raid if the reward was high enough.

Lee never relaxed vigilance over the Barb. He and Kink took turns at night, standing watch for intruders, but mainly to make sure that the picket lines and hobbles that held the stallion were secure.

They forded branches of the Colorado River and reached the drainage of the Brazos. They were now east of the Staked Plains, but following the rough country that broke away from the plateau. This was Comanche country, their old hunting grounds. To Lee, he was riding through scenes of his childhood. Often, disturbingly, landmarks would impinge on his memory as though he had passed this way only yesterday.

He became more and more silent. Occasionally they sighted buffalo. Small bands, or lone animals. Remnants of the great herds which still held out in the cedar brakes and brushy canyons. This land was still as it had been. Except for a few maverick cattle—mossy old longhorns—that had escaped from the ranches to the east, there was little sign of white men. The settlements still clung to the watercourses on the easier land to the east. The big ranches had yet to invade this area.

They forded a small creek. This, Lee recalled, was where he had been beaten by the squaw who said she was his mother because he had dropped a bundle of firewood as he had tried to wade the stream when it was in flood.

They crossed a divide and emerged onto a stretch of open country that brought memories more vivid than any other. And more bitter. This was where the buffalo hunting camp had been pitched when he had made his third and final attempt to escape. The entire village had been quartered here while the hunters slaughtered buffalo that had been stampeded into a trap in a box draw.

Lee had been about six years old at the time, and forced to do a squaw's work. He had helped scrape and stretch hides and carry water and wood from dawn until dark, day after day. He had cut and strung strips of fleece and humpmeat for drying, with squaws poking him to greater activity with sticks and the lashes of dog whips.

He remembered many things. He remembered seizing up a long spear that some buffalo hunter had thrust in the ground upon returning from the hunt, and bringing its flat metal head down on the skull of Eagle's eldest wife.

He had fled from the camp into the early darkness, leaving the stunned squaw lying on the ground. She was Wau-Qua, who said she was his mother. He remembered the pursuit. They had tried for two days to catch him. They would have succeeded, except that he had encountered the Army patrol and had surrendered.

He was remembering the hardships of his existence with the Comanches. But his very familiarity with this country seemed to prove everything in his mind that he wanted to disprove. This, surely, must have been the land of his birth.

Clemmy watched his silence continue. She said nothing, but the carefree happiness that had come to her during the days at Spirit Lake was now faded. She became again the sharp-tongued, scornful Clemmy O'Neil with a chip on her shoulder. Defensive of mind, suspicious of the motives of others.

She had reverted, as Lee had reverted. He was Comanche now in mood and grimness, in wariness and training. She was the defiant, spitfire daughter of a notorious woman.

They lived off the country. Game could be had for the shooting, but they used their rifles sparingly. Wild turkeys were so plentiful they could be taken with club in the evenings when they weighed down the limbs of the groves of post oaks.

They abandoned night travel because the country was so wild and rough it became a problem to pick a feasible route even in daylight.

They had been on the way nearly a week without having sighted anything except wildlife, but one morning, as they were following a stream that Lee believed would join with the Clear Fork of the Brazos, they emerged into a wide stretch of open prairie. And halted.

Three riders were moving into scattered timber across the clearing. They were far away, but they seemed to be hazing along a loaded packhorse and at least three other pack animals with empty saddles.

"Freeze!" Lee warned. "Maybe they won't spot us."

The trio kept heading westward and vanished into the timber.

"Good!" Kink said. "Dey didn't see us." He added, "You reckon dey was law men lookin' fer us?"

"Hardly," Lee said. "Not way up here. We're almost in the Panhandle. Hunters, is my guess. They're probably out to get some buffalo robes. And heads. Robes and stuffed buffalo heads are said to be bringing a good price back East these days. They're getting mighty scarce."

However, toward sundown the following day, he glimpsed a lone rider far behind them. The horseman vanished into the country and did not reappear.

"Maverick hunter, maybe," Lee said. "Trying to build himself up a brand with a running iron."

They had spotted a number of wild cattle during the day. They knew there were ranches on the Clear Fork to the east.

The horse the man had been riding was of a light dun color. Lee remembered, uneasily, that one of the three strangers they had sighted the previous day had been riding a horse of that distinctive hue.

He backtracked, leaving Kink and Clemmy to ride ahead at a slower gait. He picked up the trail of the lone rider, followed it until he felt sure the man had shown no interest in their own trail, then returned to where Kink and Clemmy waited.

"I doubt if he even saw our trail," he said. "He seemed to be interested only in heading west."

They camped that night on what Lee believed was the Clear Fork. That meant they probably were already on the Comanche reservation. They had proof of that at daybreak.

They were awakened by shrill shouts in the distance and and the thunder of wings. They rolled out of their blankets and crept on foot through the thickets until they could peer into another of the clearings that characterized this country.

An immense flock of wild turkeys that had left the timber at dawn in order to forage in the clearing had been surprised by a half-dozen young, mounted Indians.

The Indians had cut the birds off from refuge in the timber and were hazing them into taking wing. Racing on their ponies beneath the demoralized fowls, they kept their quarry aloft until the turkeys, exhausted, fell to earth where they were easy victims of clubs.

"Comanches," Lee said.

Again the memories came in a flood. He had seen turkey kills as a boy. It had meant hours of helping the squaws feather and prepare the birds for the gorging that customarily followed.

They crouched in hiding until the hunting party had left, their ponies loaded with the kill.

"There'll be a village not far away," Lee said. "I'll follow these fellows and get information. These might even be from Eagle's village. They were young braves, and I didn't know any of them, of course. There are other villages on the reserve, and Comanches always keep on the move."

He trailed the hunting party alone. He had traveled only a few miles when the wind brought a scent that again took him back to bitter years. It was the tang of woodsmoke, of buckskin and old buffalo-hide lodges, of fresh-cut firewood and humanity—all mingling with the incense of blooming lupine and willows and bluebonnets and buckthorn. A Comanche village.

He located the lodges and scouted them from a distance. The village stood among scattered trees along a small stream. The turkey hunters had arrived. Squaws and children were swarming about, unloading the game. Lee watched for a long time. He did not see any of the children poked with sticks, nor switched as he had been under the same circumstances. These Indian children were happy. It had been that way in the other days. He had been the only one who had been tormented.

He singled out one gray-haired, but drill-straight Indian who stood apart from the activity. The chief.

He retreated and rejoined Clemmy and Kink. They could see the news in his attitude.

"It is Eagle's—!" Clemmy began. She had started it bravely, but was unable to finish it. There was now a great terror in her. A doubt that her own belief was right. In Lee was the same grisly fear.

He nodded. "I saw him. He's aged, of course, but I'd know him anywhere."

He repeated it. "Anywhere. In hell, I'd know him."

He turned to Kink. "Shine up the Barb while I shave and slick up. We've both got to be at our best. Take him to the stream and wash him down. Comb out his mane and tail with whatever you can find to use. I want him to look like the king he is."

"You ain't goin' in dar alone, are you?" Kink demanded.

"That's the only way it can be done."

"What if they figger out dat you used to be—to be—" Kink began to flounder helplessly.

"—One of them? I'm banking on it that Eagle *will* know me."

"Won't he hold it against you?" Clemmy spoke. "What if—if he sees to it that you never come back?"

"I'm taking the Barb in with me. Comanches don't kill a guest that brings gifts. That's against their code."

"He'll only take your gift and laugh at you," she said.

"It's also the Indian code that if a gift can't be returned with one of equal value, it must be refused. The Eagle has only one thing of value to me and he knows it."

"He'll lie to you."

"I doubt that. He's a chief. A Comanche chief. Whatever else he might be, he'd lose face if he lied. There's a matter of pride and dignity involved. Eagle will either have to tell me what I want, or he'll have to refuse to accept the Barb."

He looked at the stallion which Kink had washed down at the stream and was now currying, using a handful of dry grass as a comb. "I believe it will come mighty hard for

Eagle to give up that horse, once he lays eyes on him. He will want a mount like that on the other side. That will make him a chief again."

"De other side?" Kink asked uneasily. "You ain't meanin' de happy land, now is you?"

"White men call it the Happy Hunting Ground," Lee said. "Indians have other names for it, the most of which are taboo for speaking. Only medicine men can say the words. It's the custom to be buried with a string of their best ponies when they go. They don't want to be afoot on the other side."

"You mean dey'd destroy dis fine animal when dat Injun died?"

"That's the custom."

Kink stopped furbishing the animal. He dropped the bundle of grass and walked off into the brush, muttering to himself. Clemmy refused to meet Lee's eyes. She also walked away.

Lee shaved, using a still pool of water as an unsatisfactory mirror. He put on his spare shirt which he had washed out when they had camped the previous night. He dusted his boots, saddled his roan, and led up the Barb.

Kink did not appear. However, Clemmy came hurrying to his side. "You will come back," she said huskily. "You *will*. I wish it."

"Of course," he said.

She placed a hand on the shoulder of the Barb. "Blame me for this," she sobbed. "Not yourself."

Lee rode away without looking back, leading the stallion. The sun was far down the afternoon sky.

As he appeared in sight of the Comanche village, the dogs, as usual, came charging to challenge a stranger. They came in a pack, with teeth gleaming and with shrill, coyote-like screaming. Also, as usual, they turned tail and ran howling when he charged his horse at them.

There were now less than a score of lodges in Quin-a-se-i-co's village. Once he had been chief over ten times that number. Now the lodges, made of buffalo leather, were old and patched. The colorful designs that had been painted on them were faded. The picture stories of the past mighty deeds of the warriors of the village had been dimmed by time and weather. Some of the Comanches even lived in shabby canvas Sibley tents that had been given them by the Army—a sacrifice of pride for these people who had been the great buffalo hunters of the plains—the Spear People, other tribes had called them.

Squaws were still busy preparing the turkeys the hunters had brought in. They and the naked children stared at the rider entering the village. It was the big, pale horse he was leading that fascinated them.

The squaws sudenly began scurrying to hiding, dragging children with them. Warriors appeared and stood motionless, waiting for the visitor to disclose his intentions.

The chief's lodge stood near the medicine pole in the center of the village. The lodge was made of buffalo hide in the ancient manner and bore the scars of time.

A squaw peered from its entrance. Lee remembered that woman, even though the years had withered her. She was Wau-Qua, who had said she was his mother. She was now as lean as a starving crow, and snag-toothed. How well he remembered Wau-Qua and her genius for inventing ways of tormenting him.

He gazed at hostile faces and into fierce, suspicious eyes. Somehow, this gave him hope. They did not see him as one of them. They saw him as an alien.

The Comanches had smoked the peace pipe with the Army, and had signed the treaties that restricted them to a segment of what had once been their vast domain. But, their pride had not been crushed,

There were faces that bore the scars of war. Some of these warriors, no doubt, had the scalps of white men and women hidden in their lodges—forbidden by the Army, but treasured and flaunted when coup dances were held and appeals offered that the ghosts of all departed fighters would return with spears in their hands to restore the race to its former place in the sun.

Chapter *THIRTEEN*

He held his horse to a walk as he rode through the village. The Barb seemed to sense that it was the object of attention, for it pranced along, its mane and tail flying.

Lee halted his mount in front of Eagle's lodge. The flap was closed. The interior was silent, but a faint haze of smoke from the cookfire drifted from the wings above. The feathered lance of a chief was driven in the ground alongside the entrance—the historic notification that Eagle was at home.

"I am one who lived in the lodge of Quin-a-se-i-co," he spoke loudly in English. Then he changed to the Comanche tongue. "I come to talk with him. I bring him a gift. A horse that only a chief must ride."

He rode closer to the lodge and looped the Barb's picket line around the lance.

He remained in the saddle, waiting. The village street was now deserted. Every Comanche had retreated into his lodge. This, too, was historic custom. A stranger had come to talk to the chief. He had brought a gift. A gift such as none of them had ever even dreamed of possessing. A gift that might bring fame to all of them because of its magnificence. For the Comanche was, above all, a horseman. A horse was his strength, his pride.

For a long time there was no response, as was befitting the dignity of a chief. Lee had known it would be this way. He knew all their ways—too well. Even the Comanche tongue, which he had seldom used since his escape from them as a boy, had come back easily—too easily.

The flap of the lodge was finally lifted. Eagle-in-the-Sky stepped into the open sunlight. The Comanche chief was still straight and tall, but gaunt. Time had frosted his brows and furrowed his cheeks. He wore a beaded vest, beaded elkhide breeches with belled bottoms in the Spanish style, and high, bleached moccasins. He had a beaded band

132

around his whitening hair, and a small silver bell tinkled faintly as it hung from his pierced right earlobe. His nose was hawklike. He bore many scars of battle, but there was one in particular that ran from jawbone into his hair, as jagged as a streak of lightning.

He gazed at Lee without speaking. Lee said, "I am Wa-no-lo-pay. You claimed I was your son."

Eagle continued to gaze, then said, "You are Wa-no-lo-pay. That is the truth. I know you after all these years."

His eyes turned to the pale horse. In spite of himself, he was unable to entirely maintain his pose of haughty indifference. Desire shone in his old eyes.

Then Eagle remembered the rules. The glint faded out of his eyes. Regret came. And anger. Anger at Lee for placing before him such a temptation.

Then he remembered that Lee would also know the Comanche code. Therefore he must feel that Eagle had something of equal value to the stallion and had come for it.

"We will smoke," Eagle said.

He motioned Lee to dismount, and led him into the lodge. Wau-Qua and a second squaw hovered in the background. At Eagle's order, the two women left the lodge. Wau-Qua cast a terrified glance over her shoulder as she hurried out. She feared that Lee had returned to square the account for the torments she had inflicted on him as a child.

Lee gave her a threatening scowl. He owed her that much, at least. She fled from the lodge in a panic. She probably feared that she was the gift he would ask in return for the white stallion.

Eagle lighted the pipe in the ancient ceremonial manner, sent smoke to the winds, and passed it over to Lee, who followed suit. The pipe passed back and forth three times, the ceremonial when a guest was being granted the favor of speaking to the chief.

"You have grown into a tall warrior, my son," Eagle finally said. "No one in the village can look over your head."

"I'm not your son," Lee said. "Not a real son, given to you by Wau-Qua or any of your wives. That is the truth, is it not, Quin-a-se-i-co?"

Eagle was a long time answering. He and Lee could hear the snuffling and impatient pawing of the Barb. Its shadow flickered against the wall of the lodge.

"You should be proud to be a chief's son," Eagle said.

"Am I Comanche?" Lee asked.

"You are as dark as a Comanche. You are as tall as a Comanche. Strong as a Comanche. You talk Comanche."

The chief was evading. It was the classic way of avoiding a falsehood.

"Am I Comanche?" Lee demanded again.

Eagle sat motionless on the robe. He thought it over for a long time, shooting speculative glances at Lee.

"You are not Comanche!" he finally said. "You are not my son."

Lee's heart thudded. He believed he was hearing the truth. However, there was the possibility that avarice had overcome Eagle's code of honor and that he was lying in hope he was offering a gift that would repay for the stallion.

"How can I know this?" Lee demanded.

"I tell you it is the truth," Eagle said haughtily.

"It is not enough," Lee said. "I must have proof."

"It is my gift to you," Eagle said. "That is what you came here to hear me say, is it not? I have said it."

He moved. He produced a rifle from beneath the robe. He cocked it and leveled it at Lee's heart. He suddenly spoke in English. "You are white man!" He uttered the words with hatred. "You are not Comanche."

Lee did not move. "It is no gift. Not until I have more than your word to show that you don't lie. If I am white, where did the Comanches find me?"

Eagle touched the long, jagged scar on his face. "This was given me by white woman," he said bitterly. "She is the one who bore you. She try to kill me. She do this to me."

"And *you* killed *her!*" Lee said hoarsely. "You killed my mother. The Comanches killed everyone at Rancho Verde that day except me. I was a small boy, not two years old. That's the truth, isn't it?"

Eagle did not speak. Lee waited. The seconds went by, marked by the throb of his pulse. He had come so near, and still was not sure.

"I will kill the horse unless I hear the truth," he said. His six-shooter was in his hand, looking back at Eagle over the rifle. "I will kill you, Eagle-in-the-Sky, if you shoot me now. I will live long enough to pull the trigger of this gun. You will die. The horse will not be yours. He will still be mine to ride beyond the far mountain. You know more about me than you have told. I want this knowledge. All of it."

Eagle sat motionless for a long time. Then he made a scornful gesture of acceptance. Laying aside the rifle, he arose, moved stiffly across the lodge, and drew a wolf pelt aside. Lee saw a chest the size of a small trunk. It was made of polished oak, brass-bound, the type in which valuables had been kept by ranchers in the early days. Its lock had been torn off long ago.

Eagle lifted its lid and delved into it. In the saffron light that filtered through the hide walls, Lee made out trinkets of many kinds—gold watches, bone and pearl buttons, combs, and brooches. Lace and silk kerchiefs, all soiled by time and coup-counting. Here was the record of a warrior's life. His coup chest!

There were items in the chest far more grim. Tufts of hair. Scalps. Some were those of Indians who had been tribal enemies, but the majority were from the heads of settlers. From men and women and children. These were souvenirs of raids on cabins, of ambushed stagecoaches, of men shot down in their cornfields.

One scalp was of fine, long, dark hair, faded by time, but retaining some of what must have once been young, lustrous beauty. Lee was suddenly gazing at Eagle through a haze of fury.

"My mother's hair?" he demanded.

The chief did not answer, but the truth was in his eyes.

"I know now why I've always hated you, Quin-a-se-i-co," Lee said, reverting to the Comanche tongue. "I thought it was a nightmare that I remembered from babyhood. But it was real, wasn't it? I *saw* you murder my mother. I was a child in her arms. That sight stayed with me."

Eagle had never been nearer death, not even when the bullet fired by Lee's mother had torn that jagged line up his face. He looked into the muzzle of Lee's six-shooter with the scorn of a warrior. He had faced this thing too many times in the days when life was dear to him to fear it now in his declining years.

"A great medicine man told me long ago that you would be the cause of my death, Wa-no-lo-pay," he said. "He told me you would see me lying dead at your feet."

"So now you can utter my name," Lee said. "Wa-no-lo-pay. John Lopez Calvin. That was why you forbade the tribe to speak that name. You never wanted me to hear it for fear I would know you had murdered my mother."

The chief did not answer.

"So that is why you hated me," Lee went on. "You were afraid what the medicine man said would come true. You feared that if I learned you had murdered my mother, I would kill you. You wanted me to die. You did not dare kill me yourself, because you had claimed me as a son, and it is forbidden to shed one's own blood. You put the squaws on me to torment me, hoping I would die. But, when I ran away, you wanted me brought back, for fear I would come back some day to pay you for what you did."

Lee added, "I am here."

Eagle still did not speak. He turned to the coup chest and drew out a small, brass strongbox. It was the type in which documents and jewelry were kept for safekeeping.

Eagle offered the box. "I give this to you," he said.

Lee did not respond for a time. Refusal meant failure and that he must leave the village, taking the Barb with him. Acceptance might also mean failure. Eagle was offering him a gift in return for the horse. But the strongbox might be empty.

"You want?" Eagle demanded.

Lee said, "Yes. I want it."

Eagle placed the box in his hands. His heart sank. The metal made it heavy—but not heavy enough. There could be little or nothing inside.

The small key was still in the lock. It refused to turn at first, its brass corroded by time. Finally, it yielded. He lifted the lid on its small, squeaking hinges.

All that the box offered was a sheet of paper and a faded photograph. If it had contained any valuables, Eagle long ago had made away with them.

"You read?" Eagle asked.

Lee lifted the sheet of paper. It was the quality a well-to-do, refined woman would use for correspondence, and had therefore stood up under the rigors of time. It bore an embossed seal that was a reproduction of Rancho Verde's original Spanish cattle brand.

The upper half of the letter was unmarred, though soiled, but an ugly, dark blotch discolored the lower half of the sheet. The ink was faded. Lee threw open the flap of the lodge to admit more light. The major portion of the writing was still legible. It was written in the neat hand of a woman.

It was dated more than twenty years in the past. Lee read the words:

My Dearest Rose:

I have received your note, saying you are to be the bride of Clement O'Neil, and I am sending my wishes for a lifetime of happiness. I understand some busy-bodies are advising you against your choice, for Mr. O'Neil seems to be a man who enjoys life and lets no person tell him how he must live it.

I will tell you a secret. They said the same things when I married my beloved John Calvin. They said he was a gambler and a drifter who would only break my heart. He gave me only loyalty, joy, and devotion for the few years we had together. So to perdition with the pessimists. Life is short. I intend to dance at your wedding.

I have made my will, Rose dear, and have taken the liberty of naming you guardian of my little Juano in case anything should happen to me. You are the one person I am sure would love and look after him until he can fend for himself. I have made provision for you from the ranch income so that you will be compensated, of course.

Judge Clebe drew up the document for me. He and your former precious brother-in-law signed the paper as witnesses. Both have copies of the document, for safety's sake. I refer to William Tice, of course. I admit I would have preferred someone else as a witness to my will, but he happened to be handy. It is only a technicality, at best.

I now have another secret that I want to talk over with you at first chance. It concerns my new ranch foreman, Michael Bastrop. He has been with the ranch only a few months, but

From that point on, the writing was blotted out by the dark smear. Lee could only make out a few words here and there. "Impressed," "marriage," "disillusioned."

There was no signature. The writer had been interrupted, evidently, in the act of penning the closing line.

Lee knew that the grim discoloration had been made by blood. The blood of his mother. He looked up at Eagle. There was little chance the chief could read. Therefore he held such matters in awe and respect. In this case there probably was superstitious dread involved that had prevailed on the Comanche to preserve the letter.

Lee lifted out the photograph. It was coated with dust and soiled, but was still a remarkably clear print, made no doubt by one of the old, itinerant, wet-plate cameramen.

It was a posed picture of a beautiful, young, dark-eyed matron with a small boy on her lap, both in their best garb. Penned across the bottom of the picture was an inscription:

Dear Rose: As you can see, Juano is growing up.
Margarita

Eagle placed a gnarled finger on the picture of the child. "You," he said. "You. Wa-no-lo-pay."

Here was final proof. Lee knew beyond all doubt that he held in his hand a picture of himself with his mother. He was the son of John Calvin and the beautiful señorita who had been the heiress to Rancho Verde.

His mother must have been writing this letter when death had swept down on her as she sat at her desk. The "Rose" to whom she had been addressing the message could be none other than Clemmy's mother, who at that time had not yet married Clem O'Neil.

Memories that had been imbedded in the horrified mind of a child came to life, bleak and terrible. It was Eagle himself who had delivered the death blow when he led his warriors into the ranch house in broad daylight.

The haze of fury engulfed Lee again. Eagle snatched up the carbine to fight to the last, for he expected to be shot.

At that moment an unshaven man, wearing a grease-stained buckskin shirt and leather brush leggings, appeared in the opening and shouted, "Here he is, boys! Just like I said it would be from the reward posters. Put up your hands, Jackson! We've got you!"

At the intruder's shoulder were two more roughly garbed men. All had weapons in their hands. In the background Lee sighted a dun-colored pony.

He whirled, firing his six-shooter. The unshaven man touched off his rifle at the same moment. Neither bullet struck its intended target. Lee heard his opponent's slug smash through flesh back of him. His own shot missed.

He fired again, but the arrivals were all diving away from the entrance to the lodge, and the bullet had no target to find.

Eagle-in-the-Sky, blood flowing from his mouth, was sinking to his knees, clutching at his breast. He was trying to speak. Perhaps it was the death song he was attempting. He failed, for he pitched on his face on the lodge floor.

The bullet that had been meant for Lee had torn through his lungs. The medicine man's prophecy had been fulfilled: Eagle-in-the-Sky had died at Lee's feet.

The leader of the strangers was shouting orders, but his companions were yelling too, in confusion. Lee sent another bullet through the opening to discourage any attempt to enter.

The squaws had been using one area of the lodge as their sewing shop where they carried on the never-ending task of making garments and moccasins of buckskin. A knife lay among the homemade needles and awls.

Lee seized the knife, slashed a slit in the rear wall of the lodge, and leaped into the open. He was not sighted until he had traveled half a dozen strides. Then the reward hunters came howling in pursuit and began shooting.

He swerved, circling the lodge, keeping its bulk between himself and the trio. His strategy succeeded. He drew them away from the horses in front of the lodge. Both his roan and the Barb were rearing, terrified by the gunfire.

He reached the saddle of the roan as one of the strangers came in sight. He fired and missed, but the shot served to drive its target back to hiding.

He grabbed the trailing reins of the roan. The knife was still in his left hand. He leaped into the saddle, leaned, and slashed the picket line the Barb was fighting.

He whirled the roan and hung on the far side of the saddle as he headed away. Indian fashion. Comanche style. But now that thought aroused no bitterness.

Bullets raged past. He swerved among the lodges to dis-
tract their aim. A slug struck the saddle horn, its force
sending the roan off balance. It staggered to its knees. That
probably saved the lives of both the horse and Lee, for the
next slug stung the tip of the roan's ear. That bullet might
have brained the animal had it been on its feet.

The injury goaded the roan to its feet and to frenzied
speed. Looking back, Lee saw his pursuers running toward
their horses. Their animals had been spooked by the uproar, and were rearing away from their owners.

In another direction, the Barb was running free, heading through the timber south of the village. The stallion
was a part of the lilac shadows that were gathering in the
thickets.

Lee rode west, away from where Kinky Bob and Clemmy would be waiting. He continued in that direction until
darkness had come and he was sure he had shaken them
off.

He still had the letter his mother had been writing when
she had died, along with the photograph. He had thrust
them inside his shirt when he had fled from the lodge.

Chapter FOURTEEN

He rode south until sure he had shaken off all chance they were still on his trail, then circled eastward. After some difficulty in the darkness he made his way back to where Clemmy and Kinky Bob waited.

Clemmy came running to his side as he slid from the saddle. "We thought—we were afraid—!" she babbled. "We heard shooting far away."

He kissed her. "I'm all right," he said. "I'll tell you about it while we're riding. Saddle up, Kink."

"Are they after us, Jack-Lee?"

"In a way, yes. But we're heading for home."

"Home?" Clemmy exclaimed.

"Punchbowl. That's our home. That's where we belong. Those hunters we spotted a day or two ago were smarter than I figured. They had sighted us, after all, and had guessed who we were. We seem to be pretty well advertised. They must have set up a blind trail to fool me into believing they had no interest in us, then circled back and followed us, waiting a chance to earn Mike Bastrop's offer of five thousand for me and a thousand for Kink. Dead."

After they were mounted and heading south he told them about the appearance of the hunters in Eagle's lodge and his escape.

"What did you learn from Eagle?" Clemmy demanded. "You found out something. Something good. You're different. You've changed."

"Eagle gave me a photograph and an unfinished letter in exchange for the Barb," he said. "My mother was writing the letter years ago to your mother."

"To my mother?"

"It was being written before you were born, before your mother had married Clem O'Neil," Lee said.

141

"They—they knew each other?"

"They must have been very close friends. And why not? They were of about the same age. Both had been raised in the Punchbowl. In fact, it was addressed to her dearest friend, Rose."

He repeated the gist of the letter. "My mother must have been writing it when Eagle burst into the room to kill her," he said. "She must have managed to get a gun, and shot him. He was scarred for life. He killed her, and he and his Comanches took me with them when they left. He hated that scar and made me pay for it. He hated me."

"Nevertheless, you can't really think of going back to Punchbowl," Clemmy protested. "Nothing's really changed. They'd never believe you, or that the letter isn't a fake. And they'd still charge you with killing Uncle Tice, no doubt."

"I want to ask a few questions of a certain party in Punchbowl," Lee said. "Judge Clebe."

"But—"

"Let's think back to the night Bill Tice was killed," Lee said. "Let's go over everything you remember, step by step. We know that the killing was done with that .32 you still have. You said you ran out of your room to follow Merl when he set out to chase me. You're sure you didn't have the gun with you?"

"Yes. I'm sure of that. I must have tossed it on the sofa. It was there when I came back."

"On the sofa?"

"Yes. I'm almost positive it was. I was excited, of course, by the shooting. The room reeked of power smoke. I panicked when I heard Marl screeching that Uncle Tice was dead and that I had killed him. I took the gun with me when I ran and jumped on Major Bastrop's horse."

"Could anyone have been in your room and fired the shots through the window before you came back?"

"I suppose so. I don't know where the others were. It probably could have been most anyone."

"But Clebe and Mike Bastrop were the only ones around," Lee said. "Merl was chasing me."

They let the horses settle down to a long gait that they could keep up indefinitely. "I've got a hunch we can't let grass grow under us," Lee said. "Those three men will still try to cash in. And they know where the money will come from. Mike Bastrop. They'll try to get to Bastrop as fast as possible. And I think Mike Bastrop will know why we went to Eagle-in-the-Sky. He'll know that I'm sure now that I am John and Margarita Calvin's son."

He added, "That means I might be the legal owner of Rancho Verde."

"Isn't it the law that a husband inherits all of a wife's property?" Clemmy said dubiously.

"That's true. But what about the will my mother mentioned? Your mother was named in it, but the will that was filed seemed to have left everything to Mike Bastrop."

"I see what you mean. A fake will. But that means—"

"Sure," Lee said. "That means Judge Clebe was in on it. And Bill Tice. They were witnesses to the real will."

"Oh, my goodness!" Clemmy breathed excitedly. Then her animation faded. "But proving it is something else. What chance would you have against Amos Clebe and Major Bastrop? They've got all the advantage, including money."

"If Clebe forged my mother's will, he might have pulled a few other tricks," Lee said. "Such as faking a marriage license."

"You mean you don't believe your mother was married to Major Bastrop?"

"I don't know what to think. There are a few words I could make out in the stained part of the letter that seemed to be referring to Bastrop. One was 'marriage.' Another was 'impressed.' That might mean she was secretly married to him. But it might not. There was another word, 'disillusioned.' It's my guess that what she was saying was that she had been impressed by Bastrop when she first hired him as foreman at the ranch, that he had proposed marriage and that she had decided to fire him, being disillusioned with him."

"Of course," Clemy breathed. "A lot of things are beginning to add up."

"Speaking of wills," Lee said. "Did you ever see the one your mother made out?"

"No. I was only a child at the time, of course. All I know is that they say Mother left nothing, and that Uncle Tice, as my only kin, was appointed my guardian by the court."

"The court. By Judge Clebe, in other words. That means that, as guardian, Bill Tice had control of any money your mother actually might have left you. I've heard that Rose

O'Neil was paid pretty high as a singer. What became of it?"

"I've always believed in my heart that Uncle Tice cheated me out of a lot of money," Clemmy sighed. "But by the time I was grown up enough to realize it, it was too late."

"He likely split it with Judge Clebe," Lee said. "They figured that if that sort of a scheme had worked when my mother died, it was worth trying again. They saw to it that your mother's name was maligned in order to keep you from asking questions, and to make it unpopular for anyone to take your side against them. They didn't dare do away with you. They only tried to break your spirit so you'd never cause trouble for them."

"The same way they tried to force you to break your neck riding bad horses and taking the worst of it on the trail," she said.

"We've *got* to talk to Amos Clebe," Lee said. "Alone!"

He was remembering the bodyguards Kink had said were looking after Judge Clebe's safety. He guessed that Clemmy and Kink were thinking of them also.

Darkness of the third day of their long ride came before they sighted the lights of Punchbowl ahead. They were mounted on their third relay of horses. They had seized fresh mounts at isolated ranches along the way and had been forced to take them at gun point, for they had been recognized by the owners of the animals they had commandeered.

"Send the bill to Rancho Verde," Lee had told them. "If I'm alive, it will be paid. Forget about earning the rewards Mike Bastrop has placed on our heads. Bastrop might not be in a position to pay blood money."

Lee felt certain the hunters who had tried to earn the bounty would be heading for Punchbowl to notify Mike Bastrop of their discovery, hoping to salvage at least a part of the reward for their pains. These men would have an advantage in the race to Punchbowl. Their horses were comparatively fresh at the start. Furthermore, they could ride openly on the trails, rather than the devious paths Lee and his companions were forced to take at times to avoid settlements where they might be recognized and halted.

The three of them had lost more weight from bodies that had already been thinned by hardships. Now, with the lights of Punchbowl ahead, they had the lean aspect of wolves. Their eyes were sunken in faces burned by sun and wind. Their cloths flapped on them in the wind.

They skirted the town and dismounted in the brush along Punchbowl Creek near the spot where Clemmy had waited the night Lee had gone into the town for supplies.

The hot spell had ended. A chill wind, whispering of the coming of winter, droned through the brush and rattled store signs and loose clapboards in the town. Clemmy clasped her arms across her breast and moaned with cold and weariness.

To gain information that Lee wanted, Kink left them and headed off into the darkness on foot, hoping to get in touch with his friend Celia. Clemmy huddled against Lee and they settled down to wait. She fell asleep, clinging to him, still moaning in her slumber.

The wait went on, and became an ordeal. "If anything goes wrong," Lee had told Kinky Bob, "just shoot in the air. I'll come in. Don't try any fool thing like leading them away from us. And don't shoot anybody. If there's anything like that to be done, I'm the one to do it."

Lee did not move, not wanting to awaken Clemmy. He watched the swing of the Big Dipper, using a dead tree as a guide, in order to keep track of time.

He judged that the hour was past eleven and he had almost convinced himself that he should wait no longer, but must enter the town in search of the big man, when Kink came back out of the darkness.

"I had to lay low quite a spell afore I had a chance to crawl in an' talk to Celia," Kink explained. "She's still cook an' housekeeper for de Judge. She live dar in a little room back o' de kitchen. She wants to quit, but she skeered to."

"Scared?"

"Judge Clebe, he skeered too. He keep dem bodyguards o' his mighty close to de house at nights. Dat's why I had to wait 'til I was sure I could wriggle to de back door an' git Celia to let me in."

"You were in the house? In Clebe's house?"

"Inside, safest place to be. One o' dem slingers always on de watch an' prowls around de outside o' the house every once in a while all night long. Celia know somebody goin' to git killed sooner or later. She mighty worked up, I tell you."

"Does she happen to know just who the Judge is afraid might come for him?"

"Celia don't know dat. She say de Judge is drinkin' harder'n ever, an' is mighty, mighty nervous. Jumps if'n a door slams. Two o' dem gunmen go with him to court every day, an' stay with him every step."

"What about Mike Bastrop?"

"Celia say she ain't seen hide nor hair o' him in town since somebody put dat bullet in his arm."

"And Merl and Gabe Tice?"

"She say de Judge is 'special keerful to steer clear o' dem two scamps. Dey in town most o' de time, drinkin' an' playin' cards. Dey're in Punchbowl right now. Least ways, Celia saw dem early dis evenin' when she was shoppin' at Sim Quarles' store."

"Did you remember to ask her if the Judge keeps any papers in the house, and if so, where?"

"If he's got any in the house, Celia say they're in a big iron safe dat's built into the wall back of a dresser in de Judge's bedroom. She say de Judge got powerful mad at her one time when she moved de dresser so she could sweep de carpet, an' saw de safe. Dat was de first time she knew it was there."

Lee shook hands with the big man. "I know you took your life in your hands to go into that house," he said. "That's another thing I'll always remember."

He added, "We'll leave the horses here. Mark the place well so that you can find it in a hurry if need be."

The three of them moved through the back areas of the town. The only activity in Sumner Street at this hour was in the gambling houses, and even there the patronage evidently was very light.

They made their way to Amos Clebe's residence, which had been built away from any neighbors for the sake of seclusion. It was a pretentious structure with two stories and a high-gabled attic, all adorned with fretwork and turrets. A white picket fence enclosed the tree-shaded grounds. Leaves flew in the brisk wind.

Kinky Bob led the way to the rear. They scaled the fence, Lee lifting Clemmy over the barrier. Heeding Kink's warning for silence, they crawled on hands and knees, a few feet at a time.

They were still a dozen yards from the house when they heard footsteps on the veranda at the front. They flattened to the ground, and watched the glow of a masked bull's-eye lantern that marked the location of someone who had emerged from the front door of the mansion.

It was an inspection trip. The blind on the lantern was snapped open and shut, with the beam of light darting briefly over windows and doors. Once the light passed almost over their huddled bodies, but the sentry moved on without discovering them.

Lee detected the odor of cheap whisky and rank pipe tobacco. The bodyguard, evidently bored with his lonely duty, was taking steps to make the task more bearable.

A heavier rush of wind roared through the trees. Lee arose and ran, his six-shooter lifted above his head. The wind helped cover the sound of his footfalls. His quarry heard him at the last moment and turned. But too late. Lee slashed the muzzle of the weapon across the man's neck. The blow numbed nerves. The only sound was a gasp. He caught the sagging weight of his victim and lowered him to the ground.

Clemmy rushed up and picked up the lantern which had fallen to the ground. She snapped the slide closed, masking it, and waited a moment until the flickering of the flame steadied.

Kink joined them. They crouched, waiting and listening. No sign of alarm came from the house. Lee and Kink bound the dazed man's ankles and wrists and gagged him with sleeves torn from his own shirt.

Lee took the lantern from Clemmy and led the way to the front of the house. No light showed inside. He mounted the veranda and tiptoed to the dark door. It stood ajar. The sentry evidently had intended to return by this route after circling the house.

Lee pushed open the door and unmasked the lantern. The beam of light probed a richly carpeted entry hall. To the left, a wide arched opening led to an ornately furnished parlor. A carpeted stairway mounted to rooms above. At the rear of the hall an open door revealed a sizable kitchen.

Another door stood at the right, midway down the hall. The snoring of sleepers was audible. Lee moved down the hall, Kink at his heels, while Clemmy waited. Lee stepped into the side room, flashing the beam of light around.

A man in his underwear was sprawled on a bed, asleep. A second sleeper lay on a cot. Another cot stood in a corner, evidently the bed of the man they had left bound outside.

Lee gave Kink the lantern. "Keep 'em blinded," he whispered.

He moved to the bed, seized the sleeper by the hair, and shook him. He jammed a boot into the ribs of the man on the cot.

Both men tried to leap to their feet, befuddled. Their instinct was to reach for weapons, but their gunbelts had been draped over chairs out of reach. Lee pushed them back onto their beds.

"Lie face down!" he whispered. "And don't say a word unless you want a broken skull. Not a word!"

He trust his six-shooter into the beam of light so they could see it.

"Your partner outside has been taken care of," he added. "You'll get no help from him. Don't try to earn your pay by asking for a bullet. It isn't worth it. You can believe that. Stretch out face-down and put your hands back of you. We're not interested in you two leppies. We're after bigger game."

They obeyed. "You must be thet damned Comanch' what punched the ticket o' that cattleman at BT," one of them grunted.

Lee rapped him sharply on the head with the muzzle of the pistol. "That will only raise a lump," he said. "One more peep out of you, and you'll wake up with the devil poking a pitchfork into you."

The man went rigidly silent. Neither he nor his companion offered opposition as Kink lashed their ankles to their wrists behind their backs and gagged them with strips from the bedding.

Lee saw a second bull's-eye lantern on the shelf. He found it in working order and lighted it, then handed it to Clemmy. "Keep watch on these two and anything that might come up outside," he said.

He and Kink mounted the stairs to the second floor. Their feet made no sound on the carpet. The beam of the lantern picked out the doors of four bedrooms. A narrower stair led to what evidently were quarters in the turrets and gables above.

"Ain't nobody up dar," Kink murmured.

Three of the bedrooms were unlocked and unoccupied.

The door of the fourth room was locked when Lee cautiously tested the knob. He looked at Kink, who nodded.

Kink backed away a pace and crashed his weight against the door. The lock was torn from its moorings. Kink plunged into the room, falling to his knees. Lee nearly toppled over him, but steadied himself, darting the beam of the lamp around.

The light settled on Judge Amos Clebe in a nightshift. The Judge was sitting, startled, in bed and swinging a cocked Colt .44 back and forth, ready to shoot.

He was blinded by the light. Before he could make up his mind whether to fire or not, Lee came out of the shadows and clamped a hand over the gun, jamming the hammer with his thumb so that it could not fall.

He twisted the weapon from the Judge's grasp. "My God, Mike!" Amos Clebe croaked. "Give me a chance! Let's talk this over sanely. We can come to an understanding."

"What sort of an understanding?" Lee demanded.

Amos Clebe blinked, trying to avoid the beam of light in order to make out Lee's shadowy face. "It *is* you, isn't it Mike?" he asked shrilly.

"Guess again," Lee said.

Amos Clebe ran a tongue over dry lips. "It's not—not—!"

"Yes," Lee said. "You might be better off if it had been Mike Bastrop. But, unlucky for you, it's John Calvin. John Lopez Calvin, Margarita Calvin's son. Otherwise known as Lee Jackson."

Chapter *FIFTEEN*

The shock of it silenced Amos Clebe for a space. Then he tried to bluster it out. "You must be insane. Margarita Calvin's child was killed by Comanches years ago and you know it."

"It's no use," Lee said. "I've learned about my mother's will. The real will, not the fake one you drew up after her death, which left everything to Mike Bastrop."

"How—?" Clebe began to mumble. Then he realized his mistake, and tried to cover it up. "I'd say you are really out of your mind, or that you think you can attempt blackmail."

"You know a lot about blackmail, I imagine, Judge," Lee said. "My mother was never married to Mike Bastrop, was she, secretly or otherwise? That's another lie you manufactured."

"What kind of foolishness—?" Clebe began. He had been deluded by the level tone of Lee's voice.

Lee slapped him. The blow sent the man back onto his pillow, gasping.

"You drew up a fake marriage license and dated it two months before her death," he said. "You and Bastrop saw your chance to own Rancho Verde. You had to take Bill Tice in on the deal because he knew about the real will."

Lee was pretending an assurance he did not really possess. He was guessing and believed he was right, but he still had no actual proof. But his manner was more convincing than he realized.

Amos Clebe made a last desperate attempt to brazen it out, but the blow had driven terror through him and it showed in his voice. "I—I don't know what you're talking about."

"Was it Bastrop who murdered Bill Tice that night?" Lee demanded. "Was it Bastrop who used Clemmy O'Neil's .32, firing from the window of her room, then left the gun in the room so that the murder would be put against her? Or against me?"

Amos Clebe's bearded face was suddenly gray and haggard. He tried to answer, failed.

"Or was it you who murdered Bill Tice?" Lee went on. "It was one or the other of you."

"No!" Clebe gasped. "No! I didn't do it! I was at the front of the house. I was drunk, but not drunk enough to—"

"To know murder when you saw it," Lee said. "Then you *did* see it. And so did I. So it *was* the Major who killed him."

Clebe could not answer. But the admission was written on his face.

"You were afraid you'd be the next to go," Lee said. "You and Bill Tice had milked Bastrop for years, forcing him to share the profits from Rancho Verde. That's why the Tices blossomed out after living so long on hard scrabble, and that's why Bill Tice became a partner in Rancho Verde. And that's why you've been able to live like a rich man. Likely you two began hogging more than your share of the money and Bastrop decided to get rid of both of you."

He dragged Amos Clebe from the bed, hurled him on the floor, and jammed a boot heel against his throat. "You figured you would have to kill Mike Bastrop before he killed you like he did Bill Tice. Bastrop had decided to quit being a front man for you leeches and was going for all the profits from Rancho Verde. You saw a chance to dust him in the back that night you spotted his horse in front of the Silver Bell. You hurried home to get a gun, came back, and waited until he came out of the Bell. I interfered, or you'd have put him out of the way for keeps. And you'd have seen to it that I got the blame. It was just by luck that I happened to be right there at the right time. Or was it the wrong time?"

He flashed the beam of light around the room and halted it on a big walnut dresser. "Move it, Kink," he said.

Kink shoved the dresser aside, revealing the door of an iron combination safe, set in the wall.

Lee grasped Amos Clebe by his wiry gray beard and dragged him to the safe. "Open it!" he ordered.

Clebe moaned again, looking up at him. "Open it!" Lee repeated. "You might get off with only a jolt in prison, if

you tell the truth. After all, you haven't murdered anybody
—yet."

Amos Clebe got to his knees and began fumbling with
the knob. Lee rapped his hands with the muzzle of the
pistol. "Quit stalling. Open it the easy way, or with some
fingers busted. It's your choice."

He jammed Clebe's nose roughly against the metal surface of the safe. "No, please! Please!" Clebe moaned. "I'll
open it."

The man manipulated the knob, his hands trembling.
The door of the safe swung open. Its compartments were
well filled with filed documents. One section was stuffed
with packets of greenbacks.

"You were making sure you wouldn't be exactly broke if
you had to pull out in a hurry," Lee commented.

He added, "You know what I want. My mother's will.
The real one. I know it's here. You never destroyed your
copy of it. Nor did Bill Tice, I'm sure. Both of you needed
the copies as a club to keep Mike Bastrop in line. I want
Rose O'Neil's will also. Don't make me go through all
those papers to find them."

Clebe thought of trying to brave it out, but didn't have
the fortitude. With shaking fingers he delved through a
packet of papers that he drew from an inner, locked
drawer in the safe. Presently he handed one over.

Lee did not attempt to read it. He was sure it was the
will his mother had made out. "How about Rose O'Neil's
will?" he demanded.

"I—I destroyed it years ago," Clebe admitted.

"How much money did she leave to Clemmy?" Lee
asked.

"Why—why, nothing. She—"

Lee jammed the pistol muzzle jarringly into the Judge's
teeth. "How much?"

"Please don't hurt me!" Clebe chattered. "It was about—
about sixty thousand dollars."

Lee gave Kink a tight grin. "You can tell Clemmy that
she'll likely soon be the owner of BT. It should be about
worth what the Tices owe her after all these years."

At that moment, Clemmy, from below, uttered a sound
of warning. Kink snapped the hood closed on the lantern.

She came silently up the stairs in the darkness. "There's
someone outside," she murmured.

Lee jammed the bore of his six-shooter hard into Amos

Clebe's back. "Don't make a sound!" he warned. "Not a sound!"

They waited. Utter silence held for a time. Lee was beginning to believe Clemmy had been mistaken.

Then a voice spoke guardedly in the darkness at the front of the house. "Amos! Amos! Wake up! It's Mike! Call off your bodyguards. It's Mike. I want to talk to you! Wake up"

Lee prodded Amos Clebe again. "Answer him!" he breathed. "Ask what he wants."

Clebe croaked something, but it was unintelligible even to Lee. However, it fitted the situation, for it could have been the voice of a man suddenly awakened from sound sleep.

"We've got to have a talk, Amos," Bastrop repeated. "It's important. Something's come up. Promise me I won't be shot. I'll come onto the porch."

"Talk?" Clebe called hoarsely. His curiosity was genuine. "What about?"

"Speak to your men," Bastrop insisted. "Are they in the house? If so, I don't want them to open up on me. I'm not armed. My gun is still on the saddle."

"Tell him to come onto the porch," Lee murmured.

"No, no!" Clebe groaned. "He's lying. He's come here to kill me. He'll be armed."

"I'll see to it that you come out of it, still breathing," Lee said. "I need you alive, Judge. I need you very much."

Mike Bastrop raised another impatient demand. "Amos! Let me in!"

"Answer," Lee ordered. "Say, 'I'm coming down to meet you at the door, Mike.' "

Amos Clebe gained a measure of steadiness and repeated the words. He had accepted the fact that his only hope was to obey.

Lee prodded him to his feet. "I'm going down with you," he murmured.

Carrying the masked lantern, he prodded his prisoner down the stairs ahead of him.

Clemmy had closed the front door after their entrance. Lee heard the footsteps of Mike Bastrop as he mounted the steps and crossed the veranda. Bastrop was standing at the door, waiting.

Lee unmasked the lantern, letting the circle of light fall

on the door. He pushed Clebe toward the portal. "Open it!" he breathed.

Amos Clebe feared to open the door. He was suddenly frozen by terror. Lee reached past him, freed the latch, and let the door swing inward.

Mike Bastrop stood, blinded by the lantern. He raised an arm to shield his eyes from the light. He wore no weapon—in sight at least. Evidently he had recovered from the arm wound that Amos Clebe had inflicted, for there was no sign of a bandage.

"I can't see a damned thing, Amos," he complained. "Turn that light off. I'm coming in. There's the devil to pay."

Lee drew Clebe back from the door. Mike Bastrop took that as an invitation to enter and stepped in.

"I'm afraid a certain party knows too much," Bastrop said. "He's talked to a Comanche chief. You can guess who it was, I imagine."

Lee poked Clebe into answering. "I can guess."

"A man showed up at Casa Bonita tonight," Bastrop said. "He had two more men with him. They likely make their living with a running iron and stealing horses, but I think he told the truth this time. He and his pals sighted a white man, a black man, and a girl dressed as a boy, way up north on the Comanche reserve. They followed one of them into Eagle's village and tried to grab him, for he was Lee Jackson. Jackson got away. This man and his pals killed a few horses getting to Rancho Verde to tell me they're sure Jackson was heading toward Punchbowl nesses, for Lee surmised that he had come here to com- with his two friends."

He waited for Clebe to speak. He became impatient, again trying to shield his eyes from the light. "Stop blinding me, Amos," he snarled. "If you've got a gun on me, put it away. We've got to pull together. If young Calvin shows up here, you know what that will mean."

Clebe's continued silence sparked a warning in Bastrop's mind.

"Is someone there with you, Amos?" he demanded.

Lee spoke. "Yes. It's young Calvin. I got to the Punchbowl ahead of the bounty hunters, Major. By the way, were you ever really in the Confederate Army? Everything else about you is wrong."

Mike Bastrop had lied. He *was* armed. His reaction was

very fast. A six-shooter appeared in his hand. He had been carrying it thrust in the rear of his belt.

He fired twice. But he missed, for coming at him was the bull's-eye lantern. Lee had hurled the lantern the instant Bastrop moved. At the same time he fell aside, jerking Amos Clebe with him.

The lantern struck Bastrop in the face. The man fired a third shot, but this slug went wild as had the first two.

Lee dived forward, bowling Bastrop off his feet. He knew that Bastrop would attempt to turn the gun on him. He brought his head up against Bastrop's chin, and teeth shattered. He swung an arm and it batted Bastrop's gun aside as it exploded a fourth time. He drove a fist deep into Bastrop's stomach and brought a knee into the groin.

He felt Bastrop sag, then go down with bubbling sounds of agony. Lee yanked the gun from the man's hand. He crouched, listening in case others were out there in the darkness. But there was no sound.

Bastrop had come here alone. He had not wanted witnesses for Lee surmised that he had come here to commit another murder. He had wanted to make sure that Amos Clebe would never live to face Lee.

"Lee?" Clemmy screamed from the head of the stairs. "Lee?"

"I'm all right," Lee said. "How about you and Kink?"

The beam of the second lantern lighted the stairs as Kink unmasked it. "Keno," Kink said. "But one o' dem slugs shore came mighty close to givin' ol' Kink a part in his hair."

They joined Lee. Lee searched Mike Bastrop for additional weapons, but found only a sleeve knife. He swung the light on Amos Clebe. The pudgy Judge sat numbly against the wall. At first Lee believed he had been hit by a bullet. But Clebe's injury was despair. He was a collapsed balloon. Flaccid, beset by self-pity.

Bastrop began to recover. He cursed Clebe with savage anger and contempt. "You gutless, yellow-livered thief," he panted. "You thought up this whole scheme, but I always knew you'd be the first to turn yellow if pressure was put on you."

He glared into the lantern beam. "I'm not going to let this hypocrite nor Bill Tice's two whelps put all of this on me. They're in it too."

"Merl and Gabe know about how my mother's will was faked?" Lee asked.

"They found it out a long time ago," Bastrop said. "Bill Tice was fool enough to keep a copy of the real will and those two found it when they were going through things that wasn't any of their business."

"We'll ask them if they still have that copy," Lee said.

"Ask them? We?"

"Get on your feet," Lee said. "You too, Judge. We're going for a walk. The Tices were in town earlier in the evening. Maybe they still are. If they heard the shooting, they might even be wondering if it meant that you had taken care of Judge Clebe like you took care of their father."

"It was this doughbelly who calls himself a judge who shot Bill Tice in the back," Bastrop snapped.

"Oh, no you don't, Bastrop!" Clebe panted. "You did it."

They began raving at each other. Lee put an end to it by yanking both of them to their feet.

"Keep your gun in the Judge's back, Kink," he said. "If he tries to run, shoot him. I'll do the same for Bastrop."

"You ain't really aimin' on lookin' up dem Tice boys?" Kink asked dubiously.

"I don't intend to let them get away," Lee said. "They'll be long gone for Mexico if they get spooked."

He sent Bastrop ahead of him with a shove. "Get used to it," he said. "Prison guards want action when they give an order. So does the hangman."

The stiff wind evidently had carried the sound of the gunshots away from the heart of Punchbowl, for Sumner Street was deserted when they turned into it from a side street. Dust blew and signs creaked. Loose sheet-iron banged on a roof.

It was past midnight and the Silver Bell was the only saloon still open. The two flashy California sorrels that Gabe and Merl Tice preferred as saddle mounts stood at the rail in front of the gambling house.

Mike Bastrop halted. "Don't make me walk in there," he said.

"Why not?"

"They'll come up shooting. At least give me a gun to defend myself."

"What you mean is that they know you murdered their father, but didn't give a hoot as long as it gave them more money to spend. Now, you figure that when they see you and Clebe with me they'll know that all four of you have reached the end of the rope, and they'll try to shoot you to keep you from doing any more talking. A fine handful of cold-blooded sharks."

Bastrop grasped at a new straw. "You've got it wrong," he exclaimed. "They're the ones who killed Bill Tice. Bill would never give them all the money they wanted for their drinking and gambling, so—"

"That's it!" Amos Clebe blurted, pouncing on this possible avenue of safety. "That's the way it was. Gabe is the one, most likely. He's capable of it. He always despised his father."

"I'll tell them what you said," Lee said. "Especially Gabe."

He sent Bastrop through the swing doors with a push that sprawled him on the floor inside. He caught Clebe by the throat and shoved him into the gambling house where he fell over Bastrop.

Merl and Gabe Tice had been playing poker at a rear table with two cowboys whom Lee recognized as being from the Fiddleback outfit north of the Armadillo Hills. The Fiddleback men could be expected to remain neutral.

The only other patron of the place at this late hour was Sheriff Fred Mack who was standing at the bar, drinking a nightcap.

The Tice brothers had leaped to their feet. Lee stepped in, his six-shooter in his hand. Clemmy and Kink started to follow him. "Stay back," he said. "Kink, keep out of this!"

He addressed the sheriff. "Glad you're here, sheriff. I'll turn these people over to you. All of them are mixed up in stealing Rancho Verde, in blackmail, embezzlement, and forgery. Not to mention murder."

He looked at the Tice brothers. "The murder of Bill Tice. Bastrop and Judge Clebe say one or the other of you killed your father so as to get for yourselves all the profits from BT and from blackmailing Mike Bastrop."

"What's that?" Merl yelled. "Why, the dirty liars! It was one o' them that—"

"Shut *up!*" his brother growled.

"They said you probably were the one, Gabe," Lee said. "Get enough of them against you and you'll swing whether you did it or not. Sheriff, I'm asking you to arrest these men. I've got documents and witnesses that will convict them all. In addition to stealing Rancho Verde, they helped defraud Clemmy O'Neil of a lot of money."

Gabe Tice went for his gun. Lee fired, but not to kill. The bullet struck Gabe high on the right arm, shattering his shoulder. Blood spurted. The impact drove him sprawling back on the poker table. The two Fiddleback riders were diving to cover. Gabe's half-drawn gun fell from his hand.

Merl, always slower-witted, was also slower on the draw.

"Hold it, Merl!" Lee warned. "I just fixed it so that Gabe never will be able to swing a quirt on a horse, most likely, let alone on a man. I'd mighty like to do the same favor for you. And I will if you try to pull that gun."

Merl let his hands rise into the air. "We didn't do it!" he almost screamed. "We didn't kill our own Paw. You did it, you Comanch' devil, an' you know it."

"You're a liar, Merl," Lee said. "You know who killed your Paw. And my name is John Lopez Calvin, not Comanch'. I never took it kindly when they called me that in the past. I'm going to be still more touchy about it in the future."

He added, "They're all yours, sheriff."

Fred Mack stood confused for a time. Then he acted. "We'll go a little deeper into this at the jail," he said. "One of you Fiddleback boys will serve as deputy to help me lead these men to my office. The other better go an' fetch Doc Peters to fix up Gabe's arm."

Dawn was near when Lee and Clemmy emerged from the door of the jail, followed by Kink. Lamplight still burned in the jail office where Fred Mack was at his desk, pen in hand, writing his report. Mike Bastrop, Amos Clebe, and the Tices were locked up in cells.

It had taken hours of questioning, of sifting the truth from the evasions, denials, and attempts of the four to blame each other.

But there was no doubt that Mike Bastrop had slain Bill Tice and would go on trial for his life, sooner or later. Amos Clebe would face a long list of charges and the Tice brothers stood to serve time also for abetting the fraud.

The three of them stood soberly in the darkness of deserted Sumner Street. Their worn clothes flapped about their thin bodies in the wind. The Silver Bell had closed. The town was dismal and lonely.

Clemmy was shaking. Once again Lee lifted her in his arms and carried her.

"Where are we going?" she asked exhaustedly.

"To Rancho Verde," he said. "To Spirit Lake. To everywhere. To the world. To everything we've always wanted to see and do. Together."

"We goin' to walk to all dem places?" Kink wailed. "My laigs are mighty, mighty tired, Jack-Lee."

All three of them suddenly began to laugh. They stood there together in the lonely street of Punchbowl, laughing wildly.

RIDE THE
WILD TRAIL

Chapter
One

Along with a handful of other passengers, Steve Santee alighted from the westbound transcontinental express at Junction Bend to await the local which would carry him up the branch line to Bugle in the Powderhorn country.

He stood on the plank platform as the train proceeded on its way. He was nearly home. He pulled the thin, dry air of the plains deep into his lungs. To him, after nearly three years in the humid tropics, it had the sparkle and lift of champagne. He drank deep of it.

Ike Jenkins, the station agent, was puttering with the baggage truck. He was a spare, bony man with a penetrating voice. "You got nigh onto thirty minutes before the northbound local is due, folks," he informed the arrivals. "Time to wash the dust out of your throats an' eat a bite. There's establishments for both purposes right acrost the way, as you can see."

He added conversationally, "That train for Bugle is likely to be a mite crowded an' quite a bit lively. Cattlemen from the Powderhorn Pool are aboard, accordin' to what the telegraph operator tells me, an' they'll be jinglin' their spurs, an' maybe a little likkered up. They're on their way home from the Stock Association meetin' at Cheyenne, an' also from sellin' the Pool's beef gather. They hit the market top."

"What's the Powderhorn Pool, friend?" a bystander asked. "Sounds like something you fish in. And what's the market top?"

Ike Jenkins snorted at such ignorance. "I can see that you're a stranger in cattle country, mister," he said. "A pool is a bunch of ranchers who join together to round up an' sell their beef for the sake of easier handlin'. Market top means they got a durned good price for their cattle. An' about time too. They've had tough pickin's the last three, four years, what with blizzards an' robbery. They've got a right to stand

1

up on their hind laigs an' howl. I hear they'll be splittin' up more'n eighty thousand dollars when they git back to Bugle. That'll——"

For the first time Jenkins' eyes rested on Steve. His voice died off. He stood peering. "Steve Santee!" he said, and there was a curious mixture of surprise, scorn, and avid curiosity in his manner.

"You've got a good memory, Ike," Steve said.

"So has other folks in this country," Jenkins said. " 'Specially up around Bugle."

"And your tongue is still set on a loose pivot," Steve said.

Jenkins backed away from the impact of Steve's dark eyes and busied himself spotting the baggage truck against the wall of the station. He dropped his voice, but made sure it still reached. "That local might turn out to be plenty more crowded than I figgered," he informed bystanders. "Amos Whipple, himself, is aboard most likely. He's the big cog in the Powderhorn Pool. An' he ain't the forgivin' kind."

"What's he got to forgive, friend?" someone asked.

"The thievery of ten thousand dollars," Jenkins said. "That an' bein' double-crossed by a man he had trusted."

"I don't follow you," the bystander said. "Who——?"

But Jenkins, with a smirking sidewise glance at Steve, retreated into the station to avoid answering further questions.

Steve walked to the far end of the platform where he could gaze northward. Before him lay the great land, and all of it was as much a part of his life as yesterday. Here a man could see mile upon mile, mile upon mile. There was no end to it. There were no green jungle walls to shut him in. Only people like Ike Jenkins.

It was early September. The spice of sagebrush rode the breeze. It was a warm breeze, and yet it carried the promise of fall in its touch. The Mormon Buttes, flat-topped, their flanks banded in patterns of buff and lavender, rose to the north. Antelope country.

Beyond them, far away, a deep mauve shadow lay on the skyline. This might have been a line of clouds. It was, in fact, the massive bulk of the Powderhorn Mountains more than a hundred miles distant, the crests of which peered over the rim of the plains.

Steve gazed at that shadow. He laughed with the quiet joy of a man who had found something he had never ex-

2

pected to see again. "Hello, you rough heads!" he said to those mountains.

Crowding him were memories that eased some of the tautness in him. He was twenty-five and looked older. He was tall and needed meat on his bones. He had fought malaria and yellow jack and jungle rot in the gold fields of Nicaragua and Honduras and had gone into battle in bloody revolutions. He was thin and sallow, but this was already beginning to fade. He had put on a few pounds since setting foot again in the States.

He wore a dark store suit which he had bought four days previously in New Orleans. In his war sack was other new garb that he had acquired in Kansas City. His feet were in soft-topped cowboots, a luxury he had not known in a long time. He had very dark thick hair and straight dark brows.

He was thinking of rushing mountain streams in the Powderhorns and of battles won and lost with fighting trout. He was remembering the savor of elk steaks and venison, cooked over open campfires. And of frosty mornings in the high country, and of the slap of a beaver's tail on a clear green pool on hot summer evenings.

He felt that he was returning to the joy of living.

He turned and discovered that Ike Jenkins was watching him, that malicious glint brighter in his eyes. He saw the same look in other bystanders before they quickly averted their gaze. They had been talking to Jenkins and he had told them the story.

That clouded the day. Steve left his canvas luggage sack on the baggage truck and walked across the dusty street to an eating house. He ordered food and lingered over it, and over the coffee.

The smoke of the approaching local became visible and the wail of its whistle drifted across the flats. He paid his bill, returned to the station, and retrieved his luggage.

The clatter of the arriving train drowned out even Ike Jenkins' shrill voice. The engine ground past Steve, carrying its aura of steamy heat. It was followed by a yellow-painted combination express and baggage car and two wooden day coaches. At the rear were three freight cars and a gondola loaded with heavy mining machinery.

The windows in the coaches were open and heads emerged. The majority of the faces were the weathered coun-

3

tenances of men who had spent the biggest parts of their lives in the outdoors. They were Powderhorn ranchers and riders and they were noisy and waving bottles.

"Forty-two dollars an' four bits a head!" one yelled. "Highest danged price in years fer range cattle. I'm buyin' the wife a red silk dress an' a cast iron cookstove tomorrow, an' payin' off the mortgage."

Steve recognized the majority of them. Their activities had been a part of the range life he had known from childhood, for Powderhorn Basin was occupied by small ranches, some of which counted their cattle only by the scores. The two largest outfits in the Pool ran little more than a thousand head each.

He saw that some of them had also identified him. The word ran through the two coaches. There was a rib nudging and muttered comment. A touch of frost subdued their high spirits.

Steve gazed back at them. Luck had played an ironical trick on him by forcing him to face them like this, so unexpectedly. It would be easy to back off, avoid the issue at this moment, and wait for another train to Bugle on another day. In that way he could meet them on ground more of his own choosing.

He refused to damage his pride to that extent. He singled out two men with whom he had been well acquainted and friendly in the past. "Hello, Tim," he said. "Howdy, Race."

One answered confusedly, "Howdy." The other was too uncertain of himself even to frame a reply.

Both pulled back from the windows like startled turtles and seemed to be looking to someone else inside the coach for guidance as to how they should meet this situation.

Steve turned his back on them and watched two armed express employees emerge from the office in the depot bearing between them a padlocked, steel treasure box. The door of the express car opened and the box was shoved inside and signed for by a messenger whose cap bore the name of Northern Express. The responsibility for the treasure was now in the hands of the smaller, independent express company.

Some thirteen thousand dollars in gold coin which had cost Steve more than two years of toil and privation and danger was among the contents of that box. It all belonged

4

to him at the moment, but soon he would have only three thousand dollars to show for his efforts. The bulk of the money, ten thousand dollars, was the price he was paying as balm for his pride.

The gold had been mainly in raw dust, along with some Spanish coin when he had landed at New Orleans, but he had exchanged it for United States gold coin at the mint. Because of its weight he had entrusted the money to the express company when he had entrained for the cattle country.

When he had named Bugle as his destination, the clerk in the New Orleans office of Wells Fargo had frowned a trifle and had consulted his rate book. "We can carry your specie at the customary rates only as far as Cheyenne, my friend. Up to that point we carry gold for the same fee as iced lobsters and fresh eggs. Beyond that point, as far as the Utah line, the fee will be considerably higher. This also includes the territory northward to the Montana line served by Northern Express."

"How come?" Steve had asked.

"Organized gangs of outlaws are operating in that region, according to the bulletins sent out by the company," the clerk had said. "In addition to other crimes there have been some train robberies. We sustained one loss of more than fifty thousand dollars in a holdup near Rock Springs on the main line of the Union Pacific some four months ago. And not long before that, Northern Express was robbed of about the same amount just north of Junction Bend, where you will change trains. Northern Express has the express franchise on the branch line northward into Bugle and Powderhorn Basin. Your destination seems to have become a very rough community in the past year or two."

"Rough?" Steve had questioned.

"And wild," the clerk had nodded. "Big silver and gold mining has started in the Powderhorn Mountains, and the town is described in company information as the possible headquarters of some of these road agents and train robbers. You are sending quite a sum of money to Bugle. Be careful. Being forewarned is forearmed."

This was the first intimation Steve had that Bugle might not be as peaceful as he remembered it. He had not known that big, deep-shaft mining was in progress in the Powderhorns.

It had sounded fantastic. It had been like standing in broad daylight and hearing a grown man talk seriously of goblins and spooks. Steve's memory of Bugle was a drowsy mountain town of some two score structures. Bugle, to him, meant the clang of the hammer on the anvil in Sid Wheeler's blacksmith shop, the musty, nostalgic aroma of potatoes and apples and sacked coffee beans in Ed Leffler's general store. Or the fascinating glitter of a new saddle on display in the window of Hans Weber's leather shop. There had been three saloons and a pool hall at the south end of Bozeman Street, and the First Methodist Church at the north end, and Nick Latzo's roadhouse at the river ford not far out of town for garish entertainment. Now he was being told that Bugle had changed into some kind of a Gomorrah.

It still sounded fantastic as he stood here in the clean sunshine at Junction Bend, watching the sliding doors on the express car roll shut. He heard the metallic creaking as the messenger inside thrust the locking bars into their sockets.

He had had no other choice than to entrust the gold money to express shipment. Its weight would have been a giveaway if he had attempted to keep it with him as personal baggage, and he would also have had the task of attempting to stand guard over it every minute through four days of train travel. So he had paid the additional charge for expressing the coin.

He lifted his war sack, slung it over his arm. It contained his personal effects and his shaving kit and spare clothing. And it also held a .45 Colt six-shooter and belt and holster and a box of shells. The holster had the shine of much wearing. He had wrapped the gun in soft linen cloth for protection from damage.

He walked across the platform to the steps of the first coach and climbed aboard. He was aware that every eye now was following him. He opened the squeaky door and stepped into the coach to face them.

Saddles were piled in the aisles and bedrolls were stuffed into the overhead baggage racks. Only about half a dozen seats were unoccupied. Of the nearly two score of passengers in the car, all but a handful were riders and owners, returning from delivering beef at the shipping pens.

Roundup was over, the beef gather had been successful. The owners in the Powderhorn Pool were going home with the biggest profit in the history of the organization. They had been whooping it up. The smoke of good cigars hazed the car and they had been drinking bonded whiskey.

He saw this joviality fade out of them. They did not speak as they eyed him. They merely sat silent and watching. And waiting.

One face emerged above all others. It was the stern, lined countenance of a weather-tanned, powerfully featured cattleman with shaggy iron-gray hair and brows and a drooping gray mustache. Amos Whipple, owner of the Center Fire, which was the biggest and most prosperous outfit in the Pool, was also chairman of the ranchers' organization and herd leader in all matters of decision and policy-making.

Steve watched Amos Whipple's eyes grimly inspect him. After three years there still was no toleration in the older man. He was not the forgiving kind. He had come up from Texas in the early days with the longhorns, fought the Sioux and the blizzards and the loneliness to establish Center Fire in Powderhorn Basin.

He was a strong man who took pride in never having gone back on a promise to a friend or to an enemy. He had no patience with weakness or dishonesty. He would have been a hanging judge if he had sat on the bench.

He was smoking a cigar, but he had drunk sparingly, if at all. He believed in seeing to it that he always had his mental faculties fully in control.

He continued to stare at Steve. In his deep voice he spoke through the spreading silence. "So you've come back to Bugle after all, Santee? Do you think that is wise?"

"I always intended to come back," Steve said. "I never had any other thought."

"Flocking to the feast, along with the other vultures," Amos Whipple said harshly. "Where have you been? In prison?"

"Not the kind you're thinking of," Steve said. "Not one with iron bars."

"Apparently whatever it was, it wasn't strong enough," Whipple said. "At least you're here, and you're not a blasted bit welcome. My advice to you, Santee, is——"

"I'm not asking your advice, Amos," Steve said.

A third party intervened. Steve discovered that Amos's companion in the seat was a young woman. She had been hidden from his view by the bulk of men in the forward seats.

She laid a hand on Amos's arm. "Uncle Amos!" she remonstrated, a reproof in her voice that silenced him.

She looked at Steve. "Hello, Steve!" she said. "It's good to see you." She spoke so that her voice carried to everyone in the car.

Steve stood gazing at her. He kept staring. Her eyes, a fine shade of gray green, looked back at him. "You skunk!" she said, a catch in her voice. "You act as though you don't even know me."

She was a gorgeous person. She had a small, straight nose and a nice mouth with a soft underlip. Her hair was a warm coppery shade with golden highlights, and her cheekbones gave character to the slimness of her features. She wore a cool green blouse and a pleated skirt. Excitement had brought a pulsing glow into her. The heat had accented a scatter of small freckles on her forehead. She was tanned healthily. Her fingers, where they lay on her handbag in her lap, were slender, but strong and carefully tended.

"And why should I know you?" Steve asked, a trifle numbly. "I once knew a girl as thin as a bean pole, who rode and looked like a boy. Before that I knew a pig-tailed, freckled little imp with legs as reedy as pipestems. She had a patch in the seat of her britches and used to throw stones at me and Doug Whipple when we wouldn't let her go swimming with us in Canteen Creek, because none of us owned bathing suits."

"That is not the sort of thing to tell here before other people," the gray-eyed person sniffed. "It was not that way at all, and I was a mere child at the time. As for being as thin as a bean pole, you never were very observant in matters concerning me. I do not believe I have changed that much in a few years. But, at least, you apparently do recall me vaguely."

"I don't know you," Steve said. "I only knew a person who, when we were kids, was as hard to get rid of as the hives whenever we wanted to go fishing or hunting. She should have stayed at home playing with dolls."

"It was because I always caught more fish and could track a bull elk better than the both of you," she said. "And I could swim faster than either of you, and you didn't want to be humiliated by a mere girl. That was why you and Doug Whipple used to pull my pigtails and call me a sissy."

"Your fishing ability is only a matter of your own con-

8

ceited opinion," Steve said. He found himself fighting a tightness in his throat.

"I could catch more trout then than either you or Doug Whipple," she said. "And I can do it now, as I will demonstrate at first opportunity, if the two of you have the sand to face the test, which I doubt."

She was extending a hand. Steve took it shakily. She was smiling at him, and he saw some of the same emotion in her that gripped him.

"Thanks!" he said huskily as he held that warm, slender hand in his own. "Thanks, Bricktop."

"So you do remember me after all?" Eileen Maddox said, trying to maintain the bantering manner—and failing.

She added, "Welcome home, Steve."

Chapter Two

Steve didn't dare speak. He released Eileen Maddox's hand and moved ahead. Amos Whipple sat silent and grim, his lips fixed in utter disapproval of her action.

The next seat was occupied only by a cowpuncher. It was the rearmost in the coach. Steve would have preferred greater distance between himself and Eileen Maddox at that moment, for he was still fighting that lump in his throat. But to have retreated into the second coach would have looked like he was backing away from Amos Whipple. He swung his possible sack onto the overhead rack and took the vacant place.

Eileen looked around and smiled at him again. She studied him for a moment and her smile faded. He decided that she was seeing the changes three years had brought in him and did not like what she saw. She turned away.

Amos Whipple continued to sit stiff-necked and icily angry, because she had dared to differ with him. The puncher arose hastily, stumbled over Steve's feet, and departed for the other coach to seek an atmosphere that was less strained.

Across the aisle a sharp-featured man with jet dark hair and sideburns and eyes to match was listlessly dealing blackjack to two companions who were in a facing seat. He had the well-barbered look of a gambler who was in funds. The other two were older and of rougher formation. They wore holster guns. Steve tabbed them as the type who might be gambling-house bouncers and trouble shooters. He glimpsed the strap of an armpit holster beneath the linen coat of the younger one.

They were using silver dollars as chips, and the play was not high enough, evidently, to interest the natty one in sideburns. He inspected Steve boldly and a trifle insolently, as though indifferent to whether offense might be taken. He had witnessed the way Steve had been received by the cattlemen and Amos Whipple. And also by Eileen Maddox. He was curious, and evidently did not have the answer. His interest in Eileen was even greater, but she pointedly ignored him.

The train got under way and the drab water tanks and freight sheds at Junction Bend slid past, echoing the rumble of the wheels. The cars picked up speed in open country.

Steve slid over to the window and stared out unseeingly at the land. Eileen's warm friendliness and her courage in publicly defying Amos Whipple had helped. It had helped enormously, but the truth was that the zest of his return to these familar scenes was lost.

He hadn't expected them to forget entirely, particularly Amos. But neither had he expected them to be so unyielding. What was it that Amos had said—"flocking to the feast with the other vultures"? What had that meant?

They still believed that he had helped his father vanish from the Powderhorn country with ten thousand dollars that had belonged to the Pool. Only Eileen, apparently, did not share that opinion.

She had addressed Amos as "Uncle" although they were not related. It was a title of respect. Eileen had lost her parents when she was a small child. They had been killed by a snowslide that had swept down off Long Ridge and trapped their top buggy as they were driving from town to their ranch during a winter's storm. Eileen had also been in the buggy, but she had been dug alive from the avalanche by Steve's father and mother, who had been traveling the trail that day.

Eileen had been an only child. Amos Whipple, who had been a long-time friend and neighbor of her parents, had been appointed her guardian. He and his wife had taken her to Center Fire and had raised her, along with their own son, Doug, who was four years older than she.

A veteran cowboy named Shorty Barnes had been placed in charge of Antler. When Eileen was sixteen she had preferred to return to Antler to live and had hired a widow as housekeeper. Antler's holdings, like the majority of the outfits in the Pool, were modest but sufficient to afford a comfortable living when all went well.

Steve kept gazing at Eileen disbelievingly. It did not seem possible that the freckled, peppery-tempered tomboy he and Doug Whipple had ordered around like a slave could have blossomed into such an alluring creature.

Steve's father, Buck Santee, had owned the small OK ranch on Canteen Creek, where he had shared open range with the Antler and with Amos Whipple's bigger Center Fire to the east. The only other outfit in that end of the basin had been the Rafter O, owned by a cowman named Dave Garland.

Eileen's parents had not been the only victims of the snowslide. Steve's own mother had died of pneumonia that winter, brought on by her exertions in helping save Eileen.

Those tragedies had occurred during a hard winter in the Powderhorn. A worse one was to come, but it did not strike until four years ago, when Steve had grown to manhood. During that season of relentless cold and storm Steve and his father had seen more than half of their flourishing OK brand perish in the deep drifts and frozen flats.

Amos Whipple and other ranchers had been hit equally as hard. Beef gather the following summer had brought only a return of ten thousand dollars to be apportioned among all the members of the Pool. But, meager as was the return, the money was desperately needed in the basin.

Buck Santee had been chairman of Powderhorn Pool, and that had been a thorn in the flesh of Amos Whipple, who felt that he was entitled to that honor. Just as Steve had always been ill at ease in Amos's presence, his father and the Center Fire owner had never seemed to look at things from the same viewpoint.

Buck Santee, before he married and settled down, had been a rolling stone. He had been a cavalryman, stage driver, a deputy marshal in tough frontier towns, a lookout and trouble shooter in gambling houses, and had dealt poker and faro professionally in plush, high-play establishments in Denver and other places as far away as El Paso.

He had never made a secret of such things. He was well-liked, and men who had known him in his colorful past also knew that he had a reputation for strict honesty. Therefore they had chosen him as head of the Pool in spite of Amos's misgivings.

The money for the beef gather that year had been paid in gold as usual at the Kansas City stockyards by the commission buyers and had been brought to Bugle by train, just as the proceeds were being transported at the present moment.

The proportional settlement to the individual ranchers, after all expenses were tabulated and deducted, was to have been made at the customary barbecue and dance at the Spanish Flat schoolhouse, which had been the scene of such activities since the formation of the Pool. Pool Day, in good years or bad, was a time of high fiesta in the basin.

Buck Santee and an assistant had left Bugle for the schoolhouse after dark, with the gold on the back of a packhorse. Arrival of the money was always the high point of the celebration, and after its division the ranchers and their women would dance until dawn.

Buck Santee's companion was a ranching friend named Henry Thane. Both men carried six-shooters. The presence of the gold was supposed to be a secret, but it was an open secret, for this same procedure had been followed for so many years that it was routine.

There had been no lawlessness in the Powderhorn during those years, lulling the basin into a sense of security. Even the habitués of Nick Latzo's bawdy roadhouse in the brush near the river ford did not attempt to mingle with the citizens of Bugle.

Nick Latzo was a bulky, black-jowled, cigar-chewing man, whose Silver Moon offered gambling in tinseled surroundings, the music of an orchestra, and feminine entertainment. The place was anathema to the women of the country and spoken of by them in scandalized whispers. Law officers hunting fugitives always made Latzo's Silver Moon a port of call, usually without result. The patrons of the roadhouse did not talk. Tinhorn gamblers and taciturn men of mysterious origin hung out there. But they had kept their place, evidently considering Latzo's as a refuge where they only wanted to live and let live.

Steve's father and Henry Thane had never arrived at the schoolhouse. Henry Thane's body was found at daylight, partly buried under leaves and pine needles not far off the trail. His horse was grazing nearby, still carrying his saddle. Thane had been shot in the back of the head at close range.

Buck Santee and his horse were missing, along with the ten thousand dollars. The trail of his mount was lost after a short distance, wiped out by passing ore freighters which had furrowed a rain-softened road for miles.

Weeks afterwards it was reported that Buck Santee had been seen in Denver and later in Abilene, his old haunts where he had once been a professional gambler. As time went on it was rumored that he had been in San Antonio and in El Paso.

Amos Whipple swore out a warrant for Buck Santee's arrest, charging him with murder and robbery. The loss of the money placed ranchers in the Pool in precarious condition, and restitution was demanded in the courts.

What cattle and range rights Steve's father had owned were seized and sold under legal judgement. Only the modest, log-built house and spread which stood on homesteaded land remained immune.

Steve had found himself at bay. Amos Whipple had made it plain that he believed Steve must have had a hand in helping his father vanish with the money. "Blood is thicker than water," the Center Fire owner had kept repeating.

Steve had tried to face it out. He had scanned, inch by inch, the route his father and Henry Thane had followed that night. He had gone over it day after day, week after week, until time and weather had buried all hope of turning up any information in that manner.

He had scoured the country. He believed, in spite of the stories that his father had been seen alive in other places, that Buck Santee had been murdered at the same time Henry Thane had been killed, and that the body had been hidden in order to cast blame upon a dead man.

However, the word that Buck Santee had been glimpsed in faraway regions continued to drift in. This hardened public opinion against Steve. It was whispered that Buck Santee was in Chihuahua in old Mexico. Everyone knew that a man who had been well acquainted with him had talked to him there. Next he was in Vera Cruz, dealing Spanish monte in a gambling house. After that he was reported as living in lux-

13

ury in Panama. So the tales went. Steve had never been able to trace down the source of these reports. But they confirmed the general belief that Buck Santee was alive.

Steve's persistence in hunting murder evidence began to be resented. He was ridiculed and taunted and accused of trying to set up blind trails to protect his father. Twice he fought men with his fists. These affairs had only hardened their antagonism. He had been arrested on both occasions and fined for disturbing the peace. He had been assured that any further trouble would land him behind bars.

Then Steve himself disappeared. He padlocked the doors of the house on Canteen Creek, where he had been born, and rode out of the Powerhorn between sundown and dawn.

He left a letter in the Antler mailbox, along with keys to the padlocks. The letter was for Eileen. It read:

> Eileen:
> I'm going away for a while. If my father is alive I'll find him. Either that or prove that he is dead. I'll bring back enough money to pay off the Pool for what it lost. Ask Doug to keep an eye on the house for me until I get back.
>
> Steve

And now, after three years, he was back. Eileen was gazing at him once more, and he sensed that she also was thinking of that message.

She arose suddenly. Amos Whipple tried to stop her, uttering an angry protest, but she pushed past him and seated herself alongside Steve. Amos got to his feet, stamped down the aisle, and entered the next car.

The blackjack dealer across the aisle paused a moment to watch Eileen admiringly. Then he eyed Steve with increasing speculation.

"I still have the note you left for me," Eileen said, the rumble of the train covering her voice. "Three years is a long time. Was your—your quest successful?"

"You might call it that," Steve said. "At least I've brought back the money to pay off the Pool."

"Money? How much?"

"Thirteen thousand dollars in all," he said.

"You—you have that much with you? Now?"

"It's up ahead in the express car," he said. "Ten thousand

14

of it goes to these men in the Pool. I believe you'll be entitled to a share of it too, Eileen. Your beef money was in with the others."

"I don't want that kind of money," she said. "Where in the world did you get it, Steve?"

"I made the biggest part of it shoveling placer sand into a long tom trough in Nicaragua," he said. "I shoveled half a mountain through the riffles. A year and a half of it. Fourteen hours a day. When the placer wore out, I earned the rest of it running guns to a ragged little army in one of the banana republics down there. I was on the winning side. For once, justice and liberty got the upper hand. I had to earn part of my pay using a carbine. Sometimes a Gatling gun. The pay there was mighty low for what you put into it, just like it had been on the placer bars."

"How did you ever find such terrible places?" she asked.

"Hunting my father—tracing down those stories of him being seen here and there. After I left the Powderhorn I went first to Denver. Nobody there had seen Buck Santee in many years. Sure, they remembered him. He used to deal there in a gambling house. A square shooter. Abilene, the same. San Antonio and El Paso. I went into Mexico. Chihuahua, Vera Cruz. They had never heard of Señor Buck Santee. Then to Panama. I worked my way as a deck hand on a ship. You've never imagined anything like Panama. You sweat even when it's raining torrents. Beachcombers and outcasts from all over the world, preying on each other."

He was silent for a time. "That was the end of the hunt for me," he said.

"The end?"

"I had traveled ten thousand miles trying to find a man who had never left Powderhorn Basin," he said. "I had eliminated any last possibility, as far as I was personally concerned, that my father was alive. I was certain beyond question that he had been killed that night along with Henry Thane. About that time there was a gold strike in Nicaragua. So I joined the rush."

He peered out at the buttes and the blue sky. "And now I'm home," he repeated.

"Do you really intend to give the Pool that money?" she asked.

"Yes. At the Spanish Flat schoolhouse, if it's still there. As soon as I can do it. When is Pool Day?"

"Tomorrow. And the schoolhouse is still there."

She studied him gravely. "That money would give you a new start at ranching," she said. "You know that."

"I've never looked on it as my money," he said. "Money's not yours unless you think of it that way. But I'll have three thousand dollars left over for myself. I'll buy cattle. Is the house still all right?"

She nodded. "I stopped by there only yesterday. It's ready to live in. The fact is, Doug has been staying there a lot and taking care of it."

He gazed at her and she shrugged. "Doug and his father still can't hit it off. Doug never goes near Center Fire, even to see his mother."

They sat silent for a time. The blackjack game ended across the aisle. The two hard-visaged men dozed in the heat of the afternoon.

The younger one riffled the cards and continued to eye Eileen with bold interest. "Hello, Miss Maddox," he spoke finally. "You know me, of course. I'm Louie Latzo. Nick's brother. I've seen you often in Bugle."

Eileen ignored him. Louie Latzo was annoyed. He started to speak again.

"The lady doesn't know you," Steve said. "Let it ride that way."

Latzo had been drinking. He glared at Steve challengingly. But his companions had awakened and one muttered a growl of warning. Latzo scowled, but subsided. He finally laughed loudly, said something to the two, and took a drink from a bottle. He yawned and stared through the window.

Steve quietly studied Louie Latzo with interest. After the disappearance of his father he had fallen into the habit of visiting Nick Latzo's roadhouse at the river ford. His patronage at the Silver Moon, he had known, was not welcome, even though the elder Latzo had always greeted him with loud and effusive warmth. Latzo had been fully aware that Steve's purpose in mingling with the shady patrons of his place had been in hope of seeing or hearing something that would give him a clue to the fate of his father.

Nothing had ever come of it. If Latzo had any inkling of what had happened to Buck Santee he had kept it carefully concealed back of the beetling smile with which he greeted all outsiders and unidentified visitors who showed up at the roadhouse. There had been no younger brother of Latzo around at that time.

Eileen guessed the trend of his thoughts and supplied information. "It didn't occur to me that you had never before seen Louie. He's an addition to our population since you went away. Unwanted, I might say. He showed up not long after you had left."

"Where did he come from?" Steve asked.

"Who knows? A gopher hole, probably. He came to share his brother's prosperity. Nick is said to be very fond of him. He keeps Louie well supplied with money, of which Nick always seems to have plenty. The Silver Moon is bigger and wilder than ever, what with the mines booming, and even cattlemen making profits. At least, so I hear. I wouldn't know at first hand. It's no place for a lady. And the Blue Moon is doing well also."

"The Blue Moon?"

"Nick has opened a second gambling house right in town," she said. "The Blue Moon. So we now have both the Silver and the Blue Moon in our sky in Powderhorn Basin."

"What's Louie doing on this train?" he asked. "Is he a member of the cattle pool?"

Eileen laughed. "Hardly. Louie probably doesn't know which end of a cow the horns grow on. He and his pals got aboard at Cheyenne. I suppose they were down there on a spree during the Stock Association convention. Cheyenne was humming. Louie likes the high life. His big brother sends the other two along to help him out when he gets into trouble, which is frequently. Louie is what you might call a little louse."

Steve sat thinking. He had never stopped believing that Nick Latzo could shed considerable light on what he wanted to know. There must be some way the man could be made to talk.

Eileen was silent also. Without knowing exactly why, he was aware that she knew the trend his thoughts were taking. He remembered now that it had been this way with them even as youngsters. He had always been an open book for her to read.

"Nick Latzo," she said, "is a very powerful man now—and dangerous."

17

Chapter Three

The sun was low in the sky and beating hotly through the car windows. The fluted walls of the Mormon Buttes appeared abreast as the engine labored up the grade toward the Powderhorn Divide.

Steve touched Eileen's arm and pointed. "Pronghorns!" he said delightedly. "I made a bet with myself that we'd sight some along here. Antelope always hang around the buttes at this season of year. There's a spring under the base of that bluff where the juniper grows thick. I bagged a fine head there one morning."

A dozen or more antelope were standing in the sagebrush near the track, every head at attention, watching the train. Apparently they had learned that such mechanical objects offered no particular danger.

"Nothing has changed," Steve said. "Not even the people. And certainly not Amos Whipple. He still sits in judgement on others."

"Perhaps you've changed," Eileen said.

"For the worse, you mean?"

She sorted through her mind for an answer. "I really don't know. You're grim, Steve. And much, much older than you should be. You look like—well like a man who doesn't give a hoot about the rights of other people if they happen to stand in his way."

"Nobody ever gave a damn about my rights," he said.

"Then you are bitter," she said. "You've come back with a chip on your shoulder. Next it'll be a gun at your side. You bear a grudge."

"That might be one way of putting it," he said. "If they want trouble I'll not back away from it this time."

"It isn't worth it," she said anxiously. "You owe yourself a chance to forget."

"I'll owe myself nothing, nor them either after I pay them the money they accuse my father of stealing," he said.

18

"But it isn't easy to forget bitterness. You can't rub out deeds with words, you know."

Across the aisle Louie Latzo was staring at the antelope. The train had now drawn abreast of the animals, which were less than fifty yards away.

The band wheeled suddenly to retreat. Even as the antelope began their first stiff-legged jump, Latzo snatched from his shoulder holster a silver-mounted six-shooter and began firing as fast as he could thumb the hammer.

The antelope were moving parallel with the laboring train, and even an average marksman would have registered at that short range. But Latzo was in a frenzy, as though fearing his quarry would escape. It was the passion to kill and kill, Steve realized.

The man spilled his shots in a shocking thunder of sound. Bullets kicked up dust around the running animals. Latzo was shooting into the band indiscriminately, trying to register hits on as many targets as possible.

Only one bullet found a mark. A young doe stumbled and went down. It arose bleating, then fell again. It had a bullet-broken leg.

The remainder of the band were off and bounding in frantic effort over the sagebrush. Latzo, laughing shrilly, snatched a six-shooter from the holster of one of his companions. He had emptied his own gun. He eared back the hammer, intending to send another hail of bullets among the fleeing animals.

Steve was out of the seat and past Eileen in a lunge. His hand caught the .45, his thumb jamming the hammer. He twisted the weapon from Latzo's grasp.

The doe was still hobbling along, trying to overtake its companions, its shattered front leg dragging grotesquely. Steve lifted the gun and fired twice. Luck was kind to him, for the distance had widened. The injured animal, which would have been a living prey for coyotes and magpies, reared, then went down with the limpness that was the mark of a death blow. At least one of the mercy shots had scored.

"Why, you . . . !" Latzo screeched in a rage.

He swung a punch at Steve's face. Steve, with his free hand, blocked that blow. Latzo tried to snatch the pistol from him. There was the savagery and rage of a humiliated small mind in the man's thin face. If he could have gotten possession of the loaded gun he would have killed.

But Steve shoved him roughly back into the seat and maintained possession of the weapon. Latzo's two companions had been unable to move until now because of the fast action and the close quarters. The one who still was armed saw his chance to attempt to draw.

"Stay out of this!" Steve said and backed off a pace, the captured .45 covering the three of them. The man went motionless. After a moment he carefully lifted his arms well away from his gun. He was coarse-featured, thick-lipped, with a nose that had suffered damage in the past. He said nothing, nor did his companion, who was shorter and blocky of shoulders, with muddy brown eyes and a small, sand-colored mustache.

Taut silence held the coach. Steve yanked the six-shooter from the holster worn by the thick-lipped man. He flipped open the chamber and spilled the live shells out the window. He did the same with the cartridges in the weapon he had appropriated. Louie Latzo's ornate pistol was empty. Steve lifted it from Latzo's holster.

He sent all three guns skidding down the floor of the aisle to the far end of the car. "Pick 'em up after you cool off," he said. "And not before. In case you have more shells in your pockets, don't reload as long as you're on this train."

He eyed Latzo. "After this," he went on, "if you want to kill game, pick your target and shoot it clean and honest. Don't wound animals just to abandon them in their misery."

Latzo and his companions glared around. No one had anything to say. The cattlemen were eying them stonily. Whatever other opinion they might hold in regard to Steve, it was evident that he had their grudging approval in this matter at least.

Latzo spoke in a choked, strained voice. "All right, mister. I'll remember you, whoever you are. I hope you won't be hard to find."

"My name is Santee," Steve said. "Steve Santee."

A flicker of surprise passed over Latzo's features. Evidently he had heard the story of Buck and Steve Santee.

"I'll be at my home on Canteen Creek if you want to look me up," Steve went on. "I'll also be in Bugle whenever I have a mind to come there. You won't have any trouble finding me."

He wasn't talking to Louie Latzo as much as he was addressing the men of the Powderhorn Pool.

"I'll find you," Latzo promised fervently. "You can bet your last slick nickel on that."

Steve sat down alongside Eileen again. She looked at him and said, "Thanks."

Some of the hard fury slacked out of him. He smiled at her. She leaned close. "Louie Latzo meant what he said about getting even," she said. "Watch out for him, Steve. That big ugly one goes by the name of Al Painter. The other one is called Chick Varney. They've both been in gun fights and brawls several times. They're vicious persons."

"How does a man go about watching for them?" he shrugged. "Usually that's another name for running away."

She sighed. "You haven't changed in one respect at least," she said. "You always were mule-headed about such things."

The train rolled on northward. Steve watched the Powderhorns take shape and rise until they filled the sky ahead. Some mountains, he reflected, were feminine in character. Soft and mysterious and beautiful and fascinating. The Powderhorns were ruggedly masculine. They were as wild and untamed as a great bull elk or as the grizzlies and the mountain sheep which ran free and above the world on their high flanks.

Eileen watched him. "The Powderhorns don't change either," she said. "You always looked at them as though you were looking at a friend—a very close friend. And that's the way you're looking at them now."

"They're honest," he said. "I understand them and they understand me. It's good to know them."

She sighed again a trifle impatiently and said nothing more. Amos Whipple returned from the rear car and took his place in the seat ahead. The set of his shoulders was evidence that Eileen was not forgiven for standing against him.

Sundown came. The Powderhorns began to draw purple shadows about their shoulders as twilight moved in. Bugle was little more than thirty miles away. Louie Latzo and his two pals sat sullen and forboding across the aisle. Their guns still lay untouched at the end of the car.

Many of the cattlemen were dozing now. Eileen had her eyes closed, but Steve knew she was not sleeping.

The train abruptly slowed and the whistle sounded. Men roused and crowded to the windows, shouting and pointing. Two riders were galloping alongside the tracks. One left the saddle and leaped agilely onto the steps of the coach. The other, who was a cowpuncher, swerved away, seized the reins of the riderless horse and pulled up, laughing and waving his hat.

The occupants of the car were delighted. They were cheering and guffawing. As the arrival entered the car they greeted him with friendly jibes and comment.

"Tryin' to avoid buyin' a ticket, huh, Burl?"

"You ought to try that stunt at the Frontier Days show, Burl. You'd shore win a prize—or a busted laig."

"I reckon it wasn't us boys you was so anxious to see, Burl," another said. "There must be some other attraction aboard this train."

Burl Talley was grinning and taking sips from bottles that were being pushed at him. "Sorry I couldn't make it to the convention at Cheyenne, boys," he said. "But I wanted to be in on part of the fun at least. Red Sealover and me rode all the way across the basin from the ranch today to meet this train."

Talley's glance searched the coach and rested on Eileen. Steve realized that she was the attraction the speaker had mentioned. Talley pushed past hands that tried to restrain him and moved down the aisle.

Steve knew him well. He was a straight, lithe, handsome man of forty who carried himself with poise and assurance. He had thinning, well-barbered brown hair and brown eyes that were bright and alert. He had come into the Powderhorn some ten years in the past on foot and in search of opportunity. He had swamped for freighters and had worked in lumber mills. Within a few years he owned a lumber mill of his own in Bugle. From there he had branched into other prosperous sidelines.

Talley now wore the garb of a cattleman. It was expensive regalia, but conservative.

Eileen must have guessed the trend of Steve's thoughts, for she explained. "Burl has gone into cattle also, since you went away, in addition to owning the planing mill and lumber yard. He took over the Rafter O in our end of the valley when Dave Garland had to sell. He's a member of the Pool."

Talley came striding toward Eileen and it occurred to Steve there was confidence in his smile and also something demanding, as though he was sure of himself, but felt that he was not receiving entirely all that was his right.

22

"You went to considerable trouble to join the crowd, Burl," she greeted him.

"Not the crowd," he corrected, taking her hand. "You. Again I want to say how much I regret that I couldn't go with you and the others. I just couldn't shake loose from several business snarls."

She laughed and slowly withdrew her hand. But she was not annoyed by his public display of affection. His intentions were plain enough. And though he was considerably older than she, he had much of the quality that would hold the feminine interest. Most any girl, Steve reflected, would consider Burl Talley quite a catch.

Talley had been so absorbed in Eileen that it was not until now that he really looked at Steve and recognized him. He straightened a trifle, and his mind must have flashed to some disturbing thought, for he frowned a little and stood as though trying to decide his course.

"Well," he said. "Santee! Steve Santee!"

"Hello, Burl," Steve said.

Talley did not offer his hand. He cleared his throat and said, "I believe it might be cooler in the other car, Eileen. Perhaps——"

"Steve and I have a lot to talk about," she said. "We grew up together, you know. Some folks called him and me and Doug Whipple the three little devils. Others had still stronger names for us."

Talley forced a strained smile. "Is that a fact? Perhaps you and I can talk later, my dear."

He shook hands with Amos Whipple, who shrugged helplessly. Talley gave Steve a concerned, measuring look, then walked on out of the car and into the other coach.

Steve did not speak for a time. "Burl Talley thinks you are not in very good company," he finally said.

"Does he?"

"You value his opinion, I take it?"

She turned a cool, slanting inspection upon him. "Why do you ask?"

"You're good at ducking straight answers," he said. "You like him, don't you?"

She frowned a little over that question as though it was a matter that must be examined. "I know of no reason why I should not," she said. "Burl's solid, substantial. And he doesn't try to pry into my private thoughts."

23

"I'll change the subject," Steve said. "I can see that your temper is beginning to simmer up. Next thing I know you'll be kicking me on the shins to put me in my place. Is that big rainbow lunker still in Black Rock pool, waiting for me to drift a bucktail fly into the riffle back of that boulder in the middle of the river where he hangs out?"

"He's still there," she said. "Along with a couple of his brothers who've grown up. I've saved them for you. I haven't fished Black Rock since—well, since you went away. I'm running Antler, now that I've grown up. Shorty Barnes is really the one who still does the running, but I'm learning. Between the two of us, Antler is doing well. The basin's luck changed the past few seasons. Mild winters, healthy calf crops, and plenty of grass. I've got nearly six thousand dollars coming out of the beef pool. I'm a full-fledged member of the Stock Association now. that's why I went along on this trip."

"How's Doug?" Steve asked. "Is he still rolling his spurs high, wide, and noisy, and kissing all the girls?"

Eileen hesitated a moment. "He's still trying to kiss all the girls at least," she finally said.

Steve believed he knew the reason for that pause. Amos Whipple had always hoped that his son and Eileen would marry. In fact nearly everyone in the Powderhorn had taken it for granted that she would wed Doug Whipple—provided she didn't marry Steve Santee. They had been so young that marriage was a subject that only elderly people thought about or talked about. Such a matter had been fantastic to them . . . then.

All three of them had been born in the basin. Steve and Doug Whipple had attended the Spanish Flat schoolhouse together and had hunted and fished and played and squabbled side by side.

Eileen had made herself an insistent participant in their activities in spite of the lofty scorn with which they looked down upon her from their more advanced masculine years.

It had been one of their responsibilities to see that she got safely to school and back each day on the ancient, plodding saddle stock that all three of them were compelled to ride for the sake of her tender years.

That had been very humiliating to Steve and Doug, and had brought down on them the derision of more fortunate ranch youths who were permitted to ride spirited horseflesh. Many times they had stood back to back against odds, defending their honor with their fists. And Eileen had joined with them frequently, fighting like a wildcat against their opponents.

Beyond that, Steve and Doug Whipple, when away from the dampening influence of a girl's presence, had been reckless, hell-for-leather striplings who were the prank-playing terrors of the range.

It was Steve who had been the balance wheel, the one who had kept the mischief-making within the bounds of boyish high spirits. For, in Doug, there had been a moody, heedless thirst for excitement and high experience and a disregard for the rights of others.

Doug and his father had always been at odds, and he had felt the iron hand of Amos Whipple's unswerving discipline many times. This had driven them farther apart until Doug, when he was nearing manhood, had left Center Fire, vowing that he would never again bow to his father's will.

Steve and Doug had also drifted apart as they reached maturity. More and more they lacked mutual interest. Doug began putting in his time traveling with flashy, hard-drinking cowboys.

But the affection that had been welded between them in boyhood was as strong as ever. Steve believed he knew more about Doug Whipple, and understood him better, than any man living. He knew Doug's weaknesses and irresponsibility and knew his strength. On one occasion Doug had saved his life.

"If Doug's gone and caught that big walloper at Black Rock I'll wring his neck," he said. "He knows that's my fish. He's got his own fishing hole just above that spot."

"I'm afraid the only fishing Doug does nowdays," Eileen said reluctantly, "is from a whiskey bottle."

"So that's how it is?" Steve said.

"He and Uncle Amos never came to an understanding," she said. "They're farther apart than ever. Doug doesn't seem to have any purpose in life, unless you call drinking and having a wild time a purpose. Maybe you can talk to him."

"I never was able to do much with him in the past," Steve shrugged.

"If you can't, then no one can," she said. "Doug thinks a lot of you, Steve. He talks about you every time we meet."

"What's he doing, outside of the things you mentioned?"

"He rides for one outfit or another," Eileen said. "He

worked roundup for Burl Talley at Rafter O, and gambled the money away in one night, so I was told. Maybe you can talk him into going back to where he belongs. To Center Fire with his father and mother. Julia Whipple is heartbroken over losing her son this way."

"I doubt that either Doug or Amos Whipple would appreciate my interfering," Steve said. "Both of them have minds of their own in matters concerning themselves."

The oil lamps were lighted in the coaches. Dusk deepened, and the train climbed from sagebrush into higher country of scrub cedar. And still higher into timber. The clean aroma of pines and firs came on the breeze which turned cool and penetrating.

Presently the train pulled into the siding at Three Forks to lay over for the passage of the southbound train out of Bugle. The stopping point was a dark, deserted flag station which had only the body of a converted box car as a depot. From this point Steve's and Eileen's ranches on Canteen Creek were less than ten miles away to the northwest of the railroad route, while Bugle itself was still a dozen miles farther up the basin.

Burl Talley appeared. "How about a little exercise, Eileen?" he said. "We'll probably be hung up here awhile. Might as well get out and stroll a little."

She arose. "Of course."

Talley said evenly, "Will you join us, Santee?"

"Thanks," Steve said. "Maybe later." He was surprised that Talley had treated him with that courtesy.

The majority of the passengers alighted also. Steve followed them. He rolled a smoke and stood in darkness near the coaches. Eileen and Talley walked past on the clay platform. She was resting a hand on Talley's arm. Steve heard her laugh, enjoying some remark he had made.

Louie Latzo and his companions also moved past. They had retrieved their six-shooters. Latzo gave Steve a gray and promising look.

The stop ended and the strollers filed aboard. The passengers were impatient now to reach Bugle after their long day's ride. The bottles were empty and they were hungry. They settled down for another siege of boredom.

Eileen again seated herself beside Steve, taking the place nearest the window. Burl Talley frowned, not at all pleased, and was forced to join Amos Whipple in the seat ahead.

26

Eileen leaned her head against the worn back of the plush seat and said, "I'm drowsy."

The train lurched into motion, crawling out of the siding, and the engine labored for traction on a slight upgrade.

Full darkness had fallen. Steve watched flickering glow from the firebox play against the timber and boulders along the right of way as the fireman fed fuel beneath the boiler.

The throb of the smokestack began to quicken and steady as the train gained momentum. Abruptly this broke off completely. The cars slowed and came to a jarring stop.

The majority of the passengers were dozing. Some muttered querulous complaints at this new delay. A few peered impatiently out, but when their eyes met only the blank wall of darkness they settled back apathetically.

Tim Foley, the rawboned, brick-topped conductor, went hurrying ahead through the car, scowling in perplexity. The stolid inertia of a train halted in the middle of nowhere bore down.

Steve sat staring past the dozing Eileen out into the darkness, not seeing the blackness, not seeing anything, for his thoughts were on what lay ahead of him when he arrived at Bugle.

A shape, dimly reached by the bands of lamplight from the coach windows moved across his line of vision. Preoccupied, his mind remotely noted the fact that it was a person on foot, walking alongside the train.

He was struck by the impression of something unusual in the shape of that figure, and he leaned forward across Eileen to peer from the window. His movement aroused her and she opened her eyes and turned to see what had attracted his interest.

At that moment the door of the firebox was opened again. For a few seconds the landscape was bathed in crimson light. Then the lightning-like flicker was shut off.

Steve sat motionless. Eileen uttered a tiny sound. In that brief play of firelight they had found themselves gazing at not one but two figures alongside the train. They were no more than a dozen yards away, moving parallel with the coaches in the direction of the engine ahead.

The picture remained clear in Steve's mind. He wondered if it had been imagination. His gaze jerked to Eileen and he saw that it was not, for he understood that she had seen the same thing.

27

Those two figures out there could have been something from a dream. Or a nightmare. One, at least, had been something hard to believe. A yellow slicker, and cheap white canvas gloves. A gray, shapeless mass for a head. And no face.

Steve knew that what he had seen was a masked man—a man who had a canvas bag, with eyeholes, pulled over his head and shoulders. His gloved hands had carried a sawed-off shotgun, and around his waist had been two holstered pistols and a belt of cartridges.

The other intruder had been nearer the coach. He was taller than the first, wider of shoulders and with the carriage of a younger man. He also had been muffled in a slicker and cotton gloves, and had carried a rifle and a brace of pistols.

But, a moment before the firebox had opened, this one had evidently walked into the entanglement of a half-dead scrub cedar and one of the dead snags had caught the canvas hood and had lifted it from his head. The man was in the act of frantically trying to readjust it when the firelight had revealed him.

Both Steve and Eileen had only the briefest glimpse of his features, and that had been only a profile view. He was a good-looking man of about Steve's own age and with thick, fair hair.

The blackness held. Steve saw the wide, horrified disbelief commence in Eileen, and grow. They sat looking at each other. Neither wanted to speak.

The remainder of the passengers still drowsed. Evidently what Steve and Eileen had seen had escaped the notice of the others.

Guns began exploding ahead! Steve now saw the two masked men once more, outlined against the flashes of powder flame which seemed to be originating near the engine. The taller one had drawn the concealing hood over his head. He and his companion began shooting into the air over the tops of the coaches.

"Stay where you are an' you won't git hurt!" a shrill, disguised voice shouted.

Chapter
Four

The engine stack broke into thundering life. Steve could hear the drive wheels spinning, as though an inexperienced hand was at the throttle. Steam roared.

The passengers, aroused from their lethargy, were still blinking confusedly, unable to rationalize events.

Someone lifted his voice. "Lord a'mighty! It's a stick-up, as shore as little apples. I was in the one near Rock Springs last spring. They're holdin' up the express car!"

Amos Whipple lurched to his feet. "The express car? Our beef money! Our money! That's what they're after!"

That started a stampede for the doors. But the first man to reach the outer platform recoiled, for bullets were sweeping along the sides of the coaches, laying a grim deadline.

The disguised voice arose again. "Stay inside, or you'll stop some lead, you fools! This is none of your affair. We won't bother you."

The aisle was blocked by frantic cattlemen. The grating of a released coupling pin came and the coaches lurched slightly, then became motionless again.

"Damn them, they've cut off the express car!" Amos Whipple bellowed. "Stop them! Get out of my way!"

"Easy!" a man on the platform protested. "We'll get killed if we go out there."

Another voice in the car was raised. "Use your heads, men! After all, this is the express company's responsibility. It's their problem. They'll have to pay off. Why risk your lives unnecessarily?"

Steve could not be sure, but he believed that voice belonged to Burl Talley. Evidently it seemed like logic to some of the less reckless men, and the surge for the doors lost enthusiasm.

But Amos Whipple was in no mood to listen. He was blocked in the jammed aisle. He stood frothing and shouting for a clear path. His words were almost unintelligible. His helplessness seemed to drive him into a frenzy.

He turned and backed into the space between seats and turned to the window as though of a mind to attempt to descend by that route from the car. Then he glimpsed the two masked men outside. They had now broken into a run and were on their way forward, evidently to board the engine or the express car, which was pulling away.

Amos Whipple was armed. He snatched out his six-shooter and leveled it. The taller of the two train bandits was an easy target through the open window and his back was to the cattleman.

Steve leaned over the seat and jostled Amos's elbow an instant before the hammer fell. The gun exploded, but the bullet went wild. Before Whipple could recover his balance to fire again, his quarry had vanished out of range.

Amos whirled and glared. When he realized that it was Steve who had interfered, he at first turned white with fury, then crimson. For the space of a heartbeat Steve expected to be shot down by the infuriated man.

Eileen tried to move in front of him, but Steve would not permit that. "It was an accident, Uncle Amos!" she exclaimed. "Steve started to crowd past me and through the window to fight them. He bumped your arm."

Amos knew it could not have happened that way. He started to say something to Eileen, then decided against it.

A final volley of shots crashed along the cars. The throb of the engine stack increased. This settled to a steady sound, which began to recede ahead.

"They're gittin' away!" a man said hoarsely. "They're steamin' away with the express car, just like they did twice before. It must be the same bunch."

Amos Whipple glared at Steve, his eyes blazing. "You—you——!" he said. He raised his six-shooter.

He would have fired, but Eileen frantically pushed the gun down.

Burl Talley came fighting his way through the throng, attracted by the commotion. "What's wrong?" he exclaimed. "Amos! Good Lord! Quit it! What's happened?"

Amos Whipple, with an effort, gained control of his rage. He lowered the gun and finally holstered it. He gazed at Steve for a moment or two longer, his eyes bleak and condemning.

He turned away without answering Talley. Together they shouldered their way down the aisle, following the wild-eyed, confused men of the Pool, who were now spilling from the coaches onto the dark right of way.

There they milled around, stumbling into the ditches and over crossties. Tim Foley, so excited his voice sounded like a child's tin whistle, kept chattering, "What are we goin' to do, me boys? 'Tis a terrible thing that's happened this night to Conductor Tim Foley's train. Now, what are we goin' to do?"

Steve remained sitting in the coach. He knew it was a waste of energy to do anything else. Afoot, it was hopeless to think of attempting pursuit of the outlaws.

Eileen sat with him. Suddenly she uttered a little startled sound. "Your money! It—it was in the express car too!"

"It's gone," he said. "Along with your beef money. But, as someone said, the express company will make it good. That's the least of my worries."

"Yes," she said. "I know what you mean. I—I wish we hadn't been looking in a certain direction at a certain time."

They dropped that subject and sat without speaking. Steve was sure Amos Whipple believed he had been an accomplice in the holdup and a member of the outlaw band.

After some time the slam of a dynamite explosion drifted from far away. The sound rolled across the basin to the Powderhorns and returned after a surprising interval as a faint rumble.

"This'll cost Northern Express a pretty penny," a rancher said. "There was plenty more'n our eighty thousand dollars in that car. I seen 'em load a bank box aboard at Cheyenne, an' they put another treasure box into the car at Junction Bend."

"It might not cost Northern Express anything," Burl Talley said.

A dozen voices spoke at once. "What's that? What do you mean, Burl?"

"I hope I'm wrong," Talley said reluctantly. "But I'm wondering if Northern Express can pay off."

Utter silence came for an instant that was broken by a wild babble of excited questions.

Talley finally could make himself heard again. "I happen to know that Northern Express had trouble making good on the last holdup," he said. "It's a small company, you know, and owned by a few private individuals. It's not backed by any of the big express companies."

"Do you realize what you're sayin', Burl?" Amos Whipple shouted.

"Only too well," Talley said. "And I hope I'm dead wrong."

"Why—why I couldn't stand to lose that beef money," a cattleman said. "Nor could a lot of the other boys. It's set us back to where we was when Buck Santee robbed us. Some of us will go under."

"I'm in the same boat with you," Talley said. "I have some money in the beef pool too. But I thought it best that we face the truth. You men all seem to be so sure this robbery didn't mean a thing to you. Maybe you'll get off your hip pockets now and try to find these robbers."

Steve looked at Eileen. "Looks like the Pool will have to wait awhile after all before I can pay back that ten thousand dollars."

The cattlemen were a frenzied, howling mass, shouting threats and recriminations. One shook a fist in Amos Whipple's face. "You was the one that talked us into sendin' the money in the express car!" he frothed. "You must have knowed Northern Express was shaky. You're one of the big augurs in the basin."

"How would I know it?" Amos said bitterly. "Don't you go blamin' me. I figured the money'd be safer in an express safe than among a pack o' whiskey-soaked sots like you cowmen. They'd have taken it from you whether it was here or there. I didn't see any of you wantin' to stand up ag'in them. I'll smash in the mouth of the first man who says another word ag'in me."

Then he added hoarsely. "We'll get that money back whether the express company makes good or not. I promise you that. An' I'll hang these outlaws higher'n Haman. That's another promise you can bank on."

"Do you figger you're smarter'n the law?" a rancher demanded. "This is the third train that's been robbed an' we all know danged well there must be express detectives workin' in this country since the first job. But nobody's catched anyone, has they? Ain't seen hide nor hair of these slick cusses. An' now here's a new stick-up pulled right under their noses. Are you sharper'n the Pinkertons an' federal marshals?"

"Smart enough not to bray back when a jackass brays at me," Amos snorted. "I know what I know, but I'll only tell it

32

at the right time an' place. An' that won't be in any court-room where slick lawyers throw snakey loops. It'll be in front of the kind of a jury whose only verdicts will be exoneration or the hang-rope."

An uneasy silence came. "That's mighty strong talk, Amos," Burl Talley said.

Amos Whipple had voiced the Vigilante creed, a creed that had been invoked in violent and sanguine cleanups of other frontier towns and other ranges.

"Strong talk's what's needed," Amos snapped. "We all know what's been happenin' in Bugle, but we closed our eyes to it because we wasn't hit directly. Outlaws, scoundrels, fancy women, and all the other scum of the West have come since the mines hit it rich. Shootin's, robberies, an' general all-around cussedness."

"Bill Rawls ought to be able——"

"Bill Rawls is a good, honest sheriff an' has done his best," Amos said. "So has the town marshal, but the job is too big for 'em. That's plain enough now. We all know in our hearts that this gang of train robbers likely has their nest right near Bugle, but because it wasn't our own ox that was gored we didn't give a hoot. Now it's our pocketbooks that stand to be flattened just when we was seein' our way out of the woods for keeps. We got hit by lightnin'. But there's ways of strikin' back. An' ways of gittin' our money back."

"How?" men shouted eagerly.

"I'll tell that too, at the right time an' the right place that I mentioned," Amos said.

Steve was aware that Eileen had moved closer to him as they listened. She was pale, her eyes dark with the weight of her knowledge. She suddenly seemed to reach a decision. She started to arise. Steve caught her arm, halting her.

"You can't do it," he said. "We can't do it."

"He's making Vigilante talk," she said. "He means it. You know how that works. A summary court under a hang-tree where they have you convicted before you can say a word. They strike fast and don't listen to reason. They're as likely to hang an innocent man as a guilty one."

"You can't do what you have in mind," he said.

She sank back into the seat. They were silent for a time. She looked at him. She was shaking now. "You know you should never have stopped me," she said. "Don't you?"

He didn't answer. They were thinking of the likeable comrade of their childhood who had shared their joys and their sorrows. Doug Whipple.

For the face of the train bandit which they had glimpsed during the holdup was the face of that same person.

Steve, in jostling Amos Whipple's gun arm had saved the Center Fire owner from the horror of killing his own son.

"Whatever are we going to do?" Eileen asked.

"Forget what you saw," he said.

"Will you forget also?"

He smiled wryly. "That might be a little difficult. From what was said there's a lot more than the Pool's eighty thousand dollars and my thirteen thousand involved. And I'm suspected in having had a hand in stealing it. However, you're not to get mixed up in this, young lady. You never saw a thing tonight."

There was a look in her face and a little set to her mouth that brought back memories of other days when he and Doug had tried determinedly to bar her from their more reckless ventures. "Go to Antler and stay there," he said.

Her expression did not change. "Damn it!" he said. "You look just like you used to when Doug and I would try to shake you off when we wanted to go somewhere without having a brat like you tagging along."

"Go to your own ranch and hole up," she said tartly. "And I will do as I please."

"Just as you've always done," he said.

"You can't boss me around, Steve Santee. I'm not a child anymore."

"Nobody could tell you what to do even when you were a child. You always were as onery as a bogged cow."

Burl Talley entered the car and came striding up. "A hell of a mess, Eileen," he said. "Whoever pulled this holdup had it well planned. My guess is that one or two of them slipped aboard the engine during the stop at Three Forks. The others waited here. All of them pulled out with the engine and the express car, and we can't do a thing about it until they begin to worry about us at Bugle and send out to investigate. Tim Foley says the telegraph line has been short-circuited."

She arose and walked with Talley out of the car. She looked back at Steve and nodded. "Just as I've always done," she said.

Chapter
Five

It was nearly midnight before an engine arrived from Bugle, bringing Sheriff Bill Rawls and half a dozen possemen, along with a carload of saddle horses.

The details of the holdup began to fall into place. The engineer and fireman had been slugged by masked men who evidently had boarded the engine at Three Forks, as Burl Talley had surmised. The trainmen had been blindfolded and tied hand and foot.

After detaching the express car from the train the outlaws had drawn it a mile away and then had given the messenger his choice of surrendering or being blown sky high with dynamite. The leader of the outlaws had used the same disguised voice they all had heard.

The messenger had preferred to stay alive. He had obeyed orders to alight from the car, and in the darkness had scarcely even glimpsed his captors. He had been bound and gagged and he and the train crew had been left lying alongside the right of way at the point where they were sighted and picked up by the sheriff aboard the rescue train later on.

The outlaws had steamed away with the express car. Some five miles farther on they had dynamited the safe and looted it. They had then abandoned the engine and car, but had left the throttle open on the locomotive. It had been found, along with the shattered car, only a mile from Bugle, steam down and the boiler fires nearly out.

Steve heard Bill Rawls say that it was believed there had been around one hundred and thirty thousand dollars, all told, in the express safe. It was one of the richest hauls in the history of train robbery.

"The worst of it," Rawls said, "is that nobody is likely to find out just where they left the train with the money. We know where they blew the safe. There was wreckage around. But they probably stayed with the engine and got off somewhere between that point and Bugle. That's ten miles."

also. That means had a name. The name was Doug Whipple.

That brought back the memory of a day when he had dangled, terrified, from a ledge a hundred feet above a rapids on the Powderhorn River with Doug clinging to his wrists.

They had been fourteen years of age at the time and he had been demonstrating his daredeviltry by walking the lip of the sloping ledge above the rapids. He had slipped. Only Doug's swiftness in getting within reaching distance had saved him from falling at once to his death.

He remembered the way Doug's feet had slid a fraction of an inch at a time toward the rim of the ledge, with the loose, decomposing granite giving way little by little. He remembered the look in Doug's eyes. Doug had made up his mind to hang on and go over to death with him if it came to that rather than release his grip.

Then Doug's toes had found firm support on a solid crevice. That had been enough. With a last surge of their combined strength Steve had clawed his way back to safety.

Even after the years Steve found himself sweating a little and breathing hard as he lived over that moment. He owed his life to the man he had seen a few hours earlier wearing an outlaw's mask. Even above that he and Doug Whipple had been comrades. Friends. As boys they had taken a blood oath as brothers.

He watched the lights of Bugle rise out of the timber in the distance as the train rumbled over the switch frogs into the station.

The town was bigger. It was three in the morning and in the old days Bugle would have been abed and dark long since. Now lights still glittered in gambling houses and dancehalls that had sprung up for several blocks from the depot on Bozeman Street. Front Street, still a single-sided thoroughfare facing the railroad tracks, which had been given over in the past to shacks and mule yards, was now occupied by dimly-lit honky-tonks, gambling houses and brothels.

Steve alighted. When he walked into Bozeman Street he found scarcely a familiar landmark. The business district had been pushed back half a dozen blocks from the depot and this section was crowded with higher-class gambling houses and saloons than the type on Front Street. The sedate part of town was dark now and peaceful. Here and there

"It's the same stunt they pulled on the other two jobs," Burl Talley said.

"They figured out a way to light where they won't leave any trail," Rawls said. "Come daybreak we'll go over that stretch of track 'til our eyes bulge, an' we won't see even a footprint to tell us anything."

Ashen-faced cattlemen who faced a bleak winter now that they had lost their season's profits remained at the scene to join the posses when daylight came. The majority of the passengers rode on into Bugle aboard the coaches.

Steve rode with them. He had stayed in the background during the noisy and sometimes dangerous hours while awaiting the sheriff. At times he had been aware that the suspicion and anger his presence aroused had neared the explosive point.

Amos Whipple also was with the townbound group. He had been the heaviest loser in the robbery, for his Center Fire beef had accounted for nearly a third of the eighty thousand dollars in the Pool's beef money.

He had been silent since making the threat of Vigilante vengeance. He was not an obtuse man, and he was so careful to act as though he had lost interest in Steve that it was evident the opposite was true.

Eileen sat with Burl Talley across the aisle, for Louie Latzo and his pals had shifted to the other coach. She was wan and tired now, drained by the stress of the holdup and the sleepless night, and burdened by the knowledge that she and Steve shared.

Steve was positive that only he and Eileen had been gazing out of the car at the moment Doug Whipple had been surprised by the fire glow with his mask removed.

She finally dozed off. Talley drew her head over upon his shoulder. She aroused, looked up at him speculatively for a moment. She pulled away then. But she smiled at him. However, after that she remained awake.

Steve felt the strain also. The loss of the money seemed unimportant to him. This, he candidly admitted, was because he had looked upon himself only as its custodian and not its owner.

The gold was only incidental. A factor of far greater value was involved. The fact was that he possessed the means of recovering not only his own fund, but the Pool's money

36

the brighter glow of late eating places and hotels offered signs of life.

The gay district nearer at hand was still doing business. There was noisy drunken revelry in a dancehall. Somewhere on Front Street arose the pounding of feet and shouting and screaming as a fight broke out.

Steve had not anticipated changes as drastic as this. He stood, his war sack over his shoulder, gazing perplexed, seeking some link with the past. Then he sighted the swinging, lighted sign marking Jeb Keene's white-painted hostelry, the Pioneer House. It was several blocks away.

Burl Talley had appropriated the only hansom cab available at the depot and was helping Eileen aboard with her luggage. Amos Whipple joined them, and the driver stirred the horse into action. The equipage went clattering away, heading for the Pioneer House.

The remainder of the train arrivals were scattering, the majority of them streaming toward the nearest saloon to drink and talk over the robbery.

Steve's throat was powder dry. He stopped at the last open bar, which was nearly deserted, and drank beer with the deep gratitude of a thirsty man.

He walked onward past the office of Burl Talley's lumberyard toward the Pioneer House up the street. The hotel occupied the corner of an intersection. Light spilled onto the sidewalk from the lamp over the clerk's desk in the lobby.

As he neared the place Burl Talley emerged alone, boarded the hansom, and the driver swung the vehicle around in the street and headed for the lumber office. There Talley had always maintained living quarters.

Steve crossed the street and stepped on the sidewalk in front of the Pioneer House.

A voice said, "Get him!" Three men came at him, rising from the shadows at the corner of the building where they had been crouching in wait.

He saw the sideburned Louie Latzo leaping at him, teeth ashine in a grin of anticipation. He knew then that the other two must be the hard-cased pair of the train journey, Al Painter and Chick Varney.

He lurched aside, sending the war sack whirling at Latzo's legs. That upset the man, tripping him so that he came plunging forward into the half-raised uppercut that Steve had started. He felt his knuckles loosen teeth.

Then Al Painter's bulk was on his back, knees hammering into him. Varney came in, smashing at his face with both fists while Painter tried to pin down his arms.

He reeled backwards and rammed Painter against the wall of the building. He dove forward in a somersault, grasping the man's arms and carrying him whirling with him. Painter crashed into the street with a grunting, breath-taking jar.

Steve came to his feet and was met by a smash to the face by Varney. At the same time Louie Latzo loomed over him, swinging the muzzle of a six-shooter. Steve partly evaded the gun, but the blow glanced off the point of his shoulder and he felt the shock drive down the nerves of his left arm, leaving it momentarily numb.

Varney was flailing at him and Al Painter, shaken, but more savage than ever was coming back into the fight against him.

He couldn't hold them off much longer. He wanted to damage Latzo above all, before he went under. He weaved, braced himself, found his opening and drove a sledging smash into the man's face. Latzo reeled back, blood spurting.

Steve paid for that. Both Painter and Varney were hammering blows to his face and body. He fought, but his strength was draining rapidly, for he had expended it with blast furnace fury during these hectic moments. He began to go down and he knew they would beat and kick him to pulp once they had him beneath their boots.

Help arrived. Al Painter was snatched away from him. He heard the thud of a fist and Painter went staggering. The arrival followed his target into the doorlight from the hotel.

It was Doug Whipple. He was hatless and wore a natty double-breasted shirt with pearl buttons. He had on foxed saddle breeches and new cowboots. His fair hair was waving like a banner and there was delight in his face as he moved in on Al Painter, his fists darting.

"Damn you, Al!" he said. "Three of you on Steve!"

Painter was far from done for. "Why are you dealin' yourself in on this, Whipple?" he panted.

Chick Varney left Steve, believing he was no longer a problem and lunged toward Doug. A girl darted down the steps from the door of the hotel. "Oh, no, you don't!" Eileen's voice sounded.

She was swinging the heavy ledger which she had seized from the clerk's desk. That ledger carried names of guests dating back for forty years. It came crashing down on Chick Varney's head with the sound of a mallet on a stake.

Varney stood an instant, his knees unsteady. He sat down carefully, as though not sure of his plans. Then he keeled over.

Steve arose in time to intercept Louie Latzo, who had decided to come back into the fight and was about to leap on Doug Whipple's back. He drove a punch to Louie's body. The man whirled, went staggering aside, and fell into the street on his face.

Al Painter was backing away from Doug. No guns had been drawn during the fight, but that thought was in Painter's mind now. Steve, realizing his intention, kept driving ahead, carried by the momentum of the finishing blow he had dealt Latzo. He crashed into Painter, pitching him backwards to the sidewalk. As they fell he smashed an elbow into the man's throat.

That took the last of the fight out of Al Painter. He lay gagging and wheezing.

Steve dragged himself to his feet. He wasn't in much better shape than Painter. He looked at Doug Whipple. "She always did insist on horning in on our fun," he said. "It's just like old times."

He and Doug stood grinning foolishly at each other. Steve became aware of blood dripping from his chin. A sleeve of his coat was torn and he was matted with gore and dust. Perspiration now began to pour from him. But Doug seemed unmarked and unruffled.

Eileen dropped the bulky ledger and sat down shakily on the steps. Evidently she had been preparing for bed when the sound of the brawl had brought her from her room, for she had loosened her hair, and it hung down in a coppery cascade over her shoulders.

"I—I didn't k—kill that man, did I?" she chattered.

"Deader than a tombstone," Steve said. "You'll likely get hung for it."

"I always said she'd come to a bad end," Doug said.

"I didn't mean to hit him that hard," Eileen wailed.

Chick Varney was far from dead. He stirred and lifted himself dazedly to a sitting position.

"The stampede went right over you," Doug told him.

Louie Latzo pulled himself to hands and knees and crawled to safer distance. He got to his feet and began uttering profanity and threats.

Painter also lurched to his feet. "Shut up!" he snarled at Latzo. "If you'd fight as well with your fists as your mouth . . ."

Painter then looked at Doug and said, "You do the damnedest things, Whipple."

"I think so myself," Doug said.

Painter and Varney walked shakily away, nursing their injuries. Louie Latzo followed them, a hand to his broken, bleeding nose.

Amos Whipple came charging from the hotel. He was in his undershirt, his suspenders flapping. Other guests were arriving also. Heads had appeared at doors and windows.

Amos pulled up. He gave Steve a glare, then wheeled on his son. "You?" he said. "I might have known you'd be mixed up in any cheap street brawl that took place."

He glowered at Eileen. "And what are you doing here, young lady?"

"The trouble started right beneath my window," she said. "So I came down to see what was going on."

"An' she joined in the ruckus," said Jeb Keene, the hotel owner. "She knocked out one of 'em with my register." Jeb added proudly, "That ain't the fust time thet book's been used to whack somebody over the haid. Fact is, I've slammed down a few with it myself. But I don't ever recollect that a lady ever swung it in a brawl before."

He gazed admiringly at Eileen. "I'll make a note of it in the page for special events," he said.

"Thank you," Eileen said. "I have always wanted to do something that would go down in history."

Amos Whipple was in no mood for light talk. "Go to your room," he said grimly. "You've made enough of a spectacle of yourself for one night. If your dad and your mother were alive how would they feel about you getting mixed up in a thing like this?"

Burl Talley arrived. "Why, Eileen!" he exclaimed. "What's happened?"

"It seems like we were in a fight," Eileen said.

She moved close to Steve and peered at his face. "You look very much like it," she said. "Come inside where I can take a better view of the damage. You seem to have been hit by several things much more bruising than a book. That eye is a dandy, and you're bleeding nicely from that gash on your jaw, not to mention other items."

She added seriously, "You may have some broken bones."

Amos Whipple started to protest, but she grasped Steve's arm and tried to steer him toward the door of the hotel. Steve resisted. "I'll go to a saloon and——" he began.

"And be beat up again by some of Latzo's hoodlums," she said.

She led him into the hotel and on through the dark dining room into the kitchen. "Light a lamp and fetch water and towels, court plaster and liniment and alum and whatever else you have in stock," she ordered.

Jeb Keene hurried to obey. Steve suffered her to use warm water on his injuries. She applied liniment and alum and winced with him when he grimaced at the sting. She used a strip of court plaster on his jaw.

Doug sat by, smoking a cigarette and watching. Burl Talley was the only other bystander. He remained in the background, waiting patiently for Eileen, who was being helped in her task by Jeb Keene. Amos Whipple had not followed them.

She finished with Steve. "You'll have a scar on that jawbone of yours, I'm afraid," she said. "But you escaped better than I had expected. Your beauty won't be too badly blemished."

She walked to Doug and inspected him carefully. "They barely mussed your hair," she said. "You always were one to come out of trouble looking like you'd been to a pink tea. Please tell me the secret. I always get hot and wildlooking, and the freckles pop out something awful."

"I waited until Steve had 'em licked, an' then came in with bugles blowing," Doug said.

She lifted his hands and peered. "At least you bear the marks of honorable combat," she said. "You've got some barked knuckles and one is puffing. You should have rammed this into cold water before this. Why didn't you say something about it?"

"Quit poking it!" Doug protested. "Ouch! Lord a'mighty,

Eileen! Take it easy. Lucky for me it's not my roping hand."

"Or your poker or drinking hand," Eileen said. "Here! Put it in this water. Hold it there until I say to take it out."

Doug looked at Steve. "If I resisted she'd probably whack me with the ledger an' stretch me out like a calf at brandin'," he said.

Chapter
Six

Any impression that three years had left Doug untouched faded under the glare of the lamplight. His features had thickened a trifle and there was an opaque, lifeless quality in his eyes, as though he had walled in his thoughts.

He was still handsome. His lips were perhaps thinner and tighter and there was the slight blurring of his features —the mark of hard living, hard drinking, and of harsh and tense emotions beneath the surface.

Steve searched his mind for something casual to say, something that would not betray the fact that he knew that Doug, who had saved his life in the past and had within the last few minutes joined in to save him from being beaten, perhaps to death, had also, on this same night, helped hold up a train and rob him and other men of the Powderhorn. Above all, he had robbed his own father.

It did not seem possible that the slicker-clad outlaw whose face he had glimpsed could be the same Doug Whipple who stood so obedient to Eileen's orders, grinning down at her fondly. It was evident that all the recollections of the joyful days of their childhood were in his mind, as they had been in Steve's.

But he was one and the same man. It could not have been an error of resemblance. Eileen had seen him also, and Steve knew she was keeping her eyes away from him now as she worked on his damaged hands, because in her, no doubt, was the same incredulity that was in him. She did not want Doug to suspect her dark bewilderment.

Doug's presence in Bugle meant that he had come directly to town after the robbery. That indicated that his companions also were here in Bugle, mingling with the townfolk as honest citizens.

Steve became aware that Doug was watching him. Doug's expression had shifted a trifle as though a disturbing thought had crossed his mind. He swung his glance away. He said to Eileen, "The hand feels much better. It's surprising what a little liniment and a lot of sympathy does for a man."

Mart Lowery, town marshal of Bugle, came hurrying into the kitchen, followed by several men who seemed to be there out of mere curiosity. One of these bystanders was blocky-shouldered and square-faced, with a clipped graying mustache. He wore a commonplace dark serge suit, and high-heeled cowboots and a stiff-brimmed, dented range hat.

Mart Lowery had worn the shield of the law for years. He was past sixty now, frosted at the temples, and more of a mind to live out his full span of life rather than delve deep for trouble. There was a wariness and also distaste in the inspection he gave Steve. Lean and big-boned, he had a large nose and a drooping mustache.

He spoke respectfully to Talley. "Howdy, Burl."

He touched his hat to Eileen. "Surprised to see you here, Miss Maddox," he said.

His greeting to Doug Whipple was strictly neutral. "How did you get mixed up in this, Doug?" he asked.

"It looked a little one-sided," Doug said.

"That depends," Lowery said.

Steve knew then that the marshal had been coached and primed by Amos Whipple. He surmised that Amos had hinted that he believed Steve was implicated in the train holdup or at least had guilty knowledge as to the perpetrators.

"What started it, Santee?" Mart Lowery asked without preliminary. He had been friendly with Steve's father in the days when Buck Santee was chairman of the Powderhorn Pool and therefore a man to be reckoned with. But he was hostile now.

"An antelope with a broken leg," Steve said.

Lowery frowned. "Let's pass up the small talk an' get down to cases. I understand you an' Louie had trouble on the train. He's got a broken nose an' maybe a busted jaw. Not that I grieve none for him. Nor for Al Painter or Chick Varney. They're mussed up considerable also. They're down

44

at Doc Skelley's office gettin' patched up. I asked you what started it?"

"I've already told you," Steve said.

Eileen spoke. "Latzo took some shots at——"

"I'll do my own talking," Steve said to her. And to the marshal, "What difference does it make what started it? It started. That's all."

"Not much difference, I reckon," Lowery said. "But I'm a lot more interested in how it's likely to end. Louie has a brother who don't like to see his kinfolk pushed around. Nick Latzo plays rough. I'm warnin' you, Santee, not to bring your feuds into Bugle—particularly here in the respectable part of town. I don't want any gunplay either here or down along the tracks. A train stick-up an' a street fight the first night you hit town ought to be about enough."

"Meaning that you think I had something to do with the train robbery?" Steve asked.

"I didn't say that," Lowery protested hastily. "All I'm sayin' is that I'm here to keep the peace in Bugle. An' I don't want any grudges poppin' up."

Eileen had been listening with growing indignation. "Has it ever occurred to anyone, Mart Lowery, that we members of the Pool weren't the only losers in that holdup?" she burst out. "Steve Santee had quite a sum of his own money in that express safe also."

"Yeah?" Lowery said skeptically. "How much?"

Steve tried to halt her, but there was no silencing her. "Thirteen thousand dollars!"

Lowery started to laugh disbelievingly. That died off. Something in Steve's eyes warned him that scoffing might be dangerous.

Amos Whipple came stomping into the kitchen through a side door beyond which he had been lurking, listening to what had been said. Eileen's revelation had startled him into appearing.

"What's that?" he demanded. "What kind of nonsense is this, Santee, about you losing thirteen thousand dollars? Ridiculous!"

Doug spoke. "Some day, Dad, you're going to get your nose caught in a door, eavesdropping on people."

Amos glared at his son, then ignored him. "You don't expect us to believe a story like that, do you?" he said to Steve.

45

"I'm not interested in whether you believe it or not, Amos," Steve said.

"Eileen, did you see any of this money Santee claims he had?" Amos demanded. "With your own eyes, I mean?"

"No," she said. "Not with my own eyes. But it was there. What object would Steve have in lying?"

Amos started to blurt out an answer to that, then thought better of it. "That remains to be seen," he said.

Burl Talley moved up and laid a hand on Eileen's arm. "You must be very tired, my dear," he said. "You had better get some sleep. Tomorrow may be a long day. They'll be turning this range upside down, hunting those devils who robbed us. I'm going to join in myself, this time. I've got some of my own money at stake now. Odd how it changes a man's viewpoint when his own toes are stepped on. Up to now, like everyone else, I've let the law-officers do all the work, figuring that's what they were paid for."

He looked at Amos. "Maybe you were right, Amos, in what you said about it being high time that citizens take a hand in cleaning up the Powderhorn."

"Yes," Amos said tersely. "Yes."

Mart Lowery glanced uneasily from face to face. Once more the threat of Vigilante action had been made. And the backing of a man of Talley's prominence added great power to the blackening storm.

"Thirteen thousand dollars is quite a jag of money to lose, if the express company can't pay off," Amos said to Steve. "You seem to be takin' it right calmly."

"If I look calm then appearances are very misleading, and that's for sure," Steve said. "I earned that money with more sweat and strain than I ever thought I'd go through for any man or anything."

"If you really had any such amount, I reckon I can guess where you got the most of it about three years ago," Amos said.

Eileen uttered an outraged gasp. "That isn't fair, Uncle Amos! And it isn't true! Why, Steve intended to turn ten thousand dollars of that money over to——"

Steve halted her. "It's no use," he said.

But she rushed on. "Steve was going to give it to the Powderhorn Pool to make up for what was lost the night his father disappeared."

"What?" Amos said derisively. "You don't actually believe that do you, my dear girl?"

"Yes, I do," she said.

Amos took her arm. "It's high time you got some sleep. You better go to your room."

She sighed resignedly, realizing that debate was a waste of time. Talley followed as she let Amos lead her toward the door. He turned and spoke to Steve. "Maybe you'd like to ride posse with us tomorrow, Santee," he said.

"I doubt if I'd be welcome," Steve said.

Talley shrugged. "Perhaps you're right. Marshal, if it's in your mind to arrest Doug Whipple on charges of disturbing the peace I'll go bail and also pay fines and costs. Doug's a friend of mine." And in a burst of generosity, he added, "That goes for Santee also, as far as the fines go. After all, he and Doug may have done the town a favor by taking Louie and his pals to a cleaning."

"We'll pay for our own fun, Burl," Doug spoke sharply.

However Mart Lowery hastily disclaimed any intention of arresting anyone. He had come here at Amos Whipple's request to place the heavy frown of the law on Steve. Instead, he had found himself confronted by forces and undercurrents, the sources of which he could not imagine.

"That big lunker is still waiting at Black Rock," Eileen said, pausing at the door. "And I can still beat both of you at laying a fly over that hole where he lives."

"You have just let yourself in for a fishing trip that will humble your pride," Steve said.

She left then, with Amos and Talley. Mart Lowery also followed them out of the kitchen, and the uninvited bystanders departed too, leaving Steve and Doug alone.

"Thanks, fella," Steve said. "Thanks for helping me out. It was beginning to be a very tight fit when you showed up."

"The pleasure was all mine," Doug said.

"Was it?" Steve asked, carefully keeping his tone casual. "I had an impression, from what Al Painter said, that he and the other two might have been friends of yours."

"Acquaintances might be a better way of putting it," Doug said. "I've played poker with 'em. Any one's money is good in a poker game."

"Did you play at Nick Latze's roadhouse?"

"Where else?" Doug said. "Any particular reason for asking that question?"

"You really ought to pick better poker partners," Steve said.

"And better places in which to play, maybe?" Doug asked.

"I'll buy a drink," Steve said.

They walked out of the Pioneer House and to the bar Steve had first visited. It was ready for closing. Steve's taste was still for beer, but Doug ordered whiskey. He tossed off a drink, poured another and stood, his hat pushed back on his head, revolving the glass thoughtfully in his hand as he absently studied the contents.

"Was that straight about you having thirteen thousand dollars in that express car, Steve?" he asked abruptly.

"Yes," Steve said. "I've got a company receipt to prove it."

"Why didn't you show that receipt to Amos? He didn't believe you had any such amount of money."

"I didn't figure I owed him any explanation," Steve said. "I'll show the receipt to Bill Rawls, if he wants to see it. As sheriff, he's entitled to look at it, if he's interested in my troubles. That I doubt."

"Did you really intend to turn ten thousand over to the Pool?" Doug asked.

Steve sipped his beer. "Yes."

"You always were one hell of a person for paying off any debt you figured you owed. So was your father, from what I know of him, an' what men have told me."

"There's another debt that I haven't forgotten," Steve said. "Remember that day on the ledge above Racehorse Rapids?"

"There's no debt there, and you know it," Doug said impatiently. "You'd have done the same. You know that too."

"Maybe in the matter of the ten thousand dollars it's just pigheaded pride," Steve said. "I look at it from the viewpoint I'm sure Dad would have taken. He would have figured himself responsible and would have tried to pay it back. So I'm doing it for him so that he can sleep easy."

"You figure then that he's dead?" Doug asked.

Steve nodded. "Beyond all doubt. And I'm sure his bones are somewhere in this range, though I guess the chances are they'll never be found. I'm sure he was killed at the same time Henry Thane was murdered."

"Is that why you came back?"

"Yes. It's at least one of the reasons. I like this country.

48

I belong here and I don't want to be driven out of it. In fact I won't be driven out."

"May heaven help the guilty man if you ever catch up with him," Doug said. "You can be mighty rough, Steve. As you proved tonight. From the signs, whatever you went through while you were away didn't soften you any."

"Nor has time softened your father," Steve said. "Did you know what was meant when Burl Talley mentioned that it was time for citizens to pitch in against lawlessness in the Powderhorn?"

Doug looked at him without speaking.

"Amos is stirring up the ranchers to ride Vigilante," Steve said. "He means it. It must have been talked over by him and others before tonight. Otherwise he wouldn't have come out in the open with it."

Doug tossed off his drink. "Vigilantes!" he said. He laughed. It was dry, bleak humor. "That would be something, wouldn't it? My own father leading the stranglers."

The barkeeper was making a great ceremony of placing chairs on tables and snuffing lamps as a hint that closing time was past.

Steve and Doug walked to the street. The sedate citizens had gone back to bed and the fandango district was quieting at this late hour, although Steve saw that some of the bigger gambling houses evidently never closed their doors or dimmed their lights.

Only a night lamp now burned in the lobby of the Pioneer House a short distance away. All of the guest rooms were dark, but Steve saw a shadow at the window of one of the second-floor quarters. It was a person in a nightgown, and then he realized that it was Eileen. She was there, watching them.

He surmised she had been standing there all the time he and Doug were in the barroom, worrying about them. He knew that Doug had seen also. "She ought to be in bed," he said irritably.

"She always was like a mother hen with us two, tryin' to keep us out of trouble," Doug said. "She's afraid this isn't over yet. She knows Nick Latzo's reputation. You plowed up that leppie brother of his quite deep. Nick will go a far piece out of his way to demonstrate that it doesn't pay to push a Latzo around. Nick is harder formation than Louie. He's been spreading out. He runs the Blue Moon

49

here in town in addition to the roadhouse. That's the one with the revolving blue light on the roof down the street. He lives at the roadhouse but he's at the Blue Moon every night, dealing big poker games. I saw him there not long before you hit town and got yourself into a bushel of trouble."

"It's quite a crowded bushel," Steve said. "You're jammed into it with me."

Doug shrugged. "I didn't touch Louie. I only tussled with Al Painter. Painter and Varney don't count. Nick's got half a dozen like them hangin' around his place. They'd shoot a man in the back for a few dollars."

Steve gazed at the dark window where Eileen had been standing. It stared back vacantly. She had withdrawn. "Burl Talley seems to be doing well," he remarked.

Doug knew the reason for that change of subject. "Yeah," he said. "Burl's got the talent for making money. He's the kind that usually gets anything he goes after."

"You mean Eileen," Steve said, and there was distaste in him. "He wants to marry her. That's easy to see. But what does she think about it?"

"Who knows?" Doug said. "You better ask her."

"I have," Steve said. "I was told to mind my own business."

Doug laughed. "I can believe that. She hasn't been in the habit of talking things over with me lately either, particularly matters concerning Talley's courtship."

There was a forced lightness in him, an obvious attempt to be indifferent and neutral. Steve eyed him, trying to read his thoughts.

"I punched cattle for Burl durin' roundup," Doug said in that same casual manner. "Right now I'm loafin'."

He changed the subject. "Have you got a place to hang out tonight, Steve?"

"I'll take a room at the Pioneer," Steve said. "Tomorrow I'll hire a horse and ride out to the ranch. Eileen says the house still seems to be in fair shape."

"It is," Doug said. "I've lived there a lot, in fact. I went over to the river a couple of days ago an' sat awhile on Black Rock, recalling a lot of things. I caught me a grasshopper an' threw him in that eddy back of the big boulder out in the middle. Something that looked like the front end of a catawampus came up through the clear green water and—zowie! No more grasshopper."

"We'll try it together," Steve said. "The three of us. The day after tomorrow, if possible. I can't hold myself down much longer. I've been thinking of Black Rock ever since I went away. And of a fly rod in my hands. And man, I'd like to taste an elk steak again, thin and cooked fast and juicy. Rolled in flour and——"

"I'll be there and blast you for makin' my mouth water here at two o'clock in the mornin'," Doug said. "I haven't bagged me an elk this year."

He stood a moment thinking. "Every rancher and cowboy in the basin will be out tomorrow, tryin' to cut sign of the bunch that stuck up the train," he said. "And half the men from town. What about you, Steve?"

"You heard me tell Talley I wouldn't be welcome," Steve said. "Any particular reason why I should ride posse?"

"There'll be a reward," Doug said. "There's talk of offering five thousand or more."

"Good night," Steve said. "Don't forget. Black Rock the day after tomorrow. I'll talk to Eileen about it in the morning."

He crossed the street and entered the Pioneer House. When he looked back Doug was not in sight.

The night clerk got up from a cot back of the desk and yawningly led him down the hall to a room on the lower floor toward the rear of the building.

Steve listened to the man's receding footsteps and heard him roll back into the cot with a sigh. He lifted his luggage sack onto the bed, opened it, and brought out his six-shooter and holster and shells.

He got out a cloth and cleaned the gun and tried the action, then loaded all six chambers. He buckled on the belt and slid the gun into the holster.

He left the hotel by way of a rear door, which opened into a side street, for he did not want to disturb the clerk who might not yet be asleep.

He returned to Bozeman Street and walked onward into the gambling district. In some of the places percentage girls were still dancing with miners and cowboys.

He suddenly had the impression of being followed. He turned. A man was strolling the sidewalk, some distance back of him. This person passed the band of light from a doorway and Steve identified him as the blocky, square-jawed man he had noticed earlier during his talk with Mart Lowery. There was nothing furtive about his manner, however, and Steve scoffed at himself for seeing trouble where none existed.

He walked on and entered the door of the gambling house with the revolving light on the roof. Nick Latzo's Blue Moon.

Batteries of ornate oil lamps lighted the place. Cutglass glittered on the backbar and oil paintings of beauties adorned the walls. The card tables had green baize tops. An orchestra of five pieces was playing and there was dancing on a small space at the rear.

Three poker tables were still busy, and from the stacks of chips in sight at least two of the games were for heavy stakes. The players were intent on these games.

The bull-necked Nick Latzo sat at one of the tables and was dealing a stud hand to four opponents. He had grown fleshier and his small eyes were almost hidden in the heavy pouches around them.

Steve's arrival had now been discovered by some of the men who were standing at the bar, among whom were Pool cattlemen who had been aboard the train.

The news spread by means of word and rib-nudging. The orchestra finished its number and prepared to strike up a new tune, but the leader paused, peering and ready to duck to cover. Past experience had taught him that these sudden lulls were often the prelude to stormy moments.

Nick Latzo became aware of the quiet and looked up. He saw Steve and sat watching and waiting, the deck of cards in his hands—his face without tangible expression.

Steve walked down the room to the poker table. The other four players edged back and a plump man pulled in his stomach and began breathing fast, obviously wishing he was somewhere else.

"Hello, Nick!" Steve said.

Latzo did not move. Only his small eyes were active. He was coatless, but wore a vest of green flowered silk over a white silk shirt. A green silk sash was around his thick waist and from this jutted the handle of a scabbarded dagger. He had no gun in sight.

"Well, well, if it isn't Steve Santee himself," Latzo finally spoke. "It's been a long time since you've been in a place of mine. Must be two, three years."

Steve glanced around. The warning had been flashed, for three of Latzo's trouble shooters had appeared and had moved to strategic points in the room. Al Painter, bearing the marks of combat, also emerged from a side door into the main room.

"You know about the little dispute I had with your brother and a couple of your men tonight, of course, Nick?" Steve said.

"They wasn't my men," Latzo said. "They was friends of Louie's. I was told you picked trouble with them."

"If you're taking it up, let's get it over with—right now, Nick," Steve said.

It was so blunt and unexpected that Nick Latzo had no answer ready. Then he saw Steve's purpose. He had not only been taken by surprise, but he had been placed on notice in the presence of many witnesses of being responsible for any foul play that might befall Steve. That was exactly the situation Steve had wanted to create when he had come to the Blue Moon.

Latzo knew he had been outmaneuvered. He had an agile mind back of the blank face, and was quick to attempt to turn the situation in his favor.

"Louie's man enough to settle his own accounts, Santee," he said. "And so am I. Are you huntin' trouble? You must be drunk. Have another one on the house, then go somewhere and sleep it off. You're interferin' with our game."

Steve stood gazing at Latzo a moment. He still felt that among the many dark secrets that Nick Latzo must share with the devious persons who passed through his establishments was the key to what had happened to his father.

Latzo looked back at him, and again his face was utterly without expression. But suddenly Steve was sure he was right. The man knew! He knew Buck Santee's fate.

He realized also that Latzo was fully aware that he, above everything else, would like to pry out that knowledge. He fancied that a faint irony showed briefly in Latzo's eyes, as though daring him to try.

"I'll always make it a point never to be drunk when I'm dealing with you, Nick," Steve said. "And that goes for the present moment as well as the future."

He turned, walked past Latzo's gunmen, and spun a silver

dollar on the bar. "I pay for my own drinks when I'm in Nick's place," he told the bartender. "I always have."

He filled a glass from the bottle that was nervously placed before him. He tasted it, then poured it on the floor. "Rotgut," he said. "I'll see you another day, Nick."

He walked through the swing doors to the sidewalk. He pulled up, gazing at Doug Whipple, who stood there. Doug wore a brace of six-shooters and the holsters were tied to his legs with rawhide thongs.

"You do stay up late, fellow," Steve said.

"I knew I had made a mistake when I let it slip that Nick was here in town," Doug shrugged. "You always were one to force the play. I knew you'd go down to the Moon and brace him. Lone-handed. You don't care how young you die, do you? If Nick had lifted a finger they'd have blasted you down. And Louie was aching for 'em to do it. But you got away with it."

"At least, if I'm found with a bullet or a knife in my back or beaten to death out in the brush, Nick will have some embarrassing explaining to do," Steve said. "He'll hear that there's Vigilante talk in the air, if he doesn't already know about it. That'll give him pause for thought. I hope he'll stay clear of me. I need some leeway and don't want to have to spend my time trying to avoid being bushwhacked. You might call this visit to the Blue Moon as setting up a little life insurance. It ought to keep Nick off my back. I've got things to do."

"Such as trying to decide whether to try to help run down the men who held up the train tonight?" Doug asked.

"I've already decided that," Steve said.

Doug stood for a time without speaking. Then he said, "Well, I'll turn in. See you tomorrow, Steve."

"I've taken a room at the Pioneer," Steve said. "There's a spare bed, if you're not fixed up."

"I've got other plans," Doug said.

Steve watched him walk down Bozeman Street and turn into Front Street along the railway tracks. He debated whether to follow Doug and bring him back. Momentarily he had been given an insight into the conflict and turmoil that raged in a man torn between two worlds.

Doug was a person in torment, caught in the demands of loyalty to a friend on the one hand and, on the other, some black necessity which he did not know how to evade. He had gone, Steve knew, to some sordid barroom to drink and dull the poignant sense of guilt that had been so searing in his eyes.

Steve finally turned away. Total weariness was on him as he walked to the Pioneer House. Ahead of him he saw the blocky man enter the hotel. As he walked down the hall to his own room he saw lamplight shining beneath a door near his own. He had the sensation that ears were tuned to his arrival, and to his movements as he prepared to turn in. After he stretched out on the bed he also lay listening for a time. He heard nothing, and finally convinced himself that again it was imagination.

Chapter
Seven

Steve awakened at daybreak and listened to the departure of mounted men who were being assigned by Sheriff Bill Rawls to various sectors of the hills. There was activity in the railroad yards also, and a clatter as a train rolled away. He guessed that it carried more manhunters toward outer points in the basin.

He slept again. The sun was high in the sky when he finally aroused. He arose from bed and the first thing he saw was a white envelope which had been thrust under his door.

It was a plain, cheap envelope and bore no name or writing. It was sealed and he ripped it open, his mind still a trifle fogged with sleep.

He instantly came wide awake. He stood staring at two objects that he had drawn from the envelope. One was a square of paper containing a brief written message which said:

Santee:
    There are more like the enclosed sample and they'll be easy to earn. Just keep this one on you all the time for quick identification when I get in touch with you.

55

There was no signature. The note was done in a shaky scrawl which indicated that the wrong writing hand had been used for the sake of disguise.

The other object, which was the "sample" referred to in the note, was a hundred-dollar banknote. It was a well-used bill, and there was no doubt in Steve's mind but that it was genuine.

He read the message again, studying over it. He inspected the torn envelope and tossed it on the dresser, for it told him nothing.

He found himself holding the banknote to the light as though it might reveal some secret message. He grinned wryly at his own confusion.

A hand softly tapped the door at that moment, startling him. He pocketed the banknote, then unlocked the door. His visitor was the blocky, gray-mustached man whom he had suspected of trailing him the previous night. He stared.

"I'd like a word with you," the man said, glancing apprehensively up and down the hall. Then he pushed his way past Steve into the room. "I don't want anybody to know I'm here," he explained.

Steve closed and bolted the door. The man appeared to be about fifty and had eyes that were a pale blue and very direct. He looked around Steve's room. His glance took in the torn envelope on the dresser and Steve fancied that it halted there for an instant. His gaze roved onward and Steve felt that all details were being tabulated in his mind.

His attention returned to Steve. He offered a taut, little smile. "I go by the name of John Drumm in this range," he said. "I'm supposed to be a horse buyer for big livery companies in the east. That gives me an excuse for traveling around and getting acquainted at the ranches."

"Why would you need an excuse for that?" Steve asked carefully.

"My real name is Clum. Frank Clum. I'm a deputy United States Marshal. For the past two months, however, I've been detached for special duty. Right now my salary is being paid by several express companies. All of the express outfits are interested in breaking up any organized gangs of outlaws who rob trains."

"Why are you telling me this?" Steve asked.

"Because I believe we might have the same purpose in mind and might be able to help each other."

"Do you mean catching train robbers?"

"Perhaps. And also in trying to solve the disappearance of your father.

Steve gazed demandingly at him. Clum nodded. "I know all about your search for your father. There's a full report on it in the district headquarters. I read it, along with other information when I took over this investigation. You didn't know it, but you were watched every step of your way by express men in the expectation that you would lead them to your father and the stolen money, if he was still alive. It wasn't exactly an express company responsibility that time, because the money had passed out of their hands, but we did it as a favor to the county authorities. They watched you in Denver and San Antonio and El Paso. The Rurales co-operated in Mexico. The American consul helped in Panama. It was there they quit keeping cases on you."

"Why did they quit?" Steve asked.

"Because they figured you had proved your point, which was that your father had never been in any of those places. That indicated, of course, that you were correct in believing Buck Santee had been murdered. However, there was no actual proof to back up that assumption until just lately, so the matter remained inactive."

Steve straightened. "Actual proof? What do you mean?"

"I'm now convinced beyond all doubt that your father was killed the night of the disappearance of the ten thousand dollars," Clum nodded.

"What convinced you?"

"The money he was accused of stealing has shown up."

"Shown up?" Steve demanded. "How do you know that?"

"That money could be identified," Clum said. "It was all in new twenty-dollar gold pieces—double-eagles—and was part of the only mintage in that denomination that had been turned out so far that year by the Denver mint. The coins bore the mint initial, of course. A small part of the mintage had gone to a Kansas City bank, where it was paid out to the Powderhorn Pool through the accounts of commission buyers. Cattlemen always like the feel of new gold money. The remainder of that mintage was shipped to St. Louis, where it went into the gold reserve of a bank, and was never placed in circulation at all."

Steve's voice was taut. "When did this money come to light?"

"About a month ago—although I only got word yesterday from headquarters. Someone there was slow to realize its significance in connection with my presence here."

"A month ago? You mean whoever had it waited three years to pass it off?"

Clum nodded. "Evidently they had learned it was money that could be identified. It's hang-rope money, you know. They thought three years was long enough. Even so, they went to great pains to avoid discovery. Nearly all of that ten thousand dollars appeared suddenly in Chicago. It was deposited in small amounts in different banks, and was withdrawn a day or two later. The withdrawals were taken in silver and banknotes. Because of the small amounts involved, no suspicion was aroused."

"Who——?" Steve began.

"I'm getting to that," Clum said. "Because of the three years' lapse of time several days passed before it was discovered that the Bugle robbery money was in circulation in Chicago. Federal agents traced out the manner in which it had been done. By that time the man who had made the deposits was long gone. Only one or two tellers could recall very vague descriptions of him. One said he had been an old man, bearded and heavily dressed, who seemed to be in bad health. The other gave a different description. Obviously the man was disguised."

"It could have been Buck Santee if he were still alive," Steve pointed out.

"But it wasn't," Clum said. "It was Louie Latzo."

Steve felt a fierce surge within him. "Latzo? Are you sure? How do you know that?"

"I didn't know that it was Louie until last night," Clum said. "I've always had a hunch Nick was back of these train robberies and I also figured he probably knew something about what happened to Buck Santee three years ago. But it was only a hunch until your fight with Louie and his pals. I arrived just as you and young Whipple were finishing them off. When Louie was knocked down I saw some objects fall from his coat pocket. He wasn't in condition to know that. After everyone had gone, I took a look. I found a nail file, a cigar case, and a pencil. Also a small notebook. This contained the names of quite a number of ladies. Some of these gals live here in Bugle. Some in Cheyenne. And two or three in Chicago."

"Chicago?"

"And there was something else relating to Chicago in the notebook," Clum said. "On an inner page, in very tiny writing, was a column of figures. Alongside each item was a street address. Also initials that I'm sure are abbreviations for the names of banks. In other words that was a check list of deposits that had been made in a dozen banks in and near Chicago. The column of figures totaled up to almost ten thousand dollars."

"You still have this notebook?" Steve asked.

"No. I didn't want Louie to know anyone had seen it. I copied the information, then returned the notebook, along with the other items, to where I had found them. Later I saw Louie come back and search around until he found them. He seemed very happy when he came across the notebook."

"But Louis wasn't in the Powderhorn at the time Dad was killed," Steve said. "Miss Maddox told me that he showed up in Bugle after I had left."

"He was acting only as his brother's agent in passing the money," Clum said. "Louie was a fool for keeping that book. I suppose it was because of the ladies' addresses that he stuck into it. It wouldn't the the first time that a man hung himself with a petticoat."

"I've always felt deep in my heart that Nick was the one," Steve said, and there was a savage, roweling fury in him, "I'll——"

"I'm asking you not to do a thing—at least until I give the word," Clum said urgently.

"Not do a thing?" Steve demanded.

"A wrong move now might spoil everything," Clum said. "That's why I came to you to tell you all this. Another reason is that I knew your Dad years ago. We wore law badges in a tough Kansas trail town when we were young men. We were close friends. Buck Santee backed me up a couple of times in some bad situations."

"But——"

"I'll see to it that, as far as the law is concerned, his name is cleared of all stigma as soon as I can write up my report and send it to headquarters."

"When will that be?" Steve demanded. "Hasn't this gone long enough? Three years."

"I'll take care of it as soon as possible," Clum said. "But I'm asking you not to go near Nick Latzo again. You might say or do something that would warn him. It's for your own sake as well as for the sake of recovering that money that was stolen last night along with what they got in the other two stick-ups. It amounts to close to a quarter of a million dollars in all."

"A quarter of a million? Is it true that Northern Express might not be able to pay off?"

Clum shook his head. "There isn't a chance. The express office won't open this morning. The men who are stockholders will be ruined. There are four or five of them and everything they own won't meet the loss at more than a few cents on the dollar. Some of the ranchers likely will go under also. Amos Whipple and his Center Fire are going to be hard hit, they say."

Clum added significantly, "Unless we can find that quarter of a million."

"Are you trying to tell me you believe all that money from the three robberies is still intact somewhere?"

"None of it has been spent to the best of our knowledge," Clum said. "Some of it was in bills which had recorded serial numbers. And a lot of the gold had come from the mint too and can be singled out, just like the money your Dad was packin' to the Spanish Flat schoolhouse that night."

Clum winked and added, "Leastwise that's the story that we put out right after the holdups started. It's true only to a certain extent, but they don't know that. But we're pretty sure it's being held, like Latzo held the other money, until they feel safe to either begin passing it or maybe until they figure they've got enough to skip the country with."

"You believe Latzo has it?" Steve asked.

"Who else? Your father's murder touched off a lot of things that have happened in the Powderhorn. At first it was only small holdups and burglaries. Cleanups stolen and paymasters robbed. Then the big stuff. Train robberies. It's only reasonable to figure Latzo and the shady crowd that hangs around his Silver Moon are back of it."

Steve stood gazing unseeingly at Frank Clum for a long time. "Do you know what this means to me?" he finally asked. "I've tried for three years to prove they were wrong about Buck Santee. Now you lay it right in my lap out of a blue sky. I'm grateful. I'll try to keep my hands off Latzo's throat until you say the word."

He went silent a moment, then said, "However, I've reason to believe that Latzo, even though he may have been back of what happened to Dad, probably had nothing to do with the train holdup last night."

"Not in person, of course," Clum said. "He was right in town. An ironbound alibi. But that don't mean——"

"I don't think he had anything to do with it at all," Steve said.

Clum hadn't expected that. Steve endured his searching inspection for seconds. "Want to tell me just what your reason is for saying that, Santee?" Clum asked.

"Have you talked to Amos Whipple about the holdup?" Steve asked.

Clum shook his head. "Should I?"

"If you do you'll probably learn that I'm suspected of having had a hand in it. Or guilty knowledge, at least."

Clum did not seem astonished. "I gathered it was something like that from Whipple's attitude last night," he said.

"And did you?"

Steve shrugged. "I landed at New Orleans from Panama only four days ago. Every minute of my time can be accounted for."

"Maybe you won't be given a chance to account for it," Clum warned. "Amos Whipple is workin' for Vigilante action."

"I know," Steve said.

Clum waited. When Steve offered nothing more, Clum walked to the table, picked up the torn envelope, and examined it. "Am I right in guessing that this was pushed under your door while you were asleep?" he asked.

"Yes," Steve said.

"I found one under my door also," Clum said. "Did your envelope have something like this inside it?"

He produced a leather wallet from the inner pocket of his coat and fished from it a hundred-dollar bill.

"Yeah," Steve said. "I've got its twin in my pocket."

They laid the banknotes side by side on the dresser.

"At least they took pains to see that this money couldn't be easily identified," Steve commented. "Both bills have been in circulation for some time—as much as bills of that size get around."

"It must be the opening move in some kind of a bribe,"

Clum decided. "It couldn't be anything else." He frowned. "Someone might have got onto the fact that I'm an express agent. That's what worries me. Aside from yourself I've confided in only one other person."

"I can savvy why they might try to bribe you," Steve said. "But why me?"

There was no answer. Clum produced a written note which had accompanied the bank bill. It was practically a duplicate of the one Steve had received.

"Someone has money to spend on the two of us for some reason or other," Clum said. "I reckon we'll learn in time who's tryin' to buy us off. We can guess, of course."

He tucked the banknote in his wallet and stored it back in his pocket. "I'll be happy to meet whoever sent it," he went on. "I suppose, if I follow instructions, I'll have that pleasure, sooner or later. I figure it'll be a mighty big help in the job I'm bein' paid to do."

He moved to the door and stood listening to make sure the way was clear. "I may have made a mistake in telling you my identity, Santee," he said. "But you have to take chances in this business. I pride myself on being a judge of men. I had great respect for your Dad. As long as I've gone this far I'll have to trust you completely. You understand, no doubt, that if these banknotes came from the men I'm after I might be in a dangerous position. They won't back off from murder if bribery fails."

"I understand," Steve said.

"It'd be as well that we remain strangers as far as other folks are concerned," Clum said. "But if you should have to get in touch with me and can't locate me personally you can probably get word as to my whereabouts from Burl Talley."

"Talley? You mean that he's the other man you mentioned as knowing you are an express agent?"

"I had to have some responsible person as a source of information about people in this range," Clum said. "Talley, being a leading citizen and widely acquainted, was the man. An intelligent person, Talley. Smart businessman. Everyone respects him."

Clum extended a hand, which Steve grasped. The man opened the door, made sure the hall was clear, then stepped out. Steve heard him walk away.

Steve stood thinking. Finally he followed Clum's example by carefully storing the banknote in the billfold which he carried. It seemed obvious, as Clum had decided, that this was a preliminary step in offering some kind of a bribe.

He knew Clum was still certain that Nick Latzo had been the brains back of the train robberies. Furthermore, he surmised that Clum was wondering why he had said that he doubted that Latzo had any part in at least the previous night's holdup.

Steve had no way of knowing about the other two train robberies. They may or may not have been engineered by Latzo. But it did not seem reasonable to believe that Doug Whipple would help Latzo or any of Latzo's outfit in a holdup, and a few hours later fight Louie Latzo and also back Steve's play against Nick himself.

In addition, Nick Latzo was guilty of, or deeply involved in the disappearance of Steve's father and the loss of the Pool money three years ago, as well as the murder of Henry Thane. If Doug was a member of any outlaw organization led by Nick, then he likely would have had an inkling of Nick's part in that crime.

That just didn't add up. Doug's nature was not the kind to tolerate murder or murderers—particularly of Buck Santee, who had been a kind of idol to him in boyhood. Train robbery might have appealed to Doug as a means of escape from boredom or as a chance to prove in his own mind that he was a swashbuckling, fearless individual who was strong enough to stand on his own feet. Lawlessness could be Doug's way of hurting his father for their differences.

The robbery of the Powderhorn Pool's own beef money might have appealed to Doug's sense of irony as a blow, not only at Amos, but at all others in the basin who looked down on him as a wastrel. But not murder.

Steve talked the chambermaid into bringing a tub and hot water to his room and he shaved and soaked away the grime of travel in peace, if not in comfort, for a wooden washtub was by no stretch of the imagination suited to the demands of his length.

In the midst of this operation a hand tapped the door. Eileen's voice spoke. "The hotel's on fire."

"That solves my problem," Steve said. "I'm wedged in this infernal contrivance. I'll die fast now at least."

"It sounded more to me like a buffalo was wallowing around in there," she said. "A fine time to be rising. It's midmorning. Have you had breakfast yet?"

"Not yet, but I'm willing."

"I'll order ham and eggs and flapjacks and if you don't show up in ten minutes I'll send Maggie, the chambermaid, with a bucket of ice water to dump on you."

"Make it steak and eggs," Steve called, untangling himself from the tub. "And I'll be there in five minutes."

She was awaiting him at the table in the dining room, which was nearly deserted at this off hour. She wore a divided riding skirt, half boots, and a cool blouse of blue and white polka dots. Her hair was brushed to a fine, dark red gloss. A straw hat of Spanish type hung on the back of her chair, along with a large handbag.

"Six minutes, exactly," she said. "You're either a man of your word or you're afraid of ice water."

"I'm both," he said. "And also hungry."

"And grouchy," she said. "You don't waste words, do you? How about saying good morning?"

"Good morning," he said. "Wait'll I get that steak under my belt. Then I'll have the strength to talk until you holler calf rope."

Through the nearby window they watched half a dozen returning possemen ride into town, swing up at the tie rail, and dismount. They came clumping into the hotel.

With them was Burl Talley. They evidently had been searching east of town and their morning ride had been fruitless. They were hungry now, and touched by the impatience of men who feel that they are wasting their time and yet are duty-bound to go through with the effort.

When Talley discovered Steve in Eileen's presence his tanned face went blank and stiff with an effort at masking his disapproval. Then he pushed that mood away and came walking over to their table.

"Morning, Santee," he said cordially enough. And to Eileen, "Breakfast at this hour, gal? You'll have to do better than that if you're going to be healthy, wealthy, and wise. So they tell me, at least."

"And they also say that you only get a worm for arising early," she said. "Now what would I want with a worm?"

"Steak, man-size and I want it cooked," Talley told the

waitress. "If I want raw meat I'll go out and shoot it myself. Say—what's this Santee has? Eggs! Great! Add a couple to that steak, smiling-side up, Dollie."

Talley laid his hand lightly on Eileen's. "You're staying in town a few days, I hope," he said.

"No," she said. "I'm riding out to Antler this afternoon."

"I'm disappointed," Talley said. "I wanted to be the fortunate man who would see you home, but I'm obligated to do my best in helping pick up the trail of the train robbers. Well, maybe I'll have better luck another day."

Talley rejoined the three men at the table on the opposite side of the room. He dropped his hat on a vacant chair and rolled a cigarette, then reached for the coffee that Dollie had brought.

Two of Talley's companions were riders, by their dress. The taller of the pair was a sinewy, leathery, gaunt-jawed cowboy of about forty. The other was younger and swarthy with the wide, square face and high cheekbones that spoke of Indian blood.

The third man had the garb and looks of a lumber-mill worker. He was a long-chinned individual with hair as dry and lifeless as dusty hay. All three wore pistols. Rifles were slung on the saddles of their horses in the street.

"The two punchers work for Burl at Rafter O," Eileen informed Steve. "Tex Creed, the older one, is foreman. The second one is known as Highriver. I never heard any other name for him. The third man is Whitey Bird, who is Burl's mill boss at the lumberyard."

All were strangers to Steve. In the past he had been well acquainted at the Rafter O and also at the planing mill. Evidently Talley had made some changes.

Steve was hungry, but preoccupied, as he tackled the steak and eggs. He saw Frank Clum stroll down the street, apparently without a care in the world.

Clum, glancing through the window, saw Talley and beckoned. Talley arose and walked outside and they stood on the sidewalk for a minute or two talking. Clum had his thumbs hooked in the armholes of his vest in the manner of a man discussing a business matter. Talley clapped Clum on the back and came back to his table.

Steve was thinking of Doug Whipple, wondering where he might be. Eileen's thoughts evidently were running in the same path. She spoke softly, "It's no use for the two of us to pretend we don't know what the other saw last night."

He withheld his reponse for a time, wishing he did not have to answer. "Sometimes it's better to pretend," he said. "You always were good at it. Remember when you used to pretend that your dolls were grown-up people?"

"I was lonely then, even with my dolls," she said. "The only times I wasn't lonely after Mother and Dad went—went away was when I was with you and Doug."

"How about now?" he asked.

She didn't directly answer that. She gave him the measure of a smile. "We're all grown-up now, Steve, and we're dealing with real grown-up people, not dolls. It won't hurt to pretend—for a while at least. But, sooner or later, it must be faced."

She made a little gesture, dispelling these ghosts from her mind for the moment at least. "Are you planning on riding out to your place today?" she asked. "If so, we can go together. I left my horse at Sim Kendall's livery when I left for the convention. Shorty Barnes is in town. I saw him on the street from my window. You can borrow his horse. Shorty can catch a ride out to the ranch with a freighter later."

Steve pushed back his chair. He knew what she meant. Town was no place for him at the moment. "If Shorty won't mind. . . ." He nodded.

They arose. Burl Talley turned in his chair. "Leaving, Eileen?" he asked. "The schoolhouse party is off, of course, thanks to our train-robbing friends. However, as soon as possible, I'll get me a shave and a clean shirt and come galloping over to Antler with a box of candy under my arm."

He said to Steve, "I hope you find your house in shape, Santee."

Chapter
Eight

In the dining room Talley finished the food Dollie Lee placed before him. Through the window he watched Steve and Eileen walk down the street and enter Sim Kendall's livery.

Talley drank his coffee, lighted a cigar, and paid for the meal for himself and the three men. He arose and said, "I've some business I must look after. Don't wait for me."

From the Pioneer House he strolled down Bozeman Street to the office of his lumber business. This was where he could usually be found during the day when he was in town from the ranch.

He entered and locked himself in his inner office. He dialed the combination on a small safe, opened it, and from a locker drew a packet of bills of large denominations. He picked off four bills which were hundred-dollar banknotes, and returned the remainder to the safe.

He left the office, nodding to the elderly spinster who was his bookkeeper and said, "Jenny, I'll be back in an hour or less in case anyone wants to see me. I've decided not to ride posse any more today. Tomorrow, perhaps."

His horse still stood before the Pioneer House. En route in that direction he was buttonholed several times by citizens who wanted news about the train robbery.

He was passing the Powderhorn Security Bank when Charlie Hodges, its president, hurried from his office and called him in. Hodges, a balding, nervous man, was pale and shaking.

He led Talley inside his office and closed the door. "I've been informed by Pete Crain that Northern Express can't make good the beef money," he said. "They're stretched out so thin financially they'll have to go into bankruptcy."

"Well, it's not what you'd call a surprise," Talley said. "This merely makes it official. Everybody in town has been expecting it. Do you know what this means, Charlie?"

"I know," Hodges said wearily. "The ranchers in the Pool

are in deep trouble. That means that I'm in trouble too. The bank's fortunes are tied up with the ranches. We don't get much of the mining business."

"A bad situation," Talley said. "We've got to see to it that Bill Rawls catches these robbers. I'll build a fire under Bill when I see him, though I doubt that it's needed. He understands the situation."

"This might be seized out of Rawls' hands," Hodges said. "They're making Vigilante threats. They might even try to take it out on Pete Crain. He organized the express company. He's president and general manager. I told him to lay low."

"I can't say I'm happy about the situation myself," Talley said. "I had some six thousand dollars coming to me out of the Pool money. Maybe a little hang-rope medicine is what we need."

"Don't talk like that," Hodges protested. "That sort of thing can get out of hand. You can stand a loss. Others can't. You haven't got all your eggs in one basket."

"It's still my money," Talley said.

He left the bank, walked to his horse, mounted, and rode out of town. His three men came out of the Pioneer House a few minutes later, swung aboard their mounts, and also left Bugle to rejoin the manhunt.

Possemen were coming and going and all of the community was set on edge, for confirmation that the express company could not pay off was spreading swiftly.

The three men headed southward toward Art Stubbs' ranch, which was being used by the sheriff as the day's base of operations in that section of the basin, but Talley crossed the railroad tracks and followed the trail in the opposite direction up the basin toward the ford of the Powderhorn River.

Talley was alone on the trail. A few hundred yards before reaching the river he turned off the main route, passing beneath a massive archway of pine logs and jogged down a side road which curved through thick timber and brush.

After a quarter of a mile it opened into a clearing in which stood a rambling, ramshackle, shake-roofed structure. This was Nick Latzo's original gambling house, the Silver Moon.

Only the main entrance showed any attempt at glamour.

The weathered painting of a dancing girl adorned the false front. Above that arose the outline of a crescent moon which had been painted silver, but which was now considerably tarnished. Nevertheless, the tie rails bore the polish of constant use, and the clearing was beaten bare of all grass. The Silver Moon was a prosperous enterprise.

However, at this hot hour of noon the Silver Moon was nearly deserted. Not a single saddle horse was in sight. Talley dismounted and let the reins dangle, and walked through the doors and met the cool, echoing dimness of the main room.

A lone bartender was dealing a hand of solitaire as he sat on the lookout's stilt-legged chair. The roulette tables were covered and the faro layouts looked. The green curtain that served the small stage at the rear was lifted. An emaciated man wearing a derby and a woman with very golden hair, were practicing a soft-shoe routine on the bare stage while they kept time by humming a song. The roadhouse held the odor of stale beer, stale cigar smoke, and stale humans.

The bartender sluggishly left his seat and moved back of the polished counter. Then he recognized Talley. He was surprised. He straightened, and his manner became respectful.

"Beer," Talley said. "Is Nick up yet? I've got a little business deal to discuss with him."

"Nick's awake," the bartender nodded. "I had his breakfast sent into him half an hour ago. We don't see you here very often, Mr. Talley. I can't remember when——"

"Not often," Talley said. He picked up the glass of beer and walked down the echoing room and passed through a side door alongside the stage. He drained the glass and set it on a window ledge in the narrow passageway in which he stood.

This passageway carried him past half a dozen dressing-room doors. He reached the last portal, which, in contrast to the shabbiness of the others, was of heavy, varnished oak with a steel peek panel.

Talley knocked on the door and spoke loudly. "It's Burl Talley, Nick. I came to talk about that property on Bozeman Street you're interested in buying."

There was a growling response inside. Feminine footsteps

came hurrying. The panel opened and the round face of a girl with dyed red hair was framed there briefly. Then she freed the bolt on the main door and admitted him.

"Good morning," Talley said. "Even though it's afternoon to most people."

He eyed her with appreciation. She went by the name of Daisy O'Day, and she was a singer and dancer at the Silver Moon. She wore only a thin silk dressing gown over a lacy nightdress. She was buxom and attractive enough with sensuous blue eyes and full lips.

It was a large room with heavy furniture and garish velvet carpets. A bedroom opened to the left in which Talley glimpsed a silk-canopied bed.

Nick Latzo, wearing a flowered dressing gown and pajamas sat in an easy chair, a cigar in his mouth and the remains of a breakfast on the table before him. He had been totaling up the previous night's receipts and had pushed aside the coffee cups and dishes to make room for his ledgers and the stacks of silver and gold coins and packets of bills.

Talley discovered that another man was present. He had been hidden by the high back of a leather chair in which he was sprawled. It was Louie Latzo. He was fully dressed. He wore a patch over his left eye. His lips were puffed and discolored and he was suffering the bruises and the aching aftermath of his encounter with Steve.

"Morning, Nick," Talley said. "Good morning, Louie."

Nick Latzo's voice was surly and there was a wariness in him. "I figured you'd be ridin' hell-fer-leather with the posses, Talley," he said.

"The hills are full of posses," Talley said. "I'm not needed. I've changed my mind about selling that vacant land next to the Blue Moon to you, Nick."

"Land?" Latzo said a trifle blankly. Then he added swiftly, "Sure, sure."

"The train robbery left me in need of some ready cash, so I think we can come to terms," Talley said.

Latzo made a few notations in a ledger, swept all the money from the table into a leather handbag, and carried it as he arose and moved across the room. "Let's go into the office where we can talk it over and come down to cases," he said.

He led the way into a small room in which stood a heavy safe and a roll-top desk, and several chairs and a table. This room had no windows and was equipped with heavy double doors as a protection against both bullets and eavesdroppers.

"Keep your eyes off that girl," Latzo said after he had closed and bolted both doors. "I got money invested in her."

"And time?" Talley inquired.

"She's a good entertainer an' helps business," Latzo growled. "Don't go wheedlin' her into goin' with you on any of your trips to Chicago like you did with my last singer. That one never came back to Bugle either."

"I won't steal this one away from you, Nick," Talley said. "I have other plans."

"Are you crazy, comin' here in open daylight?" Latzo said. "What's wrong? Has anything happened?"

"You always were too excitable, Nick," Talley said. "Everything's under control. However this visit was necessary, for your sake at least."

"Fer my sake?"

Talley produced his wallet and extracted two of the hundred-dollar banknotes. He placed them on the desk in front of Latzo.

"There are two men in town who are each carrying a bill like these with them," he said. "They probably think it is a bribe of some kind. That's the impression I hoped to give them at least."

He helped himself to one of Latzo's cigars from a humidor and lighted it. "It isn't a bribe," he went on. "It's an incentive."

"What's that?" Latzo asked suspiciously. "What's this incentive?"

"You are to give these two bills to any persons you choose and tell them how they can double it," Talley said.

Latzo leaned back in the creaking swivel chair, a scowling distaste settling in his heavy face. "So that's it?" he said. "I might have knowed it'd be somethin' like that what brought you here."

Presently he asked, "Who are the two?"

"One of them goes by the name of John Drumm and is posing as a horse buyer," Talley said.

Latzo nodded. "I know the one you mean. He's been in the Blue Moon. Drinks a glass of bourbon an' bitters, an' plays piker faro for a while, then leaves. He comes in often."

"But only when you are there," Talley said. "You should have noticed that. He's been keeping cases on you. His real name is Frank Clum and he's working as special agent for the express companies."

Latzo uttered an oath and his scowl blackened. "Maybe he's keepin' cases on you too," he said.

"Not yet," Talley said. "But he is beginning to get too close to a lot of things."

"How do you know this?" Latzo demanded.

"Clum confided in me," Talley said. "He needed a source of reliable information and picked me for the role. That's the reward for building a reputation for integrity."

"How close is he?"

"Not close enough to move in—yet. But he will be eventually."

"An' the other man?"

"Steve Santee," Talley said. "He stumbled onto a piece of knowledge last night that might be embarrassing and also very dangerous to me. But more so to him. I believe he recognized one of my men during that little episode this side of Three Forks. There are reasons why he isn't too anxious to tell what he saw. He may never talk. But it's better to make sure that he won't."

Latzo tapped the banknotes scornfully with a thick finger. "You don't figger I'd be interested in piker money like that, do you, Burl?"

"Perhaps not. I can remember a time when you would be interested. In addition, you're growing too fat and soft for this sort of thing. But there are others."

Latzo smiled thinly. "Al Painter an' Chick Varney might hanker for that job at that, at least as fur as Santee is concerned," he said.

"And so would Louie," Talley said. "And get their heads in a noose. They'd be the first one suspected after that brawl they had with Santee. And you too. Santee made sure of that when he put you on notice at the Blue Moon last night. It was a smart play on his part. You've got to be smart too."

"But how——?"

"Keep Louie and his two pals away from Santee. It won't make any difference about Clum. Nobody knows there could be any connection. Amos Whipple and the ranchers are working themselves up to hang somebody. You don't want it to be your neck that's broken in a noose, do you? Or Louie's?"

"An' you don't want it to be yours, either, my friend,"

Latzo said. "We're in this together. Don't ever overlook that."

"I can't overlook it, unfortunately," Talley said.

Latzo was worried. "Plantin' them bills don't make sense. It's a circus stunt. Why did you do it?"

"My experience is that money talks," Talley said. "If your assistants are to double their profit they will have to make sure that they perform their tasks quietly so that they can search for and find their additional payment without being interrupted. Therefore they will be careful about the time and place so that they will be unobserved. That is highly desirable."

He turned toward the door, then paused in thought for a moment. "I'm afraid Douglas Whipple is too much of a burden to us also, to my regret," he said.

"Doug Whipple? You mean you want . . . ?"

Latzo let it trail off. Talley nodded. "He's a likable chap. But he has a conscience, unfortunately. He never fitted in with us. He went along the first time because he was drunk and in rebellion against life in general. Then he became so involved he could not quit us. He's been wondering ever since how to pull out."

"Involved is kind of a soft way of puttin' it," Latzo said ironically. "He's the one what touched off the dynamite that killed that Wells Fargo messenger on the Rock Springs job, wasn't he?"

Talley didn't answer. He produced his wallet, drew out the other two hundred-dollar notes, and tossed them on the desk. "It must be done," he said. "I've made up my mind. That's for Whipple. In his case I can't plant one of the bills on him for collection. He might suspect. So I'll give you the full amount—but it is to be paid only for value received."

"I still don't see any point in all this damned hanky-panky about plantin' money on people," Latzo said. "It might backfire."

"Maybe it's only my flair for the dramatic," Talley said. "And maybe, in case of this backfire, it might be helpful by confusing the situation."

"An' I don't see any sense in waitin' all these months to split up the money," Latzo said doggedly.

"You waited three years to pass off certain other funds that you had acquired by means I won't mention," Talley said.

"That was different. That was marked money."

"How do we know that some, or all of these other funds can't be traced also?" said Talley. "It's better to wait."

Latzo glowered, wanting to argue the matter further, but lacked the fiber. "I hope that wherever you've got the stuff hid out, it's safe," he growled.

Talley laughed. "Some day, Nick, I might even tell you where it's cached. You'll get your share, never fear. It'll be the easiest money you ever earned. Imagine getting paid for doing nothing."

"For bein' a sittin' duck, maybe," Latzo said.

"As for dividing it up, I'll decide the time and place," Talley said.

"Tex Creed an' the other boys might be a little hard to convince o' that if they really git the idea they want their divvy in a hurry," Latzo said. "They ain't the kind to set on their hands if they figger there's trouble comin'. They'll want to light out o' the Powderhorn mighty sudden."

"That bridge will be crossed if we ever come to it," Talley said. "Which I doubt. Meanwhile I would suggest that you do not let anyone know the subject of our conversation. By that I particularly mean your brother Louie. I don't trust him to be able to hold his tongue if pressure is brought to bear on him."

"Pressure? What do you mean pressure?"

"Use your head, Nick," Talley said. "You know, of course, that you are Clum's chief suspect in these train robberies. It is the natural viewpoint, because of the riffraff with which you consort, and I helped it along with a few veiled remarks, for that is exactly the situation we wanted to create. He is keeping close watch on you. He might decide to sweat someone. Louie, for instance."

"Maybe he's out there right now, watchin'," Latzo exclaimed. "Maybe he saw you come here."

"On the contrary he asked me to visit you," Talley said. "We had a conversation in the street this morning."

"What? He asked you to? What fer?"

"To snoop around and see if I noticed anything unusual, or if there were any strangers hanging around the Silver Moon. In other words he is letting me act as his assistant sleuth. I had mentioned to him a few days ago that you had approached me in regard to buying that vacant land next to the Blue Moon. I set that up as a genuine excuse for coming here."

Latzo sat troubled, his big, hairy fists clenched on the table before him. He finally drew a long breath and said, "We ought to take what we got an' quit. There's plenty fer the two of us, even after Creed an' the others are paid off."

"Nonsense!" Talley snapped. "It's too soon to get rid of that money. And there's bigger game in sight right now. I can own this whole damned basin before I'm finished. It's full of ripe plums. I'm in a position to start shaking the tree. Ranches can be picked up for a song before long."

"I ain't a cow raiser," Latzo said.

"You'll get your cut of the plum juice as well as what's in the cache," Talley said.

Latzo distrusted him, but seemed unable to do anything about it. In silence he unbarred the door.

Louie Latzo and Daisy O'Day were waiting in the larger room. For their benefit, Talley said heartily, "I'll think it over, Nick, and let you know. Four thousand is hardly enough. With the town booming that lot will be worth twice that much in a year or so."

He walked through the room, slapped Daisy O'Day on the hip, and laughed at Nick's black scowl and left the Silver Moon.

He rode into town. It was early afternoon and Bugle had settled into apathetic, heat-drenched exhaustion after the hours of sustained excitement.

Sheriff Bill Rawls came down the street on a tired horse, along with half a dozen other riders. Rawls' eyes were red-rimmed. He was mud-caked and needed a shave and sleep. He had the look of a harassed man who knew that much was expected of him and who also knew that he was beaten.

Among the sheriff's posse were Talley's two Rafter O cowboys, Tex Creed and Highriver.

Rawls, in response to Talley's questioning glance, shrugged and said resignedly, "Nothin', Burl. Not a damned thing. No trace of 'em. They flew off into thin air."

Talley spoke to his two riders. "Your pay at Rafter O goes right on as long as you want to keep looking for these men. You're under Bill's orders."

Talley rode on to his lumberyard. In his office he reached into a drawer and took a drink from a bottle of liquor. He sat for a time, thinking of Bill Rawls, riding stirrup to stirrup with two of the men who had helped hold up the train the previous night, and never suspecting. The other two members of the outlaw party had been Doug Whipple and Talley's planing mill boss, Whitey Bird.

He thought of his interview with Nick Latzo. He took another drink. He and Latzo had known each other nearly twenty years. As young men they had been members of a group of high graders and desperadoes that had operated in Colorado mining camps. They had used other names in those days.

Talley had served five years in Leavenworth Prison on a mail-theft charge. When he was released he had made an attempt to reform and achieve a respectable life. Chance had brought him to Powderhorn Basin and Bugle.

Nick Latzo had come into the Powderhorn also and had opened his Silver Moon near the ford. Slowly, inexorably they had drifted together again. The magnet and the needle. At first Latzo had been the magnet, Talley the needle. Now it was the other way around.

Talley had gained a dominating hold on Latzo when Buck Santee had disappeared with the Pool money. Talley had guessed that Latzo was responsible, for it had carried the earmarks of Latzo's methods in the past.

While the law was riding in circles, trying to find Buck Santee, Talley had trailed Latzo day and night and had caught him in the act of caching the stolen ten thousand dollars.

Latzo had admitted that he had murdered both Buck Santee and Henry Thane, and had hidden the former's body where it could never be found. That had not been Latzo's first experience with murder, but it had been his most profitable crime. Talley, although he had robbed and stolen, had avoided killing. The death of the Wells Fargo messenger in the dynamite blast had been his first close connection with the supreme crime.

Now he was forced into a position where, to protect himself, he was conniving the slaying of men. Once the acts were committed he was fully aware that his domination over Latzo would end. They would be on an equal footing. Such was the way he had drifted farther and farther from his long-ago intention of going straight.

Up to this time he and Latzo had served as very useful foils for each other. They had been careful never to associate openly. Thir meetings had been at night, in secret in Latzo's quarters. Publicly, Talley had let it be known that he did not consider Latzo a credit to the community. He discouraged his riders and mill hands from patronizing Latzo's establishments.

On the other hand, Latzo played his part by labeling Talley as a penny-pinching busybody who spent his life working on account books.

Tex Creed, Highriver, and Whitey Bird also were acquaintances from the past of both Latzo and Talley. Creed had been Talley's cellmate in prison. Whitey Bird and Highriver had known Latzo in the early days. It was Latzo who had sent them to Talley.

Talley had not taken part personally in the train holdups. Like Latzo, he had made sure he had an alibi to which many persons could attest. It was his strategy to continue, by innuendo, to point the finger of suspicion at Latzo by branding him as the brains back of the holdups.

This served to keep the law busy on a futile quest and to divert attention from himself. Not even Louie Latzo suspected that his burly older brother was serving as a decoy. Nick's reward for his role was to be a full share of the loot.

All of the money taken in the robberies was still intact under a troubled agreement that it would not be touched until such a time as the stake was big enough to support the lot of them in luxury. Then they were to go their separate ways.

The first train holdup had been carried out by only Creed, Highriver, and Bird. These three posed as peaceful, colorless men who drew their monthly pay from the Rafter O and the planing mill and blew it in on sprees and at the poker tables in Bugle.

But such thin numbers had nearly been disastrous. Creed, defying Talley's misgivings, had taken the hard-drinking wildling, Doug Whipple, along on the Rock Springs job.

That robbery was the one that had brought the full weight of the law into the chase, for Creed had used too heavy a charge of dynamite beneath the car in which an express messenger was holding out. The blast had ripped the car apart and had tossed the torn body of the messenger into the brush.

Doug Whipple believed he was the one who had touched

the match to the fuse that night. The truth was that he had been so benumbed by alcohol that he had taken little part in the holdup. It was Creed who had fired the fuse, but only Creed and Burl Talley knew that. Talley had seized the opportunity to hold a club over Doug Whipple's head by making him believe he was responsible for the messenger's death.

Talley shivered a little. What had happened to his resolve to go straight? First small robberies and holdups. Then the big money. Each crime, little or big, had been planned by him in every detail and rehearsed at the Rafter O.

With each success the urge for more and more easy money had grown. Avarice inspired increasing ruthlessness. Now, Talley, a little sick inside, knew there was no turning back. There must be more killings, and perhaps more, if he were to be safe.

He looked out and saw Amos Whipple ride past and dismount at the Pioneer House. Amos evidently had been on posse duty, for he was dusty and saddle-stiff. He was the person Talley had been hoping to see. He arose and left the office swiftly.

Amos saw him coming and waited. He laid a hand on Amos's arm. "You need something cold, Amos," he said. "They've got ice today, so the sign says."

They went into the barroom, which adjoined the eating room. It was dim and cool here. There were only two other drowsy patrons and these sat at tables.

Talley glanced around to make sure they were not being overheard. "Amos," he said. "I'm going to tell you something that I know won't go any farther. It was told to me in strictest confidence, but I've thought it over and believe it is too important to be the knowledge of only one person. Here it is. You may have met a man who calls himself John Drumm and represents himself as a horse buyer?"

"I know the man," Amos said.

"He's a federal marshal, detached from duty to work for the express companies, investigating these robberies," Talley said. "He told me his identity some time ago. This is what I wanted you to know particularly: Clum, which is his real name, Frank Clum, found an envelope under his door here at the Pioneer House this morning and it contained a hundred-dollar bill. There was a note in a disguised hand which stated that he would soon learn how to earn much more such money."

"I don't follow you," Amos said. "What——?"

"Clum thinks it's a bribe, of course," Talley said. "He told me about it as a precaution, however."

"Precaution?"

"It is evident that whoever sent that money is aware that he is an express agent. Perhaps this person will decide that if he can't buy Clum off he'll have to get rid of him by some other means."

Amos stared. "Rub him out, you mean? Did this Drumm, or Clum, say who he might suspect?"

Talley hesitated. "I don't believe I should repeat that. It was also in strict confidence. In addition Clum only suspects. He has no actual proof."

"But the man you're thinking about is Steve Santee," Amos said.

Talley shrugged. "I didn't say that."

Amos finished his drink. He said, "Thanks, Burl," and tramped woodenly out of the hotel.

Talley remained there a few minutes longer. He left the bar, walked into the lobby and down the hallway past the guest rooms on the lower floor as though he intended to leave the building by the rear exit.

Instead, he tapped softly on the door of the room that Frank Clum occupied. Clum had been awaiting him. He was quickly admitted. He declined Clum's invitation to sit down.

"Nothing to report, Frank," he said. "I talked to Latzo in his quarters. It's quite a place. I've never been inside it before. I used the sale of that vacant lot as an excuse. But I didn't see a thing that'd help you. I'm sorry."

"I hardly expected you to," Clum said. "But it was worth a try. It's the little things you pick up that usually solve the big ones. You saw nobody suspicious around?"

"Louie was with Nick," Talley said. "And a girl entertainer named O'Day. She seems to live with Nick. That was all."

He turned to go. "If I can be of any more help just give the word, Frank. This gang must be caught and caught soon. I'm still just as sure as you are that Latzo is back of it. There's nobody else capable of it to my knowledge."

He returned to his office at the lumberyard. There he spent

79

the remainder of the afternoon diligently working on accounts and discussing business matters with buyers.

At late afternoon he watched Amos Whipple ride out of town accompanied by two other ranchers. They looked grim and purposeful. They had the attitudes of men who had come to a stern decision.

Chapter
Nine

After they had left Burl Talley sitting in the Pioneer House dining room, eating his steak and eggs, Steve and Eileen walked to Sim Kendall's livery. Shorty Barnes' horse, a stalwart roan was quartered there along with Eileen's mouse-colored gelding.

Steve borrowed Shorty's saddle, rigged both animals and held the stirrup for her as she swung astride. She did not need that help, but she was pleased, and laughed down at him.

"My, but you've changed, now that old age is creeping on you," she said. "At least you no longer seem afraid of me. The last time you helped me on a horse you acted as though I was something you had to touch lightly and hold at arm's length. That was the day I graduated from the grammar grades at the Spanish Flat schoolhouse and your father forced you to escort me to and from the program."

"I remember," Steve said. "I had figured on going on a prospecting trip west of Cardinal Pass that day with Doug. I was a mite disappointed."

"I suppose I'm still facing the same kind of counterattractions," she said.

"Alongside of you a gold pan just doesn't seem to have a bit of allure," Steve said. "Not any more."

She laughed. "Now, there's a real compliment. In your travels you seem to have learned a few things about the opposite sex. At least how to flatter them."

She paused and gave him one of her slanting looks. "I wonder who taught you?" she added.

After this a soberness came upon them. They rode out of

town sedately and Steve was gripped by this knowledge of a new awareness of each other. She was conscious of it also. Suddenly she decided to end this trend of affairs. She slashed her hat down on the gelding's flank. "Last one to Spanish Flat is a chump!" she shouted.

They raced away from Bugle, across an open flat with the peaks of the Powderhorns towering to their right, hoary with the remnants of last winter's snows.

Steve stood in the stirrups and saluted the mountains again. "Here I am, home, rough heads," he said exultantly.

They sped into a stretch of timber and were berated by the driver of a jerkline freight outfit whose mules they threw into confusion as they thundered past. They skirted Long Ridge and crossed Blue Creek. Eileen's hair was flying and she was laughing.

Steve realized another rider had joined them in the gallop. He twisted in the saddle. It was Doug Whipple. He was mounted on a long-legged black. He must have emerged from the brush at Blue Creek.

He grinned at Steve and said, "If she beats us we'll duck her in the crick like we did the day she won those two big agate shooters that we were so proud of, at marble playing."

"You really mean it!" Eileen said. "And you'd do it, too."

She fanned the gelding ahead faster. Doug's black might have overtaken her, for it began to pull away from Steve's mount, but he caught Doug's saddle skirt and impeded it. "You're not leaving me behind, my bucko," he said.

Eileen beat them by a length to the door of the old frame-built schoolhouse. The building was locked and deserted, for the fall school term had not yet started. A few lengths of bunting blew in the wind over the door. The picnic benches and tables and the barbecue pit which would have been used on Pool Day stood forlornly deserted under the box elders. The benches and trees bore the carved initials of generations of pupils, including Steve's and Doug's and Eileen's.

Beyond the school building was Short Creek, a small, meandering tributary to the nearby Powderhorn River. Steve and Doug overtook Eileen, snatched her, screaming and kicking, from the saddle and carried her to the creek. There they ducked her face under water.

She arose gasping and hurled mud at them. She sank back, breathless and laughing on the grass at the brink of the stream, blowing water, and spreading out the wet strands of her hair to dry. She looked down at her blouse, which was soaked and clinging to her.

"I'm a sight, and it wasn't fair, and quit looking at me until I dry off, and I'll get square with the both of you when I get a chance," she panted.

She pulled Doug's hair until he yelled for mercy and filled her cupped hands with water from the icy stream and poured it down Doug's back.

Quieting at last, they lay side by side on their stomachs, gazing at the old schoolhouse. The only sound now was the rasping of locusts in the grass and the soft, liquid footsteps of the stream. The memories came back, poignantly sweet and also disturbingly bitter. Steve saw the bleakness return to Doug's face—and the regret. He watched the animation fade from Eileen, saw the shadows arise. The moment when they had captured the lightheartedness of their youth had escaped them again.

"Where did you drop from, Doug?" Steve asked.

"Just happened to be letting my horse take a drink when you two hellions went by like a stampede," Doug said.

Steve guessed that Doug had been waiting there at the ford for them—since morning perhaps. He was drawn out, gaunt. Steve guessed that he had drunk all night, and perhaps had not slept at all.

A reticence holding them, they mounted again and headed up the trail which carried them into greener and heavily timbered country along the river. The stream, brawling with the memory of its plunge down the canyons of the mountains, foamed and surged in youthful vigor as it swept through its rugged channel. Steve kept pulling up, gazing longingly at stretches of smooth water, picturing the trout that must be lying there.

"Save it for Black Rock," Eileen told him.

They rode onward and he tried to put out of his mind all recollection of that moment when he had seen Doug unmasked alongside the halted train. He glanced at Eileen and guessed that she too was trying to assure herself that it could never have really happened.

They topped the Canteen Creek divide and left the main road and angled down a wagon track through stately spruce and pines. Presently they came out in an open meadow in which a beaver-dammed stream meandered. They took a short cut across this meadow, avoiding marshes and leaping their horses across the stream, then climbed to a higher, firm grass flat. In this stood a solid, log-built, shake-roofed house, flanked by a pole corral which had a saddle shed as its wall nearest the house. There was a small old dugout nearby which had once been used as the residence before the house was built. The sod roof of the saddle shed and dugout were adorned by blooming lupine and Indian paintbrush.

This was home at last for Steve. The OK ranch. He pulled up, and Eileen and Doug halted at a distance behind him and sat watching him.

He said nothing. It wasn't necessary. He then led the way ahead to the house and dismounted before the door. Instead of the battened, weed-grown desertion he had anticipated, the building and surroundings presented a used, tended look.

"I did what I could," Doug spoke. "And Eileen came over regularly with a mop and soap."

He added. "You see, we figured you'd be back some day, Steve."

Steve opened the door and stepped into the house. He heard Eileen and Doug ride away, heading for Antler two miles farther up the creek.

The shadows of late afternoon lay in the living room, which still held the furnishings that were identified with his life. He ran his hand over the smooth, cold face of the iron heating stove. From its isinglass window it had cast the fascinating colors that had entertained him as a small child on so many wintry days. The rocker, and the clock on the wall with its china face and gilded hands were in their usual places. The clock's pendulum was motionless now, but he found the key in the blue glass vase on the mantle where his father had always kept it. He wound the clock and it began its soothing clucking.

He walked into the kitchen. Doug had stocked the cupboard with canned food and other supplies. The cookstove showed the benefit of use.

He stood remembering his mother in this place, and he remembered his father coming in from the corral after the day's riding to lift and kiss her lustily and swing her so that her skirts flew like a feather in the wind.

83

He could not hold off these memories nor their regrets. He walked outside and stood breathing fast with the effort of a man trying to break this surge of weakening emotions.

He was glad when Doug came riding back from Antler. They ate in silence the meal Doug cooked—a man's meal of fried beefsteak which he had brought back as a gift from Eileen, fried potatoes with onions, and baked soda biscuits and canned tomatoes. With coffee and canned peaches.

They sat in the twilight smoking, watching the horses graze on picket in the meadow. They turned the animals into the corral as early darkness came.

"I'd like to live two hundred years with everything just like it is here tonight," Doug said.

He got out his trout tackle, along with Steve's, which he had kept oiled and cared for, and they spent a pleasant hour debating the merits of flies and lures and natural bait, and recalling Homeric contests of the past with battling monarchs of the streams.

For in the morning they were going fishing, the three of them. They finally turned in for the night, carrying with them these memories of the past and the hopes for the morrow.

"We'll have elk steak as well as trout for supper tomorrow," Doug said. "Eileen says she's got an elk yard staked out up on Cardinal."

Steve started to drop instantly asleep. Then other memories returned . . . the train robbery . . . the black and hostile attitude of Amos Whipple . . . the fight with Louis Latzo . . . the mystery of the hundred-dollar banknote in his wallet.

And there was the confident, handsome face of Burl Talley smiling at Eileen. Sleep vanished. He lay awake with these phantoms. He realized that Doug also was beleaguered and torn by his own thoughts.

He suddenly aroused, aware of the sound of approaching horses. He rose to an elbow. He heard Doug sit up.

Riders were turning off the main road and coming up to the house. He arose and peered from a window. All he could see was an indistinct group of mounted men. They pulled up in front of the house.

A voice shouted, "Light a lamp, Santee, an' show yourself. We aim to search your house an' ask a few questions."

It was the heavy, dominating voice of Amos Whipple. Steve stood debating it a moment, a deep and molten opposition in him. Doug spoke softly. "If you want to run them out of here I'll back your play, Steve. They're on the prod and want a victim. They don't care who that victim is."

"That's your own father out there, Doug," Steve said. "Stay out of this."

He lifted his voice and said, "All right. Wait'll I get into my pants."

He lighted the lamp and dressed. He buckled on his six-shooter. Doug, a queer, sardonic glint in his face as though he was bracing himself for chastisement, did not bother to arise from his bunk. He sat there, bare to the waist, his wide, freckled shoulders clear of the covers, waiting.

Steve opened the door. With a groan of leather and the tramp of boots Amos Whipple dismounted and led four men into the lamplight. They were armed with six-shooters and rifles. They glared at Steve, challenging him to try to question their right to be here.

He knew all of Amos's followers. They too had once been friends of his father. Now they were beset by the knowledge of loss and the fear of ruin and by anger and frustration. They were men ready to take the law into their own hands.

Amos paused in stride when he saw his son sitting on the bunk. "You should not be here, Douglas," he said sadly. "There should be a limit to the shame you heap on me."

"I've lived in this house quite a lot for the past three years, Dad," Doug said. "It's been almost like home to me. Almost, I said. There's nothing like a real home. Fact is, this house always seemed like home even when I was a button."

Amos felt the sting of this, Steve noted, but decided not to pursue the subject. He went rummaging through the house, poking beneath the beds with the muzzle of his rifle, pushing aside curtains, peering into corners and cupboards and tapping the floor in search of hiding places.

He did find the trap door leading to an opening, and for a time there was excitement as this was investigated. But it proved to be only the root cellar, long unused.

The presence of his son had taken the wind out of Amos's sails. He was unable to maintain the determination that had brought him here.

He abruptly motioned his companions to leave and followed them to the door. Turning, he said, "Coming, Douglas?"

Doug shook his head. "Leave this to the law, Dad. You don't know what you're monkeying with."

His father gave him a withering look. He glared at Steve, started to say something, but decided against it. He turned and walked out into the darkness.

Steve listened to the receding sounds as they rode away. He knew that Doug's presence had stayed off a showdown between himself and Amos and his Vigilantes. A violent showdown, perhaps. Undoubtedly, they had meant to make him explain why he had jostled Amos's arm during the train robbery. One of them had carried a coiled rope under his arm. A rope with the many folds of a hangman's knot as the hondo. He had been marked for Vigilante trial. He was to have been persuaded to talk with a noose around his neck.

"They were of a mind to hang you," Doug said. "Why?"

"If they were they decided against it," Steve said.

Doug stared unseeingly at the door through which they had gone. "You know about me, don't you, Steve?" he asked suddenly. "Me and the holdup?"

Steve had felt that this was coming and had been trying to find a way to meet it. Now that he had to answer, he still did not know what was best.

Finally he said tersely, "Yes."

"Eileen too?" Doug asked.

Steve nodded and waited.

"How long have you known?" Doug asked.

"Since the night of the holdup," Steve said. "Your mask had snagged on a tree limb, which lifted it off just at the time someone opened the firebox in the engine."

"Yeah," Doug said. "I was scared when it happened. But I was beginning to think nobody had seen."

"You were lucky, in a way," Steve said. "Only Eileen and myself happened to be looking in the right direction at that moment."

"But something else must have happened," Doug said. "My father seems to think you had a hand in the holdup. Why is that?"

"Maybe he's suspicious of anyone named Santee," Steve said.

Doug shook his head. "It's more than that. Amos has his faults, but he wouldn't go so far as to try to hang you just for being Buck Santee's son. He must have reason to suspect you."

"He's probably only trying to scare me," Steve said.

"I know him better than that," Doug said. "He never tries to run a bluff. He's an unforgiving man in matters of right and wrong. He convicted and sentenced your father after the Pool money disappeared three years ago. He had been Buck Santee's friend, but that didn't count, once he had pronounced his judgment."

Doug quit talking for a time, then said slowly, as though apologizing for his father. "But he was pushed into it. He's honest almost to a fault. He can't see the flaws in others. He can be led by a glib tongue."

"Who led him?" Steve asked.

"I'm not sure," Doug admitted. "But I'm beginning to understand a lot of things that've happened. Amos fired a shot at someone during the holdup. It's my guess that you did something to upset his aim, or he might have shot one of the outlaws down. Me?"

"It's past and done," Steve said.

Doug showed a twisted smile. "Amos used to say that blood is thicker than water when he was accusing you of having helped Buck Santee get away with that beef money. He and I are father and son. Nothing can change that. Beneath his stiff-necked pride Amos loves me. I know that. I also know what it would have done to him if he had shot that outlaw and then learned that he had killed his own son."

Steve said nothing. Doug spoke again. "And I know what it would have done to my mother. She still believes I'll come home to Center Fire some day and that everything will be as it was before."

He again gave Steve that fragment of a smile. "You've squared for that day on the ledge when we were boys, a hundred times over, Steve. I don't count, but for saving Mother —and Amos too, from heartbreak the other night, I thank you."

"You know one reason why I came back to the Powderhorn, Doug?" Steve said.

"Two reasons," Doug said.

Steve eyed him questioningly. When Doug did not elaborate, he went on, "I intend to run down the man who killed my father and Henry Thane. I know Dad was murdered."

"You've learned something?" Doug asked.

Steve nodded. "Yes. But I can't pass it along right now. I'm going to see that the guilty man is hung for it. If any others were mixed up in it they'll also go on my list. The law might not see it my way. Then I'll tear a page from Amos's book and take justice in my own hands."

"That sounds like a warning," Doug said.

"I've got a question that you can answer, or not, just as you choose, Doug," Steve said. "Here it is, cold. Was Nick Latzo or any of his crowd mixed up in the train stick-up?"

"Latzo? I've fallen pretty low. I've helped rob my own father, my own friends. But I draw the line somewhere, Steve. Would I have helped you against that slimy little Louie and those other two if I had been hooked up with a cutthroat like Nick?"

The next question was obvious. Just who was Doug hooked up with, if not Latzo? But it was one Steve did not ask. He felt that it would not be answered.

"Doug," he said. "Get out of the Powderhorn before it's too late. There are forces working against you that you don't know about. Get out while you can. That's all I can tell you."

"How does a man get stuck in the mire this way?" Doug said exhaustedly.

"It's never too late to wade out," Steve said.

"I don't expect you to believe this, even though it's true," Doug said. "But I didn't know I was going to rob my own father and the other ranchers. I didn't know they were aboard that train. I thought they were still in Cheyenne."

"But they *were* aboard," Steve said.

"I know it doesn't change things," Doug said. "But I've got to talk to somebody. I was told it was a shipment of money to the bank. I had been drunk as usual. For a week. Maybe I didn't do any real thinking. Maybe I didn't want to think. But I sobered up in a hurry when I learned I'd robbed men I've known from boyhood. And then I found out I'd stolen money from you, too."

"How did you get started in this sort of thing?" Steve asked.

"I was drunk that time too," Doug said, his voice flat and neutral as though he was discussing a stranger. "It was months ago. One night I found myself wearing a mask and riding with—with other masked men and helping rob a train. They told me I was the one who lighted the fuse that killed an express messenger who refused to surrender. I had too much alcohol in me to remember anything clearly. I guess I did it. It makes no difference anyway. I was a member of the gang. They won't let me forget about that messenger. They hold it over me."

"Who are 'they,' Doug?" Steve demanded.

There was no reply. He hadn't expected one. And he asked no more questions.

He barred the door, laid his pistol within reach alongside the bunk, and marked the location of Doug's rifle so that he could get to it in the dark in a hurry if the need came. He snuffed the lamp.

He lay a long time and knew that Doug was not asleep either. He listened to the clock ticking on the mantle and tried to find an answer for many things.

"I'll see to it that you get your money back," Doug spoke.

"It's the Pool's money," Steve said. "See that they get it back."

Finally he fell asleep. At intervals he would awaken and start up, reaching for the pistol. Then he would sink back, listening to the silence, realizing that what had aroused him was only the stirring of the wind in the timber. For the night passed and Amos Whipple did not return.

Chapter Ten

A rider jogged into the yard before dawn and Steve came out of the bunk with a rush and stood with the six-shooter in his hand, thumb on the hammer.

But it was Eileen's voice that called lightly. "You, there in the warm beds. It's almost daybreak and if you're going to eat elk steak and trout today you've got to face the facts of life. Let me in. I'm shivering like a quakie tree. It's frosty this morning."

Steve fumbled for his clothes, got into them and lighted a lamp. He admitted her.

It wasn't until then that he discovered that the bunk in which Doug had been sleeping was empty—the blanket and quilts thrown back.

He looked blankly at Eileen and walked outside to the corral. Doug's horse and saddle were gone.

"I thought I slept light," he said. "But he injuned away without arousing me."

"Why would he do that?" she asked. "He was looking forward to going with us."

Steve avoided answering that, banging the stove lids around as he built a fire. She huddled over the stove while it warmed. She had her hair stuffed into a wide-brimmed hat and wore a turtle-neck sweater and a duck saddle-jacket and riding jeans cuffed high on her half boots.

She had brought a slab of bacon and a jar of wild honey. She shed jacket and sweater as warmth pervaded the kitchen, and pushed Steve aside to take over the cooking.

She forced herself to be gay and chipper at first, but she was aware of Steve's silence and became more and more subdued. A pinch of worry formed above the bridge of her nose.

She placed a platter of hotcakes and crisp bacon on the table, along with a pitcher of warmed honey, and seated herself opposite him.

"Exactly what happened last night?" she demanded.

"Happened?"

She leaned across the table, pushing her face closer to his. "Don't try to hold out on me, my lad, or I'll twist your ears like a corkscrew. Where did Doug go? And why?"

"I don't know," Steve said. "Out of the country, I hope."

"Out of the country? Then something did happen!"

"Some ranchers came by early in the evening and searched the house," he said.

"Ranchers? Oh! Uncle Amos?"

"He was with them," Steve said. "In fact he seemed to be the ramrod. They searched the place. They found nothing. They left. That's all there was to it."

"What—what did they expect to find?" she asked wanly.

"They didn't say," Steve said. "The money from the train robbery, maybe."

"Or more likely they intended to try to force you to talk," she said. "Amos knows you jostled his arm deliberately. Was Doug here when they came?"

"He was here," Steve said.

"What happened between him and his father?"

"Amos was considerably upset," Steve said. "It spoiled his plans. I believe it saved me from a session that might have become very rough."

Eileen was silent for a time. "Steve," she finally said. "I

know how you feel about Doug. But this isn't fair to you. You can't take the blame for——"

"A man gave me some valuable information about my father's death yesterday," Steve said. "In return for that he asked me to say nothing and do nothing until he gave the word. He is an express company agent. You will not mention this to anyone."

"And—and you say Doug has left the country. You warned him?"

"I only hope he's gone," Steve said. "I don't know for sure. All I know is that I remember a day when I was hanging above Racehorse Rapids and——"

"I know," she sighed. "I was there. You can't forget a debt. But you can't pay for it with your own life. And Uncle Amos and the others aren't in a mood to listen to reason. They're facing ruin. Men like that strike out blindly."

Steve leaned over suddenly, took her in his arms, and kissed her. She burst into tears. "Damn it!" she sobbed. "Why did we have to grow up? Why couldn't we just have gone on as we did, playing together, fishing, hunting, and——"

"It's going to be just like it was for today at least, for you and me," he said. "And I'd be in a hell of a stew right now if you hadn't grown up. Come on! How about that elk you talked about? And that lunker in Black Rock?"

She dabbed at her eyes. She looked at him through the mist, then kissed him softly, tenderly.

"It's a deal," she said. "Steve, three years is a long time to wait. I—I don't want to lose you now."

She clung to him for a time, kissed him again, then moved back. "There's something I want to show you today," she said. "It's across the river, high up on Cardinal. That's elk country up there too. I stumbled on this thing a week or so ago. We can hit Black Rock toward sundown on the way back and that's when that big trout is most likely to be hungry."

Steve saddled, pocketed a fly book, and packed reels and sandwiches into saddlebags and tied rods across the cantle. Eileen had a .44-.40 rifle in the boot on her saddle. She led the way.

They crossed the meadow, forded Canteen Creek, and struck directly westward across a timbered rise for the river. Pink dawn was overhead now, but the frost lay white and pure as new snow on the grass and deadfalls. Night's heavy shadows still fought the oncoming day in the thick depths of the lodgepole pines.

They rode in silence, the air crisp and exhilarating in their throats. The glow of dawn presently reached through the foliage and touched them. All the shadows on their minds were driven away and they lived only for the moment.

Cattle huddled in the timber. Some wore Eileen's Antler brand. Others were Amos's Center Fires and Steve spotted a few of Burl Talley's Rafter O steers. This was open range.

"There'll be OK cattle here soon, I hope," he said. "I'm going to restore the brand."

They crested the rise, with the horses beginning to steam, and dropped downward into the rough and wild valley where the Powderhorn River began its long sweep northeastward through the basin. The sun was now striking the high peaks above them. Cardinal, the tallest, wore ermine and gold.

Half an hour of steady riding brought them to the river where it foamed and thundered over a boulder-studded course. They followed its margin upstream and presently climbed above its surface, skirting the rim of the stretch of gorge known as Racehorse Rapids.

Steve dismounted and walked to the rim at one point and gazed down the sheer drop to the rapids. This was where Doug had saved his life. Eileen watched and said nothing as he stood there for a time.

He mounted and they rode onward. They reached quieter water above the gorge and forded the river at a wide, sandy crossing where the horses blew complainingly as the icy water touched their bellies.

Beyond the river they began the climb up the flank of Cardinal Mountain. This was slanting country in all directions and clumped with aspen and coniferous timber and spangled with green parks and clearings.

Grazing horses drifted out of their path. There were not many cattle west of the river, for this was used principally as range for saddle stock by all of the outfits in the upper basin. Many of the horses bore the girth marks of recent work. They were from the remudas that had taken part in the beef gather and were turned out now to rest and fatten.

They mounted higher. A six-point buck, shaggy and wild-eyed, broke from cover and went tearing through the brush out of sight.

Twice Steve saw the fresh tracks of shod hooves. Once,

from beyond the river, came the faint report of a signal shot. Posses were still riding in their hunt for the train bandits, a search that was growing increasingly vain with the passing of time.

Hooves grated on rock higher up and two men appeared from around a clump of aspen on a ridge ahead. They were Burl Talley's two riders, Tex Creed and Highriver.

Both made quick motions toward their holsters. They paused, then sat motionless and Steve had the impression they were tautly waiting his next move.

Eileen lifted her voice. "Hello there! You're getting jumpy! Did you think you had bumped into your holdup men?"

The pair stirred their horses and descended the slant to meet them. "Didn't recognize you in britches, Miss Maddox," Creed said. "We been ridin' posse so long we're gittin' bug-eyed. We didn't expect to meet anybody up here. Ed Walters an' a puncher from Center Fire are supposed to be workin' along east o' the river toward the ford. Did you see 'em?"

"No," Eileen said. "We're out to bag an elk I've got staked out higher up—I hope. We're going to fish the river this afternoon."

"You'll have better luck with elk lower down," Creed said. "We sighted a nice bull this side o' the river awhile ago. Quite aways off just this side o' that old avalanche scar."

"Thanks," Eileen said. "We'll take a look."

"Good huntin'!" Creed said. "An' fishin'." He lifted his hat to Eileen, Highriver did likewise. They nodded to Steve and rode on past. They had the gaunt, drawn aspect of men who had been too long in the saddle.

"We're about ready to call it quits," Creed spoke back to them. "We're goin' on into town after we report to Ed. Whoever stuck up that train are likely a long ways from the Powderhorn. It's my guess they never came in this direction."

The two men rode on down the slope and were presently lost to sight among timber and ridges.

Eileen took the lead again and she and Steve sidehilled the mountain. They were paralleling the river now, but well above it. All of Powderhorn Basin was spread below them, stretching in a wrinkled carpet of somber green and saffron hues. The river was a strewn ribbon which coiled through the rough country, glittering here and there in the sun, the rays of which were now striking downward into the basin. Bugle was hidden in the distance by an arm of Long Ridge.

They were at nine-thousand-feet elevation now, with big timber below them and timberline showing on a naked mountainside to their right where a rockslide reflected the sunlight. The air here had a brittle quality and was so clear that Steve plainly saw a marmot's head jut above a rock on the rockslide, although the distance was a long rifleshot away.

The animal's shrill whistle came faintly. That was followed by a louder sound, and it wasn't the marmot. It was the whistle of a bull elk and fairly close at hand.

"All right," Eileen whispered, and her eyes were bright with excitement. "He's there—just where I expected him to be."

They dismounted, leaving the horses tied to ground pine. Eileen pulled the rifle from the boot and thrust it into his hand. They moved a step at a time up a rise.

Nearing the skyline, they crawled on hands and knees, careful not to displace rock. Steve could hear Eileen breathing in high suspense. Their shoulders touched and she moved close, her lips touching his cheek. "Welcome home, Steve," she said. "Welcome back to all the things you like to do."

They made the last few yards to the rim on their stomachs. Steve peered cautiously, and Eileen assayed a look.

A stately bull elk grazed in a shallow, sizeable draw where a small stream supported aspen and a growth of grass. The place was sheltered from the wind by rocky ridges and warmed by the radiation of the sunlight. Farther across the draw were three cow elk with calves and in the distance were more.

It was an easy shot. Steve estimated the distance and centered the sight on his quarry. But he could not squeeze the trigger. He lowered the rifle and gave Eileen a wry look.

He tried again. And again he could not fire. "This is no good," he said. "For three years I've been dreaming about this, and now I can't bring myself to knock over that noble creature as though I was slaughtering a steer for beef."

He arose into plain view and shouted. The elk whirled, hair ruffled. In the next instant it was off with all the power and speed of its wild nature.

He raised the rifle, followed his quarry a moment in the sights, and let drive. The elk kept going, vanishing into quaking aspen over the ridge southward. The remainder of the band was gone also, crashing away through the aspen.

He lowered the gun and looked guiltily at Eileen. She began to laugh. "Don't try to tell me it was buck fever," she said. "You missed him deliberately." She added, "I'm glad. It just isn't a day for destroying beauty—or illusions."

"It looks like we eat trout or nothing," Steve said. "That shot likely spooked every elk on this side of the mountain. You can bet I won't be in a mood to miss by the time we hit Black Rock pool."

"Remember that I said I had something up here I wanted to show you," she said. "It isn't far. It's something that has puzzled me."

They returned to the horses and she led the way for another mile or more along the flank of the mountain. She dismounted and said, "Here it is."

They were in a small draw which faded out into a great thicket of willows, ground pine, and aspen. A game trail led into this tangle. Steve followed her into this opening on foot. Paths such as this had a habit of dwindling out, leaving a man with the alternative of turning back or trying to fight his way ahead an unknown distance through heavy vegetation.

But Steve noticed that horses had used this game trail —both shod and unshod animals.

The brush extended to the base of a low clay bluff. Abruptly the trail widened and Steve found himself gazing at a man-made habitation. It was a dugout, almost a cave, in fact, for it was backed into the base of the bluff where a natural alcove had been enlarged and closed in with rude walls of ax-cut lengths of lodgepole pine and aspen.

Dead brush and branches had been heaped against the face of the structure to mask its presence. A casual intruder might have passed it without discovering it.

"I stumbled on this about a week ago," Eileen explained. "That was after the beef gather had been shipped. I helped Shorty shove the spare saddle stock across the river into pasture. Some of the horses which had been here all summer had taken it into their heads to hide up high, and I rode up here to push them down nearer the river. Two of them took off down this game trail, and that's when I found this hide-out. I had a feeling that the two horses had been here before. They seemed to know this dugout. I left for Cheyenne the next day and had nearly forgotten about this thing."

Steve moved aside dead brush to get at a crude door hung on leather straps. He opened this portal and stepped inside. There was no sign that the place had ever been used as a shelter for men, but it had been occupied by saddle stock recently. Within the past hour or two, by the fresh tracks and sign. Two sacks of grain stood nearby and one had been partly used.

It was not a line camp, for such duty was unnecessary west of the river. The towering Powderhorns were sufficient protection from drift in that direction.

Steve gazed around, a cold excitement forming in him. "You used the right word," he said to Eileen. "Hide-out."

This dugout was outlaw handiwork. This was a relay point where fresh horses were spotted before a robbery for emergency use in escaping over the mountains in case something went wrong and it was necessary to flee the country ahead of pursuers.

He studied the interior and decided that four horses had been quartered in the structure for perhaps three days. The animals had just recently been released, and the dead brush had been carefully replaced across the front of the structure.

Palpably it had not been necessary to use the relay horses and there had no longer been need of holding them ready. The law had never come that close to picking up the scent of the men who had staged the train robbery. For there was no question but that this relay station was a part of that affair, at least in Steve's mind.

He looked at Eileen and saw that she was beginning to understand all these things. A somber shadow lay upon her. He knew she was thinking of Doug.

She turned abruptly and headed for the open. She walked faster and faster until she was running back down the game trail as though pursued by evil.

Steve carefully replaced the dead brush over the face of the hide-out and followed her. They mounted in silence and headed toward the river. Neither mentioned what they had discovered in the thicket.

Halfway down the mountain, four riders came spurring out of timber into view ahead. One was Ed Walters, first deputy sheriff under Bill Rawls. With him were Tex Creed and Highriver and a cowpuncher who worked for Amos Whipple.

"Was it you folks that done the shootin' awhile ago higher up?" Walters demanded as he rode up.

Steve nodded. "I cut loose on an elk. Missed."

The deputy was disgruntled. He was a ruddy, heavy irascible man. "A hell of a time to sling lead in these parts," he complained. "You cost us two miles' ride up this damned slant on footsore hawses."

"My fault," Steve said. "But we had passed Creed and this other rider here on our way up and told them we were after elk. We took it for granted you'd know it was us who did the shooting."

"You didn't tell me that, Tex," Walters said, aggrieved.

"It slipped my mind," Creed said. "An' we'd have had to make sure they hadn't bumped into these train robbers, no matter what." He turned on Steve. "Did you sight anything up there outside of elk?"

"Nothing worth shooting at," Steve said.

Ed Walters eyed Eileen sourly. "You all right, Miss Maddox?" he asked.

"Why shouldn't I be all right?" Eileen asked, bristling.

Walters didn't reply to that. He gave Steve a critical look, turned, and led his posse away. "This is the last place they'd have come to," he was grumbling. "Bill Rawls would never have sent us on a wild goose chase west of the river if you hadn't put him up to it, Tex."

Steve and Eileen followed at a distance, but their trails soon parted, and the posse headed for the ford downstream. They picked their own trail directly down the mountain toward Black Rock pool.

The pool was a fine stretch of clear water where the river swept past an upthrusting ridge of bedrock that was black with the constant spray. This created a wide inshore eddy. In the depths of this deep hole were boulders and waterlogged driftwood where big trout lurked.

They ate their sandwiches, boiled a pot of coffee and then lay dozing in the sun-warmed sand alongside the river until the afternoon shadows reached the stream. They then set up their rods and after a long debate, during which Steve refused to take precedence, they compromised by agreeing to cast simultaneously.

Steve watched Eileen as she stripped line and danced the fly above water, working for distance. She picked a whorl forty feet from shore as her target. She had laid aside the sweater and jacket and was in a checkered blouse and was barefoot, her jeans rolled high. She waded into the margin of the stream.

Steve fought the urge to walk to her, take her in his arms, and tell her all the things he had been wanting to say to her almost since that first moment aboard the train. He found in him a fear of unutterable loss—a desperate fear.

He moved to the stream playing the rod. He judged his time and placed his own fly on the surface at a likely spot at the same moment Eileen let her own lure settle to the water.

Almost instantly there were violent eruptions around the dancing objects. Eileen uttered a cry of delight. Steve experienced the electric excitement of a hookup as he straightened line.

They had fish, but not the monsters they had anticipated. Eileen's trout, when she finally beached it, proved to be a thirteen-inch beauty. Steve's catch was only slightly smaller.

They cast again, but nothing arose. They fished for half an hour longer and Black Rock pool lay sullenly unresponsive. Now and then Steve saw great shadows move in the depths. But none of the big trout would rise.

Somehow the zest had gone. In fact it had vanished at the moment they had stood in the dugout on the mountain and had comprehended its significance. Since then they had been maintaining only a pretense of the lightheartedness with which they had set out at dawn.

Sundown came. They saddled up and rode toward the ford. A cold wind drove down from the peaks. Abruptly the weather changed. Rain clouds came rolling over the rims.

It began to rain and they donned slickers. The downpour increased, slatting through the timber, funneling in streams from their hatbrims, finding its way down their necks.

It was dreary nightfall when the lights of Eileen's ranch appeared. Shorty Barnes' widowed sister, who acted as housekeeper at Antler, came to the door, peering and called, "I was worryin' about you, Eileen."

Steve drew the saddle from her gelding, turned the animal into the corral, and carried the rigging into the shed. She stood with him there in the shadows and kissed him. "Whatever is going to become of Doug?" she said tiredly. "And of you, Steve? Please be careful."

She seemed reluctant to part with him, but finally turned away and walked to the house. She stood in the doorway, watching as he rode away.

His own ranch was dark and forlorn in the rain. He cared for the horse and fled from the storm into the house. Lighting the lamp, he got a fire going and cooked a supper from the remainder of the steak and other food.

He ate and afterwards sat with a mug of coffee in his hand, trying to decide his course. He was gripped by complete frustration, unable to make a move in the matter of his father's death, because of the promise he had made to Frank Clum, and he was equally handicapped in the matter of the money he had lost, because of Doug's involvement in the robbery.

He added pitch fuel to the stove and it roared busily, casting flickering bands of light in the kitchen. The storm rumbled through the tops of the timber. Heavier gusts of rain beat on the roof, and the drip of water was a soothing undertone.

He thought of Eileen, remembering her as she had stood at Black Rock pool. He thought of her steadfast loyalty and of her grief over Doug. Burl Talley's face came into focus in his mental picture, serene and confident. That brought a cold desolation in him. It was as though he was seeing Eileen's true future.

He became aware of a vague scraping sound. Absently he decided that it might be a squirrel at a window. In the next moment he aroused, knowing there would be no squirrels out at this time of night and in this weather.

That saved his life. There was a shadowy something at the window. It was the head and shoulders of a man who wore a black slicker buttoned to his chin and had a neckerchief pulled over the lower half of his face. Only his eyes were tangible beneath the brim of his rain-sogged hat.

The man had a six-shooter in his hand and it was pointed. Steve hurled himself aside as the weapon exploded. Glass burst in a shower, the fragments striking him and tinkling against the stove and on the floor.

Chapter
Eleven

He felt the vicious, pushing thrust of a bullet at his arm. It was as though some arrogant hand had tried to grasp him. It whirled him, overbalancing him, and he fell.

He twisted around, scrambling with legs and arms, and drawing himself toward the wall beneath the window. It was an instinctive maneuver for self-preservation, because that area was a difficult point for the assassin to command through the broken glass of the small opening.

As he moved the roar of gunfire beat at him, and the room was alight and quivering with the explosions of a six-shooter which was being emptied at him in a frantic attempt to pin him to the floor with bullets.

He did not know if he had been hit. He felt nothing, for the only thought in him was to try to stay alive until he could reach his own .45, which he had hung on a peg not far from the window.

He made it to the wall. The crash of the gunfire ended and he heard a hammer fall on an empty. He pulled himself along the wall, gazing upward at the opening above him. The concussions had blown out the lamp and only the dull flicker from the stove lighted the room.

He expected a second gun to be pushed through the window and to face bullets that would finish him.

This did not come. He got to his knees, and his hand found his holster where it dangled on the wall. He snatched out the pistol and sent a bullet angling through the opening. The flash lighted the window and he saw that it was vacant. The masked man had backed away.

He raced to the door, tore it open, and leaped out, crouching low and diving aside. No shot came.

He stood braced there in the darkness, searching the night for sound or movement. The rain began soaking him to the skin. He felt a burning pain along his left upper arm, but the arm was unimpaired and he believed it had been only a graze.

The first slug that had twisted him around seemed to have done no physical damage. He discovered that the bullet had torn through the heavy fold of his shirt sleeve, which he had rolled above his elbows while cooking.

He restrained his breathing, listening. The only sound for a space of time was the drone of the wind in the timber and the rain drip from the eaves of the house.

On a hunch he went plunging straight ahead, with a noisy stamping of his boots in the muddy ranch yard. He had guessed that the assassin must be crouching near. His maneuver panicked the man into revealing his whereabouts. A six-shooter exploded twice from the vicinity of the saddle shed. The man had managed to reload.

Steve was not hit. He heard one of the bullets grind into the wall of the house at his side. He fired back once, but knew that he was only wasting powder, for he could hear the other breaking into running escape.

He fired again into the air, hoping the flash would reveal his opponent. He gained only a glimpse of a figure darting around the corner of the saddle shed.

Steve raced in the opposite direction around the corral, circling it. He had the advantage of knowledge of the terrain. He also had the advantage of initiative and impetus.

It was certain that the man would have a saddle horse nearby. The natural point at which the mount would have been tied, and the easiest to locate in the darkness, would be the opposite end of the corral, for that was far enough from the house so that the sound of the approach of a rider would have been covered by the wind and rain.

He almost collided with the man's horse, which was tethered to the pole rails of the corral just about where he had estimated that it would be.

The horse reared. At the same instant he realized that his man was coming up at a run from around the opposite side of the corral. He ducked past the plunging horse, risking a blow from a hoof, and crashed bodily into his opponent in the darkness.

The man fired his pistol, but Steve had anticipated that and had flailed out with both arms in a sweeping motion. His left wrist struck the other's gun arm an instant before the weapon flamed and the bullet went into the sky.

His fingers grasped the folds of a slicker. His own pistol was clear. But the other's gunhand was free also. Steve had no choice, for he knew that in the next instant a bullet would tear through him. He jammed his gun against the slicker and fired twice.

The sledging force of the .45 slugs tore the man from him. He heard a terrible, choking sound. His own forward motion was still carrying him and he fell over the man who was going down at his feet.

A gun flashed almost beneath him, but the bullet went into the mud. A voice, drowned now in both blood and despair, said thickly. "Don't shoot me again, Santee. I'm—done—fo——"

That ended it. The last shot had been fired by the man in the final reflex of expiring life.

Steve crouched there for a time, the fingers of his left hand still locked in the slicker of the figure that lay unseen beside him in the blackness and the rain. His foot rested on the other's gun-arm. But there was no longer any harm in the assassin.

He got to his feet at last and walked shakily to the house and lighted the lamp in the kitchen. He did not replace the chimney, but carried the glass base, with its flaring and smoking wick turned up, shielding it as best he could from the storm.

He bent over the sprawled figure, peering in the wavering light. The hat and the handkerchief mask had fallen aside.

The features that looked up at him were those of a stranger. He stood there for some time, peering incredulously. His first thought had been that the assassin had made a mistake in picking him as his target. But he remembered that the man had uttered his name before he died. There had been no mistake.

The lampwick guttered out. He carried it to the house and relighted it. He examined his own wound. It was a bullet scrape just beneath his armpit. A painful injury which was bleeding, but was not much more than a deep scratch. He tore a clean shirt into strips and formed a bandage.

He carried the lamp to the saddle shed and left it there while he walked to the far side of the corral with a blanket. He wrapped this around the limp form and lifted its weight in his arms, and carried it to the shed. He laid the body on the lid of the six-foot-long feedbox which his father had built years in the past for the storage of bran and corn for the saddle stock.

He moved the lamp closer. The dead man was tough-featured and marked by hard drinking. He wore cowboots, run-down at the heel, but otherwise, neither his shabby garb nor his general appearance was that of one who spent much time working cattle.

He had carried only the one six-shooter and its action now was choked with mud. Steve searched the pockets for some means of identification. He placed the results on a bench. A plug of tobacco, an elk-tooth charm, two brass checks of the kind that could be won in slot machines and were good for drinks at bars. These particular ones, according to their inscriptions, were cashable only at the places operated by Nick Latzo.

Steve found himself shaking. The aftermath of that moment of supreme effort when he had fought for his life, hand-to-hand, with this stranger in darkness, was hard upon him. He had to drive himself to go ahead with the grisly task of ransacking the pockets of a corpse.

The inner pocket of the coat yielded a partly punched meal ticket issued by a Front Street restaurant and half a dozen coins in small change. Also a thin packet of bills, held by a paper clip. The bills seemed to be of small denominations.

But no! Steve picked up one of the folded banknotes. It was a hundred-dollar bill—a twin of the one he had in his own wallet, and of the one Frank Clum had shown him. It bore a stain of dark blood which was already drying.

He stared. The probable real purpose of these banknotes occurred to him. He and Clum might have been too quick in jumping to the conclusion that they had been meant as a mere bribe. The person who had requested that they carry the bills on their persons could have used that method of making their murder worth while to a paid killer. The shoddy form on the feedbox had all the appearance of a man whose fee for assassination would not have been high.

A new thought startled him. "Clum!" he said aloud. "They might be after him too!"

He debated it an instant. He placed the bloodstained bill in his pocket and raced to the house to get his coat and slicker. He got the saddle out of the shed, blew out the lamp, and closed the door, dropping the wooden peg into the hasp.

Moving fast, he rigged the horse and mounted. He hesitated a moment, gazing at the dark outline of the shed, regretting the necessity of leaving even the body of a person who had tried to murder him alone and unwatched.

He rode away toward Bugle. He still had Shorty Barnes' horse, and the animal was equal to the task in spite of the day's journey on the mountain.

It was past ten o'clock by the clock in the window of Eli Morton's jewelry store when he rode down Bozeman Street on the tired horse. The rain had slackened to a thin drizzle. The street was muddy and desolate. The conservative section of town was turning in for the night, but the gambling houses were doing business, though even there the weather had subdued the activity.

The front of the Pioneer House was still lighted. Steve dismounted at the rail, looped the reins, and walked into the lobby. The clerk was disappearing upstairs on some errand, a bundle of towels over his arm.

Except for a sleepy, round-stomached man who had the appearance of a clothing drummer, the chairs in the lobby were vacant.

Steve walked down the hall. This passageway had a runner of faded red carpet down its length and was lighted only by a single ceiling lamp.

Someone was just leaving by way of the rear door. It was a man's figure. The light was too dim for positive identification, but Steve had the impression that it was Louie Latzo. The door closed behind the departee.

Steve's step quickened. He did not realize that he was a hard-looking figure. His face still bore the marks of his fight with Louie and the two roughs. His dark beard had grown during the day, giving his features a thin, wild cast. His shirt, stained with his own blood and that of the man who had tried to kill him, was visible beneath his open slicker, which he had unfrogged so that he would have access to his holster. He was streaked with mud as a result of his struggle at the corral. More mud had spattered him during the ride to town.

He remembered that Clum's room had been three doors from the one he had occupied. He hardly counted on finding the man in his quarters, but it at least offered a starting point in the hunt he expected to have to make.

However, lamplight showed beneath the door. He stood a moment at the portal, listening. From another room half a dozen doors away came voices. Someone was entertaining visitors over a convivial bottle. A door slammed on the upper floor. He heard the clerk descending the creaking stairs at the front, en route back to the desk. There were other sounds in the building—normal sounds.

Frank Clum's room was silent. Some warning of disaster impelled Steve to draw his six-shooter.

He tapped on the door. The silence was unbroken. He tapped again, harder.

The door swung slightly ajar. It was not locked, and had been only partly caught on the latch.

Steve pushed it open. Frank Clum was at home. He sat slumped forward, his head resting face-down on a small table that served as a writing desk. A bottle of ink was spilled, the black stream still dripping over the edge of the table to the brown carpet.

There it was joined by another stain. This one was blood. The handle of a knife jutted from Frank Clum's back.

Steve moved numbly into the room and to the side of the slumped figure. Clum had been writing a letter. Steve mechanically read the words:

To My Dearest Wife:
        I am writing this in my room at . . .

Frank Clum had died as he had started that message to his loved one. A knife had been driven into his back and into his heart. The top of his head had been caved in by a violent blow. He had been blackjacked to make sure of the job.

Clum's coat was on the floor, the pockets turned inside out. His wallet lay nearby. Steve picked up the wallet. It was empty. The hundred-dollar bill was gone.

Steve grasped the handle of the knife in the instinctive, humane attempt to free it from human flesh. It was a wooden-handled, cheap affair of the kind that could be bought in any outfitting store. It did not easily yield and he realized that removing it was useless anyway, and that it should be left where it was until the law was called in.

Before his fingers relaxed from the handle a woman's shrill scream of terror brought him around, startled.

He was looking into the horrified face of a gray-haired woman who wore the apron of a chambermaid and carried a broom. She was the night maid who had passed by the open door, and had looked in.

She screamed again with all the frenzied strength of complete fear. She dropped the broom and fled, still screeching at the top of her lungs.

Doors opened and confusion began. Guests poured into the hall from other rooms. A man appeared in the door staring. It was the plump man who had been drowsing in the lobby. Others joined him.

Steve gazed at them. He realized he still had his six-shooter in his hand. He holstered it. "Come in here, you," he said, pointing at the drummer. "And you," he added, singling out another. "The rest of you stay out. Someone send for the marshal."

The two men he had indicated did not move. Nor did the others. The hall was filling with new arrivals. Those in the rear were babbling questions. "That man just killed another one in the room there," someone was saying hoarsely. "The maid saw it. He used a knife. Stabbed him in the back."

In the lobby the chambermaid was still screaming hysterically.

"I didn't kill him," Steve said. "I just happened by."

He was remembering the dim figure he had seen leaving by the rear exit, the one that might have been Louie Latzo.

He tried to push past. "Let me by," he said. "I saw someone go out by the back door just as I came down the hall. Maybe he's the one who killed this man."

Nobody moved. Nobody yielded an inch. They merely stood looking at him. "You better stay here," the drummer said. The man lifted his voice. "Fetch the marshal! Tell him there's been a murder."

Steve drew his .45. "You fools!" he said. "The real killer is getting away. Stand aside."

They saw the grimness in his eyes and gave way suddenly. The drummer's face was chalky. He backed away hastily, forcing those behind him to yield.

Steve gave them an additional shove and raced through them and down the hall to the rear door. It opened into a deserted back street. The rain had settled in again and he ran along this dark, muddy thoroughfare, peering in both directions. No one was in sight. There were many paths between buildings by which the figure he sought could have reached other streets. Behind him men were spilling from the Pioneer House. Someone shouted, "There he is!"

Another touched off a pistol, firing three times with the wildness of an excited, frightened man. Steve heard a bullet strike a building and another ricochet from stone.

He called, "Hold your fire! You've got it all wrong!"

He backed into the shelter of a building corner. Other shots were fired. Men were spreading out in the street and shouting to each other.

A deeper, authoritative voice arose. "Come out of there, whoever you are, with your hands up."

That was Marshal Mart Lowery, who had arrived.

"Tell those idiots to quit shooting, Lowery," Steve said. "I was only chasing the murderer. I'm coming out."

He expected to be shot down by some overwrought person. He holstered his gun and walked toward the dark mass of men.

Mart Lowery's figure detached itself from the group and loomed before him. "Well, well!" Lowery grunted, peering at him. "Steve Santee! You know, I felt in my bones you'd be mixed up in this."

Before he was aware of the officer's intention he felt hard metal close around his left wrist. He was handcuffed to the marshal. An instant later his right hand was similarly linked to another man who wore a deputy's shield. His six-shooter was taken from its holster.

"Why did you knife that man?" Lowery demanded.

"Clum was already dead when I found him," Steve said. "Listen to me! I think I know who killed him. Take off these damned handcuffs. Use your head, Lowery!"

"Clum, you say," Lowery said. "I understood the man's name was Drumm—John Drumm. What did you do? Kill the wrong man?"

Steve went wild. He yanked Lowery toward him and tried to swing a fist, forgetting that his arm was manacled to the deputy. Even so the power of his effort carried that officer with him and into the marshal. The three of them went floundering down in a heap in the mud.

Lowery, panting, rose to a knee. "You need coolin' down!" he said, and brought the long muzzle of his six-shooter smashing down on Steve's head.

Chapter
Twelve

Steve's next memory was of throbbing, heavy agony in his head. Through the haze that seemed to cloud his vision he made out blurred faces. Gradually his sight cleared, and his thoughts focused. They had carried him to the jail and he was stretched on a bunk in a cell.

Tobias Skelly, the wizened medic who had doctored the ills of the Powderhorn people for years, was rolling down his starched cuffs. "He'll be all right," Tobias was saying. "He escaped a fracture, thanks to having a hard skull. Mart, you ought to be more careful when you buffalo a man. You might have killed him."

"It'd have saved the county the cost of a trial," Lowery said.

The doctor left. Another man remained in the cell with the marshal. Steve groggily recognized him. It was Burl Talley.

Steve finally managed to sit up. The cell kept whirling around him, and he clung to the bunk. Slowly that vertigo faded, slowly all memory came back—Frank Clum's body with the knife in the back—the futile pursuit of that furtive figure—and the handcuffs on his own wrists.

And his own fight to the death at his ranch with the stranger. That aroused him and his hand sped to the inner pocket of his coat where he had been carrying his wallet. During the ride to town he had placed in it for safekeeping, along with the original banknote, the blood-stained hundred-dollar bill he had found on the assassin.

The wallet was gone. "Lookin' for somethin'?" Lowery asked ironically.

"Yes," he said. "My wallet."

"The one in which you put the hundred-dollar bill that you took from Frank Clum?"

Steve looked from the marshal to Burl Talley. The latter's lean face was grave. He shook his head and said, "You might as well tell Mart all about it, Steve. I'm sorry. Sorry for you."

Steve pulled himself to his feet with an effort. Tobias

Skelly had added a band of court plaster to his other relics of combat. It ran from his temple on up into his hair, where a patch had been shaved out. This covered the gash where Lowery's gun muzzle had broken the skin.

He steadied. He had been at a disadvantage sitting down. He was as tall as the lanky marshal and an inch taller than Talley.

Lowery sensed this opposition in him and moved back a pace. "Don't try nothin', Santee," he warned. "I've stood enough o' your roughness."

"So you know that his name was Frank Clum?" Steve asked.

Lowery nodded. "I've learned some things lately. I know now that Clum wasn't a horse buyer. He was sent here by the express companies. He was tryin' to run down the train robbers."

He added, "That's why you killed him."

"On the contrary I went there to prevent just what happened," Steve said. "I was too late. I sighted a man leaving by way of the door to the back street as I came into the hall from the lobby. He had made his getaway by the time I got out there."

Lowery grinned derisively. "Got a story all fixed up in a hurry, didn't you? But it'll take plenty more than that. How about the two hundred-dollar bills we found in your wallet? We know Clum was carryin' one. An' we know how he got it."

"Neither of those two bills were taken from Clum," Steve said. "I was sent one of them at the same time Clum got one. I——"

"Sure," Lowery jeered. "Sure you got one. That was half payment for killin' Clum. The other half you got from his wallet. Clum's blood was on it. The blood from where you knifed him. You didn't know about the blood did you? Now let's see you explain that away."

"It isn't Clum's blood," Steve said. "It was the blood of a man who tried to kill me at the OK tonight. I shot him. His body is in the saddle shed at my place. I found a hundred-dollar bill in his pocket."

Lowery stared and his jeering grin widened. "How's that? Say, you must have been awake longer than we knew about to have dreamed up a yarn like that. What kind o' a sandy are you tryin'——"

Steve turned to Burl Talley. "I know you must be the

one who told Lowery about Clum. How do I know that? Because Clum told me he had taken you into his confidence. We two were the only ones in the Powderhorn who knew Clum's real identity."

Talley shrugged. "It's true Clum confided in me. He told me only yesterday morning that someone apparently was trying to bribe him. He said he had received a hundred-dollar bill, along with a note hinting that more money would be easy to earn if he was agreeable. But it seems now that it was part payment for killing him."

"He told you about talking to me, of course?" Steve asked. "And about finding the same thing under my door?"

"He did mention your name to me, but not in any such connection," Talley said reluctantly. "As a matter of fact he was inclined to believe you were in league with those train robbers."

Steve stared disbelievingly. "That's impossible!" he exclaimed. "Why, Clum told me——"

"Frankly, Santee," Talley said. "I must warn you that you're in a very serious situation. It would be better if you made a clean breast of everything."

Steve had the sensation of wading upstream against a current that grew increasingly powerful and that, sooner or later, would sweep him away. "Listen to me!" he said. He forced himself to speak slowly, carefully. He related his talk with Clum.

"Clum had turned up some new evidence in the disappearance of my father which might spoil a lot of work by the law if I told it now," he said.

"I'm sure, if there actually was any such new evidence in regard to your father you'd be better off telling it to Mart here and now," Talley said.

"It would be still better if I talked to express company agents first," Steve said.

Talley shrugged. "What's this story you were telling about killing a man at your place tonight?"

Steve recounted the details of his escape from assassination and of his fight to the death with the stranger and of finding the blood-stained banknote in the dead man's possession.

"You were right about it being payment for murder," he said to Talley. "I realized it also. Apparently someone wanted both Clum and myself put out of the way. Why?

110

Maybe that someone was afraid we might learn too much about a lot of things in addition to the murder of my father."

Mart Lowery, who had been listening impatiently, said, "Bosh! I ain't got time to listen to any such pack o' lies."

"Be fair, Mart," Talley remonstrated. "Santee's story should be easy to corroborate or disprove. You can send someone out to his ranch to take a look at this dead man—if one is there."

"That's county territory," Lowery said. "It's the sheriff's responsibility. I don't aim to go to the expense o' sendin' a man on a wild goose chase twenty miles on a night like this. I'll turn it over to Bill Rawls as soon as he shows up."

Talley turned to leave. "I'd advise that you retain a good lawyer, Santee. I'm afraid you're going to need all the help you can get. I know that Eileen Maddox feels obligated to you because of childhood association. For her sake I'll do what I can. I'll try to get in touch with Carter Benton and have him talk to you tonight, late as it is. Carter's the smartest lawyer in these parts."

"I don't need a lawyer," Steve said. "I'll be out of here by morning."

"I hope so," Talley said, and walked out of the cell and down the stone floor of the jail out of the cellroom. He had the attitude of a man who had shown Christian tolerance in a trying situation and who was now glad to wash his hands of the affair.

Mart Lowery followed him. The iron door swung shut behind them and the lock grated into place. A bleary-eyed, ragged saddle tramp who occupied the opposite cell on a charge of drunkenness, peered scornfully and spat on the floor. "Gittin' so a man finds hisself in the damnedest company in these here jails," the man said. "I don't go fer knifin' in the back. They ought to hang you higher'n a buzzard's nest."

Steve found himself breathing hard. He had heard of men who went berserk under confinement and had battered themselves to death against the bars like wild animals. He could understand this now.

Time passed. The jail was used jointly by both the county and the town officers. The marshal and his deputies shared the office space at the front with the sheriff's staff, with merely a partition between the two sections.

There was no sign that anyone knew or cared whether

Steve was dead or alive. Finally the night turnkey came into the jail room from the office, swinging a bull's-eye lantern with which he made the rounds of the cells. He flashed the light through the bars, scrutinizing Steve from head to foot.

"Where's Lowery?" Steve demanded.

"Lowery? Home o' course. In bed fer an hour or more by this time. Where'd you think he'd be at this time of night?"

"Did they send someone out to my place?"

"To your place? Do you mean to hunt that ghost you was yarnin' about?"

"Damn you, did anyone go?"

The turnkey scowled. "Keep a polite tongue in your head, Santee. Or maybe you'd like me to git a bucket of cold water an' chill you down. Ever sleep in a bunk that's soppin' wet?"

"I asked you a question," Steve said grimly.

"Mart notified the sheriff's office," the turnkey said sourly. "But Rawls is asleep an' wasn't to be disturbed. Bill's been ridin' quite a fur piece an' deserves some rest. I reckon someone'll go out there in the morning. That'll be time enough." The man laughed. "Yore dead man won't up an' walk away, now will he?"

Steve turned away. The turnkey guffawed again and left the cell room, extinguishing the single oil lamp that had given light, leaving the place in darkness—a darkness that Steve could feel reaching deep inside him.

The saddle tramp began to snore. Other prisoners slept noisily also. Steve stretched out on the bunk. He lay rigid and awake. He found himself sweating, although the damp chill of the night had crept into the place.

He finally dropped off for an hour or two, but awakened when dawn seeped into the dismal room. He walked the cell, trying to force the numb cold out of his marrow—and out of his heart.

Daylight strengthened. He could hear the stirring of the awakening town. A jerkline team ground past the jail down Bozeman Street, dragging a loaded wagon and trailer by the sounds. Other outfits moved out, bound for the mines. Wheels rumbled and bit chains jangled.

A steam whistle blew. That would be the working signal at Burl Talley's planing mill at the head of the street. Six-thirty.

Steve had already been in the cell a lifetime. His head still ached from the blow Lowery had struck. He gave way to his futile rage and rattled the iron door.

It was a long time before the door from the office opened. It was the day turnkey who had come on duty. "What in hell do you want?" the man demanded. "Tim told me that you likely would try to stir up trouble. Keep quiet. You'll git some breakfast when I git good an' ready to fetch it."

The door closed again. An hour passed. The turnkey came in with a plate of flapjacks and a mug of coffee which he had carried from a restaurant. He thrust the food through the small panel in the cell door and started to turn away without a word.

"I want to talk to Lowery," Steve demanded. "Is he on duty yet?"

"It's Bill Rawls you'll deal with from now on," the man said. "You're a county prisoner. County's payin' for your board now."

Then he left. The coffee was cold, the flapjacks soggy. Midmorning passed. Noon approached. Nothing happened. Merely the passage of time. One long minute after another. The hands on Steve's watch seemed frozen. Occasionally he called out and rattled the door. It brought no response.

An unpalatable noon meal was brought by the same turnkey who refused to answer his questions.

It was midafternoon when Sheriff Rawls came striding into the jail room, followed by Mart Lowery and Carter Benton, the lawyer.

Rawls was a big, gaunt, high-shouldered man with a thin, arched nose. An honest, but unimaginative man, he had been sheriff of Powderhorn County for half a dozen terms. He was fresh-shaven and dressed in clean garb, but his eyes were still tired and the marks of strain were on him.

"Hello, Santee," he said, and his tone was strictly neutral. He jerked a thumb toward the lawyer. "I reckon you know Mr. Carter Benton, of course? Burl Talley asked Carter if he'd consider defending you."

"I agreed to discuss it with you, at least, Santee," the lawyer said. He was a crisp and starchy man of sixty with a clipped gray mustache and wooly, iron gray hair. He was prosperous and wore an expensive business suit.

"Anything you say can be used against you," Rawls warned

113

Steve. "But you might also be able to help yourself if you cooperated with the law."

"Don't say a word, Santee," Carter Benton spoke. "Not until you and I have had a chance to talk in private."

"I've already told it all," Steve said. "Sheriff, did you send out to my place to find that fellow's body who tried to kill me last night?"

"Surely, you don't aim to try to stick to that story?" Rawls said testily.

"You mean you haven't bothered to send anyone?" Steve demanded angrily.

"I did, to my regret," Rawls said. "I sent Ed Walters out there this morning to take a look."

Steve gazed at him. "And he didn't find anything?" he said slowly, for he had seen the answer in Rawls' face.

"There was no corpse in your saddle shed or anywhere else," Rawls said. "What did you gain by tellin' a windy like that?"

Somehow, Steve had expected something like that. It was the way the current was running resistlessly against him.

"Bloodstains!" he said. "There must have been some stains on the lid of the feedbox. That's where I laid him after I carried him in from the corral."

Rawls shook his head. "Ed said he looked the place over. Nary a speck o' blood. I don't recollect him mentionin' this feedbox, but I take it that he examined it too."

"Tracks! There must have been tracks around!"

"Plenty," Rawls said. "Horse tracks, boot tracks. An' all blurred by rain so they didn't mean a thing."

"And the broken window in the house," Steve said hoarsely. "The man emptied his gun at me through that window. There'll be bullet holes in the kitchen. The broken glass will show . . ."

He quit talking, silenced by the sheriff's expression.

"There ain't much of a house left," Rawls said slowly. "You had visitors last night. They're the ones what made all the tracks I mentioned. Your house burned out inside durin' the night. There's nothin' left but some rain-soaked log walls. The saddle shed wasn't touched."

Steve was ashen, sick at heart. Amos Whipple and his Vigilantes evidently had carried out their threat, and had returned to his ranch. He could see that Rawls believed this.

And it was also plain that Rawls had no intention of doing anything about it.

In fact, he sensed that the sheriff approved of what had been done and was relieved that some of the burden of punishing the will o' the wisps he had been unable to pin down was being taken out of his hands, even though by illegal means.

But that did not explain the disappearance of the stranger's body. It did not seem reasonable to believe that the ranchers would have removed the corpse without at least letting Rawls know.

A new arrival came rushing into the cell room. "Steve!" It was Eileen. She wore mud-flecked riding garb and a quirt still dangled from her wrist. Evidently she had just leaped from the saddle at the jail door.

She pushed past Rawls and grasped both of Steve's hands through the bars. "I just heard about it!" she said. "I couldn't get here any faster."

"You shouldn't have come at all, Miss Eileen," Rawls said. "I don't like to be rough, but Santee was caught red-handed, knifin' an express detective in the back. There's good reason to believe he's tied up with these men who've been robbin' trains. I figure you ought to know the cold truth. Don't let your sympathy get away with you."

"Bosh!" Eileen snapped. "You're all wall-eyed idiots. What's all this about knifing a detective?"

Rawls shrugged and withdrew from the jail room, taking Mart Lowery with him.

Carter Benton cleared his throat. He patted Eileen on the shoulder. "Santee will want to talk this over with me, my dear," he said. "He's due for arraignment shortly, and if I agree to defend him, I must have time to prepare a plea. Perhaps you would prefer to wait in my office."

"Stay here," Steve said to her. "I want you to hear every word."

Step by step he went over the story while Carter Benton listened and asked questions. He omitted two items, however. One was Doug Whipple's part in the train holdup.

Carter Benton seized upon that point. "It's common knowledge that you prevented Amos Whipple from shooting one of the outlaws," he said. "Is that the truth? If so, why?"

"Let's just continue to say that I jostled Amos's arm accidentally," Steve said.

115

Benton frowned. "It is not my custom to defend a client who withholds facts from me. Let's hope you change your mind before we go to trial. It may be the only means of saving you from the gallows—if there actually is any hope."

"You believe Steve is guilty, don't you?" Eileen demanded.

The lawyer only smiled dryly and prepared to leave. "Coming, my dear?" he asked.

"Not at the moment," she said. She remained with Steve.

The second item that Steve had withheld from the lawyer was Frank Clum's revelation linking the Latzos with the Pool money his father was accused of having stolen.

He told all of this now to Eileen, keeping his voice down on the possibility the sheriff might have planted someone in nearby cells to eavesdrop.

"Why, that's—that's both wonderful and terrible," she whispered. "It means your father is dead, of course. He was such a fine man. But it, at least, proves that he was innocent of the terrible things they've said about him."

"The things Amos said, you mean," he said.

"Yes," she nodded. "Uncle Amos was the one. He's to blame. But why didn't you tell this to Mr. Benton? Or to Sheriff Rawls?"

"Clum knew I suspected Latzo," Steve said. "So he came to me and told me this, and asked me to lay off for fear I might drive Latzo deep into cover. Clum hoped that by watching Latzo he would eventually be able to round up the whole outfit in the train robberies and recover the money. If that money could be got back it'd save people in this basin plenty of grief."

"But——" she began. Then she fell silent.

"I know what you started to say," he said. "It's about Doug —and whether he's mixed up with Latzo. I believe the answer is no."

"But you're not sure?"

"I've got Doug's word for it. He never lied to me in the past. I know him well enough to feel that he's not lying now."

"He knows that you and I saw him that night?"

Steve nodded. "We're not very good at concealing things, I reckon. He guessed it from our attitudes. He came right out with it the other night after Amos and his Vigilantes had searched my place. That's why he pulled out. He was ashamed to face you, I suppose. I asked him whether he was tied up with Latzo. He was insulted. He looked like he wanted to slug me. He despises Latzo."

"Then who is he tied up with?"

"He didn't say," Steve said. "I didn't ask. But, if there's any connection between his outfit and Latzo, he doesn't know about it. I'm as sure about that as you can be about any human being."

She drew a long breath. "I'm frightened. Terribly! I talked to Burl Talley. I met him outside the jail. He wasn't at all reassuring. He didn't want to come right out and say so, but he thinks you are guilty. And so does the town. And the town is quiet. Too quiet. The way people avoided me gave me the shivers."

Her slim hands were ice cold in his grasp. He could feel them trembling. He kissed her through the bars. "If it's lynching you're worrying about, forget it," he said, forcing himself to laugh at her fears. "Rawls won't stand for anything like that. He's a sincere officer, at least. But, even better, there must be other express company agents in town. Or will be soon, to take over where Clum left off. I'll straighten out everything as soon as I can talk to them."

She brightened. "I'll find them. But——"

"I don't dare confide in Rawls or Mart Lowery," he said. "They might give it away, or make a wrong move, and Latzo would be warned. He'd cover up good and tight and they'd never be able to prove anything."

"I—I hope you're right," she said. "But—but, if it's necessary, there's another way. All of this goes back to that moment when you hit Amos Whipple's gun arm. If it comes to that I'll tell them exactly why you did it."

"You won't have to," Steve said confidently. "Doug will do that himself."

"But, if he's left the Powderhorn——?"

"He'd come back when he found out that I was in a tight fix. And then too, I only think he may have pulled out. I don't know for certain."

"Are you sure he'd come back to help you?"

"Yes," Steve said.

"But he's weak. You know that also. Only a weak man would let himself become involved in the things he's mixed up in."

"Weak in some ways," Steve admitted. "And very headstrong and wild. Strong in others. Doug is a man who isn't

117

afraid to die. He proved that to me a long time ago. He told me how he got started in these robberies. He thinks he's responsible for killing an express messenger. They hold it over his head as a club to keep him with the gang."

"That sounds like an excuse," she said. "A club is a club only as long as you fear it."

She kissed him again. Her lips were soft and very yielding. "If—if anything happened to you . . ." she said shakily. She drew away.

"Where are you going?" he asked.

"To try to find these express men," she said as she hurried out of the jail room.

Chapter
Thirteen

Steve was taken into court that afternoon, handcuffed between Bill Rawls and Deputy Ed Walters. Carter Benton represented him at the arraignment, which was a brief, routine matter. Steve entered a plea of not guilty and waived a hearing. The judge bound him over to trial before the circuit court on a charge of murder.

The small courtroom, which adjoined the jail, was jammed with onlookers. What Eileen had told him was true. Bleak silence was the keynote of Bugle on this day. There was not a voice raised among the spectators, scarcely a murmur.

As Steve was led away that mood continued to hold. After he was back in his cell he could hear them leaving the courtroom and shuffling away along the sidewalk without talking.

Eileen returned late in the afternoon. This time Bill Rawls stood uncompromisingly at her elbow, listening to every word that was said.

"I—I couldn't find the men you mentioned, Steve," she said, worried. "They've either not arrived in Bugle yet, or are still out hunting the train robbers. The express office is closed and barred. Pete Crain can't be located. He's probably hiding somewhere, afraid of being mobbed because the company can't pay off."

Steve pondered it. Crain, as manager of Northern Express, was the one person likely to know the identity of any express operatives who might have been helping Clum.

"There won't be no mobbin' of nobody as long as I'm sheriff," Bill Rawls stated.

"How about Burl Talley?" Steve questioned Eileen. "Maybe Clum might have told him if there were other express agents handy."

"I asked Burl," she said. "He said Clum had never mentioned any. Apparently Clum was working alone."

She was trying to hide the deep concern that weighed on her. She kissed him and said, "I'll be back bright and early in the morning. I'll keep hunting them until I find them. Is there anything I can bring you?"

Steve looked at Rawls. "Yes," he said. "A sharp hacksaw, a six-shooter, and a fast horse."

Rawls smiled tolerantly. It was a jest he had heard many times. "Nobody's goin' to get out of this jail," he said. "An' nobody is gettin' in either without permission, if that's what's worrying you."

"That could be one of the things on my mind," Steve agreed.

"And mine," Eileen said.

Darkness came and Steve ate his evening meal. He smoked the last of the tobacco and paid the night turnkey to bring him a fresh supply. He kept rolling new smokes, lighting them, then crushing them out. He knew he was losing the battle to retain a semblance of sanity and calm.

The hush that had settled over the town during the day seemed to have hardened into something so tangible that he had the eerie sensation of its having taken the substance of a smothering blanket.

Sounds which would have been commonplace at another time had the jangling effect of breaking glass as they cut through this barrier. The indistinct voices of jailers and deputies in the office conducting routine duties appeared muted as though in tune with this mood.

This shield was torn violently aside. Gunfire broke out somewhere in the town. The heavy, slamming reports of .45's being fired with speed rolled through the night, the echoes recoiling from frame walls and false fronts.

Voices barked orders in the main office. Steve recognized one as belonging to Bill Rawls. Another's was Mart Lowery's. That faded away with a rush of men running from the office and down the street. The officers were hurrying to the scene of the disturbance.

The gunfire broke off. Steve decided that it had come from the gay district on Front Street. He could hear citizens in the street shouting questions at each other.

Then many riders swept into Bozeman Street and pulled up before the jail. The fast tread of boots sounded in the office. Hoarse, harsh orders were given and Steve heard the turnkey protesting halfheartedly.

The bolts were pulled on the inner door and men came flooding into the jail room. They had neckerchiefs tied over their faces and were prodding the turnkey ahead of them.

"Open that cell!" the leader commanded.

That was Amos Whipple's heavy voice. He had made no attempt to disguise it. Nor was the turnkey making any genuine effort to oppose them. The man shrugged and quickly unlocked the door of Steve's cell.

"Come out, Santee," Amos Whipple said.

Steve found himself facing leveled .45's. Hands seized him and tried to yank him through the door. He wrested free, slapped one pistol aside, and backed into the far corner of the cell.

"Come on, stranglers," he said bitterly. "Let's fight it out here."

He believed they would strike him down with bullets. He would welcome that rather than the lynching they evidently intended.

"Don't shoot him!" Amos Whipple shouted. "He's to get a fair chance to talk. A fair and square trial. Drag him out of there."

They rushed him. He fought grimly, swinging fists and boots at the mass of them. But he was overwhelmed by weight of numbers. His arms and legs were pinned down.

One of them drove a fist into his face and said, "You dirty killer. You'll have to talk fast."

Steve surged forward and rammed his head into the masked face and heard a grunt of pain. The man drew back a fist to batter Steve, but a tall member of the Vigilantes seized him by the shoulder and hurled him violently aside. "Yella blood!" the intruder raged. "Hitting a man who can't fight back."

"No brutality!" Amos Whipple boomed. "Keep your heads

120

men. We're not avengers. We are here only to see that justice is done."

Steve fought them futilely, but was dragged from the cell and through the office into the street. Horses were waiting along with other disguised, mounted men. The shooting on Front Street had been a ruse to draw Bill Rawls and the town marshal and their deputies away from the jail.

Bozeman Street was deserted. Appearance of the Vigilantes had driven all citizens discreetly to cover. Doors were closed and window curtains had been tightly drawn.

But from Front Street the tinny refrain of pianos and hurdy gurdies was rising again. Steve heard the hoarse monotone of a dancehall barker. Business was resuming as usual after the interruption of the gunfire. The word of what was happening at the jail had not yet spread that far.

Steve's wrists were lashed together. They lifted him into a saddle and one captor looped his ankles together with a thong beneath the horse.

The tall man who had saved him from being slugged in the cell began fumbling at the task of tying his bound hands to the saddlehorn.

Instead, Steve felt the metallic coolness of a knife blade against his wrists. The bonds loosened. They had been cut. The knife was left there between his locked hands, hidden.

Strong fingers closed reassuringly on his arm for an instant. Realization came! The tall Vigilante was Doug!

"All right!" Amos Whipple said, mounting and seizing up the trailing reins of Steve's horse.

The Vigilantes swung into the saddles and Amos led the way. The Pioneer House was a block west of the jail and Steve saw a feminine figure come from its door.

It was Eileen. She screamed something and raced toward the dark mass of riders, holding her skirts clear of the mud.

"Damn that girl!" Amos Whipple said.

Eileen was too far away, too late to intercept them. Amos led the way around the corner of the jail into a side street and pushed the pace to a gallop, leaving her still running futilely there in the street alone and screaming frenziedly for them to stop. The roar of hooves drowned out that outcry.

Steve realized that Doug was riding at his stirrup. They were passing through straggling back areas of town, heading northward. They entered a dark area of wagon yards and stock corrals and cattle pens and loading chutes which flanked the railroad yards.

Doug said, "Now!"

And he brought a rope slashing down on Steve's horse and his own. Steve saw the opening. It was a narrow lane between corrals, barely wide enough for a mounted man.

He tore his wrists free of the lashings and his horse made its first lunging stride. Wild shouts arose.

"Hey! Stop him! He's tryin'——! Shoot him! Shoot him! He's tryin' to make a break fer it!"

Steve's horse sped into the narrow lane at full gallop with Doug riding a length behind him.

"Hold your fire!" someone shouted. "That's one of our own boys chasin' him, right at his heels. You'll hit him instead o' Santee. He can't git away."

The Vigilantes were spurring in pursuit, but the lane was a bottleneck and their own numbers impeded them. Horses milled and reared in the darkness at the entrance.

Steve and Doug emerged into the open. They veered among shacks and ash heaps and crossed a series of sidetracks where empty cattle cars stood idle. They changed direction again, crossing the main line of the railroad and reached the rolling sagebrush flats northeast of town.

They pulled up to gain their bearings, and listened to the shouting and the distant mutter of hooves. Steve slashed the thong from his ankles. "Here's your knife, Doug," he said. "It came in handy."

He added, "I thought maybe you'd taken my advice and had pulled out of the Powderhorn."

They rode ahead again. Tumbleweeds formed grotesque shapes against the skyline as they mounted a low ridge. The search seemed to be swinging westward away from them.

The lights of Bugle began to fade behind. They passed over the rim of the rise and let the horses settle to a jiggling pace. They had shaken off the Vigilantes, whose big handicap had been their own numbers.

They traveled in silence for a time. Doug removed the neckerchief mask and hurled it away. "I know what you're thinking," he said. "I don't blame you. I let you take the jolt just to protect me. The real reason they believe you killed Frank Clum is because Amos has convinced them that you're in cahoots with the bunch who robbed the train. You expected to be strung up without me turning a hand to help you."

"I'll never come closer to going down the big chute," Steve admitted. "Amos talked about a fair trial. What he meant was a trial with a rope around my neck."

"I'd have talked before it went that far," Doug said, his voice dull. "I was in a saloon on Front Street last night when I heard that you had been arrested for Clum's murder. I knew what the next move would be, for I know my father. So I high-tailed it out to Center Fire."

"Center Fire?"

"I siwashed out in the brush not far from the house last night, keeping an eye on the place," Doug said. "I knew any move that would be made by the Vigilantes would start from there. I was there when Burl Talley brought the news of Clum's murder to Amos this morning."

"Talley?" Steve repeated. "Was he with the Vigilantes?"

"I doubt if he was in the bunch that came to the jail," Doug said. "Burl never was one to get mixed up in real trouble. But he helped notify other ranchers in the organization. I kept cases on Amos, knowing he was the leader. They all met at the Spanish Flat schoolhouse after dark. I eavesdropped and heard them arrange that fake gunfight to decoy the law away from the jail. I pulled on a mask and joined the party, mixing in with them in the dark as they rode up to the jail. They never knew they had an extra member."

"You must have been watching them when they set fire to my house," Steve said. "What else did they do there?"

"Set fire to your house?" Doug exclaimed. "That's the first I've heard of that. Do you mean that? When did that happen?"

"Last night sometime, evidently," Steve said.

"Amos couldn't have had anything to do with it," Doug said. "At least he was at Center Fire all night, asleep in his bed, to the best of my knowledge. You mean your house is gone—burned down?"

"So Bill Rawls told me," Steve said.

Doug waited, but he added nothing more to that. Doug misunderstood his silence. "I know what you're wondering," he said. "You're thinking that maybe I'm mixed up in Clum's murder."

Steve twisted in the saddle, gazing at him in the darkness. "Now that you've brought it up," he said. "Maybe I am."

"I had nothing to do with it, actually," Doug said dully. "But maybe I'm mixed up in it by what the law would call guilt by association."

"Who killed Clum?" Steve demanded.

"I don't know that."

"Maybe you know someone who does know?"

"I'm not even sure about that," Doug said. "I could be wrong. Dead wrong."

"You mean you don't want to tell me because of outlaw honor? You won't turn against your pals even though they killed a man in cold blood. Is that it?"

"It wasn't the ones who were in on the train robbery with me," Doug said miserably. "I'm sure of that, at least. They were playing poker in the same Front Street gambling house I was in when Clum was murdered. They had been there all evening. None of them could have done it."

"You don't want to tell me who those men are?"

"No," Doug said. "I guess you named it. Outlaw honor. I can't be an informer, Steve."

"A man tried to kill me last night at my house," Steve said. "Someone must have sent him to do the job. I was lucky. He missed. Before it was over I got him. Something I found in his pocket warned me that Clum might be in for the same treatment. That's why I rode to town. I was just a few minutes too late to save him."

"Who was it who tried to get you?" Doug asked.

"I never saw him before. Hard-cased type with big crooked teeth, nose flattened at the bridge, coarse black hair. Might have a touch of Indian or Spanish blood. Wore——"

"Choctaw!" Doug exclaimed.

"Who's Choctaw?"

"One of Nick Latzo's flunkies. At least the description fits him. Hung around the Silver Moon. Worked as case keeper for faro dealers at times. Bad medicine. The kind that'd cut a throat for a price. But Bill Rawls could have told you who he was if it was really Choctaw. Didn't Rawls——?"

"Trouble is Rawls said his deputy couldn't find any sign of a dead man in the saddle shed, where I had carried the body," Steve said. "It wasn't until this morning that he sent Ed Walters out there to take a look. Someone must have got there first and moved Choctaw elsewhere. There wasn't even a bloodstain, according to Walters. That's when he found that the house had been burned. It must have been the same person—or persons."

As he spoke Steve again shifted the direction in which they traveled. They had been heading north toward the river. Now he swung eastward, paralleling the course of the stream in its widening loop through the basin.

"We'll be hitting the main road to the ford any minute," Doug warned. "Somebody might sight us. Where are you going?"

"To the Silver Moon," Steve said.

Doug drew a harsh, startled breath. "Jupiter, but you do pick 'em tough!" he said almost joyously. He touched his horse with a spur, an eagerness and a wildness rising in him as he moved up to ride side by side.

Chapter Fourteen

They left the horses hidden in the brush and moved in on the Silver Moon, halting on the fringe of the clearing. The hour, Steve judged, was nearing nine o'clock and business at the roadhouse was at its evening peak.

A score of saddle animals were tethered at the rails, along with buggies and buckboards which had brought patrons from the mining camps in the hills. The orchestra, which had been playing for dancers, now struck a crashing chord, then quieted.

A man's voice made an announcement. Cowboy yells arose and the music struck up again. A woman began singing.

The way was clear and they moved swiftly to the side of the building, huddling in shadow. Through a slit in a curtained window Steve saw an entertainer on the small stage. It was Daisy O'Day.

Some of the gambling had slowed while players turned their attention to the stage, but other games were progressing without interruption.

Nick Latzo was not present. Steve surmised that he was at

the Blue Moon in town as usual. But Louie Latzo stood at the rear corner of the bar, a drink in his hand. Louie was smoking a cigar and wore a silk vest and a pleated linen shirt with a pearl stickpin in the flowery cravat. A gray derby hat was perched on his head.

Daisy O'Day finished her song and returned for an encore in response to loud applause which was led by Louie himself. Steve kept his attention on Louie. Doug nudged him and pointed. Al Painter sat in the lookout high seat. In another part of the room Chick Varney mingled with patrons. Both men were on duty as trouble shooters, for they each packed braces of six-shooters. They bore the court plaster and livid marks of their combat with Steve and Doug.

The singing ended. Louie hastened to offer his arm to Daisy O'Day and they walked through the door that led to the areas back stage.

This was the chance for which Steve had been hoping. He moved along the outside wall, ducking below the line of the windows. Doug followed.

Steve had visited the Silver Moon in the past, and while he was not familiar with the interior in this part of the structure, he remembered that there had been an outer stage entrance at the far corner.

He reached this door and found it open. Louie and Daisy O'Day were approaching along the inner passageway. Steve and Doug crouched down and heard a key creak in a lock.

Steve chanced a look. The pair were entering a varnished door which he was sure admitted them to Nick Latzo's living quarters.

The girl, who had drawn a wrap around her, preceded Louie through the portal. There was no one else in the passageway.

"Stay out of this," he told Doug. "Don't let anyone see you."

He leaped forward, covering the dozen feet in two strides and drove his shoulder against the startled Louie, propelling him violently ahead into the center of the room where he went staggering to his hands and knees.

Steve pounced on him and locked his fingers around the man's throat. "Steady," he said. "Or I'll break your neck, Louie."

Doug, ignoring the warning, entered a pace behind him and closed the door.

Daisy O'Day had stood frozen. "What the hell . . . !" she began. Her voice squeaked off. Steve was not armed, but Doug wore a six-shooter. He had not drawn the gun, but it wasn't necessary. The entertainer knew that big trouble had arrived.

"Just stay quiet and keep out of this, lady," Steve said. "You're not in this."

He snatched Louie to his feet, searched him, and removed a short-muzzled pistol from an armpit holster and a derringer from a sleeve. Also a wicked dirk from a belt scabbard. "Do you like knives, Louie?" he asked.

He pushed Louie against a wall and held him pinned there, his fingers wrapped in the front of the fancy vest. "Don't make a sound," he said.

He turned Louie's pockets out, spilling the contents on the floor. Finally a billfold emerged, and this he kicked toward Doug. "See what's in it," he said.

It contained several bills but none were in the hundred-dollar denomination that Steve had hoped might be there. But he had hardly counted on Louie being careless enough to have kept such evidence on him.

"You've spent it already, I suppose," he said. "It was you, all right, that I sighted spooking out of the Pioneer House as Clum was dying with a knife in his back in his room. You killed him, Louie, and spent some of that two hundred dollars on this fine plumage you're wearing. And you likely know who murdered my father. It was your brother, Nick, wasn't it?"

Louie was ash-pale. His eyes were blank and distended with fear. He expected to be shot with his own gun, which Steve jammed into his stomach.

"What happened to Choctaw's body?" Steve demanded.

"I don't know what you're talkin' about!" Louie gasped.

"You're lying," Steve said. "I'd kill you myself, Louie, but you're going to swing for the murder of Frank Clum and Buck Santee. And Nick too. I make that promise to you."

He shoved Louie toward the door. "You're going with me," he said. "We'll see if you can't be persuaded to remember a few things that I want to know."

Then he and Doug stood listening to the sound of footsteps in the passageway. A hand tapped on the door. "Louie!" a voice called. "Is it all right if Dude Lacey takes over the deal at the number two table? Whitey's gone into another of his coughin' spells."

That was the voice of Al Painter.

"Say yes," Steve whispered.

Louie tried. He tried again. A third time. But no sound issued from his fear-frozen lips.

Painter pounded the door harder and impatiently. "Louie! Do you hear me?"

Daisy O'Day gathered her courage and screamed wildly. "Two gunmen have got Louie!" she screeched. "They're sluggin' him around and are goin' to take him with them."

Her voice carried through the thin-walled building. It evidently reached the main room for Steve heard the music and the shuffle of dancing feet halt abruptly.

He spoke to Doug. "Come on! We're going out!"

He opened the door and pushed Louie ahead of him into the passageway, clinging to the wilting collar of the man's shirt with one hand, the gun in his other grip.

Al Painter had backed away a few paces and had drawn his brace of pistols. But he could not fire without killing Louie. Beyond them Steve saw Chick Varney come rushing into the passageway, a pair of guns also in his hands.

"Don't shoot, Al!" Louie babbled.

Steve and Doug backed through the outer door by which they had entered. Steve knew it was impossible now to take Louie with them.

Once they were in the open starlight he sent Louie spinning to the ground with a shove. He and Doug raced for the brush. But, even as they turned, a gun exploded almost at their feet.

It was Louie who had fired. He had snatched from some hide-out in his coat a double-barreled derringer that Steve had missed while searching him.

He had aimed at the back of Doug, who was nearest him. He was now twisting around as he lay on the ground to bring the second barrel of the little, vicious gun into play against Steve at that short range.

Steve flipped back the hammer of the pistol he had seized from the man and fired. The bullet must have torn through Louie's arm or shoulder, for the derringer flew from his hand

and exploded as it hit the ground. Louie's body was jerked around and he uttered a moaning sound.

Steve and Doug raced for the trees. "Are you all right, Doug?" Steve asked.

"Yes," Doug said.

Six-shooters opened up on them from the roadhouse. Al Painter was trying to bring them down as he crouched in the doorway through which they had emerged. At another point Chick Varney sent window glass shattering as he cleared an opening through which to shoot. His guns joined in the uproar.

A bullet ripped bark from an alder, the fragments showering Steve's face. Another glanced from a tree trunk, buzzing between him and Doug.

They reached deeper shelter in the thickets and changed direction. Slugs raked the brush in an attempt to bring them down. Painter and Varney were shooting blind now, and that failed. The guns went empty.

They located their horses, hit the saddles, and rode away, heading southward. The shouting around the roadhouse receded and was lost as they built up distance. Evidently the patrons of the Silver Moon did not deem it worth while to join in a fight the origin of which was not clear to them, and Varney and Painter lacked the courage, for there was no pursuit.

After a mile or two they left the brush and circled Bugle to the south, swinging gradually westward toward the upper basin and the mountains. The lights of the town were bright and steady only two miles to their right.

They crossed Long Ridge and entered the clearing in which stood the Spanish Flat schoolhouse. It was dark and silent in the moonlight. The main trail from town curved past within a few rods of the structure, and they pulled up to listen. There was no sound.

"Where to?" Doug asked. It was the first word either of them had spoken.

"I wish I knew," Steve said. "You shouldn't have shown your face in that roadhouse, Doug. They'll shoot you on sight now, the same as they will me. Up to that time I doubt if anyone knew you were the man who helped me get away from the Vigilantes. Rawls will probably know it soon."

"It was time I showed my face on one side or the other, wasn't it?" Doug said. There was a thickening quality in his tone that Steve took for anger and weariness.

"You were wrong about one thing; Doug," he said. "Nick Latzo is mixed up in the train holdups. And Louie too, most likely. You know that now, don't you?"

"Yes," Doug said in blurred tone. "But I didn't know it until I saw that look in Louie's eyes. You were right. He's the one who knifed Clum."

"Somebody with a lot of savvy has been maneuvering these holdups," Steve said. "He directed suspicion at Nick Latzo so as to keep the law running in circles on a wild goose chase. He fooled Frank Clum and he fooled Bill Rawls. Clum was so certain that Latzo was his man that he played right into the hands of the person he least suspected. Latzo was a party to the scheme. But he was only a decoy."

"He was more than a decoy when he sent men to kill you and Clum," Doug said.

"Somebody must have told Latzo that Clum had evidence which might hang him for the murder of my father," Steve said. "That's my guess. And that someone also feared Clum would eventually learn too much about the train robberies. That same person probably guessed that I had recognized you as one of the long riders. So, for his own safety, he decided that both Clum and I must be put out of the way. Nick Latzo had the means of that kind of an operation. He has men at his call who'll kill for a price. So this man turned the job over to him."

He quit talking for a while. "And now, do you want to tell me the name of that man?" he finally asked.

"You probably won't believe this, but up to this moment I was no more sure of who he is than you were," Doug said.

"What?"

"I suspected it," Doug said. "But it seemed so fantastic I couldn't convince myself. The only ones I was sure about were the men I went with on the two holdups. I never saw the one who planned the jobs. But I know now who it is. And I can see that you know also."

"Clum told me that he believed none of the money from the three holdups has appeared in circulation," Steve said. "He thought that all of it was still intact somewhere—hidden in or near the basin."

"That's the way it's supposed to be," Doug nodded. "The

agreement was that the money is to be kept in one chunk until we have enough to keep us well off for the rest of our lives. Then it'll be divided and we split up. Some of us talked of going to South America. It was up to one man to decide when we had enough. I was to get my cut from the last two holdups. I wasn't in on the first one."

"You mean you don't know where the money is hidden?" Steve asked. "Clum said it amounts to close to a quarter of a million dollars, including the Pool fund."

"I don't know where it's cached," Doug admitted. "I've been played for a sucker both ways from the middle. I realize that. But I didn't have much choice after that express messenger was killed. I've done a lot of drinking lately, Steve. An awful lot. I can't think straight anymore. I know that—that—you—and—Eileen——"

His words dwindled off. In the starlight Steve saw him sag suddenly in the saddle. Before he could prevent it Doug slipped to the ground with the flabbiness of an empty sack. His spur hung in a stirrup. His horse began to rear, but Steve leaped to the ground and freed his boot.

Steve fumbled for a match and finally got one lighted. Doug lay crumpled on his side, his face the color of a wax candle. One side of his coat was soggy and sticky with blood.

The derringer slug that Louie Latzo had fired had found its target, but Doug, rather than chance any slowing of Steve's escape, had refused to admit that he had been wounded.

The bullet had torn upward, burning a gouge along his ribs, and had buried itself in the heavy muscles below the shoulder blade. Steve could feel the hard pellet just under the skin.

He ignited another match and another, ignoring the danger that this might reveal him to manhunters. He decided that the injury itself was not the kind that would be fatal to a man of Doug's endurance. But the loss of blood was another matter.

He became aware that a rider was approaching at a fast lope up the trail from the direction of town. He lifted Doug and carried him to the schoolhouse.

The frame-built structure, like its kind, was determinedly oblong with a shingled gable roof which supported a small bell tower. A wooden awning guarded the main door at the front, but there was a rear door which opened abruptly into a bare clearing which served as a play yard. The front door bore a padlock but Steve had better luck at the rear entrance. It was latched, but the hasp was loose and the screws that held it came free almost at the touch of his hand.

He carried Doug inside and laid him on the floor in darkness. He raced back and led the horses to the far side of the building out of sight of the trail.

The lone rider came abreast of the school property at that same high pace. The horse Steve had been riding scented the other animals and blew suddenly and loudly.

The rider drew up instantly, then swung around and came directly toward the schoolhouse. Steve drew his six-shooter. He peered at the silhouette of the arrival against the stars.

"Eileen!" he exclaimed.

She dismounted and rushed to him. "I knew it must be you when I heard the horse," she said. "I was on my way to Antler, thinking you might try to get in touch with me there. Steve! Steve! Are you all right?"

"I am," he said. "But Doug's here. Wounded. My fault. I went to the Silver Moon to try to make Louie Latzo talk. It ended in a gun fight."

He led her inside the building and chanced igniting a match. He found a quantity of loose paper and lighted spills. They cut away Doug's jacket and used his shirt for bandages.

The bleeding stopped. Steve brought water in his hat from the creek. That strengthened Doug and he mumbled, "Eileen, get out of here. Stay away from me. I'm poison! Bad!"

He tried to rise to his feet. He did not make it. Steve caught him as he fell and lifted him, supporting him.

"Somebody's bound to search this schoolhouse before the night's over," he said. "Do you think you can hang on for a few miles in the saddle, Doug?"

"Ten miles," Doug mumbled gamely. "Twenty. You name it."

Eileen led up the horses and Steve carried Doug into the open and boosted him into the saddle. Doug reeled, but hung on. Steve and Eileen mounted and moved in at his side and steadied him.

"Where are we going?" Doug asked.

"To a place where you'll be safe," Steve said. "And cared for."

He looked at Eileen and she understood and nodded.

132

They moved away from Spanish Flat at a slow pace. For some time Doug was too weak and spent to think or ask questions.

Suddenly he aroused, gazing at the mountain skyline against the Milky Way. They were fording a small, shallow creek. "Little Canteen Creek!" he said. "We're near Center Fire—near home!"

They emerged from timber and the scattered buildings and corrals of Amos Whipple's sizeable headquarters lay before them beneath the midnight sky. No light showed.

"Your mother will be there," Steve said.

Doug said violently, "No! I won't——!"

"You've got to have help—and love," Eileen told him.

She dismounted and ran across the clearing to the house, making no sound that might arouse the two or three riders who, no doubt, were sleeping in the bunkhouse.

Presently she returned and said, "All right."

Steve lifted Doug, still mumbling protests, from the saddle and half carried him to the house. The kitchen door was open, but no lamp had been lighted.

Julia Whipple, a kindly, careworn pioneer woman, took her straying son in her arms and wept over him for a moment.

The house was a two-story frame structure. Julia Whipple led the way with a shaded lamp and Steve carried Doug up the stairs and placed him on a bed.

There, with blinds drawn, he stripped off Doug's clothes and left the remainder of the task to his mother and Eileen.

It was more than an hour before Eileen finally joined him in the dimly-lit kitchen where he was drinking coffee and eating cold beef and bread which he had found in the pantry.

"We've done all we can do here," she said. "Aunt Julia can handle it now. He's much better. We've given him broth and the juice from canned tomatoes. That's what he needs most of all to replace lost blood. He'll probably come out of it in a hurry."

"What did you tell her?" he asked.

"Only that he was shot helping a friend and that it would be better if no one was to know where he is."

"But how can she prevent Amos from knowing?" he asked.

"Aunt Julia says Amos has never set foot in Doug's room since Doug left Center Fire. The door has been kept closed and locked. I'm sure Doug will need to be there only a day or two."

Steve debated it and decided it was the safest place for the wildling. Now that he had a chance to think it over he doubted that the Latzos would want to talk to Bill Rawls about what had happened at the roadhouse, for that might lead to some questions about the reason for Steve's visit there that might be awkward to answer. Only Louie and the two gunmen knew that Doug was the man who had accompanied him. They likely would prefer to settle the matter themselves, but they hardly would risk coming to Center Fire, even if they suspected Doug was there.

"All right," he said, and arose.

He concealed Doug's saddle in the wagon shed and told Julia Whipple where it could be found. He and Eileen rode away, leading Doug's horse. They turned it loose on open range a few miles away.

He reached out, laid his hand on Eileen's on the saddle-horn. "It's been a long night," he said. "You'll be home and in your bed in thirty minutes. Will you be afraid to make it alone? You'll be safe enough, even if it's three in the morning and dark as the inside of a whale."

"I'm not afraid of the dark. I never was. But where are you going?"

"First I want to take a look-see at my saddle shed where I left Choctaw's body."

"Choctaw?"

"Doug thinks that's the name of the man I told Bill Rawls about. The one who tried to kill me. Maybe I want to convince myself I didn't dream about that fight. Maybe I want to prove something. Next, come daybreak, I want to be up on Cardinal Mountain, watching at a wolf hole."

"I just love to watch wolf holes," she said.

"You're going home."

"There are no wolf dens at Antler. At least none worth wasting time watching. And I couldn't stand it—the waiting. It's all settled. You can't leave me behind."

"You might be shaped up considerably better," Steve said. "But you're still the same bullheaded imp who made a pest of herself to Doug and me when we were kids."

"Thank you for complimenting me on my shape at least," she said. "Do you really think it has improved?"

"Indeed I do," Steve said. "But the question under discussion was about you going home peacefully."

"I'm not going home peacefully or otherwise," she said. "That's all been decided. And don't try to force me to go. I can kick and scratch."

"How well I remember," Steve sighed.

Chapter
Fifteen

They rode toward Steve's ranch. Avoiding the trail as much as possible, they kept to the shadow of brush and timber.

As they neared Canteen Creek the odor of wet, charred wood rode the night—a dismal presence as of the smell of death.

They came out into the open meadow beneath the stars and Steve watched the ears of their mounts, feeling that the animals would be the first to warn them if there were humans or other horses around. But they gave no sign of uneasiness. His ranch was unguarded as yet.

He led the way nearer. The ruins of the house bulked up in a deformed pattern. There seemed to be little chance that anything could be salvaged. Only portions of the half-burned log walls still stood. Steve's father had cut and shaped those logs with his own ax and adz.

Steve dismounted and entered the saddle shed. He ignited one of his dwindling supply of matches. The lamp he had placed on the bench still stood where he had left it. He lighted it.

The feedbox on which he had laid the body was a six-foot-long container, built of sheet metal nailed to a wooden frame and divided into two compartments for the storage of corn and bran. The last fragments of the grain had long ago been cleaned out by packrats and mice.

The cover of the box had been built stoutly of the pine siding of a packing case. It was missing. Steve was certain that the porous, unpainted pine would have carried bloodstains. But the lid had been carried away.

Eileen watched him from the doorway as he peered around. The dust of disuse had accumulated in the shed, but many boots and many hands had disturbed this layer on the floor and benches until there was little hope that anything could be learned from this source. Evidently Deputy Ed Walters had gone over the place and no doubt there had been other curiosity-minded visitors.

"Someone—or maybe more than one—got here long before Rawls sent his deputy to take a look-see," he said. "They probably buried Choctaw's body somewhere. It had been raining and it would have been easy to have caved in a cutbank over the grave, or a sandy bluff. The place might not be far away, or it could be miles off. Whether it will ever be found is anybody's guess. Trying to hunt it would be like looking for a lost needle. We might as well ride. There's nothing here to help us."

They mounted again and he led the way across country to the Powderhorn. They forded the stream with the morning star beginning to burn with diamond-white brilliance in the sky. The cold river rushed around the legs of the horses, sighing a sad song.

Eileen pulled her horse closer, reached out, and Steve felt her fingers creep into his hand and hold tightly. "I'm always afraid of rivers at night," she said. "They frighten me. They are so strange."

The horses waded ashore and left the sighing behind. Dawn was at hand. The Milky Way began to fade. The mountains took somber form, rearing up as a black wall against the sky. Soon the peaks stood defined in pastel gray. A lilac hue formed at the crests and the snowfields caught the first rosy tint of the coming sun. Around them this wild, tumbled world emerged, ridge upon ridge, deep shadow upon shadow. Daybreak!

New shell ice tinkled beneath the hooves of the horses in the shallows along the small streams. Steve felt the cold bite through his jacket. The sun edged above the horizon as they climbed higher on the mountain. Its warmth, feeble at first, touched their cheeks.

Steve became cautious as they neared the location of the hide-out to which Eileen had led him the day of the elk hunt. He circled the area, scanning the ground for tracks.

He became satisfied the place was deserted. He rode to a rise which commanded a wide view of the river and the basin. The smoke of morning cookfires in Eagle rose above Long Ridge. "All right," he said and lifted Eileen to the ground. "I'm going to search that dugout. You stand lookout. If you see anyone, whistle a couple of times. Stay off the skylines."

"The money?" she questioned.

"Yes. I doubt if it's here. But it might be. I've got to make sure. Up to now I can't offer one shred of actual evidence against anyone. Nothing but suspicion, and conclusions at which I've arrived by fitting together a lot of happenings that didn't seem to make sense at first. There's only one solid proof that would be enough to convince a man like Amos Whipple. Or Bill Rawls. Possession of the stolen money itself."

"And who do you suspect?" she asked.

"Maybe you've already guessed," he said.

"I—I don't know," she said uncertainly. "The things I think frighten me."

He left her and walked on foot down the game trail to the hidden dugout, his footprints plain in the thin coating of frost which rimmed the grass. There he went over the interior foot by foot, probing and tapping in search of any cavity in which treasure might have been cached.

He roved the thickets in the vicinity. He took pains to avoid leaving any easily-seen evidence of his presence. The frost was evaporating with the warming of the air and his footprints disappeared along with it.

He was keeping at the search, determined to exhaust every possibility, when Eileen whistled a warning. He hurried back to the ridge where she waited, concealed among the rimrock.

"Two riders just forded the river and are heading up the mountain," she said. "They were too far off to make out who they are."

They waited. Presently Steve sighted the pair a long distance away and down the mountain. They were tiny, moving dots which vanished into timber.

After an interval, the two appeared in a wide grassy clearing along a stream in which a score or more of loose horses grazed. They cut five animals from the bunch and hazed them off into the trees, heading up the mountain in the direction of the hide-out.

Steve looked at Eileen, elated. "Maybe this trip up here

will pan out after all," he said. "Every smart wolf has more than one way out of his den. Maybe we came to the right place after all."

"Did you recognize them?" she asked. "Who are they?"

He looked at her. "Burl Talley expects to marry you, doesn't he?" he asked.

She became indignant. "I make my own decisions in matters like that," she said.

Steve laughed. "That's another question that hardly needed an answer. I should have known better than to ask."

"And just what was the answer?" she demanded.

"The right one," he said.

Leading the horses on foot, they retreated nearly half a mile from the hide-out and took deep cover among boulders and aspen. Steve found a cranny among the rocks. The sun reflected warmth upon them, and Eileen leaned against him, heavy-eyed from loss of sleep. He knew she was also hungry.

"We got separated from the chuckwagon somewhere along the way," he said. "You'll have to take a notch in your belt."

A quarter of an hour passed. Then he nudged her. They watched a rider appear in the open draw which led to the hide-out in the thicket.

It was Tex Creed. The man pulled up, gazing around, and circled the draw, but his attitude was that of one who felt that he was unobserved. Then he rode down the game trail into the thicket toward the hide-out.

"I've known it for some time," Eileen whispered. "At least I began to guess it yesterday. But I still couldn't believe it. It just couldn't be. It's—it's impossible."

He nodded. "Everything points to it. When we met Creed and Highriver the day of the elk hunt they weren't really riding posse. That was only an excuse for diverting other men away from this part of the mountain—and also to turn loose the horses that had been corraled there for emergency in case anything went wrong and they had to slope out of the country in a hurry."

"How long have you suspected all this?"

"About the same time you did, I suppose. I started piecing items together."

"What's Creed doing now?" she asked.

"Making sure someone isn't using the hide-out. Doug, for instance."

Creed reappeared and waved his hat in a signal. After a

short wait the five loose horses came streaming into the draw. They were being driven by the swarthy Highriver.

"Two pack animals," Steve said. "The rest are saddle stock."

Creed joined Highriver in pushing the horses out of sight down the game trail. The two men soon returned and rode off down the mountain in the direction of the river ford. They kept to cover as much as possible.

Steve studied them as long as they were in sight. They were riding high in the saddle, stiff-legged and straight-backed. They were pushing the horses. They had all the ear-marks of men who were on edge and had some pressing purpose in mind.

"They're running scared," he told Eileen. "I've got a hunch our wolf is going to be forced out in the open where I can get a chance at him. And soon. Mighty soon."

She was gazing at him questioningly. "Too many things have happened that they don't like," he explained. "Clum's murder, for one. My escape from jail for another. And Doug's disappearance. They may have heard about Choctaw too. Things are happening that they probably don't understand. My guess is they're getting ready to light out to save their necks."

He caught up the horses and they rode to the dugout. The five animals were locked in the structure and munching grain. The two pack horses and one of the saddle mounts bore Amos Whipple's Center Fire brand. The other two belonged to Eileen's Antler string.

"Just look at that," Eileen said indignantly. "Our best cutting horses. That's Biscuit, and the roan is Old Sarge. Shorty Barnes would hit the ceiling if he knew outlaws were making free use of our top stock."

"If you were going to pick relay horses to get you over Cardinal Pass ahead of the sheriff you wouldn't pick crow-bait," Steve commented.

He freed the animals and sent them scattering down the mountain. "That'll give them some trouble if they try to use this route out," he said.

"This wolf isn't likely to be stopped as easily as that," Eileen said shakily. Tension was growing in her. "And the proper way of referring to him is in the plural. This wolf is not one man alone. We've already seen two. And we're sure who the leader of the pack is."

"Are we?" he asked.

"It's time we started calling him by his right name," she said. "Burl Talley. He's back of all this."

Steve nodded. "He was the only one in a position to do a number of things that happened that couldn't all be put down to coincidence. In the first place Clum confided in him, believing him to be a man of integrity. That was a fatal error for Clum. It gave Talley the whip hand. He knew every move Clum made. And evidently he guessed that I had recognized Doug during the train holdup. He didn't want that information to go any farther. He decided we had to be put out of the way. He's the one who planted those hundred-dollar bills."

"What about Nick Latzo?" she asked. "Where does he figure in this?"

"I'm not sure, but my hunch is that they're secret partners. Even Doug didn't know that Talley was the brain back of the train robberies. Creed was the active leader. Talley never risked his own hide by taking part openly in the holdups. Creed and Highriver are reckless men, but they aren't cold-blooded killers. When it came to having murder done Talley had to go to Latzo, who had cutthroats in his crowd."

They rode lower on the mountain and halted at a vantage point. After more than an hour they watched Creed and Highriver recross the river.

The two men were now leading three spare horses which they had picked up from the stock grazing the benches. They headed up the basin in the direction of Bugle, but kept to the timber and broken country along the river.

"There's no way of telling for sure at this distance," Steve said, "but I'd be willing to bet that two of those horses are pack animals too. They're going to set another relay near town. Our wolf must still be in Bugle. At least that seems to be where the pack is congregating. I'd have thought that Talley's Rafter O would be a more likely hiding place."

"You think that holdup money might be right in town?"

"It's got to be somewhere close. It looks to me like they're staking out pack horses for insurance in case they have to ride far and fast. Most of the money taken in the three holdups was in gold, I understand. You can't just pack a hundred thousand dollars or so in gold around in your saddlebags. I figure that's about what the share for three men would amount to. For it looks like three of them are intending to pull out. My guess is that the other one is that mill boss, Whitey Bird. He seemed to be pretty thick with Creed and Highriver."

They left the mountain and also forded the Powderhorn. Eileen turned in the direction of Antler. "Food!" she said. "I'm famished and so are you. It's only a mile or two out of the way, and we can overtake them before they reach town if that's where they're going. I doubt if your wolf will make any kind of a move in broad daylight anyway. Wolves prefer to work in the dark."

She added, "Speaking of broad daylight, you haven't forgotten, I hope, that you are still being hunted. No doubt there's a reward on your head by this time. Burl Talley will see to that. You must be careful. There are some people who will be only too happy to shoot you on sight."

Steve thought of the easy ways of life he had visualized when he had stood on the station platform at Junction Bend only a few days in the past. He looked down at himself. He ran his hand over his unshaven jaws.

"You look like a pirate," Eileen said.

"Or a train robber," he said.

Nearing Antler ranch he waited at a distance while she rode in. She returned presently, bringing food and a .45 pistol and a holster and belt. "They belonged to Dad," she said.

She also brought a fresh saddle horse for him, a roan. And gray range hat and a blue flannel shirt to replace the black headgear and the ragged shirt he had been wearing.

"At least they'll have to take a second look at you before they begin shooting," she said. "These clothes belong to Shorty Barnes. He's at the ranch. He asked no questions and therefore I did not have to tell him any fibs. He looked at me more in sorrow than accusation. He thinks I'm a fallen woman. After all, I was away all night, you know."

"What else does he think?"

"That I'm helping a man wanted for murder. Al Painter and Chick Varney were snooping around the ranch early this morning, Shorty says. They claimed they'd been deputized to hunt you. Shorty says he's sure they were also trying to find out if I was home. Shorty told them I was still asleep. They were heading for your place when they pulled out. He figures they'll be back."

She watched him buckle on the holster. He thrust the short-muzzled six-shooter he had been carrying into a saddle pocket.

She moved close, put her arms around him and clung to him tightly. "Where's this going to end?" she asked huskily.

"In Bugle, I hope," he said gently. "And soon."

"I—I don't want to lose you now after waiting all my life for you," she said.

He kissed her, gravely at first and then with a wild rush. "There's no other way," he said. "They've got to be caught redhanded—if they're to be caught."

He added, "It would be best if you stayed here."

For once, she did not oppose him. He mounted then and rode away. He looked back before the run of the timber intervened. She had climbed into the saddle of her mount and was spurring away at a lope.

He rode up the basin, staying off the trails. He crowded the horse faster.

It was noon and the day was turning hot when he reached the crest of Long Ridge two miles from town. He sighted Creed and Highriver. They were just entering the outskirts of Bugle. They no longer had the three spare animals with them. Steve was certain he had estimated the situation correctly. The horses had been left in hiding not far from town.

The two men vanished among the buildings in the heart of the settlement. Steve dismounted, drew the rigging from the roan, rubbed it down with dry grass and hung the sweaty saddle blanket on a bush. He sat with his back against a fir tree, preparing his mind for patient vigil.

Chapter Sixteen

Bugle lay peaceful in the sunlight. Ore wagons crawled down the trails from the mines at intervals and unloaded their cargoes down the chutes in the railroad yards, the sound drifting in lazy, booming echoes.

Riders and harness rigs arrived and departed. A lumber

dray, carrying fat lengths of freshly-fallen yellow pine and drawn by a jerkline hitch entered town, bound for Burl Talley's sawmill. A load of milled lumber, including window and door framing from the planing mill pulled out, bound for mining camps in the Powderhorns. Housewives hung clothes on lines in the yards of homes in the town.

The man in whom Steve was interested did not emerge. He began dozing off into short snatches of rest, disciplining his mind to bring him awake at intervals of a quarter of an hour or less, at which times he would sit up and scan any travelers on the roads. Then he would drift off again.

Thus passed the afternoon. The shadows of the mountains marched across the basin. Sundown's coolness touched him and he aroused completely.

He waited until twilight lay deep upon the town. Mounting, he rode nearer, measuring his pace so that he entered the outskirts under cover of full early darkness.

He followed a back street and finally tethered his horse in deep shadow just off Bozeman Street. He walked to the corner and peered.

Burl Talley's lumberyard fronted on Bozeman Street at this point. The office occupied a frame structure which abutted on the sidewalk at the corner farthest from the point where Steve stood. The lumberyard, where it faced the main thoroughfare, was guarded by a high board fence, pierced by a wagon gate with double wings. The gate was closed. The planing mill occupied a ramshackle structure at the rear of the property.

The door of the office was closed, but two swinging oil lamps burned in the room. A sash in one of the two windows overlooking the sidewalk was raised for air.

Only one person was visible in the office. Tex Creed. He sat in a swivel chair, smoking a cigarette. He flipped this away, but soon was nervously rolling another. He occupied the chair in the same taut, on-edge manner that Steve had marked in his posture on a horse earlier in the day.

A passer-by was approaching on the sidewalk. This compelled Steve to pull back into concealment until the man had gone by.

He returned to his viewpoint. Presently Creed went to the door and gazed down Bozeman Street with the fretful manner of a man waiting for someone who was wasting precious time.

Steve became aware of activity in the dark, closed lumberyard. He heard the occasional stamp of hooves and the clink of bit chains. He saw the flare of matches being applied to smokes. At least two men were waiting in the depths of the place, along with livestock.

Passers-by and riders and vehicles moved up and down Bozeman Street, driving him into cover each time. Bill Rawls came riding by, accompanied by Ed Walters and another deputy. They were soggy with weariness. Steve guessed they were returning from running down some blind trail. Rawls had not only the train robbery as his responsibility now but Steve's escape from jail also. No doubt persons with vivid imaginations were seeing fugitives back of every tree and bush and keeping the law busy on useless searching.

The sheriff turned off at the jail three blocks away. Steve gazed longingly. He could have used help. But to approach Rawls without tangible proof might be a dangerous mistake. It would, at best, mean long and wordy explanations that would probably not be believed, with almost the certainty that the real quarry would get wind of what was up and would take steps to make sure they were not caught with tangible evidence.

It would be his unsupported word—if he lived long enough, for there was also the probability that he might be shot down before he could make explanation of any kind.

A heavy-shouldered rider appeared in the street, accompanied by a smaller person. Steve stiffened, peering. It was Amos Whipple, and with him was Eileen.

He hugged the shadows, but he had the impression that both she and Amos had picked him out there. However, they moved steadily on down the street and he decided that he had only imagined that they had spotted him.

He peered out. They had already vanished somewhere—into the next cross street evidently.

He again pulled back suddenly. Burl Talley was in sight. He had emerged from the dining room of the Pioneer House. His jaunty, straight figure was unmistakable in the window lights as he came strolling down the street with the air of a man who had just finished a satisfying supper.

Steve edged back and watched Talley move past, puffing a cigar and slapping a pair of riding gloves into a palm. The man was the picture of a person with only business matters on his mind as he walked across the street and entered the office of his lumber business.

Steve swiftly left his covert, crossed the thoroughfare also, and stood at the corner of the office, just off Bozeman Street. The open window was almost above him.

He heard Creed say in a strained, angry voice, "You took your damned time about it. We've been coolin'——"

"Shut up!" Talley's lowered voice was thin and savage. "You fool! If I was to start scurrying around, somebody might . . ."

Talley came to the window and lowered the sash as he talked, and from then on all that Steve heard was a drift of unintelligible talk that was obviously bitter.

Some agreement evidently was finally reached. The glow of light faded. One of the lamps had been snuffed and the wick of the other turned down to leave a faint night light.

Steve heard the two leave by a rear door which opened directly into the lumberyard. He moved into the street toward the wagon gate with the thought in mind that he would slide over it into the enclosure. But he halted after one step, then inched back out of sight into his original position around the corner of the office structure. A man's head was visible above the closed gate. Someone was standing there on lookout.

Steve held his breath for seconds, then relaxed as he became certain that he had not been seen.

He waited. He was sure that feverish activity was under way somewhere around the planing mill in the depths of the property. But the sibilant sounds he picked up had no meaning.

Suddenly the wagon gate was swung open and two mounted men rode into the street. They jogged at a leisurely pace up the thoroughfare in the direction of the road to the upper basin. They were Tex Creed and the mill boss, Whitey Bird.

The stamp of idle hooves sounded faintly inside the lumberyard. Five minutes passed. Ten. Saddle rigging creaked as someone mounted. A voice spoke a command, along with the slap of a rope-end on hide. Breeching groaned and Highriver came riding out of the lumberyard leading two horses bearing packsaddles on which were lashed full sacks of grain, three on each load.

Highriver also headed up Bozeman Street, moving without haste. To all appearances he was bound for the Rafter O with grain for the remuda. The two pack animals bore the Rafter O iron and Steve realized that these animals and the saddle horse Whitey Bird had been riding, were the ones Creed and Highriver had brought down from winter range during the day. Evidently the horses had been shifted into town and to the lumberyard after dark.

Steve recrossed the street in a hurry to where his horse waited in the side street. He placed a foot in the stirrup and started to rise into the saddle.

Not until then did he know that two other riders were waiting nearby in the shadows. One moved in alongside of him. His six-shooter came swiftly into his hand, but it was Eileen's voice that halted him. "Steve!"

The bigger figure was that of Amos Whipple.

"I rode to Center Fire and found Uncle Amos," Eileen said. "I told him everything. I knew you'd need help. We came to town as fast as we could make it. We spotted you watching Talley's office but were afraid to make ourselves known for fear we might spoil things. We circled the block and located your horse and waited."

Steve still waited, gazing grimly and inquiringly at Amos.

"Eileen didn't quite tell me everything," Amos said. "She only told me I was a pigheaded, blind, opinionated fool who wanted to go around and hang people on mere suspicion. She said you wasn't a train robber, but that you were being forced to try, lone-handed, to run down the real gang. But she hadn't told me anything I hadn't already learned earlier."

"Already learned?"

Amos nodded. "Douglas had told me everything before Eileen showed up. I didn't know he was in his room. His mother kept it quiet. But when he got on his feet he came down an' faced me. He called me about the same things Eileen did. He was referrin' to my leadin' the Vigilantes an'——"

Steve stopped him with a gesture. "Later!" he said. "They're pulling out and I think they've got the money."

He looked at Eileen and said, "Stay in the clear."

He mounted and headed down the back street, circling four blocks before turning back into Bozeman Street. He discovered that Amos was at his heels.

"Do you really want to get into this, Amos?" he asked. "There's going to be gunplay."

"Never wanted anything so much in my life," Amos said. "Maybe I can sort of make up for a lot of things."

They entered Bozeman Street. The lighted jail office stood directly toward their right, and advancing toward them was Highriver and the two loaded packhorses.

Steve chose this spot to challenge the man. He pulled up his horse in midstreet and sat there as Highriver came riding closer. His quarry rose in the stirrups, peering through the darkness, trying to make out who he was.

Realization came to Highriver. He swung a quirt, lashing at the slow-footed packhorses, sending them into a startled surge ahead. It was a futile thing—the action of one whose mind had been stampeded.

Steve pulled his horse out of the way of the lurching animals. "Don't try to make a fight of it, Highriver," he said.

Highriver was carrying a brace of pistols. He drew and fired. Steve also fired, but his horse was rearing, startled by the violence of his movement and neither his nor Highriver's bullets found their mark.

Steve's mount began buck-jumping. He left the saddle, landing off balance, but still on his feet. A bullet tore his hat from his head. Highriver's six-shooters were blazing at him. It did not seem possible the man could continue to miss him at that close range.

Then Highriver's pistols went silent and he seemed to be impaled on some agonizing force. He rose numbly in the saddle, dropping his guns and clutching at his side. He collapsed abruptly and pitched limply into the street.

Steve realized that it was Amos who had fired the shot that had halted the man.

Eileen's voice screamed, "Behind you, Steve! Uncle Amos!"

Steve pivoted. Tex Creed and Whitey Bird, mounted, were riding into the street and bearing down on them. They had evidently been waiting on the fringe of town to join Highriver, and the gun fight had brought them back.

Creed was shooting. Amos said something in a shocked voice and reeled in the saddle. His right arm, which was his shooting arm, had been broken by one of Creed's bullets.

Marshal Mart Lowery was the first man to emerge from the jail office. He had a .45 in his hand and he was shouting, "Stop it! Stop it!"

Whitey Bird shot the marshal through the body. Lowery pitched backwards into the jail office, falling against Sheriff Bill Rawls who was coming at a run. Rawls eased his fall and rushed onto the sidewalk, a gun in his hand. He crouched there confused, trying to decide his target.

Steve and Creed shot at each other. Steve fired again. The bullet struck Creed in the shoulder, whirling him around. His weight upset the horse, which was rearing, and both animal and rider went down. Creed was thrown clear and lay there on his face. The horse arose and rabbit-jumped down the street, trying to buck off the saddle.

Steve veered his gun upon Whitey Bird, but held his fire. The powdersmoke from a shot, which had centered on the man, was spinning in a ring in the beam of light from the jail office. Mart Lowery, with blood flowing from the wound Bird had given him, had pulled himself up on his elbows and had fired back. Bird clung to the saddlehorn a moment, and then fell to the ground.

Silence came. Rawls, who had not used his .45, still stood on the sidewalk, bewildered. He kept repeating the command Mart Lowery had used. "Stop it! Stop it, in the name of the law!"

Across the street and not a score of yards away was Nick Latzo's Blue Moon. The swing doors had parted and Latzo himself had emerged. He stood there an instant, staring at the scene in the street. Then he understood!

He tried to turn and dart back into the shelter of his gambling house. But Steve said, "No, Nick!"

Latzo halted, gazing at him. "All right," Steve said. "You killed Buck Santee, Nick. Lift your hands."

Latzo was not one to surrender. "To hell with you!" he said in his heavy voice.

He drew and fired. And missed. He fired again. And again he missed.

Steve killed him. He shot Latzo twice and both bullets tore through the man's chest. Latzo lived long enough to try to fire again and did succeed in exploding one wild shot before he collapsed on the threshold of his gambling house.

Steve caught up the hackamore ropes of the pack horses, which were pitching wildly, terrorized by the gunfire. He soothed them with his voice, and they quieted.

"Good Jupiter, Santee!" Rawls began in a stunned voice. "What——?"

"A knife," Steve said. "I want your pocketknife."

Numbly Rawls produced one. Steve opened a blade and slit one of the bulging grain sacks on a packsaddle. Oats streamed into the street at his feet.

But in the split bag was something else that did not yield. Steve reached in and pulled. Smaller canvas bags which contained the hard weight of metal began dropping from the larger container. Gold coin!

He looked at Rawls and at excited citizens who were arriving. "There's your train robbery money," he said. "Part of it, at least. From all three holdups, most likely. This is the share belonging to Creed, Highriver, and Whitey Bird. They were afraid the game had played out, and forced their boss to hand over their share of the loot. They intended to be long gone from the Powderhorn before morning. You'll find the rest of their money in those other grain sacks."

"How——?" Rawls began.

"I believe I know how they vanished without leaving a trail after the Three Forks holdup," Steve said. "They probably had a wagonload of lumber waiting at some trail which crossed the railroad. They pulled the express car alongside, hid the gold and themselves among the lumber, then let the engine and car drift farther along the line. Whitey Bird drove the wagon right into town and into Talley's lumberyard bold as brass."

Steve turned and began running down Bozeman Street toward the lumberyard.

"Don't!" Eileen screamed. "Wait!"

Steve kept going. He was still a block from the dark establishment when a rider came spurring from the gate.

It was Talley. It had taken the man those few minutes since the gun fight had started in the street to saddle a horse and make his bid to escape.

He saw Steve racing toward him and fired a hasty shot which went wide. He used a spur on his mount. The horse was a powerful, well-bred sorrel. With darkness to help him Talley might have had better than an even chance of escaping if he could have got clear of town.

But a new rider appeared in the street ahead of him,

blocking his path. It was Doug Whipple. He was hatless and pale and wore only a duck saddle-jacket over the bandage that his mother had wound around his body.

"Pull up, Burl!" Doug said. "We'll face the music together."

Talley lifted his gun and fired. Steve heard the impact of the bullet. Doug was lifted from the saddle. He landed heavily in the street, rolled over, and pulled himself tenaciously to an elbow and shot the horse Talley was riding.

The animal broke in stride and pitched forward in a somersault, breaking its neck. Talley was thrown onto the sidewalk, where he crashed against a water barrel. He lay dazed.

Doug sank down like a man utterly spent after a long race. Steve got to his side and lifted his head.

Doug looked up at him and said in a voice that drifted off, "I heard Eileen when she came to the ranch to get Dad. I followed. It's better this way, Steve."

He said nothing more. A few moments later he was dead.

Steve did not move for a time. Eileen arrived. She knelt beside him and took one of Doug's hands, holding it against her. She began to weep.

Burl Talley was reviving. Steve slowly lowered Doug's head, arose, and walked to Talley. He placed a boot hard on the man's back, pinning him down.

"All we need to know from you, Burl," he said, "is where the rest of the money is cached in your lumberyard. That would be your share. And probably Nick Latzo's."

Sheriff Rawls came lumbering up, panting. "Not you, Burl?" he said. "Not you, of all people?"

"Him, of all people," Steve said. "He's all yours, Rawls."

Eileen arose from Doug's side. Tears stained her cheeks, but she had a grip on herself. "Are you hurt?" she asked Steve.

He decided that he had escaped unharmed, but she drew him into the light to make sure. All she could find was a bullet burn on his left wrist. She drooped a little then, all the strain and sadness hitting her.

He placed an arm around her and they walked back to the jail. Whitey Bird was dead, along with Nick Latzo. Creed and Highriver were alive and would probably pull through, the doctor said. Also Mart Lowery.

A doctor was working on Amos Whipple's arm in the sheriff's office.

Amos looked at Steve and Eileen and Rawls when they entered. "Douglas is dead, ain't he?" he asked dully.

Steve nodded. Amos drew a tired sigh. "What am I ever goin' to tell his mother?" he asked helplessly.

When he was better able to talk, Amos related the whole story to Rawls, with Steve filling in the details in the matter of Frank Clum and Nick Latzo's part in the death of Buck Santee. Amos did not withhold anything in telling of his son's confession to taking part in the two train robberies.

"I guess Douglas came here tonight to pay for what he'd done," he concluded. "And he paid."

He looked at Steve. "I'd give a lot if I could make up for what I did to your father," he said. "But I can't. You can't ever go back—not after they've died to show that you were wrong."

Burl Talley, handcuffed to deputies, was brought in. They had found his pockets stuffed with banknotes, which, no doubt, was a part of the loot from the robberies.

Talley looked at Eileen and some of his jauntiness returned. "I'd have been a rich man if things had worked out my way, Eileen," he said. "And you'd have worn diamonds and sables."

She shook her head. "You don't know people, Burl," she said. "You always were wrong about important things."

Talley was taken away to a cell. He was refusing to talk, demanding a lawyer. But Highriver and Creed, hoping for leniency from the law, were making a clean breast of events.

Steve turned to leave the office. Rawls halted him. "I know where you're going," he said. "To the Silver Moon. Louie Latzo."

"Yes," Steve said. "He'll talk."

"We'll see to it that he talks," Rawls said. "But this is for the law." He glanced toward Eileen. "You don't owe it to her to get yourself killed, now that you've gone this far. Louie won't get away. That's a promise. I'll ask him about Clum's murder. And your father's."

Rawls and his deputies were gone less than an hour. They brought Louie Latzo back with them in handcuffs. By that time the remainder of the train robbery money had been recovered from the sawdust pit at Burl Talley's planing mill, where Creed and Highriver had told them to look.

Rawls nodded at Steve. "Louie talked, with a little persuasion. It was Nick who ambushed your Dad and Henry Thane three years ago. I don't like to have to tell you this, but Buck Santee's body was dropped in an old prospect shaft in the hills, and the shaft was closed with a stick of dynamite."

Steve said nothing. Eileen's fingers squeezed his arm comfortingly.

"An' we won't ever be able to recover Choctaw's body either, I'm afraid," Rawls said. "According to Louie it was Al Painter an' Varney, who were sent out to move him from your saddle shed that night. They sunk Choctaw in an alkali bog way out in the east flats. They set fire to your house too. Varney an' Painter skipped out while we were grabbing Louie, but we'll round 'em up sooner or later."

Doug's body had been placed on a stretcher in the side room at the jail. Steve entered this room, pulled back the sheet, and stood looking down for a time. Doug seemed serene enough in his long sleep.

Steve replaced the sheet and turned away. He and Eileen walked out of the sheriff's office and stood in the cool night air.

"Where do you want to go?" she asked.

"Home, Eileen," he said.

"That will be Antler," she said. "Antler and the OK will be home for both of us now."

He drew her into his arms, and she clung tightly to him for a moment. She kissed him.

And a few minutes later they rode out of Bugle side by side.

◑

SIGNET Westerns For Your Enjoyment

Buy them at your local

bookstore or use coupon

on next page for ordering.

SIGNET Americana Novels of Interest

Ⓢ

SIGNET Westerns You'll Enjoy

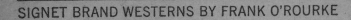

SIGNET BRAND WESTERNS BY FRANK O'ROURKE

☐	**WARBONNET LAW**	(#AJ1131—$1.95)
☐	**GUNSMOKE OVER BIG MUDDY**	(#AJ1133—$1.95)
☐	**VIOLENCE AT SUNDOWN**	(#AJ1134—$1.95)
☐	**GUN HAND**	(#AE1135—$1.75)
☐	**LATIGO**	(#AE1136—$1.75)
☐	**BANDOLIER CROSSING**	(#AE1137—$1.75)
☐	**LEGEND IN THE DUST**	(#AE1138—$1.75)
☐	**BLACKWATER**	(#AJ1139—$1.95)
☐	**DAKOTA RIFLE**	(#AJ1140—$1.95)
☐	**THE BIG FIFTY**	(#AE1141—$1.75)
☐	**GOLD UNDER SKULL PEAK**	(#AE1142—$1.75)
☐	**ACTION AT THREE PEAKS**	(#AJ1144—$1.95)
☐	**VIOLENT COUNTRY**	(#AE1145—$1.75)
☐	**HIGH VENGEANCE**	(#AE1143—$1.75)
☐	**AMBUSCADE**	(#E9490—$1.75)*
☐	**DESPERATE RIDER**	(#E9534—$1.75)

*Price slightly higher in Canada
